Married to Alison for 30 years and with one son Jonathan, Neville Drury now divides his time between Leicestershire and the Lincolnshire coast.

Retiring as a commercial property lawyer, this is his first novel since writing *SEABORN* published in 1984. He is currently working on a sequel to *Last Role of the Dice*.

LAST ROLE OF THE DICE

For Alison, Jonathan and Torrie.

Numerous people in Denmark and Germany have kindly allowed me free access to their memories. In particular I must express my sincere thanks to Mrs. Ann-Mari Madsen of Sdr Bork, Denmark for her generous help in translating Danish documents and ensuring I achieved historical accuracy for southern Jutland and the island of Bornholm.

In England I would like to acknowledge the help of Sam Clarke, John Greene, William Hancock and Mrs Lydia Knott all of whom helped me greatly with wartime and post-war background.

To Ian Thirsk and his team of the RAF Museum Hendon for allowing me direct access to their precious aircraft and helping me so generously with my technical enquiries.

To my wife Alison my thanks for her unstinting support and a lot of typing and to my son Jonathan for the first of many notebooks pleasurably filled in manuscript with the first draft of Last Role.

To my good friend Rita Evans for so neatly capturing the spirit of Last Role in her design for the book cover.

Last, but not least, the editorial and production staff at Austin Macauley for having faith in my work and guiding me in the process of bringing my manuscript to market.

Neville Drury

LAST ROLE OF THE DICE

AUSTIN MACAULEY
PUBLISHERS LTD.

A CIP catalogue record for this title is
available from the British Library.

ISBN 978 1 84963 305 5

www.austinmacauley.com

First Published (2013)
Austin Macauley Publishers Ltd.
25 Canada Square
Canary Wharf
London
E14 5LB

Printed & Bound in Great Britain

We make a living by what we get,
We make a life by what we give.

Winston S. Churchill

CAST OF CHARACTERS

ENGLAND

RONALD "RONNO" WALLACE	Retired RAF veteran
ALFRED WALLACE	Ronald's father
CISSY WALLACE	Ronald's mother
RICHARD "HUTCH" HUTCHINSON	Ronald's friend and wartime commander
KEITH WATSON	Wartime colleague "sent" by Hutch to help Ronald
COLIN FARRELL	Hutch's Solicitor
TORRIE	Ronald's sister
ELISABETH "LIBBY" DAVIS	Ronald's love

GERMANY

OTTO HECKER	General der Flieger (Luftwaffe)
ELISE HECKER	Otto's wife / sister to Anna Iversen
WERNER FISCHER	Otto's chauffeur/butler
MAXMILLIAN von LEHDENDORFF	Otto's nephew and Test Pilot for the Luftwaffe
MARGHERITTA	Otto's sister/ mother of Max &Regina
REGINA	Hutch's love / Otto's niece
WOLFGANG	Otto's son
DIETER	Otto's younger son

DENMARK

PEDER IVERSEN	Father
ANNA IVERSEN	Mother / sister to Elise Hecker
SVENN	Son
KARIN	Daughter

PROLOGUE

First, there was the photograph.

That, on its own, without even reading the man's obituary, was bad enough. Though it was only a tiny, fleeting pinprick in his carefully constructed bubble of urbane normality, it had the intensely unsettling effect of starting a trickle of unwelcome memory. Eventually, it would prove to be like the first crack in the wall of a great dam, which has held back so much.

Then, there was the letter.

Unexpected, unsolicited and unwanted, it was so much worse. It accelerated the process of erosion which now threatened to overwhelm him.

These two events, the one coming close on the heels of the other, had combined and conspired to drive him out of his comfort zone. Together, they were forcing him to confront issues from his former life that he had for so long managed to repress and then, over the years, he had done his utmost to forget.

In one respect, he had become profoundly grateful that the onset of his old age, which he had entered with some dread had, in fact, turned out to be something of a protective barrier. Like a fire blanket wrapped around his shoulders, his advancing years helped to insulate him from the inferno of his torments and which he prayed, almost daily, would carry him safely, securely and with a largely untroubled conscience to his final end. But it was, as he was presently being forced to acknowledge, a less-than-perfect structure and it seemed to him that, like it or not, his world might be about to undergo a cataclysmic reverse.

The drive to the air museum had been long and tedious. Heavy traffic, at times made worse by torrential rain, tested his resolve each time he stopped en route, once to drink coffee from his ancient Thermos flask after pulling his battered old Ford Mondeo in to a lay-by and then, for the second time, not long afterwards, to deal with the consequences of the first stop. As he hunched behind a bush, shivering in the chill, late-winter air, praying that no-one in the passing traffic would notice the curse of his many years, he challenged himself to take the easy way out, to turn the car round and to go away quietly. But the damage was already done; the rivers of his personal history were beginning to filter through and he could no more deny them, than he could deny anything that had happened to him in the last twenty four hours.

It had all been written such a long time ago – when he was young and playing a part in a world driven by events beyond his control. The only question now, was whether the archive of his past had to be opened, and read, one final time.

It was late afternoon when he entered the museum – only an hour or so before closing, as he had intended. Unsure of what his own reaction might be, he wanted as few people around as possible, and hoped that any parties of schoolchildren, as well-meaning as their teachers might intend, would be long gone. Patience had never been one of his strongest virtues and the thought of being caught up in the children's disinterested chatter filled him with a horror. Just like a beautiful film actress from his own teenage years had once said: he wanted to be alone – with his ghosts.

Paying his concessionary entrance fee, but waiving the offer of the museum's guide book as it was irrelevant to his single-minded purpose, he ignored the outer reaches with their display cases, dedicated to almost a century of aviation memorabilia, and headed directly into the inner sanctum of its aircraft exhibits.

He saw immediately that the display was organised clockwise, in date order, from the earliest years of flight and so, with barely a glance to one side or the other, he followed the grey painted walkway in its great circle. He trod quietly to avoid disturbing the silence of the cavernous hall. The many aircraft were like the members of an orchestra, stilled now, their symphony of death concluded.

On the way through to his chosen quarry, he nodded an acknowledgment to a seated attendant, who was dressed in the museum's uniform of a dark blue blazer, grey slacks and mirror-polished black shoes. The attendant, fixed in boredom, did not return his greeting.

Pausing only for a second or two in front of a biplane of the Royal Flying Corps from the First World War, or the Great War as he had known it as a youngster, (how his Dad would have been at ease in this section) he then quickened his pace until he reached the display area dedicated to the aircraft of World War II.

There, as before, each exhibit was fronted by two plaques, one elevated on a metal and Perspex stand, explaining the aircraft and its role in the destruction of people and property, and the other, at floor level, telling the visitor: DO NOT CROSS. Moving on, he ignored a row of single-engined fighters, "ours" and "theirs", which were only of passing interest even though one was of a type he had flown so many times, until he came slowly, hesitantly, to the reason for his visit. The rivers of his past were beginning to flow more strongly.

Standing squarely in front of the aircraft, dressed in its wartime camouflage colours of brown and olive green, he read the information panel, even though he knew by heart what it would tell him. It said in large bold type, as though shouting at him: HAWKER TEMPEST Mk V 1944-45. He gazed up at the huge red-painted propeller boss standing a couple of feet above his head, the bulbous air-intake immediately below, and the enormous four-bladed airscrew, each blade almost seven feet long, black like a dagger, each tip painted bright yellow.

His heartbeat quickened as he read the familiar performance figures of the large single-seat fighter: Seven tons in weight, 350-400 miles per hour (much more in a dive, he remembered, if he had the need or the nerve), enough bullets to cut a steam-engine in half (another memory) and eight, sixty pound rockets, four slung there under each wing, more than enough to raze an entire building to the ground (yet another memory). Bigger, more rugged than any Spitfire, it was almost the last in a line of piston-engined fighters from the Hawker factory. He had put his trust, his life, his future into one of these machines for more than a year and she had not failed him.

Then, as though no longer in control of his own actions, and propelled by an unseen, irresistible force, he stepped over the demarcation line and walked forward a couple of paces until he was directly under the nose of the aircraft. The scent of the old aeroplane washed over him like a long-forgotten cologne and he drew the notes of oil, varnish and the faintest hint of cordite deep into his soul. A shudder ran through his body.

Vaguely aware of someone shouting in the distance, he placed the palm of his right hand against the smooth under-surface of one of the propeller-blades and closed his eyes, as he pressed his cheek against the cold, unyielding steel.

The effect was electrifying.

For a second or two he saw his life as a series of still photographs, spinning forward through his mind like the flickering images of an old seaside peep show. It occurred to him momentarily that he might be dying – like the drowning man who is said to see his life flash before his eyes.

But then, as the shouting grew louder and more insistent, intruding more acutely into his consciousness, the images began to slow until they stopped at one of a young man, with slicked flaxen hair, sitting in the open cockpit of a Tempest, waving into the camera. Perched on the wings were other pilots, just kids really, so very young, but their faces were a blur (just as they had so often been in those short-life days) and only the one was recognisable – himself. He gripped the propeller tightly to stop his knees buckling.

"What the bloody hell do you think you are doing? There are rules, you know. Can't you read – Sir?"

The words were bellowed into his left ear by the attendant, irate and tugging at his sleeve. The "Sir" had been added very much as an afterthought. He felt the attendant take a firmer, more forceful grip on his arm, ready to prize him loose.

Recovering his composure, he turned just as the attendant was about to launch into another tirade.

"You must return to the walkway. It's the ru…" but something the attendant saw in the old man's eyes stopped him mid-sentence. Barry, according to the engraved metal badge pinned to the left lapel of his blazer, relaxed his grip just a little.

"You flew one of these, didn't you?" Barry breathed, with a tone of respect, verging on reverence, entering his voice as he pulled more gently, this time on the sleeve.

"Yes, I rather think I did, for a little while," his charge replied with a trace of nostalgia – and was there regret? "I'm sorry I broke your rules. Not sure what made me do it. Seemed I had no choice in the matter." There was an apologetic shrug of the shoulders.

"Well," replied Barry, straightening his tie as he ushered the old man back to the safety zone of the walkway, "we all have to follow the rules – at least some of the time."

By now Barry was smiling. They were going to be the best of friends, once his precious rules had been obeyed. Barry continued, "Just as well there weren't hordes of school kids around. They can be little buggers, especially if they see the grown-ups breaking the rules."

"Yes," he retorted wearily, "I suppose that's what it was all about – grown-ups breaking the rules."

Although Barry looked at him quizzically, he did not intend to elaborate.

"We still get the odd wartime pilot in here," Barry commented as though he continued to expect some response, "but they always go to the Spit," nodding back down the line.

"Flew one of those too. Damn nearly killed me." Again he did not feel the need to proffer any word of explanation, despite the encouraging, enthusiastic, puppy-like expression on Barry's face.

Barry was obviously keen to reminisce, to talk over old times, even though, (given the fact that Barry revealed he had done little more than his time in National Service with the RAF in the fifties), it was obvious they had almost nothing else in common. There was no possibility, not the slightest chance, that Barry could begin to understand what he had been through all those years ago, and he wanted nothing less than to be caught in what could only be a completely pointless exchange. He dearly wished Barry would 'buzz off' and leave him alone with his thoughts.

Thankfully, just at that moment, Barry spotted some minor misdemeanour being committed on the far side of the hangar, so he trotted off to uphold his precious rules, making his excuses with one parting observation – that the old man should remember to sign the museum's visitors' book before he left.

He sighed with relief at his liberation, cringing as another outburst from Barry shattered the stillness.

Turning once again to the Tempest, he found that he was looking at it from almost exactly the same viewpoint as in that photograph. His stomach churned.

In the gathering gloom of the late afternoon, not quite dispelled by the artificial lighting, it was not difficult for him to see, once more, that image of another young man, standing nonchalantly between the propeller blades, cap set back at a rakish angle. He shuddered as the river of memories assailed him, as though someone had walked across his grave, which perhaps thanks to the letter, or cursed by the letter, they had.

"Enough," he thought to himself. Then, realising he had in fact spoken out loud, he turned abruptly on his heel and continued, shoulders hunched, to complete the circle of exhibits, seeing nothing, until he reached the exit.

He was about to leave when he caught sight of a cream coloured plinth on which rested the visitors' book. Recalling Barry's entreaty, he thought, "Why not, what's the harm?"

Putting the museum's cheap, plastic biro to one side and taking out his much-loved fountain pen, he began to complete the register. No-one had signed that day and so he wrote, after a moment's deliberation – one day seemed much the same as any other – 23rd February 2003. In the next column, he signed with as much of a flourish as he could manage, printing underneath: RONALD ORVILLE WALLACE and then added, "Squadron Leader RAF".

He was about to append the word "Retired", when his hand hesitated. Might the letter mean, he pondered with a growing sense of disquiet which gnawed at his stomach, that, in order to address the challenge it had thrust so brutally into his life, he was in some small way still on active service? Only the trip to London if he chose to make it, as required by the letter, was going to provide an answer to that one.

The river was beginning to flow faster.

CHAPTER 1

Ronald's day started, as it seemed it always had, with a light breakfast of cereal and toast, which he combined with the lifelong ritual of a browse through The Times newspaper.

His consideration of The Times started, as it always had, with a look at the day's obituaries. Quite why he adopted this approach he could no longer explain or remember, but perhaps he had never grown accustomed to the change in the paper's style when it put conventional reporting and photographs on the front page, banishing the Court and Social to somewhere beyond halfway.

With the family grandfather clock ticking rhythmically in the background, he sat at the dining room table, carefully laid for one, crisp white napkin neatly rolled into its silver ring, as it had been for so many years. Toast in hand and the newspaper set to his left side, he opened The Times, page by page, skimming the headlines until he reached the section called the Register, and there he started to read the obituary of a recently deceased educationalist: a whole page no less, rambling on, recording the man's good works and deeds, service to the community, the honours accorded to him, on and on, so that the words blurred into one another, as he munched slowly through his first piece of toast.

Quite how, he reflected, so much could be said about a man with such an apparently unremarkable career, largely as an overpaid civil servant, was entirely beyond him. He could almost be angry at the vast amount of newsprint devoted to this one individual, who clearly had the ear of the Establishment (whatever that meant). He must have been a "jolly good fellow", and hopefully he had also been a good husband and father, because the article concluded by saying that he was survived by his widow and five children.

Patently, if this was the standard of the first article, there was not going to be much to interest him today. Still grumbling to himself, he turned the page, the second piece of toast moving automatically from plate to mouth.

What he saw on the next page stopped the toast in mid-air; his hand shook slightly, as though with a tremor, and the toast slipped from his fingers and fell butter-side-down onto the table top.

There, staring out of the page, was the face of Richard "Hutch" Hutchinson (Group Captain DFC and Bar), deceased just four days previously, on October 15th, a widower without children. A note at the end of the article recorded that his wife, Queenie, had died several years before.

Cursing himself silently for the careless old fool he felt himself to be, he removed the toast from the table top, cleaning up with his napkin, and pushed the plate aside.

With a feeling of the old "butterflies in the tummy", he settled down to read the article in detail. In all the years since the war not one of his wartime comrades had made it into the pages of a national paper so far as he could remember, dead or alive, until now.

The photograph was of the official war time variety showing a handsome young man, with slicked back hair, (but not one of the Brylcreem Boys of the Battle of Britain because the left breast of the uniform showed the DFC ribbon not awarded to him until the spring of 1944, although the Bar was absent so this picture must have been taken prior to January 1945) a pencil thin moustache, cap set back at a non-regulation angle. What Ronald noticed most of all, was the tired, tired eyes, as though the owner had already done too much, seen too many horrors. The photograph had been taken with Hutch standing, framed closely by the propeller tips of a Hawker Tempest fighter.

How long had it been since he last heard of Hutch? 1952 or 1953 at the latest, perhaps when Hutch resigned his commission and left the RAF? Ronald struggled to remember. The intervening 50 years had dulled his memory and there was so much he had tried hard to forget, to obliterate.

Continuing to read, the unknown author of the obituary duly recorded the appropriate elements of his wartime service and that Group Captain – a post-war promotion – Richard Hutchinson had left the RAF in 1954 from his last posting in Kuala Lumpur, (where he had been a counter-insurgency military advisor to the Malayan government for a time during their Emergency) and went on to pursue a career as a securities trader in Hong Kong – and what did Hutch know about securities, he wondered? At least it explained how they had lost touch so long ago.

In fact, despite being like brothers before and throughout the war, they really had not been very close once hostilities had largely come to an end in the last days of April 1945, just before the German unconditional surrender on the 8th of May to Field Marshal

Montgomery at Luneburg Heath on the flat, battle-scarred plains of north-west Germany.

With that thought, an overwhelming host of memories flooded in, memories that he had, for the most part, successfully, suppressed for almost sixty years.

For a moment, the scream of an aero engine at full throttle, the chatter of machine guns and the slower thudding of cannon fire saturated his senses, causing him involuntarily to close his eyes tightly and to clap his hands over his ears to block out the sights and sounds that threatened to engulf him. So rapid, so uncontrolled, were his movements that his elbow caught the edge of the breakfast plate, knocking it sharply to one side. It fell from the table, to shatter into a dozen pieces on the polished parquet floor below.

Quite how long he sat there, locked into immobility, fighting off his demons, he did not know, but the shadow of the crossbars in the window frame had moved substantially across the dining table in the weak late autumn sunlight so that The Times, still open at his side, lay wholly in shadow. Utterly drained, he dragged himself from the table and slumped into an armchair, head pounding, heart still racing until he grew calm as he tried to rebuild the barriers to his past. It frightened him how easily they had been breached.

Contrary to his usual habit of taking The Times intact round to one of his neighbours, he carefully cut the obituary from the page, folded it neatly and, with the feeling that he should try to read it again at his leisure, he tucked it into the back compartment of his wallet. His neighbour would probably have a moan about the vandalism to "his" Times, but on this occasion Ronald felt fully justified.

Vaguely it crossed his mind that he might attend the funeral, but at his time of life it would be a major undertaking to make the travel arrangements, assuming that he was even able to establish the name of the funeral director, which in turn would probably require a phone call to The Times. The hill that he would need to climb loomed more steeply with each passing second and so, with mounting irritation, (or was it guilt?), he concluded that sixty years was far too long to start making the effort.

He was able to justify his decision. They might have been the closest of friends all those years ago, but if only Hutch had kept in contact then he might have been willing to make a different decision, so really it was *Hutch's* fault that he could not go.

Still troubled by his weakness, his lack of loyalty, and with a less than clear conscience, he left The Times on the hall table for delivery next door at the beginning of his daily walk, during which he hoped he might, but rarely did, come across a neighbour or acquaintance for a bit of a chat.

These days, he thought ruefully, an old man engaging a total stranger in conversation was hardly acceptable socially, but the burden of isolation brought on by his increasing age was beginning to bear down on him and he dreaded the thought of the next, inevitable stage in his life.

For as long as he could manage it, he had determined that he would maintain his independence. With that thought, he dressed warmly, picked up The Times and set off, trilby hat pressed firmly onto his head, for his constitutional into the drifts of fallen autumn leaves that were chasing in swirls across the drive to his house in the blustery wind of the equinox. The ivory-topped walking stick was pure affectation, but he liked to think that, at eighty-two years of age, he still cut a dignified figure, not yet ready for the scrap heap nor, more realistically, the retirement home.

As the weeks passed, and Christmas in Bognor Regis with his sister Torrie, turned to the New Year – alone once again – the memories of Richard "Hutch" Hutchinson triggered by the obituary began to fade from his mind. All, that is, except the nagging thought that he still did not know what had happened during the two, or was it three, days when Hutch went missing right at the end of the war.

In the endless chaos that was Germany in the last week of April and the first of May 1945, Hutch had gone AWOL – absent without leave – but with their squadron effectively operating like independent buccaneers, flying missions almost as they saw fit, his absence had gone virtually unremarked. It was not until the third day that an anxious voice was raised and enquiries made – only to be stilled with his return in the late evening light. His Hawker Tempest had slipped quietly into their recently occupied Luftwaffe airfield, parking in a space cleared by their own bulldozers over the last couple of days, amongst the shattered remnants of the once mighty German Air Force.

That airfield had become the graveyard for the earthbound victims of their own squadron's ground attack. Even right at the end, the Luftwaffe seemed unable to resist the temptation to muster their aircraft in neat rows, or perhaps they had simply run out of the fuel or the pilots to move them. As the Yanks were prone to saying, it had been a turkey shoot.

Less than ten days after their arrival at that German airfield – he could no longer even remember its name – the unconditional surrender had been signed, hostilities had ceased and their own, wholehearted celebration of personal survival commenced in earnest. Somewhat to Ronald's surprise and relief, as he had no desire to see his friend court-martialled, Hutch's absence was overlooked and eventually forgotten by his superiors.

Oddly, he remembered that, although they had been together on that last sortie, Hutch filed no combat report and it seemed he carefully sidestepped any questions about his absence, referring only to "a spot of engine trouble" and of "having to divert to an emergency landing strip further south to await repairs".

Just once, Hutch, in a moment of drunken relaxation, let slip the crumb of information that there had been, what he called, a meeting of interested parties. Just that, and no more, in response to Ronald's equally drunken questioning about the days he went missing. From the expression on Hutch's reddened face, it had been evident that, even with that one tiny slip, he had said more than he intended and he contrived to lapse into a deep stupor, so as to avoid any further questions.

Never again did the opportunity arise for Ronald to question his friend about his absence and when Ronald was offered, and grabbed, the chance to return home to England on a brief period of leave to see his wife Libby, from whom he had been apart for almost six months, his and Hutch's worlds went in different directions. Once their squadron was disbanded in the late summer of 1945, the link was broken and his curiosity had remained unsatisfied.

CHAPTER 2

Given his great age, his daily post box was generally minimal, apart from the persistent rainfall of junk mail that was always consigned unread to the dustbin. What need had he, a still sprightly octogenarian, of health insurance at fifty pence a week or some other such useless benefit?

Thus it was, with some surprise, that an official looking envelope addressed to Sq. Ldr. R. O. Wallace dropped through his letter box one Friday morning a few weeks later. It was years since anyone had written to him so formally and, from the postal franking on the front, he could see it was from a firm of solicitors, Dawlings & Co in London rather than from the Ministry of Defence which wrote to him occasionally about his war service pension.

Over his traditional breakfast, The Times for once put aside, he carefully slit open the stiff, cream manila envelope and extracted the sheaf of papers it contained. Stapled at the top left hand corner, a covering letter was attached to six sheets of photocopied documents. The letter began:

17th February 2003

Dear Squadron Leader Wallace,

Re: The Late Richard Hutchinson

This Firm has been retained as Executors and Trustees to wind up the estate of our late client. As you may be aware Group Captain Hutchinson died a widower without issue and at his instruction we are authorised to tell you, in advance of the Grant of Probate that, with one exception, the whole of his estate is to be turned into cash and distributed amongst certain carefully selected charities, the details of which are of no concern to yourself.

What does concern you personally is that the Will was revised in accordance with a set of instructions we received only days before our client's death, which we discharge as follows:

N

	a	b	c W		e	f	g	h	
8	O	15	45	PQ	X	MF	X	11	
7	O7	30	54	28	N	11	10	E	
6		PQ	O >>	52	45	12	35		
E		BkN	X	Bf	8	x	PQ		S
4	08	45{	Bf 8	X	BkN}	x	PQ	>>	
3	318	NW	110	55	29	08	26	Dk	
2	1015	>>	Bf8	DH	82	BkN	<<		
1		35	45	PQ	>>>	180		O	

2. Further, at his request, we enclose copies of six specific pages of his 1945 flight log. These, our client told us, would be of particular interest to you, and to assist you, we are instructed to release to you, and no one else, the original of his flight log for 1945.

For this purpose, you are requested to travel to our offices, the expenses for which, including First Class rail fare, we are to reimburse to you.

Our instructions are that, if you so wish, you may also take the flight logs for the earlier years of the war. If you elect not to take them, they are to be donated to the RAF Museum in Hendon.

If you choose not to take the 1945 log, then our instructions are that the log is to remain unread and is to be sent for secure destruction.

It is with regret that we have to inform you that we are completely unable to throw any light on the meaning of the notation at item 1 of this letter. It is quoted verbatim from the relevant clause in the Will which was received as a manuscript from our client and carefully checked by him to ensure that we had transcribed it correctly.

It is also with regret that we have to inform you that we are required to have your answer to Item 2 within ten working days of today's date. To assist you, a reply slip and freepost envelope are enclosed.

We await your response.

Yours very sincerely,

The reference on the letter and the signature at the end appeared to be that of their senior partner, Mr C. Farrell. Ronald could only speculate whether being written to by the top man in their firm, rather than a more junior member of Farrell's staff, might have some special significance. If it did, then it might be good, or not so good. He tapped the page thoughtfully, reflecting that senior officers were rarely the bringers of good tidings. With a deep, resigned sigh which accompanied the distinct feeling that events beyond his control were about to overtake him, he turned his attention reluctantly back to the letter.

Slowly, he folded back the top sheet and considered the photocopies underneath. Intriguingly, the six pages were all from late April 1945 and more interestingly they were not all sequential. Starting with the 28th, there followed the 29th and 30th but not the 1st nor the 2nd or 3rd of May. Photocopies for the next three days then followed. Immediately it occurred to him that these three missing days might be the days Hutch went AWOL. Did this mean that they were still in the original log? The solicitors' letter indicated they had copied the pages strictly in accordance with an instruction, but did Mr Farrell know what was in the missing section?

There was clearly only one way to find out, but at his time of life, did he really want to be bothered? Mother Nature had been kind to him. A hip replacement was the only form of surgical intervention necessary to restore his quality of life. As a non-smoker since shortly after the war – pity he could not quite say the same about his liking for scotch and wine – his lungs and heart were still in good shape, so he had no real problems with getting out and about. He had changed to an automatic car following the hip operation and his doctor was still able to say that he was fit to drive, although he now rarely ventured out at night by car, preferring to make use of the local taxi service.

Did he really want to make the effort of going all the way down to London at his time of life, just to see if he would be able to fill in a three day gap in the life of a man he had not seen or spoken to in the best part of fifty years?

Then again, he thought, arguing with himself, Hutch had spoken directly to him through the will and to no one else. Not only that, if he chose not to go, then the 1945 log book was to be destroyed, so it seemed it must have some very special significance.

As the memories of those long gone days, triggered by the notes on the copies from Hutch's log, began to return, he found himself pondering the cryptic entry from the will. Obviously it should have some significance to him in particular, he supposed, or to anyone else who had the wit or the patience to puzzle it out. On the face of it, the lettering and numbering within the grid could mean anything, They could be clues or possibly moves in a game of chess or perhaps a bid at bridge, but nothing sprang immediately to mind, save that the letters and numbers around the edge of the grid were similar to the chess puzzles he saw published daily in The Times. Similar, certainly, but not the same and he just could not imagine that Hutch would send him a chess puzzle from his deathbed. But what else it might be, whatever it might be designed to tell him, was, for the moment, quite beyond him.

He read and re-read the passage trying to make sense of the entries until at last, as the light began to fade, a small bell began to ring in his mind. From time to time in recent years, he had been alarmed by the infuriating way in which his mind seemed to become a cloud of useless cotton wool, incapable of productive activity. Tonight, his thoughts kept returning to the significance of just two letters, -PQ- which appeared at random throughout the grid. But whatever it was, it would not quite come to the surface.

To explore his thoughts further, he would need to find his old de-mob suitcase which he had steadfastly refused to open since that day he had returned to his parents' home with his wife Libby, in 1946, filling it with his flight log books – more than 3000 hours recorded since applying to join the University Air Squadron in 1939 – medals and ribbons and goodness knows what else.

The process of locking it had been a symbolic act of imprisoning five years of memories and events, which, in the living of them, had been at times, if he were honest, exciting and occasionally enjoyable, but most often were terrifying, and the memories of which had proved to be so very difficult to handle. Perhaps this was, if for no other reason, because they brought on what could only be described as a deep feeling of guilt that he had survived despite the appalling odds, whereas so many of his friends had died violently in combat.

Voices and faces, long forgotten, flickered through his mind.

He fretted the evening away, racked by indecision. What to do? Libby, for all her youth and inexperience would have known with complete certainty – just as she had that first time. But there was no Libby to guide or counsel him any more.

Late that night, he read the solicitor's letter and papers a fourth and then a fifth time, trying to divine greater meaning from the words, but it left him none the wiser. Any further progress would have to await finding his old suitcase in the attic storeroom to which it had been consigned on the day he had moved into the house. Out of sight, out of mind, he felt was the best way to deal with it. Yet somehow, he had always been unwilling to throw the case and its contents away, and so it had remained up there, over his head, year after year, stalking him by its continued existence.

He retired to his bed later than his customary 11.30 p.m., but as usual with his customary whisky and water which would usually help him to drift off to sleep – but not on this occasion. He lay wide awake in the dark, his mind like a terrier, unable to let go of what he now considered to be "Hutch's Enigma" or was it to be "Hutch's Joke"? Hutch had been quite a prankster in his day, but then they all were, mostly as a means of trying to relieve the stress and tensions of wartime that had besieged them all, day after day.

Finally, in desperation, he got up, shuffled through to the bathroom, found and swallowed one of his ex-wife's sleeping tablets. They were years out of date, but more often than not, they did the trick. Maybe it was just psychological, but he doubted they did any harm and sleep would generally follow.

This night was no exception, but instead of a deep dreamless sleep, unconsciousness really, he dreamed *the* dream, re-living the nightmare that had haunted him, in the early years, almost nightly.

He was in his beloved Tempest, 'Miss Faithful', so named for all the times she had soaked up punishment, both aerobatic and from enemy fire. M-F were her squadron letters, but she was also known less kindly by the ground crew as "mother…" for all the punishment she had handed out. Once again, the cockpit was tilted steeply downwards, his finger was on the firing button, the tracer of his cannon fire drifting down toward a Luftwaffe Messerschmitt 262, the only frontline jet fighter in service anywhere in the world, and probably flown by one of General Major Galland's elite pilots. It would be a real prize if he could get it.

In his dream, Miss Faithful plunged downward at increasing speed, still the guns were firing, but with no visible result; the ground was rushing toward him, he could sense bursts of flak to left and right, but the prize was too great to miss. Then, to his horror, he realised the controls were locked, unmoveable under his hands, the airframe shuddering and finally he saw the skin of the wings beginning to peel back and tear off like tinfoil into the slipstream. He knew these were his final moments as the earth reared up like a devil's maw to swallow him.

Whether he screamed out loud, he did not know, for there was no one beside him to tell, but his wife had told him that he had screamed every time, his body convulsing from the dream-state impact with the earth.

He woke, heart pounding wildly, soaked in sweat, lying for a while panting from the exertion. Would he, he wondered, ever be free of this terrible ordeal, or would his own death be the only means of release?

Somewhat to his surprise, and as much as it had unnerved him, the dream in fact served to strengthen his resolve to work out what Hutch was trying to tell him. As sleep, of a sort, finally claimed him, he drifted off to thoughts of Miss Faithful and her code letters M-F.

All the aircraft in his squadron had, painted on the fuselage, the same two identification letters: 'B M' with a final suffix letter, running from A through to M or N. He was allocated the letter "F". The "Miss" tag he had adopted from seeing some of the Americans' nose art on their Mustangs and it had found favour with some of the other pilots. He could recall Miss Behaving, Miss Chievous and Miss Demeanour. He chuckled as he began to reminisce.

On the squadron, there was a fitter who had been an artist before the war for one of the companies that produced the popular style of saucy seaside postcards and before long he had been "persuaded" – a couple of bottles of scotch from the Officers Mess had sealed the bargain – to interpret Miss Behaving in glorious technicolour on one of the engine panels.

In fact, in the initial version, the beautiful busty blonde, clad only in a translucent negligée, was shown *astride* one of the 60lb air-to-ground rockets which their aircraft regularly carried on their ground attack sorties. Patently not wearing any knickers, the image was considered to be, not to put too fine a point on it, so pornographic that the artist had to be persuaded (once again) to remodel his design, but not before the squadron photographer had been called in to use up one or two of his precious colour negatives.

The modified version showed Miss Behaving, sitting on a cloud, with knickers to preserve her modesty, and holding one of the rockets aloft. He smiled at the memory that for five shillings the photographer would run off a ten by eight inch print of the original artwork, to adorn a locker door or wall.

Competition to produce designs for Miss Conception – even though there was no such designation – was well underway, leaving nothing to the imagination, when the Station Commander found out what was going on and promptly banned any further ventures into the world of nose art.

That was not quite the end of the matter, because the Station Commander had been so enamoured with the initial version of Miss Behaving that he had it copied and mounted on the wall over the fireplace in the Officers' Mess. It was also rumoured that for a further consideration of whisky, the photographer could be induced to produce a one-off 20 x 16 colour print of the original; these later ensured the artist's success in the immediate post-war gentleman's calendar market.

Before he finally fell asleep again, his last conscious thought was that Hutch had steadfastly refused to use their squadron's lettering for his aircraft and this memory brought on the niggling feeling that Hutch's personal identification letters, retained for much of the war, were somehow associated with a name or a place of some importance.

He woke the next morning still with the puzzle rattling around inside his head like a ball-bearing in an arcade pinball machine.

Rather than meet the problem head-on by tackling the attic to find his de-mob case, he decided he would, instead, try to telephone the London solicitors. He could only hope that they might shed more light on Hutch's instructions to help him come to a decision.

The receptionist on the switchboard of Dawlings & Co informed him that their Mr. Farrell was on the telephone at that moment, but if Mr. Wallace did not mind holding she would put the call through as soon as Mr. Farrell became free. He waited patiently through a couple of minutes of pre-recorded music (how he hated that stuff wherever it was to be found) until a distinct click announced he was being connected.

A deep cultured voice greeted him with unexpected warmth.

"Good morning Mr. Wallace. Thank you so much for calling."

Ronald responded in kind before Farrell continued:

"You have obviously received my letter. How may I help you this morning?"

"I have read everything you sent me very carefully, but I have to confess that I am in two minds as to whether I should take this any further. A trip to London these days is quite an outing for me so I wondered if there was anything you could tell me which could help me make sense of all this," he replied.

For a few moments there was complete silence on the line, and Ronald wondered whether he had been cut off, but it appeared that the solicitor had been considering his reply as he responded:

"I am uncertain as to what I can or should tell you, given the professional requirement for strict client confidentiality which continues even though Mr. Hutchinson is dead. I hope you will understand."

He went on, "I think at this stage, over the phone, there are only two things I can say to you, although whether they help you in any way is for you to decide."

Another pause, as though Farrell was choosing his words with great care. Speaking slowly and deliberately he said:

"Firstly, I would like you to know that I have known Richard and his late wife for many years. We met during a time when I was working in Hong Kong and we became good friends. Although we lost touch for a while when I came back to London, he contacted me again following his return to the UK after the handover to China in '97. Sadly, at that time, he was asking me to handle the winding up of his wife's estate.

Early last year, after a short period of illness, he was diagnosed with an incurable cancer and so he came to see me once again. This time it was with the intention of putting his personal affairs in order. I am appointed his executor, and, as I mentioned in my letter, I am duty bound to follow his instructions precisely. I have no ability to vary the timetable. My hands are tied."

Ronald continued to listen, wondering what revelations might be forthcoming. After another brief pause Farrell continued:

"I would like you to know that Richard held you in the highest regard, affection even, I might say. You may find this surprising, given that neither of you had spoken for almost fifty years, but as he and I progressed the preparation of his will, Richard said repeatedly that only you, no-one else, could or would understand.

I have read parts of his earlier flight log books and it is very evident to me that he held you to be a very close friend. He also said that, on more than one occasion, in his words, you saved his worthless backside."

Again he paused, but then continued, still measuring his words:

"Secondly I will tell you this, even though I am not sure by any means that I should. As I have said, I have looked briefly at all of the log books. I remain thankful I was only a child during the wartime and can only imagine what you and he went through. Some of the entries are extremely graphic with personal notes added, apparently at a later date. What you might like to know is that some days of the 1945 log are closed to me, sealed up before it came into my custody, and indeed will remain closed to everyone forever, unless you make the choice to come to London."

Again, Farrell seemed to hesitate, as though reviewing whether he might already have overstepped the mark, before continuing, "Approximately three pages have been carefully glued together by Richard to keep them completely confidential. For your eyes only, you might say!" he added with a note of amusement in his voice.

"I was given particular instruction as to which pages either side were to be photocopied. Richard had, I believe, the intention of jogging your memory and whetting your appetite in the hope that you would make the trip here.

Finally, I would like to add that Richard was very much aware of your age, if not your state of health and therefore has made provision not only to cover all of your expenses for travel first class, but in addition he has requested that I entertain you to lunch at my club. That alone ought to be reason enough to pop up to London, I should think," Farrell concluded with a light touch of irony.

In listening to what Farrell had said, Ronald found so many thoughts whirling through his mind that for a moment he forgot to speak, prompting Farrell to enquire if he was still on the line.

"Yes, Yes," he stammered in reply. "It's just that I am overwhelmed by all of this as you can probably imagine. Fifty years, and not a word and then… this! We certainly were good pals and comrades during the war, but he flatters me if he says that I saved his life."

More to himself than to Farrell he mused "You know, the last weeks of the war were unexpectedly violent and very confused. We hoped the German defences would crumble, but somehow they seemed more, rather than less, determined."

Ronald paused as the uncertainty fluttered in his chest.

"But perhaps some things are best left where they belong, buried in the past, and I'm not sure I can face the prospect of starting something I may not be able to finish. I am very afraid it might open up some old and painful wounds. Sometimes, it really can be better to let sleeping dogs lie."

"I quite understand," came the reply. "But nevertheless I have my instructions and I must abide by them."

"Yes," said Ronald. "Duty is duty" as he recalled words said to him so many years ago.

Desperate for time to think he added, "I will be in touch with you again early next week and give you a decision one way or another. If I decide against, then I understand you will destroy the 1945 log unread, but if I decide to come to London I will do so within your timetable if we can make the appropriate arrangements."

Farrell responded immediately by saying "I am sure we can. I await your decision. Goodbye Mr. Wallace," and with that the line went dead.

CHAPTER 3

The trip to London, arranged less than a week after his visit to the air museum, proved to be much easier than he had expected and entirely uneventful. The taxi collected him immediately after an early breakfast and delivered him, in good time, to Newark to catch the direct train, which departed and then arrived in London, to his surprise, exactly on time. Because of his evident great age, he was somewhat mollycoddled by the young steward, who brought him coffee and a copy of The Times to browse through.

Starting with the obituaries as always, he saw that another of his contemporaries, from Coastal Command, had passed away, recording long and meritorious service in the oil industry, both abroad and at home.

In a moment of reverie, he considered that he was becoming a rather rare animal, an endangered species. Apart from his own log books, which he had still not read, he speculated whether he too should perhaps consign his memories to paper, as so many had done already, and far more eloquently than he could ever hope to achieve. Maybe when this was all over and the Good Lord gave him the time, he would try to put a few thoughts down.

As the two hour journey continued, he again drifted into a gentle reverie – he seemed to do this more and more as he aged – perhaps this would be how his own death would come upon him. He was not particularly religious or devoted, but in the quiet moments of the early hours he gave thought to such matters. Oddly, when flying missions during the war he never thought he would die – the arrogance of youth or was it simply a self-defence mechanism without which he would probably have refused to sit in an aircraft a dozen times or more, at the risk of getting himself court-martialled for what was called 'LMF' – lack of moral fibre.

Even when he had seen his friends meet their end in a burst of anti-aircraft fire or at the hands of a German fighter pilot pouring cannon and machine gun fire into their cockpit, his own feeling of invincibility had not been shaken.

What next shook him was the steward's hand gently but firmly on his shoulder to waken him and advise that they would be in King's Cross Station within five minutes. He thanked her warmly for her attention and she smiled slightly awkwardly at his old-world courtesy.

Alighting slowly from the train, his limbs stiff from the extended period of enforced sitting, he made his way slowly along the platform and out through the crowded concourse to the taxi rank where there was a rather long queue of waiting customers. He took his place at the end of the line of "city gents", male and female, and waited his turn as patiently as he could.

At last, he was at the head of the queue, which by now was as long, if not longer, than when he joined. Where did all the people come from? He smiled at the memory of five young pilots plus luggage and kit bags squeezing into one tiny taxi in 1943 – who was it had sat on his lap? With a shudder he remembered that two of them were dead within a fortnight, just children really, so proud of their shiny new fighters.

"Shiny" was not just a euphemism. Research had shown that careful polishing could reduce air drag to a degree that could add 25 – 30 mph to the top speed of a Spitfire, and that could make a real difference in attack or evasive action. However, in reality, wartime did not provide time for a wax and polish, but there was not a pilot that did not prize the allocation of a brand new, squeaky-clean machine with "delivery mileage only" on the clock.

Yet again, he realised that he had drifted away, as he became aware of the taxi driver's "Where to, guv?" spoken in a rather strident tone, which, he realised, indicated that it was not the first request. There were audible mutterings from the lengthy, impatient queue behind him. Their time was more precious than his, so it seemed.

Apologising profusely, he gave the driver the address just off the Haymarket and sat back, fastening his seatbelt as instructed for his own safety and comfort, as they plunged into the traffic. Looking up at the familiar sights of the London skyline and so many new ones, he remembered the occasion when he had flown in the Victory Parade in July 1945, wing tip to wing tip in the tightest formation, straight down the Mall over thousands of upturned faces of the revellers, then over Buckingham Palace, so low that he could clearly see the faces of the King, Queen and the two Princesses gazing up at him, waving in that stilted regal manner.

He recalled the tears coursing down his cheeks as he remembered his fallen comrades and expected that there was probably not a dry eye in any of the other cockpits. They were the lucky ones entitled by an over generous measure of luck to go on and make what they could of their remaining time on Earth. He had wanted to waggle the wings of his Miss Faithful in response, an acknowledgment of the royal salute, but the solemnity of the occasion forbade it and it would have been too bloody dangerous given the number of aircraft passing in formation over London that day. He knew that never again would such a massed formation of aircraft be seen over the skies of London. The flypasts for subsequent royal events were but a pale shadow by comparison.

He had hoped that the assembled throng had appreciated what a spectacle they had witnessed, but he doubted it. They were just glad to be alive, like him, safe from the fear that their lives might end at any moment from bombs of the Blitz, the staccato buzz of the V1 Doodlebug, with its unnerving silence after the ramjet engine cut out, or the unannounced explosion of the one-ton warhead of the V2 rocket that arrived at supersonic speed, its inbound flight eerily unheard until it followed the devastating blast.

After D-Day at the beginning of June 1944, had been a bad time for the people of London. Just when they thought their war was over, the V1 flying bombs began to arrive from their launch sites on the Channel coast of France. Initially almost unstoppable, it took the fastest fighters to knock a few out of the skies. Thankfully, within a few weeks a combination of anti-aircraft fire using proximity fuses, the speed of the Tempests and finally the introduction of the new, highly secret Meteor jet aircraft, the number of V1's getting through to the heart of London had been vastly reduced. For the time being, as the taxi weaved through the congested, late-morning traffic, he did not care to dwell on his own, very personal, encounters with them.

Purely in terms of quantity, however, Mr. Hitler had not been too far off the mark when he talked of these wonder-weapons turning the tide of war, but it was too simplistic a view and full of vapid rhetoric designed to bolster his defeated nation.

As the drive in the taxi neared his destination, he again wondered why the Germans had been so defiant in the last weeks of the war. So many times he had thought to himself, "Will they never give up?" and especially so on that last sortie – God, the flak that day – when he felt nothing could get through or live through it. This thought shook him rigid. He had thought the unthinkable: that which had been suppressed for almost sixty years.

His heart was pounding, his palms damp with perspiration, as he realised, thankfully, that the taxi was slowing and drawing to the kerb. The driver twisted in his seat and pointed out the short flight of steps and the discrete brass plate that identified the offices of Dawlings & Co.

He alighted, and after paying the driver with a generous tip, he slowly mounted the freshly washed steps, pausing briefly to regain his composure, and pressed the button on the intercom. Obviously no admission here without an appointment.

In response to the disembodied enquiry, he announced himself as "Mr Wallace to see Mr. Farrell at midday." A buzzer sounded and the door popped ajar slightly, so he pushed it open and entered a different world. Plush, royal blue carpet led up to a reception desk made of some exotic wood. Tasteful, original abstract oil paintings decorated the walls and a large, well-tended potted palm helped create an air of calm and professional serenity.

Behind the desk, sat an immaculately coiffured woman, in her late thirties he estimated, dressed in an equally immaculately tailored, haute couture suit of pale lilac silk, with a small diamond clip discreetly displayed at the lapel. The desk was clear, save for a computer screen, a small telephone exchange and what appeared to be a visitors' book.

"Good morning Mr Wallace," said the receptionist in a most attractive voice as she signed him in, (if only he were thirty years younger). "Mr Farrell is of course expecting you. He will only keep you waiting a minute or so and will then see you in his room."

There was something in her tone that suggested that Mr. Farrell did not normally see clients, especially complete strangers, in his room, but before he could speculate further on this, the phone rang, the receptionist picked it up immediately and after a moment said, "Of course, Mr Farrell."

Replacing the receiver the receptionist stood, smoothed her skirt and said, "Mr. Farrell will see you now, if you will follow me, please."

So saying, she set off toward the rear of the building, leaving Ronald trailing in her wake. He could not help but notice – dammit, he was too old for this sort of thing – the tramline-straight seams in her stockings. When had he last seen those? A memory began to surface which he suppressed with some difficulty – if only he were forty years younger, he thought with a barely contained smile.

Pausing at an oak panelled door (as though to check mentally that everything was as it should be) the receptionist knocked twice and, without waiting, opened the door and ushered Ronald inside saying, "Your midday appointment, Mr. Wallace, Sir."

"Thank you Grace," came the reply and, as Ronald turned into the room, he found a slightly balding man of medium height and build, attired in a very formal pinstripe suit, standing next to a large mahogany desk hand outstretched in greeting. A file of papers, tied in pink ribbon, lay at the centre of the desk on a large rectangular, pale blue blotter-pad. A pen stand, an ancient-looking telephone and a small silver clock were the only other adornments.

"Good afternoon, Squadron Leader. I'm Colin Farrell. It's a real pleasure to meet you at long last."

"Please," said Ronald "it's a very long time since I used the title. It's just plain 'Mister' these days."

"As you wish Mr Wallace. I still like to observe the formalities although, like you, it's a long time since I used rank." His smile suggested that his rank might not be related directly to active service, Ronald thought.

He settled Ronald into a comfortable club chair and seated himself similarly, away from his desk, with a coffee table between them.

"I have to say," Farrell continued "that, privately, I am delighted you have made the decision to take Richard's papers. Professionally it did not matter to me one way or the other, but I knew how much he wanted you to say yes. In fact, as I mentioned, he said on more than one occasion that only you could or would understand. He seemed very certain of that.

"Actually, that's not quite true. Just once, I thought he said that someone, possibly called "Keith", would understand, but whether I heard him correctly I really do not know. In any event I did not enquire further."

For a moment, Ronald pondered whether there was any significance in the name *Keith*, before Farrell continued:

"I think we can be brief before we go for lunch."

Motioning toward the coffee table, he indicated a medium sized parcel contained in what appeared to be a robust and tamperproof plastic bag.

"I'm afraid I was not entirely candid in our telephone conversation. In fact I had to indulge in a small deceit, for which I do apologise. My instructions, not to be disclosed to you when we first made contact, were that, on delivery, the complete package of logs was to be handed over sealed, and not to be opened by anyone other than yourself, and then only when you were away from our premises."

40

Half-turning to look towards the file on his desk, he continued: "Possibly Richard was concerned that you might change your mind at the last moment, which would place me in some form of predicament. He was very confident that you would come to London, but inevitably some element of doubt remained and, after all, fifty-plus years is a very long time."

Ronald sat still and silent, struggling with his thoughts and emotions. Twice he made as though to speak, but no words came out. Farrell continued to sit patiently opposite him, elbows resting on the arms of the club chair, hands clasped and his chin resting on the tips of his two index fingers, watching Ronald thoughtfully over the top on his half-moon reading glasses.

After what seemed an age, he stirred and said, "Would you mind awfully if I had a cigarette. Filthy habit I know – never managed to kick it."

"Good Lord, no," replied Ronald, "you carry on. I don't mind at all. I'm very tempted to join you, but it's years since I smoked. Of course, during the war I smoked like a chimney. Thoughts about one's health were not exactly uppermost when faced with the prospect of death and destruction on a daily basis. Times change." He sighed.

Farrell leaned forward and took an untipped cigarette from a silver box lying on the coffee table, reached in to his waistcoat pocket and lit the cigarette from a slim gold Cartier lighter.

As he sat back, blowing a cloud of smoke toward the ceiling Farrell said, "My staff hate this and are always on at me to stop. I know I am dreadfully non-pc, but at my time of life, in my own office, I am inclined to do as I please. Grace, my receptionist, gets very cross with me and usually insists that I see clients in one of the interview rooms. She was indicating her disdain by not even entering the room with you," he added with a chuckle.

"You know, you don't have to make a final decision about these papers right now. In fact, by rights, you have the rest of the fortnight. Why don't we take a break now and go for a spot of lunch at my club, The East India, which is just around the corner. A walk across the square may help to clear your thoughts."

Ronald welcomed the offer as a way of escaping the pressure to make an immediate decision and anyway his stomach was beginning to rumble. Of late, his breakfasting had moved earlier in the day and today's was a long way back.

As he rose from the chair, Farrell said, "We can leave the package here. It will be quite safe. If you decide finally over lunch that you will take it, then I already have a form of receipt and discharge prepared which you can sign when we get back." He clearly hoped that the package would not be sitting on his coffee table at the end of the day.

On leaving the office, they found that the light rain of the early morning had ceased and weak sunlight of late February was breaking through the overcast to leave the pavements glistening. They crossed St. James Square largely in silence.

Farrell led the way into his club where he was recognised immediately and welcomed cordially. After signing Ronald into the visitors' book, Farrell conducted him through to a quiet and comfortable lounge next to the dining room, with oak panelled walls, deep pile carpets and heavy curtains serving to create a tranquil atmosphere. Farrell directed Ronald into a high-backed chair in buttoned green leather. He sank into it gratefully; the tension of the day was beginning to weary him.

When the waiter arrived to take their order for an aperitif, Farrell offered Ronald the menu, while ordering a bottle of dry Chablis and telling the waiter he would have his "usual". Ronald selected smoked salmon to start followed by a plain omelette. Large meals were no longer to his liking, but he felt a glass or two of wine would not go amiss.

As they waited to be called to their table, they fell into easy conversation and Farrell began to outline his limited involvement with the armed forces many years before. From an early age, Farrell had wanted to become a lawyer and after leaving Rugby School, which incidentally brought with it membership of the East India Club, his parents had paid a premium to a small London firm of solicitors so that he could enter into training as a clerk. At that time, in the early post-war years, National Service was in operation and Farrell was not exempted from this, but because of his legal background he was assigned to the Judge Advocate-General's Office and so never saw any form of active service. In fact, he only fired a rifle once in the two years and swore, with a glint in his eye, that the only thing useful he ever learned was never to go anywhere without a piece of paper in his hand.

His spell in the army had passed pleasantly enough. He returned to his old firm on being released at the end of his stint, studied hard for his final exams, passed them with a reasonable level of distinction and shortly afterwards was admitted as a practising solicitor. Much later he found his niche in trust and probate work and the rest, as he put it, was history.

The waiter then called them through to the restaurant and once they were seated, Farrell turned the tables and began to question Ronald about his time with the RAF.

Ronald felt more relaxed in Farrell's company and with a glass of wine in hand responded by saying,

"You know, I really have not talked to anyone about those days for a very long time. It was years before I attended a squadron re-union where I hoped I might find a sympathetic ear, but it was not a pleasant experience and one which I did not want to repeat. My fault, I suppose, nonetheless, but hardly any of my contemporaries attended, and the younger ones seemed to think they knew it all – really, we were worlds apart.

"In all honestly I have to admit that a small part of me did enjoy my war," he continued, "I was young, flying some of the most powerful aircraft designed by man. I was reasonably fit and doing what I thought and believed was right for our world, to make it a better place, free from the tyranny of Hitler's form of fascism. What I did not have was the benefit of twenty-twenty foresight, although, with what was to lie ahead, it was probably just as well I did not have a crystal ball."

Even though he felt quite comfortable, at ease, in the presence of an only slightly younger man, he paused for several seconds, then took a deep breath as though preparing himself to make what might amount to a confession which risked opening a door to his past.

Searching for the right words, his face lined with the tension of his inner struggle, he said in an out-rush of breath, "You know, I did some pretty bad things during the war, not criminal, but not good, even though they were probably unavoidable in the context of total war. I killed a lot of people, military and civilians and this knowledge still haunts me to this day. Much has been said about the fighter pilot being divorced from the dirt of the ground war, and yes, from time to time, in the early days, it was that way.

My father used to tell me about the aerial dog-fights of the Great War but it was never like that for me. I think only twice, and only once memorably did I go, one on one as they say these days, with an enemy pilot – and he damn nearly got the better of me. Hutch told you I saved him, but on that occasion the boot was well and truly on the other foot!"

He paused again, before continuing with a noticeable catch in his voice, "But even so, I knew that it was flesh and blood in my gunsight, not just a machine and I was sending my unseen victims to their deaths.

You cannot imagine the destructive power that was at your fingertips in a fully armed Tempest. God, how I loved my plane. I called her Miss Faithful for all the times she saved my hide, but with four twenty millimetre cannon and eight rockets, she could literally stop a train in its tracks. But again, I always knew it was people, not a machine that I was finishing off." The apology, the regret, the years of torment tumbled from his lips. He gave Farrell a thin smile, before continuing, as though driven to bare his soul.

"I can remember an occasion in early '45, sometime in March I think, when we were sent out to hit just about anything that moved. By then there weren't so many targets and the Luftwaffe was almost nonexistent. That day I was returning to our forward base with all the rockets still on board and most of the ammunition. I had only seen one German staff car and knocked it off the road with one short burst from the guns.

I was back near the frontline and thinking of landing, when a shaft of sunlight exposed a large tank, a Tiger Royal or a Panther, or perhaps one of their self-propelled eighty-eights, hidden under camouflage netting. I could see it was well dug in and intended to be a strong point against our next advance. These tanks were so heavily armoured they were almost impregnable – almost, but not totally. There was no anti-aircraft fire so presumably they did not want to reveal its location.

In the couple of seconds since first spotting it, the plane's speed had carried me to a point where I could no longer see it due to the netting, so I throttled back and began to circle which was, frankly, bloody dangerous. I was a sitting duck for any half-decent flak gunner and the Germans still had these in abundance. I came round twice, or three times, peering down trying to recreate the same angle, but to no avail and I remember thinking – 'This is daft; you're going to get your tail shot off good and proper' – but I thought I would go round just once more and then, there it was; incredible, just as though it was naked. A trick of the light.

So that I did not lose sight of it, I rolled the Tempest onto her back and, looking up as it were, armed the port bank of rockets, opened the throttle, flying inverted and fired almost in the same instant. As I rolled out, I saw the trace of the four rockets disappear into the netting and explode. I headed for home, job done.

A few days later, the front line had advanced and one of my pals found the tank and decided to have a look. Most munitions bounced off one of these monsters but not a rocket. Just one had hit; the other three had flattened everything and everyone nearby. The rocket had apparently punched straight through the armour plate – well, the warhead was probably doing the best part of 500 mph when it hit and exploded in the interior. The armour-plated shell had been strong enough to contain the blast, apart from blowing open the top hatch, and my friend made the mistake of looking inside."

Ronald left the sentence unfinished, seemingly unaware that the intensity of the memory and its telling had so overtaken him that his hands had moved of their own volition to work the throttle, control stick and rocket release. Even his head had moved slightly up and down and from side to side to mirror his recollection.

Suddenly becoming conscious of time and place, Ronald smiled awkwardly and apologised to Farrell:

"Sorry about that. I'm afraid I got a bit carried away, but there are things I have kept under lock and key for so many years."

Farrell waved his apology away, but before he could say anything more Ronald spoke again.

"I started by saying how excited I had been even though from time to time, on virtually every sortie in fact, I was in fear of·death, but the feeling of relief at surviving was so intense, it was like a great surge of electricity through my body. Only once or twice did I truly believe that my end was nigh, but that's another story altogether and I'm not ready to relive that for you or anyone else just now."

"Of course war is dreadful," he continued. "I hated the killing. Can you imagine what it is like to watch your gunfire tear a man in half? And so in the end, when the war was over, I felt I had to apologise, maybe to pay, for what I had done. This, in short order, led me to feeling guilty, perhaps not only for what I had done, but more particularly that I had survived almost unscathed, physically at least, whereas so many others had died horribly or survived only to live on with terrible injuries.

I was never burnt to be scarred for life, or injured apart from a few minor nicks and bruises, but I could, I thought, feel the anger and resentment from those who had been so grievously injured so I locked everything away, buried it – as deep as I could. I was, as they say, in denial and made a life without my war service.

It just reinforced my desire to walk away from it all. I never mentioned my experiences again to anyone and symbolically, I suppose, I put everything associated with the war, my log books, medals, ribbons, commission, everything, into a suitcase, locked it and then pushed it up into the attic of the house where we were living at the time. Although it has moved house with me, it has remained unopened until your letter arrived. Just occasionally I handled the war by treating Ronald Wallace in the third person. Thankfully these occasions were few and far between and got less as time went by.

I mentioned a moment ago the one reunion I attended. A one-time squadron colleague, Eddie Miles was there. He had been badly shot up over Dusseldorf having strayed over a flak no-go area. He got his plane home. It was a real triumph of flying skill given the amount of damage to the aircraft and his own injuries, but the undercarriage collapsed on landing and the plane pan-caked on the runway, bursting into flames.

He was trapped in the cockpit and although the fire crew got to him as quickly as they could, he had been horribly burnt. He spent months being treated by Sir Archie McIndoe's burns and plastic surgery unit at East Grinstead. When I saw him, they had worked wonders in replacing some of his damaged facial features, but I simply could not look at him – what a coward I was."

Ronald continued as Farrell sat in passive silence, absorbing Ronald's outpouring of reminiscences, like the pad of blotting paper which half covered his writing desk.

"Even with what has happened in recent times, such as the Gulf War or Kosovo, you can hardly begin to imagine what northern Germany was like in the early months of 1945. There were people everywhere," spreading his hands for emphasis, "not just hundreds, not just thousands, but maybe millions, standing out like rivers of ants against the snow, which had been heavy and prolonged that winter. If you could not see where the people were, you could see where they had been, with great patches of snow stained, and frozen, yellow from their," he hesitated, "toilet, to put it politely.

There were Wehrmacht army columns, armoured and on foot also heading in the same direction, north-west, perhaps to make a last stand around Hamburg or retreating into Denmark.

We didn't know what they were planning. We did think that, possibly they were hoping to bargain for better terms in the final hour. We just knew they had to be stopped and forced to surrender.

These were legitimate targets, but some…" His voice trailed off as painful memories and images took their hold.

It was evident to Farrell that the dining table had become a confessional even though it was not in his power to give absolution.

Ronald cleared his throat and looked at his host as though expecting, begging, to be asked not to continue, but Farrell remained silent.

Clearing his throat again, preparing himself for the worst, Ronald said, almost in a whisper that Farrell strained to hear, "Then there were the prisoners of war of all nationalities – the PoWs. The Germans' High Command had decided to empty the prisoner of war camps, not the concentration camps, but the Stalags, dozens of them. Closed at a moment's notice, I learnt later, and all of the inmates forcibly marched west and north under armed escort. The German guards were only too happy to accept that particular order as it took them towards our front lines and away from the advancing Russians.

It was literally 'devil take the hindmost' for them, and the Russian devil was gaining ground at an alarming rate, so they cracked on at the best pace they could force out of their prisoners. Some have called it a death march, and many did die – of the bitter cold with no winter clothing or even shoes, just rags tied to their feet, but their guards knew the game was up so they wanted good reports from their charges when they came to face the final judgement. But there was no care for those too ill to move an inch further. Left to die or shot."

As Ronald spoke, his voice had hardened and it was clear to Farrell that he was struggling to keep emotions, memories under control.

"So there they all were, millions trudging along, all muddled up and we still had a job to do. A Tempest was designed for ground support and attack. Sometimes we were called in to knock out a pocket of resistance, but often we were free to find targets of opportunity, shall we say. There was precious little contact with what was left of the Luftwaffe as they were too tied up with trying to stop the American bombers or the Russian army in the east. By then, nowhere was very far from anywhere, so much had Germany's borders shrunk, perhaps only 30 minutes at throttle from the Allies to the Russians. Everything was dreadfully compressed."

A frown crossed Ronald's face, "I must be boring you?"

"No, not at all," replied Farrell, "I mentioned I did my bit of National Service – spent two years of my life polishing things. Do please go on."

Ronald took another deep breath before continuing.

"Yes, and then there were the refugees, like columns of ants I said. You know, at three hundred miles per hour, a Tempest is a very noisy animal, with an engine deeper and rougher in tone than a Rolls Royce Merlin. But, at only a couple of hundred feet up, it gives its target only a second or two of advance warning. Just enough time to turn round and see that its four cannon are already firing.

From the pilot's point of view, target choices are made in a split second, and from the air there is really not a lot of difference between a column of soldiers in field grey and a column of PoWs in grey prison garb."

He paused. "There were mistakes, friendly fire they now call it, but there's nothing friendly about a twenty millimetre cannon shell. I…" Ronald bit his lip, unable to finish his thought.

"Did you… make a mistake?" Farrell asked as gently as he could, seeing Ronald's inner torment.

"No, maybe, possibly I thought so," replied Ronald covering his face with his hands for a moment. "I really didn't know at the time, but it has haunted me all these years fearing that I might have. All that I could bring myself to write in my log was '*Ground attack. Military convoy*'.

"I never talked about it. I just couldn't. It was too awful. Except once, a couple of years after the war ended I started to tell Libby, my late wife about it. She held me as I cried, held me until I stopped, and then she made love to me so gently, with such tenderness as though her compassion could wash away my pain, my guilt."

Speaking in a whisper he added, "I think we made the baby that night." Then, realising he had spoken such a secret, intimate, thought out loud, Ronald blushed deeply and started to apologise, with a little laugh to cover his discomfort.

Farrell was sympathetic as he tried to take the edge off Ronald's embarrassment, making no reference to Ronald's personal admission while he responded to Ronald's long-held dread.

"I am sure, even if it did happen, that you are forgiven, but perhaps more importantly, you need to find it within you to forgive yourself. If you will allow me to say so, I am also sure it's time you put aside this burden. With my legal hat on, as long as the civilians, the enemy's or our own, were not your intended target, you should have a clear conscience under the Rules of War. An easy thing for me to say, perhaps, but think about it – it may bring you some comfort, even now, after so many years."

Ronald smiled his thanks and found in some small way his burden might seem a little lighter, but for a long period he sat scrunching his table napkin into an even smaller ball.

To break the silence, Farrell asked, "If you don't mind me enquiring, what was it that decided you to come to London?"

"Hah!" was Ronald's response, with a chuckle. "The bane of my life," and so saying he reached into his jacket pocket, took out a small yellow die.

"Used to have two of these" he muttered, as he flipped it onto the table between them, where it bounced off the salt cellar and came to a rest with six black spots uppermost.

"Hah!" he said again, leaning back and seeming to make a decision.

"During the war, in the way that silly superstitions can arise out of nothing, I had two yellow dice and, although I can no longer remember how or why it started, I used to roll them whenever we flew a sortie. Someone decided that if I rolled a six everything should be OK – a double six was even better, but it earned me the nickname of Lucky Six and I even used that as my call sign. I guess I knew that one or both of the dice was loaded, so often did the six come up, but I have to confess I became as much of a believer as they were. Just a crumb of comfort, and we all clung willingly to the good omen to save us from the worst of fates. Strangely enough, never did a sortie go especially badly when the six appeared. If it had, then it would have shown it up for what it really was – a bit of childish nonsense. Just once... they let me down very badly," he added quietly. The bitterness of the memory caught in his throat.

"But I did open the suitcase when your letter arrived and although I could not bring myself to open any of my log books, I did find the die, rolled it – like a fool – and of course it came up six, just as I knew it would really. It's silly how such a tiny thing can play so great a role in one's life."

Farrell raised a quizzical eyebrow as Ronald reflected:

"How can the course of life be decided on such trivia, but the die has spoken and I think that the decision has been made for me. Deep down, I do want to know what happened in those three days – to honour the trust that Hutch has put in me, even though I know that I am going to revisit almost everything I have managed to steer away from for so long."

Had he realised that they were well into their second bottle of Chablis and that almost two hours had passed since they sat down to eat, Ronald might not have been so casual in the way the decision was reached, but now, it seemed, it was too late to turn back.

Farrell smiled broadly, offered Ronald his hand across the table and said, "Congratulations, I know that you have made the right decision. Richard would be so pleased. It has been a pleasure to listen to your reminiscences. A couple of times you asked me if I could imagine, and the honest answer is that, no, I can't and in part, I would not presume to. But, sadly I do still have some small matters that require my attention back at my office before the day's end," and at this he signalled to one of the waiters who brought a slip of paper on silver salver. Farrell simply signed the chit, then rose from his seat and motioned Ronald toward the door.

Dusk was creeping across the sky as they stepped out on to the square and they completed their walk back to Farrell's office chatting amiably. A cool breeze had blown up and Ronald chose to stop for a moment to slip on his overcoat. He had no wish to run the risk of getting a chill at his time of life and he had the distinct feeling that he was going to need his health to cope with the task that lay ahead.

Back in Farrell's office, the formalities were brief; just the receipt to sign which Farrell placed carefully with the file on his desk. A cheque from the firm to reimburse his expenses was tucked safely into his wallet, then after a few parting pleasantries, and a lingering glance at Grace, Ronald was outside on the street, climbing into the taxi that had been ordered for him, with the unopened parcel of Hutch's logbooks placed carefully, almost reverently on the seat beside him.

But, as his sobriety gradually returned, he came to regard the parcel with growing jaundice, so that when he eventually found his seat on the train home, he pushed the parcel firmly into the overhead storage rack and declined to give it a second glance. It was regrettably, he thought, still there as the train pulled in, only a little late, to Newark. Farrell, true to his word had called ahead so that there was a taxi waiting for him at the exit.

Back home, the parcel went, to remain unopened, onto the dining room table and, as he went wearily to his bed, he knew that it would still be there in the morning, no matter how much he might want to wish it away.

As he lay in the darkness, his mind refused to switch off and continued to recycle the events of the past few months. How had it all begun? First, there was the photograph, then there was the letter, but that begged the question of why the letter. How did they know he was still alive? Everything in the solicitor's letter assumed, (was certain?) that he was still alive – and in reasonably good health. What would have been the point of it all, if he were bedridden in a nursing home? That 'they' – Farrell – knew his condition, was the only, and inescapable conclusion.

The phone call.

He sat bolt upright in his bed. That phone call a couple of weeks before he read of Hutch's death. It had irritated him at the time, thinking that the pension people really ought to have all the information they needed, but then he remembered the question seeking confirmation that there had been no major changes to his health. 'Of course not', he had snapped, nothing since his hip operation. It seemed that there was more to that Mr. Farrell than met the eye.

Game, set and match to Hutch.

CHAPTER 4

That night he slept badly, thoroughly rattled by the interference in his life, and dreamt of long lost friends, burning aircraft and pilots' log books that were unreadable. In fact it was a relief when he finally woke even though it was still dark outside. He felt heavy and lethargic, burdened by the previous day's revelations which had resulted in a terrible headache. So, instead of his daily shower, he ran a bath as hot as he could take, in which he soaked for half an hour after he had shaved.

While he shaved, carefully lathering his face with an old badger-bristle brush, he regarded his reflection in the mirror. His once five feet ten and a half inch frame was now nearer five nine, his shoulders a little hunched, but he could still straighten his back if he made the effort. The jowls and the bags under his eyes sagged more than he liked and sometimes he thought his neck scrawny. He had gone down a half collar size in recent years and still the collars looked too big. His blue eyes continued to be clear, but his mane of blonde hair was now pure white. Then, as now, he wore it unfashionably long, although he had long since given up the use of the hair cream that had usually held it in place under his flying helmet all those years ago.

He ran his finger over a scar, now faded so that it was little more than a crease, which ran from the centre of his forehead, up above his left eye, still largely concealed by his hair. A long time ago he had examined the scar, when it was fresh, tracing the line of stitches with a trembling finger into his hairline, then across the top of his skull for eight inches and more. An inch or so lower and he would have been blinded. Taking off his flying helmet might not have been one of his better decisions, he reflected with a wry smile, but he had needed to tease every last scintilla of sensation, even the whiffle of the airflow, from his dying aircraft to keep it in the air those precious two or three seconds longer. And it mattered not, for *she* had loved it, calling it his pirate's scar.

He had two vanities. He retained his pencil moustache, painstakingly trimmed once a week and he removed all the excess hair that sprouted from his nose and ears. He was convinced that this knocked years off his looks; it was his little secret. He grunted with satisfaction at the result.

The bath seemed to do him good. His headache cleared, the tension in his neck had receded and he felt quite refreshed. By the time he had towelled off, standing on his ancient cork bathmat, and dressed, the eastern sky was brightening with the prospect of a better day. Somehow that bathmat, carted from house to house was symbolic of his life, a relic from another time, but as so often, when there was no future, what was the point in trying to keep up with it. To complete the ritual, he dried the bathmat carefully and left it propped, in its allocated spot, against the bath's side.

As he went into the kitchen to make his breakfast, he heard The Times drop through the letter box. As usual, the paper boy, who was the grandson of one of his neighbours, hammered on the door to let him know it had arrived. It was a nice thought – the lad obviously believed that most old people, and Ronald in particular, were stone deaf. In fact, his hearing was still in good shape provided there was not too much background noise.

Unlike some of his fellow pilots, he had not suffered any serious damage to his ears from the innumerable high speed changes of altitude which were part and parcel of aerial combat – except once, when he was in the grip of a heavy head-cold and had flown contrary to the Medical Officer's advice.

The squadron had been short of pilots, so he had considered he had no choice but to go. He had flown as top cover that day, but the Germans had attacked their formation from the same level, taking them all by surprise. He had been obliged to dive at full speed through more than 5,000 feet and the pain in his ears had been excruciating, to the extent that he had been unable to hear any of the calls from his Number Two.

As a consequence, he had spent much of the engagement flinging his Spitfire around the sky, more in an attempt at self-preservation than to contribute to the sortie. One ME109 had floated past his nose firing at another Spitfire and even then he had missed by a mile, but at least it distracted the German pilot who had broken off the attack. He had been, in the current jargon, an almost complete waste of space that day, and he was grateful that the sortie had ended with no losses on their side. The MO had forcibly rested him for a week to give his ears a chance to recover.

As he retrieved the newspaper, his thoughts turned to his morning routine, but in the same moment he concluded that this day, of all days, was one where routine would have to take a back seat. With the feeling that he might be in need of greater sustenance to fortify him for the task ahead, he went into the kitchen and set about cooking himself a full English breakfast; bacon, egg, tomatoes, sausage and a thick slab of fried bread – not good for the cholesterol, but his health was the least of his worries, and the feast was washed down with a large mug of sweet builder's tea – lashings of sugar and a generous dollop of condensed milk. All was taken at the kitchen table – no Times today, which stayed unopened on the sideboard.

At the back of his mind, he knew that really he was just wasting time to put off the inevitable and so, after washing up, he went through to the dining room, opened the curtains and contemplated the still-sealed package on the table. From the far corner of the room he fetched his small suitcase, where he had left it half-hidden under the knee-hole of his writing bureau and then placed it next to the package.

He had brought the case down from the attic a couple of days previously, not long after he had tentatively made the decision to go to London. It had taken a quarter hour's patient searching to locate the case, which, perhaps symbolically, was in the farthest, darkest corner, buried under years of accumulated family memorabilia. Really, the bulk of it was just rubbish, but moving it to reach the case cost him a nasty crack on the top of his head when he stood upright, forgetting the roof truss immediately overhead. He had, childishly, vented his anger and frustration with a stream of expletives, which he immediately regretted – but he did feel better for the outburst.

In the dining room, he had only opened the case long enough to remove the yellow die. Then he had slammed the lid shut, thrusting the case away into the shadows, not yet ready to encounter any more reminders of his past.

Returning momentarily to the kitchen, he took a pair of scissors from the drawer and then proceeded carefully to cut the sides of the plastic bag and remove its contents. He found seven blue coloured Pilots Flying Log Books for the years 1939 to 1945 each bearing, embossed in gold, the RAF's coat of arms and motto "Per Ardua ad Astra" – *Through difficulty to the stars* – with the owner's name hand written on the front together with rank – rising from Flight Lieutenant to Wing Commander over this period. He recognised Hutch's backward sloping hand instantly and he felt the first, cold touch to his heart.

Taking a deep breath, he flipped the catches on his own case, lifted the lid and surveyed the contents. In his search, he moved some items to one side, including a rather tattered schoolboy's diary. An old silver photograph frame with an engine-turned finish, he left face down. Now was not the time, not yet. Only when he was ready, but not yet.

At last, half hidden under a bar supporting a row of dress medals, he found and took out a similar bundle of pilot's logs, all held together with rubber bands, Air Ministry issue, that had long since gone brittle and which shattered into dozens of tiny segments as he tried to separate the individual volumes. Pilot Officer rising to Squadron Leader – he had never quite matched Hutch, but then if he had, their paths would certainly have gone in different directions. It was rare for two officers to have served together for such a prolonged period.

He regarded the two stacks of log books as though they were a pair of ticking bombs on countdown to explode into his life. His hands hovered over first one, then the other as he was racked by the indecision that accompanies life-altering moments.

Eventually, he concluded that he could not consider the two records of wartime service together and that the only way to break the ice was to conduct his initial inspection with physical separation; the life of Hutch Hutchinson would remain for the time being in the dining room and the life of Ronno, Lucky 6, Wallace he removed to the lounge, until he was ready to bring the two together again.

Clutching the bundle of his own log books to his chest, he made his way through to the lounge, setting them on the side table next to his favourite armchair into which he lowered himself with a deep sigh.

For several moments the only sounds that broke the silence in the room were the rhythmic ticking of the ornate skeleton clock in its glass case in the centre of the mantle over the fireplace, and his own slightly asthmatic breathing. He noticed that his hands were trembling, so he took another deep breath – he was doing a lot of that he thought – and selected one of his own log books. Any one of them would do.

He had to start the process of going back and he felt deep down he had to open his own case-history as a first step and to come to terms with that; for better or for worse – as the words of his two marriage ceremonies echoed in his ears. It was almost sixty years ago, dammit, and what did he have to be frightened of? But he knew it was not going to be as simple as that. The notes would take him on a journey of reliving his war years and at the same time addressing the emotions and experiences he had suppressed almost entirely.

Looking at the book in his hands, he saw that it was for 1942, at the very start of his war, not long after he had been posted to an operational squadron. Turning the first page he read the words:

"January 1st - Test flight Spitfire IX, JD –C Fuel flow problem persists. 30 minutes."

He remembered an uncomfortable flight with the engine spitting and banging even though it had warmed up and successfully gone through a full power test, according to his mechanic. He had been glad to get back on the ground in one piece.

"January 2nd – same problem. Took JD-K, clapped out. Coast patrol. Nothing. 2 hours 45 minutes."

"January 3rd – Fog."

"January 4th – Test flight JD –C. Problem cured. Difficult landing, low cloud. 30 minutes."

That was an understatement if ever there was one. He had known virtually from the moment he got the wheels up that everything was OK and he should have contented himself with just a circuit and back in pretty foul conditions, but he had to push his luck, had to indulge in some rather enjoyable although wholly inappropriate aerobatics above the cloud – strictly against regulations. Then he discovered on his way back in that the cloud base had dropped to the deck and it was more by luck than judgement that he had found himself reasonably lined up with the landing strip. Ten minutes more and he would have been in real trouble, so he took the ticking off from his CO with as much good grace as he could manage.

"January 5th A.M. RIP."

There was nothing else on the page. He stared at the notation trying to understand its significance. Obviously someone had died, but who. And then it dawned on him. A.M. stood for Amy Mollison or Amy Johnson as she had been more popularly known. Learning of her tragic, and seeming unnecessary death, had been a profound shock. As Orville Wright had been his father's hero, so Amy Johnson had been his heroine.

From his earliest teens, he had avidly followed her career and when she had returned in triumph from her record setting solo flight in her De Havilland Gypsy Moth named Jason, to Australia in 1930 he had cajoled, pestered, and generally been a pain the neck (as only a ten year old can), until his father had relented, allowing him to take a day off school and took him to the homecoming held at Croydon's airport.

Although just one in a crowd of many, many thousands, as he sat on his father's shoulders for a better view, it seemed to him that she spoke to him in her clear Yorkshire accent, directly and personally through the hastily erected public address system. Her ground-breaking trip had made her a pioneer of the people and especially to women, who at the time were numbered only as a handful in the world of aviation.

He had watched her achievements and records continue to grow in the following years, until tragedy nearly overtook her in 1933, when, with her husband, Jim Mollinson, they attempted the fastest east to west crossing of the Atlantic to North America in their specially prepared DeHavilland Rapide named 'Seafarer'. The flight had ended disastrously with Amy suffering a broken leg from a crash landing in Connecticut, but she had been befriended by America's golden girl Amelia Earhart who had become the first woman to fly the Atlantic solo from west to east.

Amy's achievement had been accorded the accolade of a tickertape parade through the streets of New York which he had seen as a newsreel report at his local cinema a couple of weeks later. She became an international celebrity.

How sad and ironic that in less than five years, her friend Amelia would be dead, presumed to have run out of fuel, lost somewhere over the incredible vastness of the Pacific, attempting to fly west to east round the world, and at the same time Amy's star would have begun to wane. She and her husband had taken part in a race, organised by the Daily Express, to set the fastest time from England to Australia. Flying in one of three specially built twin-engined DeHavilland DH88 Comets, they had led the race initially, but amongst rumours of dissent, sabotage and illness they had pulled out of the race when they had reached the Middle East. After that, they had slipped from the social scene and disappeared quietly from view, divorcing in 1938.

His contact with her would have remained completely remote and impersonal, but for the strangest of coincidences.

He had been at an Advanced Flying Training Unit just outside Wrexham in late 1941 on a training course, and was standing on the apron in front of the control tower watching one of his colleagues. He had seen a small twin engine passenger plane land in the circuit of other aircraft, and out of the corner of his eye observed it taxi round and park a little to one side. Several passengers had disembarked carrying kitbags, trainee pilots or navigators arriving, apparently.

He then noticed the pilot climb down and walk toward him. Still he took no particular notice until he realised the pilot, slight of stature, intended to speak to him. Asking the way to the station office in a strong Yorkshire accent, he realised to his amazement that he was in her presence. Initially he was too tongue-tied, embarrassed even, to express his admiration for her achievements – he explained the origins of his own second name and they joked that if ever he had a baby girl he would have to name her Amy.

She informed him that once war broke out she felt compelled to do her bit (as she put it), and so had signed up, as had Jim Mollinson, to join the Air Transport Auxiliary to ferry aircraft, materials and personnel around the country in order to free other pilots for combat. She admitted candidly that it often meant flying in less than ideal conditions, but she said it was all part of the job. They had parted company with a brief handshake and Ronald had continued with his own preparation for war.

Of course, her death less than three months later had come as a real shock, especially given the circumstances. A simple flight from Blackpool, flying alone in another twin-engined transport to Oxford had gone tragically wrong, when a parachute was seen in foul weather descending over the Thames estuary, miles from her correct destination. Her body was never found. She must have died within moments of entering the freezing January waters.

Just as for Amelia, there had been a board of enquiry into the accident and for years there were books written and seemingly endless columns of speculation that always seem to accompany the untimely loss of a special treasured person; but cock-up or conspiracy, it never brought them back.

In the 1970s, he had gone to visit the memorabilia of her life which had been set up in Sewerby Hall just outside Bridlington, not far from her home town of Hull. He had stood alone in the trophy room in silent memory and tribute, quietly recollecting the brief moment their paths had crossed.

Putting the log book back on the side table, Ronald rested his head on the wing of his chair and reflected on the early years, the few exhilarating flights with the University Air Squadron in an aircraft not much advanced from those maintained by his father, before the imminent threat of war curtailed all such activity.

He had endured the frustration of being put on reserve and trying to concentrate on his studies for a history degree until finally the ultimate joy, against the depressing news of the progress of the war, of receiving his call up papers. He could remember the mixed emotions of his parents as the pilot casualties from the Battle of Britain rose steadily, but he was kept safe, tied to the classroom as he learnt the rudiments of aerodynamics, navigation, meteorology, radio-telephony and the other essential elements that combined to make the tyro pilot. And just occasionally he was allowed a flight in a two-seater trainer with an instructor recalled to his country's service, a veteran of the Great War.

His progress under the tutelage of the instructor, something of a martinet, was steady, but not spectacular, each minute of flight carefully recorded and officially countersigned until after some twenty hours of tuition he had hesitantly managed to go solo.

With his first log book open on his lap, Ronald charted his progress page by page, reliving the thrill of the first flights and, as his skills advanced, there were new, more challenging elements; aerobatics, again with an instructor, cross country navigation, night flying (how he hated that), blind flying, ground gunnery and finally airborne gunnery, where he could begin to believe that, at last, he was getting somewhere on the long road to joining a squadron. He discovered he had a natural talent for deflection – the art of aiming and firing the guns ahead of the target to compensate for its forward travel.

If flying was his delight, then parachute training was his nemesis. Taken at an airfield near Liverpool, he listened intently to the advice, but from the moment he climbed into the basket of the barrage balloon that was to carry him aloft for the static release, his mind became a complete blank and his legs turned to jelly. For a second or two, perched on the lip of the hole cut in the floor of the basket, peering down at the diminutive figures below as though seen through the wrong end of a telescope, he feared that he would baulk at the jump while the instructor's demeanour changed from encouragement to outright threat.

Was it a push or just a sympathetic pat on the back, but then he was gone, plunging earthwards to the hiss of the static line spewing out behind his back, his gorge rising faster than the ground below, then the wonderful heart-stopping wrench as the silk canopy deployed and lowered him, with a hefty thump, safely back to the ground. He could not but be grateful that wartime pressures permitted only the one live jump, but at least it was done, and he could move on to yet more advanced training.

Then came that unforgettable day (the entry was almost engraved on to the page of his log) when he was allowed his first flight in a Spitfire, a Mark 2, an old warhorse in early retirement, now completely outclassed by the technical advances forced from the pressure-cooker of wartime development to stay one step ahead of the enemy.

But it was a Spit, his own for an hour in which to live for real the dreams born at Hendon that sunny summer's day with his father and Hutch in 1936. He was in heaven, a child in a sweetshop spoilt for choice; power, agility, balance – he'd tried it all with growing confidence and by the time he landed, the grin on his face was as wide as the Spit's wingspan.

As he climbed down from the cockpit, bursting with confidence, he was brought firmly back down to earth by an old hand, a fitter also recalled from the Great War who reminded him forcefully that, "out there" waiting for him, waiting to kill him, were other pilots who were vastly more experienced, already battle hardened. He did his best to take the advice to heart.

He woke with a start to find that the log book had tumbled from his lap as he had drifted off. To his surprise, he found on the side table a cold mug of coffee, a half-eaten sandwich and an empty glass, which when he sniffed it, had at some time contained his favourite whisky. He had no recollection of preparing any food or drink, so it appeared that for much of his day he had been completely absorbed in the process of reading and remembering.

Peering through sleep-dimmed eyes at the mantle-clock, he saw that it was late afternoon. It had taken him nearly the whole day to get just the first couple of his books into perspective, but as he sat, slumped and unwilling to move, he found that, just as he had known all along in his heart of hearts, there really was not so very much to be frightened of. It was all so long ago, and the young Ronno Wallace was more like a fondly remembered younger brother than his own timorous self.

At this point he reached a decision; one that, initially, he had thought might be days rather than hours in the making. Pushing his ageing frame from the chair, he walked slowly, stiffly and a little unsteadily from the lounge and through to the dining room where Hutch's papers still lay, inviting his inspection, on the dining table.

Seating himself at his breakfast chair, he placed his right hand on the pile of log books and gently fanned them sideways, like a croupier spreading a deck of cards, his hand steady and untroubled as he thought to himself:

"Hello, Hutch, old friend, shall we see what you have to tell us?" Realising he had in fact spoken out loud, he chuckled at his foolishness and then picked up the first book and began to read.

Later that night, again finding a cold drink, and another half eaten meal, he could at least recall having been in the kitchen and preparing a simple meal, almost one handed, while he read one of Hutch's logs held in the other. The whisky glass was there again and the falling level in the bottle at its side evidenced his intake.

Perhaps he should not have expected anything else, but Hutch's logs essentially told no different a story from his own: basic and advanced flight training and then on to a squadron, which although of historical interest, provided not a clue, not a shred of useful information, as far as he could tell, toward the interpretation and unlocking of the code.

Fortified and emboldened by the whisky, Ronald went back to the pile of log books and found the one from 1945. The sealed pages were evident as soon as he opened the cover, as were the earlier and later pages that had been photocopied.

Fearful of damaging whatever gems of information might be concealed, he initially made a small cut with the pair of scissors and established that the glue used to seal the pages was only a quarter of an inch wide around each edge. Feeling more confident, he set about cutting off the border to free the pages.

As the last of the waste fell away, he teased the pages open with an unsteady hand.

"What the hell!" he exclaimed involuntarily. The pages were completely and utterly blank.

"Damn you, Hutch!" he bellowed, giving vent to his anger. "Is this your idea of a joke?"

His words echoed back in the empty house, reinforcing the often unpleasant sense of his isolation.

And so it was that he called it a day, declining to consider the remainder of Hutch's log books, and retired to his bed more than a little drunk, none the wiser, but angry and frustrated by the apparent lack of progress and this unexpected turn of events.

Yet again, he dreamed the dream and awoke with pulses racing, certain that his screams had gone unheard, unanswered.

CHAPTER 5

One evening a few days later, while he was seated at the dining table, still struggling with the code, but with little feeling he might be on the verge of a breakthrough, the telephone rang, breaking his chain of thought. Muttering darkly about the interruption, he picked up the handset and lowered himself into his favourite armchair as he answered.

He heard the voice at the other end of the phone say in an accent he faintly seemed to recognise, "Is that Squadron Leader Wallace?" Ronald froze – no one had addressed him in that way in very many years, except of course the solicitor in London. Could there be a connection?

The voice continued, "I am trying to contact Squadron Leader Wallace, I hope I have the right number?"

"Yes," replied Ronald. "This is Squadron Leader Wallace," then checking himself, he continued, "this is Ronald Wallace. I haven't used the rank for years – just plain Mr. Wallace these days."

"Thank goodness for that," came the reply and after a noticeable pause the caller explained, "this is, well I was, Flight Lieutenant Keith Watson. I don't suppose you will remember me."

Focke-Wulf 190 with its wing breaking off; Hutch's voice; Hutch and Keith shepherding him home; his Spit going arse-over-tit at Shoreham. Vibrant images, fresh as though yesterday's, swirled through his mind, making him feel quite sick.

"Yes, yes of course, Keith – it's been such a very long time."

"I am awfully sorry this call is so late, but it has taken me an age to make up my mind whether or not I would call you. But, forgive me, I should explain myself better. A couple of days ago, I took a phone call from a solicitor in London saying he had a message for me from Group Captain Richard Hutchinson and would I go to London, all expenses paid, to collect it.

"I'm afraid I wasn't terribly polite. I said: "Don't be daft – he's dead," and the solicitor said yes, he knew that, but that the message was only to be delivered after the Group Captain's death."

Now Keith had Ronald's complete attention. What the hell's going on? he wondered.

"Anyway," Watson continued, "for the sake of a free lunch I thought I would go. To cut a long story short, I went down to London at the end of last week. The meeting with the solicitor was very brief. All he did was to hand me an envelope, saying it had been sealed in accordance with the Group Captain's instruction. I could take it and open it, but not in his presence, or it would be destroyed forever. He wouldn't give me any further explanation – claimed his hands were completely tied by client confidentiality. (Heard that one before, thought Ronald) Then he took me to lunch at his club where he did the oddest thing. He said he had something to show me: he took a little yellow dice out of his pocket and pitched it onto the table between us. It came up six and he laughed out loud.

"I took the envelope, and thought about it over the weekend trying to decide whether I really wanted to get involved. After all, I hadn't seen Hutch since 1945, or maybe it was '46. It's hard to remember after so many years and to be honest I probably thought he had died ages ago. In the end, curiosity got the better of me and I opened it yesterday. It contained a single sheet of paper and on it was written one date which was 1-5-1945, then just two words – BLACK KNIGHT – and a phone number – yours."

Ronald hesitated, weighing his reply. "There's much to tell you and so much more that I don't understand. If you feel up to it, I think we should meet."

"That's another odd thing," came the reply. "It turns out that, after all these years, we only live an hour or so apart by car. Somehow I feel I am being managed, dangled just like a puppet, in some great scheme by Hutch, so if it's OK with you, I'll drive over in the morning."

"That's fine by me," said Ronald, and was about to replace the handset when a thought struck him.

"Before you go, Keith, will you answer me one simple question? Did you by any chance get a phone call last autumn, perhaps September time, out of the blue, about your war service pension?"

"No, I don't think so," Keith responded after a moment's hesitation, and Ronald felt a twinge of disappointment, before Keith continued with a note of surprise and then understanding in his voice, "but, come to think of it, at about that time I did have a really odd call from my doctor's surgery. They wanted confirmation about some personal details, and about my health which I thought they really ought to know, especially as I'd gone in for an annual check-up only a few days previously. I had a bit of a moan about it and they fobbed me off with the excuse that some of their computer records had become corrupted. I left it at that and thought no more about it. Why? Is there some connection?"

"Well, yes, I think there is. I think it was Hutch, or someone on his behalf, checking that you were capable of whatever he wanted from you. Around the same time, I had a call about my pension. Same sort of questions. Has to be Hutch, making sure his plan had a fair chance of working," Ronald replied.

"What did I say about feeling like a puppet? The feeling is getting stronger by the minute. I'll see you in the morning." Keith broke the connection.

Ronald replaced the handset in a reflective, troubled mood.

Shoreham. Such a little place, just a dot on the map, but a dot where it – his war, his life – so nearly all came to a very unpleasant end, but where there also began a chain of events which would take him to happiness, the like of which he could not begin to imagine, as he had battled to keep his Spitfire in the air that fateful day.

He pondered what Keith's visit might bring; perhaps only the renewal of a wartime friendship, but how much more? Would it be the solution of Hutch's puzzle or just a passing opportunity for two former comrades to jaw endlessly about the old days? Or, and perhaps worse, should he take the risk that in opening Pandora's Box, he might release the horrors foretold by the legend.

He was still by no means sure, and at one point strode purposely toward the telephone fully intent on telling Keith to forget it, to leave it all where he had left it, sixty years in his past, buried under layer upon carefully constructed layer of mental denial, but his step faltered and his hand did not pick up the receiver.

Why not talk to Keith? He had precious few acquaintances these days, no real friends and Torrie, so far away on the south coast had more than enough on her plate trying to cope with her husband's Parkinson's disease. Perhaps he would visit her after Keith had gone.

She would tell him, as she had so often, that he was a silly old fool, although even she had admitted, albeit reluctantly, in the years after their father's funeral, that there were gaps, loose ends, unanswered questions about their father Alfred's history, during and after Berlin. Their regular Sunday night phone calls, taking it in turn to dial, never missed, often containing the "Do you remember when Dad...?" question – always unanswered – had become such a support, a rock on which he could rely. Yes, a visit before it was too late for either or both of them. There was still enough credit left in the time and health banks, he hoped.

With the thought of his sister's enduring love, he left the phone untouched, the meeting with Keith to remain as scheduled and wandered back to the lounge and picked up his log book for 1943.

Turning the pages slowly, he recalled, like the flicker of the leaves in a photograph album, fleeting moments of time, his baptism in a frontline squadron:

Of the first encounter with the enemy – tiny flitting specks that changed in a split-second to become venom-spitting predators.

Of trying to stay with his leader, his Number One, to protect him; and failing – miserably.

Of getting and taking the bollocking – it was not a game.

Of the first time, being on the receiving end – the sweat-drenching, heart-bursting, near trouser-soiling fear and the indescribable relief at being saved. Another bollocking. It was not a game. Do your duty. Follow the rules.

Of the first time on the giving end of the equation. Don't hesitate, don't question, do your duty. Remember the bollocking – remember Otto's words. Befehl ist befehl.

Of patrols in the icy cold crystal-clear skies at 25,000 feet – he shuddered involuntarily at the recollection of a Spitfire tumbling out of formation, the pilot deaf to all calls, unconscious at his controls through oxygen starvation.

Of patrols through the murk of dense banks of cloud, water condensing on the screen and dribbling into the cockpit with the ever present danger and fear of collision.

Of his first combat victory; the elation of the kill, the disgust of the killing – Befehl ist befehl.

Of his second kill, then a third. The possibles and the probables, all noted in his log book, until the tide turned and he had become that battle-hardened veteran – an Ace with five confirmed kills, waiting "out there" for some young greenhorn German pilot, who in his turn would be praying to survive another day.

Of simple victories. Of gut wrenching victories where the outcome lay in the balance until the final second. Duty is duty. Kill or be killed.

Of colleagues that came and went; obliterated, hospitalised, maimed for life, or prisoner of war, to be replaced by the young and inexperienced, who he tried to protect, to advise, to give of his own hard-won experience.

Of a young Keith Watson, who learned quickly, who notched up a couple of possibles before his first confirmed kill – solid and dependable.

And then Shoreham, in the summer of '43. His hand turned the page and the memories came flooding back.

The Log recorded:
Thursday 11th August 1943
Patrol over Bellancourt/ Auxe-la-Chapelle R H U B A R B.

They called it a 'Rhubarb'; a free ranging attack in one or more pairs over enemy held France, in the Pas de Calais region, almost at the limit of their combat endurance to carry the war back to the Germans in some small way. No escorts, no plans, no timetable just go and seek out targets, cause as much trouble as possible, provoke a reaction, deal with it and get back unscathed, just as long as your ammo tracks were empty. That last bit was the theory; the practice proved more difficult.

This day, the practice stretched the theory to the limit.

Two pairs of Spitfires, new Mk IXs, Hutch covered by Teddy Jones, who was on his first Rhubarb, and Keith Watson to cover Ronald, sped in their pairs, three hundred yards apart out over the south coast, between Hastings and Littlehampton, dipping to fifty feet above the sea to minimise radar detection.

Their intended target area was a sweep around the Luftwaffe base at Bellancourt from which their fighter squadrons of Me109s and Fw190s had been harassing coastal shipping and the south coast airfields for weeks. Seek and destroy.

Hutch's commands were clear, crisp and concise and, as the French coast appeared low on their horizon, he ordered a climb to five hundred feet and widened the gap between the pairs to spread the search.

With the interference of the German radar system buzzing in his earphones, Ronald struggled to balance the tasks of holding station, following Hutch's instructions, checking the route on their flight map, keeping a proper lookout for enemy fighters, anti-aircraft fire and power lines as well as being alert for anything amiss within the mechanics of the engine or the airframe.

Keeping five tons of Spitfire in the air at over 270 miles an hour was largely second nature to him now, but he wondered how Teddy was coping. Putting him with Hutch was a logical decision given his lack of experience and Ronald was relieved when Keith was scheduled as his Number Two.

Nursemaiding was not his natural forte and he knew he could rely on Keith to watch his tail.

Flashing across the French coast, Hutch dropped them back to 100 feet and they charged on over hedgerows, farm buildings, a military convoy; bursts of flak falling behind, eating up the miles, five per minute, as they swept toward their intended target.

After five minutes Hutch ordered a climb to 5000 feet so they hung on their propellers, gaining height, alert to enemy fighter patrols. As they climbed, the outline of the triangle of the runways at Auxe-la-Chapelle began to appear off the leading edge of his left wing.

Separating into their pairs, Hutch ordered the attack to begin, he from due west, Ronald from the south west, converging over the airfield, but fifteen seconds apart to minimise the possibility of collision, then parting to divide the effect of the inevitable anti-aircraft fire.

"Full throttle, go," was Hutch's cryptic command.

Curving away to the west with Keith at his wingtip, Ronald sought and found the obscurity of a patch of light cloud, delaying those few precious, dangerous seconds to allow Hutch to lead the attack from his left. Still, incredibly, they seemed to have the element of surprise.

Peering through the veil of cloud, he glimpsed Hutch begin his dive alone. No sign of Teddy, but they could not delay and there was no choice other than to go themselves. Signalling to Keith with a wave of his hand, they broke cover as one and began their downward charge as one, throttles wide open, heartbeats rising almost uncontrollably, pounding in their ears.

Moistening his lips and turning up the oxygen flow, Ronald released the safety lock to the firing button at the top of the control column and pulled the shoulder straps of his harness just a little tighter. Still no reaction from the ground. Ahead, he could see Hutch flaring out for his attack, still alone. Where the hell was Teddy?

Sunlight glinting on wings and cockpit canopies. Tiny figures beginning to run for cover, scattering in all directions like the microscopic offspring of an assassin bug.

Out of the corner of his eye, to his horror, he saw Teddy coming in on completely the wrong course, a collision course with himself as Keith's voice broke through his headphones "Go high, Ronno, now" and together they lifted over Teddy's Spitfire so that he remained oblivious of their presence until their shadow impacted on his concentration. An expletive from below broke through the airwaves.

Ahead, Ronald could see Hutch opening fire, his cannon fire beginning to cut through a line of parked aircraft as the first necklaces of ground fire, like continuous streams of Morse Code, began to swim through the air, chasing and closing.

As Ronald found his view of the airfield clearing, a line of parked 109s slightly to his right came into focus – perfect for Keith he thought – he turned his attention to a row of fuelling bowsers lined up in front of an open hangar. One thousand yards to target, and closing at the rate of 150 yards per second, Ronno opened fire six heartbeats later, his two twenty millimetre cannon and four machine guns thundering destruction into the line of tankers, aviation fuel spewing skywards, a boiling, blistering mushroom of black and fiery red erupting into his view.

A touch of left rudder to avoid the fireball brought the control tower into range. The fully glazed top deck dissolved in a prolonged burst. Out of the corner of his eye he saw Hutch catch a 109, wheels down, on its final approach. Unable to take avoiding action, it flipped onto its side and ploughed a fiery furrow down the runway.

By now the ground defences were well and truly awake. Flak was pouring at them, twenty millimetre, thirty millimetre pretty (some might think), but lethal balls of flame ripping past his canopy, passing straight through the fuselage behind the protective armour plating. Keith was weaving from side to side, in an effort to put the German gunners off their aim.

Ronald pushed the throttle through the emergency gate for maximum boost and pulled the stick back into the pit of his stomach, aiming for the sky and the relative safety of the limited cloud cover, Keith still sticking like glue to his starboard wingtip, their exhaust stubs leaving trails of vapour in their wake, pursued by ever larger calibre of flak as the range increased, death-laden black powder-puffs from the 88s.

"Nearly there," said Keith, "just a few more seconds. Oh Christ, there's Teddy. Get out!" he yelled.

Over to their left ,Teddy's Spitfire was emerging from the cloud of flak below, a plume of dirty grey smoke streaming back from the engine cowling, flames licking at the cockpit side. Ronald could see Teddy struggling to open the canopy, his hands working frantically at the emergency release mechanism, then Teddy's voice came faintly, the fear evident :

"I'm done for. Hope the 'chute's OK," then the cockpit hood flew off, the Spit rolled onto its back and Teddy tumbled out, curling into a tight ball, his maps and other papers fluttering into the airstream as he fell earthwards.

Ronald heaved a sigh of relief as he saw the parachute open and billow to a perfect canopy, Teddy's limp body swinging to and fro like a pendulum bob. Then, for a split second Ronald thought he saw Teddy waving. His future would lie in a prisoner of war camp, but at least he appeared to be alive.

As they continued to climb, Hutch reappeared and slid his plane into formation on the far side of Keith. "Steer 275. Watch for fighters. We've rattled their cage enough for one day. Let's get some height. Out." And Hutch led them away to the north-west, engines straining at maximum boost.

Below them, Teddy's Spitfire plunged into the garden of a small house at the edge of the village, just outside the airfield's perimeter. The fireball engulfed the house and Ronald prayed for the occupants.

Glancing back over his shoulder, Ronald could see the columns of black smoke rising from the airfield as bursts of 88 continued to pursue them. He began to breathe a little easier. The sunlight was blinding as they broke through the thin overcast.

"Beware the Hun in the Sun" had been the mantra of the pilots of his father's generation and Ronald knew instinctively that conditions were perfect for an ambush, so he shielded his eyes as best he could and peered directly into the sun, and, being on the edge of their formation, weaved the Spit from side to side to improve his view.

To clear his vision he pushed up his flying goggles and wiped his eyes on the back of his gloves. There, there, crossing the burning disc of the sun was a speck, no, two, three, five bearing down on them, at full throttle from four or five thousand feet above.

"Snappers –five – coming down, ten o'clock. Break left now!" he yelled and already he could see that they were Focke-Wulf 190s, the latest addition to the Luftwaffe's arsenal and more than a match for their Spitfires. Five to three were bloody awful odds he thought, as he slipped his goggles back in place and flung his Spit round to port to meet the attack head-on.

At a closing speed of more than 600 miles per hour there were but seconds before the attackers were on them, cannon muzzles flashing. The initial pass required no deflection and Ronald fired a speculative burst as the nearest 190 closed and centred fleetingly in his reflector sight. As a shell from the 190 punched a hole in his left wing without exploding, he was surprised to see flames burst from the port wing of the 190 and sensed it rolling to its left as the wing folded and dropping out of control. It missed his own wing by the narrowest of margins – so close that he could see the terror on the pilot's face as he wrestled instinctively with controls that no longer had any purpose.

Craning his neck, and thankful for the silk scarf tied around his neck which prevented any chafing as he twisted in his harness to spot the remainder of the German formation, he caught sight of Hutch trying to out-turn his opponent and further away Keith was getting the better of his. For the moment that left two unaccounted for. Where the hell were they?

The answer came, at least in part, as he looked up into the rear-view mirror mounted at the top of the front screen where he could see a 190, the large red-painted cowl of the radial engine swelling in his mirror by the second, curving in behind him for the kill, but not yet close enough to fire. Blending hand and foot Ronald hauled the Spit round trying to get behind the 190, his vision greying with the tightness of the turn, but then the 190 was gone, using its superior agility to out-climb him.

And so it went on, a fandango of death – twist and turn, climb and dive in almost perfect unity – with the realisation gradually growing within Ronald, as the sweat poured down his face from the effort, that his opponent was, bit by bit, getting the upper hand. He could hear his breathing rasping in his oxygen mask. Try as he might he could not find a way to get on terms and felt a kind of lassitude draining his limbs as the panic began to set in, the expectation of a cannon shell exploding into the cockpit sapping his confidence.

Christ! Where did that come from? Glancing up to where he instinctively felt the blow had struck, he saw that the rear view mirror, just inches from his head, had gone, snapped off clean at the base. At the periphery of his vision, he saw two more holes punched in the tip of the starboard wing with the gas of tracer disappearing down and away to his right.

Twisting so violently round to his left, in an effort to find his attacker that he cricked his neck, he heard a shouted warning. As the pain shot through the right side of his upper body; he glimpsed a FW 190 only a hundred yards astern on his port side, its cannon winking with the staccato muzzle flashes of the next burst.

"Break left Ronno," came Hutch's voice in his headphones – no Red two or Blue three for them. They had long given up such confusing designations which could change from day to day. There was only one RONNO, him. And he was about to get himself killed for a moment's inattention.

As these thoughts and sounds raced through his mind at lightning speed, the instinct for self-preservation took over. Left hand on the throttle fully forward through the emergency boost gate, right hand on the control stick forward and left, he slammed his right foot hard down on the rudder pedal, letting his left foot lift in reaction. Praying that the Rolls Royce Merlin engine would not falter, which it should not after its recent modification – Mrs. Shillings orifice as it had mysteriously been called after its invention – he felt a further hammer blow on the rear fuselage and the heart-stopping screech, like fingernails on a blackboard, of pieces of shrapnel venting their furious energy on the armour plating at his back.

But the Merlin did not fail him and its twenty-seven litres of pistons turning the crankshaft at nearly 2000 rpm hurled the Spitfire round and down to the left, the horizon tilting crazily, worse than any fairground ride ever invented, the G-force squeezing him down into his seat and onto the right wall of the cockpit, draining the blood from his head towards his feet, causing his vision to blur and go grey.

He knew that if he blacked out completely he would be dead meat, and although he could feel another hit somewhere on the fuselage, a tiny voice inside his head told him to ease the manoeuvre just enough to keep his consciousness. If a cannon shell got him now he was finished.

Less than four seconds had elapsed – his heart rate was up to nearly 200, his skin was wet with a sheen of sweat as the adrenalin kicked in.

By now the Spitfire was inverted, exposing its vulnerable duck-egg blue underside, as another voice, one from his past, came to his mind and, taking its counsel, he closed the throttle and let the Spit spin, round and round, counting as it went, exposing its belly to fire from above, to give the appearance a stricken craft not worth a further shell, hoping against hope that Hutch or Keith had at least distracted the Focke-Wulf before it finished him off.

Funfzehn, Sechszehn. Survival paramount. Opening the throttle and applying full rudder, Ronald broke out of the spin and rolled the Spitfire level, flipping a switch close to his right hand to increase the flow of oxygen to his mask. Quickly checking his instruments as his vision cleared, whilst noting that the beat of the Merlin remained steady, he saw that the artificial horizon was completely tumbled – no matter, it was a clear day, but he had lost almost 5000 feet of altitude.

The sudden change of air pressure had clogged his eardrums, so he swallowed hard to clear them. Into his earphones poured a cacophony of sounds – calls from his colleagues that he could no longer see, ground control asking for an update and more worryingly some very unpleasant noises from somewhere inside the Spitfire's fuselage – mostly toward the tail plane he thought. At this point he began to realise that the controls had started to feel mushy, so something back there was definitely not quite right.

Although he had pretty good vision to the side through the canopy, no matter how he twisted in his seat he could not get to look at the tail plane. How he wished he had one of the new Spits with the teardrop canopy which gave all round vision.

Fearing that a control line might be about to snap, he throttled back just enough to put the plane into a gentle climb, checking his compass to be sure that he was heading in a generally westerly direction. Seeing that he was flying more north than west he put in some left rudder to bring the plane round only to find the response sluggish and unpredictable. This confirmed his suspicion that he had some serious damage to the tail plane.

As he thus mused, he noticed to his surprise another FW190 passing down his starboard side trailing smoke from its BMW radial engine, oil staining the olive green body. The pilot appeared to be slumped in the cockpit. More in hope than anything else, instinctively checking that the safety catch to the firing button was still released, centred the enemy plane in the reflector sight, yawed the Spitfire slightly to the left to draw a bead on the target, and fired. The cannon and machine guns shuddered through his hands in reaction until the magazines were empty.

Two things then happened simultaneously. Firstly, the left aileron broke off the Focke-Wulf, fluttering away into the slipstream causing it to roll violently to its left and begin to tumble from sight. Just before it disappeared from view, he noticed the canopy being jettisoned, but whether the pilot followed he did not see, because in the same instant there was a distinct, heart-stopping twang from the back of the plane and his Spitfire lurched violently to starboard. Struggling with the controls, he managed to bring the Spitfire level and heading roughly in the direction of the Channel as a welcome voice came through his headphones.

"Take it steady, Ronno, old lad," came Hutch's reassuring tone, "your tail's a real mess. Your starboard elevator is hanging by a thread and there's not much left of the rudder. Gently does it. Keith and I will give you cover until you decide where you're going to put her down."

Without needing to look, Ronald knew with relief that his two friends would be above and slightly behind him, weaving from side to side to provide protection. Thinking back, he realised when his plane had first been hit, he had dipped the wing to the right purely by chance at the very moment when the German pilot had fired; and just by that tiny margin he had been saved from a direct hit full on the side of his cockpit. By such small things is a life spared.

"Oh, by the way," Hutch's voice broke in "that 190 was mine. He was finished long before you fired. Pilot got out though. Saw a 'chute just before it went in."

"The way things are going," replied Ronald, "I might be going the same way. It's getting pretty rough in here. It's taking all my efforts to keep her straight and level, but I'll stick with it for the time being. I'll jump only if I have to, but the nearer the coast the better and I certainly don't fancy my chances in the Channel even at this time of year. At least the engine feels OK and there's nothing major on the instruments so I think it's just going to be a case of getting her down somewhere – if she lasts that long."

The uncertainty was choking his voice as the French coast slid under his wing. A belated burst of anti-aircraft fire rose uncomfortably close behind. Hutch and Keith scattered to divide the gunner's aim, leaving him feeling vulnerable and exposed until they came back on station.

They flew on, holding loose formation, for another ten minutes before Ronald broke into the silence.

"Look lads, I've spoken to control. I can't hold this together much longer. There's bits coming off the top of the starboard wing so I don't think I can make it home. The nearest emergency airfield is the Air/Sea Rescue base at Shoreham which is only a few minutes away and has a crash team standing by."

Peering through the thick Plexiglas front screen, Ronald could see emerging from the late afternoon mist, the first signs of the English coast. Switching on his radio again, he said,

"Right, you two, it's time you were gone. Whatever happens now, you can't make any difference and you must be low on fuel – so bugger off, wish me luck and let me get on with it. See you back in the mess for a late snifter."

"OK, Lucky 6," came the reply. "Good luck. Try not to bend it too much, but you're leaving a trace of smoke so don't hang about. Jump if you have to." And with that, the two shepherding Spitfires drew level on his starboard side, Hutch threw a mock salute and then the pair dipped their wings and peeled away in line astern to the north east heading for their base at Hornchurch.

Lucky 6, thought Ronald, I guess this is one time when a bit of luck will come in handy, but he trained his eye on the temperature gauge and saw to his consternation that the needle had moved just a fraction further across the dial.

By now he was close to the coast and saw, to his right, the twin piers at Brighton shining like two daggers in the late afternoon sunshine. The unmistakable regency outline of the Pavilion confirmed his location. He could even see people walking along the seafront; perhaps they were trying to imagine that the war did not exist.

Turning with some difficulty to the west, his eyes sought out the landmark of the Chapel at Lancing College, now operating as HMS King Alfred, high up on the Sussex downs and immediately overlooking the landing strip at Shoreham. As he flew over the college, where naval cadets craned their necks, staring up at the stricken aircraft and its trail of smoke, he called up control, declaring a Mayday, and was told to make his approach from the north-east, to come in over the River Adur. He would be cleared to land with the firing of a green Very light.

Now he was faced with getting a plane with an unknown amount of damage and himself down, if possible in one piece.

Slipping to starboard as he throttled back to reduce airspeed, the Spitfire seemed to become increasingly unstable, swinging alarmingly from side to side accompanied by some very unpleasant grinding noises from behind him. The squat tower of Shoreham's Norman church flashed by inches below. Just a few more seconds, he begged of his dying aircraft.

With the landing strip centred roughly on the nose of the plane, he coarsened the pitch on the prop, but when he lowered the flaps, worrying vibrations ensued, and worse, when he pulled the selector to lower the under carriage, yet more vibration. To his consternation there was no green light on the dash to confirm the wheels down and locked. To add to his problems, the needle of the engine temperature gauge began to move rapidly toward the danger zone – one of the wheels was blocking the flow of air to the radiator intake. Too late to try cranking the wheels by hand.

With the Brighton Road disappearing under the nose of the Spitfire and the far bank of the river rapidly approaching, he tightened the five point Sutton safety harness, slid back and locked the hood and took a very deep breath to steady his nerves, as much as his hands. If the rescue crew were going to have to pull him out of the wreckage then it was not going to help having to smash their way through a couple of inches of reinforced Plexiglas – better to get it out of the way.

Acrid smoke began to enter the cockpit around his feet and he feared he could feel heat penetrating through the soles of his flying boots. No sign of flames – yet.

A passing cyclist on the crest of the riverbank, in the wrong place at the wrong time, threw himself to the ground as the Spitfire sank through the air just feet above.

Control now seemed almost impossible, the plane increasingly unresponsive to his movements of the control stick. This was going to be a case of going straight in, and no chance, no hope of a second attempt.

At that moment, the control tower fired a red, not a green light and his earphones crackled:

"Pilot, go round again, port wheel half down, starboard fully up. Go round and try to shake them free. Abort your landing."

"Sorry tower," he replied, "no can do – this crate has had it. Mayday, Mayday. Can't manage another circuit, nor can I get enough height to bale out. Fingers crossed – out."

So saying, he pulled off his leather flying helmet and oxygen mask and threw them into the well of the cockpit. His heart was pounding like a riveting gun as he took the best aim he could at the landing strip. He could see a crash tender moving out from the perimeter road.

The plane was now staggering like a drunk through the air, only a few feet above the grass. Realising that there was nothing further that he could do, Ronald switched off the engine, folded his forearms across his face and braced the back of his head against the padded rest behind it. For the next ten to fifteen seconds he was going to be nothing more than a passenger, living cargo awaiting delivery.

The propeller ceased turning and the Spitfire dropped instantly, the left wing dipping with the extra drag of the partially lowered undercarriage leg. Wing tip and wheel contacted the grass simultaneously gouging furrows in the surface, twisting the plane slightly to the left. Then the fuselage met the ground with a bone-shuddering thud, the plane bouncing back into the air shedding metal, propeller tips and wheel. At this point Ronald took his last conscious part in the final act of his Spitfire.

Becoming aware that the plane was slewing to the left, he stamped hard on the right rudder pedal in the hope that the plane might straighten enough to prevent it cartwheeling. Whether this had any effect he did not know because the next impact was so violent that it knocked the wind completely out of him and rendered him unconscious, as his head was flung forward to impact, only half protected by his forearms, against the reflector gunsight.

The Spitfire continued for another 200 yards, bucking and rocking like a venomous, disintegrating fairground ride, spewing chunks of deformed metal until finally the nose dug into the soft ground stopping the Spitfire in its tracks. The body rose vertical, the ground crews watching the pilot's head and arms flailing like a puppet's, then tipping over and landing on its back, steam and coolant vapour pouring from the shattered engine, the pilot's arms hanging down as though trying to support the weight of his inverted aeroplane.

Blackness
Searing pain
Awake or asleep – dead or alive – time suspended
Silence – no sounds
Smells – no smells
Petrol, hot oil, glycol coolant – a plane bleeding to death.
Blackness in a pounding head
Taste – blood, choking
Sounds – voices. Voices becoming clearer. Spades digging frantically.

"Get some foam on the engine."

Then another,

"For God's sake don't release the buckle. If he drops, you'll snap his neck. Get something under his shoulders."

Hands moving round his body – feeling. More searing pain – was he burnt? Padding being pushed under his head.

"Don't worry, sir." Another voice: "We'll have you out in a jiffy."

He tried to speak but only a groan escaped his swollen lips. He was feeling cold – very cold suddenly and shivering – no feeling of body except for the pain.

His arms were as heavy as lead. Try as he might, he could not lift them.

Someone cutting at his flying jacket – then a measured voice, reassuring.

"Listen to me carefully. You are still in the cockpit. We don't think there's going to be a fire. You are upside down and in a minute we are going to cut the harness shoulder straps one at a time. When we get your shoulders free I'm going to reach up and release the centre buckle. You'll then drop onto my chest."

Why the blackness – was he blind? His heart pounded in his chest.

Perhaps he blacked out again. Because the next thing felt was the jolt of the quick release giving way and dropping. Intense pain in his back and shoulders, then it seemed he was out, flat on his back in the open air.

As he lay there, gulping for air, strong hands holding him still, another voice, a gruff Scottish lilt, broke into his awareness saying.

"Just relax, lad, stop fighting us." Had he been struggling that much? "We need to move you to safety as soon as we can, so I'm going to put you to sleep to make our job easier. You'll maybe feel a sharp pain in your hand and then nothing more."

With those words he felt a needle being pushed into the back of his hand and then he was floating, the words "We'll see you soon" echoing in his mind. The pain receded and he passed out.

Later, but how much later, was it hours, days, weeks even, he wondered, he felt he was awake. He could hear sounds like the squeaking of mice and the sound of a curtain being opened and closed – it crossed his mind that somehow he was back at home with his mum and dad. Hs face itched terribly and so he put his hand up to try and scratch, but met only bandages wherever he probed. He tried to speak, but his chin was so restrained that nothing intelligible came out. Frightened and exhausted, his hand dropped back to the bed. Blackness claimed him once more and he relished its company.

CHAPTER 6

As he floated in and out of consciousness, he recalled what he had been told of his own beginnings:

The Camberwell Clarion, Thursday 23rd September 1920
To Sgt. Major Alfred Wallace (on active service) and Mrs. Cecelia Wallace of 14 Kimberley Terrace, Camberwell, a son Ronald. Mother and Baby in good health.

Thus had his arrival into the 20th Century been announced.

His parents Fred and Cissy had married under the shadows that presaged the outbreak of the Great War. Unlike the countless thousands who had vanished into the sea of mud and the violence of high explosive of the Western Front, Fred's experience as bicycle fitter turned motorcycle mechanic had ensured his recruitment, as a volunteer, to the fledgling Royal Flying Corps.

Somewhat behind the front line, Fred was largely safe from the direct and personal carnage that consumed armies like an insatiable gourmand. There, he learnt the intricacies of rigging an aircraft, engine maintenance and latterly he trained as a master armourer.

During his service, he learned the art of timing the interrupter gear which co-ordinated the firing of the twin Spandau machine guns, mounted on top of the engine cowl, through the arc of the propeller. Getting it wrong almost guaranteed that a pilot would shoot off his own propeller. An earlier solution had been simply to fit deflector plates on the back of each blade, with results that were as unpredictable as they were dangerous.

Fred, despite the never-far-away horrors of war, had an ever-growing affection for the miracle of flight even though he saw only too frequently the injuries suffered by "his" pilots or, when they did not return, knowing they had certainly died a horrible death, in the early days, without even a parachute. The highly combustible combination of wood, canvas, acetone and aviation fuel, turned the little biplanes into flying furnaces in seconds. In those last, terrifying moments of their young lives they faced simple, but stark choices – either to stay onboard and burn, or jump to avoid the flames, or, in desperation, to take the quick death of a bullet to the head from their own service revolver.

As the war ended in November 1918, Fred was by some small miracle spared from the last cruel act; the irony of the Spanish Lady – the 'flu epidemic that gathered into her cold arms so many of the fit young men who had so recently survived the horrors of the trenches.

However, Fred's service in France did not end with the Armistice. Early demobilisation was denied him. Often the youngest, those who had been the last to suffer the call of conscription, were chosen to go home first, then preference went to those who could create jobs back in Blighty for the thousands yet to return; but some, including Fred were retained.

These men, Officers and NCOs, were held back to supervise and verify the handover and destruction of the German war machine in all its forms – artillery, machine guns, rifles, tanks and munitions. In his own case it was the aircraft, the cream of the German Air Service – Fokker Biplanes and Triplanes, even those from the squadron of renowned Red Baron, Manfred von Richtofen or the aircraft of a young Herman Goering. Their extensive Gotha bomber force went the same way, to be remembered only in the picture books of history.

Squadron by squadron, all came before the team of which he was a small part to be stripped of their guns, ammunition and instruments, then logged and despatched to the wreckers yard or burnt on site, to become a humiliating funeral pyre of Germany's military ambition. This process was also intended to be a belated revenge for the terms imposed by Germany on France fifty years previously.

And so it continued, month by month, with only the occasional grant of home leave as the team moved steadily eastward, until they finally entered into that part of Germany ordered to be demilitarised as one of the key terms of the Versailles Treaty of 1919, the Rhineland. In that way the whole of the north-eastern border of France would have a buffer zone against any future German aggression. Once their work was completed, the Rhineland would continue to remain under Germany's own jurisdiction, but entirely bereft of military hardware.

England and France had dictated, in signing the Treaty, that Germany was to be left with no more than a minimal army to preserve national law and order, and an equally truncated navy restricted purely to self defence, but of its once mighty air force there was not to be a trace, save for the Zeppelin airships which Germany, as the world's leading exponent, was permitted to develop for civilian travel. As some, perhaps many, would see it, Germany's humiliation was complete, thus setting in train a sequence of events in which the young Ronald Wallace would play a small, but significant part from 1936 onwards.

Finally it was done. Fred's reward was a commission in the field, and it was Flight Lieutenant Alfred Wallace who would return home just in time for Christmas 1920.

Just as with their firstborn, Stanley, it was on an all too brief period of leave in the winter of 1919, much of which was spent getting back from and returning to France, that Ronald was conceived from the nights of passion that reflected their months of separation, even though Fred and Cissy had written to each other almost daily.

Home was a tiny, two up two down, mid-terrace property built at the end of the previous century and rented from the Church Commissioners for two shillings and eight pence per week. There was, of course, no bathroom and the privy was at the end of the yard, shared with two other families.

Cissy, who was an experienced machinist, continued working during her confinement at the local clothing factory which was still producing army uniforms. This involved long hours in dark and dusty conditions and as a result she was looking forward to the birth as a break from the drudgery.

With ten days to go to the expected date of confinement, Cissy felt that her time was getting near, so at the end of the Friday shift she informed the factory manager that she would not be returning until after the baby was born. No work meant no pay, but her extended belly was making it almost impossible for her to operate her machine. In fact she was so large that she wondered if, despite assurances to the contrary, she might be having twins.

Seventy-two hours later, Cissy went into labour in the front bedroom of their little house, attended by the local midwife and her widowed sister-in-law Joan. Cissy's older brother, Thomas, had been posted "missing believed killed" at the blood-soaked battle for Cambrai in Northern France during November 1917.

The birth was a sweaty, screaming, agonising process, unrelieved by drugs or painkillers until baby Ronald, equally wet and screaming, entered the world lit only by the flickering light of four oil lamps, at 2.31 a.m. on Thursday 23rd September. Weighing in at a very healthy eight and half pounds, baby and mother lay together, crying and laughing as Joan fussed round them tidying and cleaning up. Behind Joan's joy at the safe delivery, there was a mask of burning sadness at the knowledge that for her, a baby would have to wait for another man at another time.

Ronald's first name had been chosen by Fred and Cissy as soon as she had her pregnancy confirmed – Victoria if the baby was a girl – but as she lay there giving Ronald his first feed, Joan brought to her an envelope on which was written in Fred's hand "Open when Baby Wallace arrives". Opening it carefully, and reading it by the light of one of the oil lamps held close by Joan, she found a note from Fred which asked that, if the baby were a boy it was his dearest wish that the child should have a second name of Orville in honour of the younger of the Wright Brothers, the pioneers of aviation, who he so admired. How could she do otherwise?

To preserve Cissy's honour in the absence of Fred, her father-in-law Frederick had the birth announced in the evening paper.

And so it came to be that, on 18th December 1920, following Fred's return from Germany with the newly named Royal Air Force, Ronald Orville Wallace was baptised, screaming lustily in the arms of his loving parents, at the local parish church. Little did they realise that his future school mates would combine his two names into a nickname which would stay with him for the rest of his life – Ron O corrupted to Ronno.

Four years later, to their great joy, the family of Alfred and Cissy Wallace was completed by the arrival of their third child, a baby girl, christened Torrence, but who would always be known as affectionately Torrie.

CHAPTER 7

Later, as his mind began to clear, he sensed that someone was by his bed so he raised his hand to signal that he was awake and had it gripped and held by one smaller and softer than his own. At the same time, the same voice that he had heard on the day of his crash – he could remember the approach but nothing after – spoke to him, quiet and reassuring.

"Hello, Flight Lieutenant Wallace, welcome back. We've kept you under for a while" (How long he wondered?) "so that you had a bit of a chance to recover."

Again Ronald tried to move his hand up to his face, but again the unseen hands gently but firmly restrained it.

"Don't worry," came the voice again, "you haven't been burnt, but you took a hell of a battering and we bandaged you to stop you scratching. Nurse Clarke is going to remove the bandages and then you should feel a lot better.

"You can check yourself in a mirror if you want, but you're not a pretty sight just now. The bruises will go of their own accord, but you have a broken nose and we may do a little op to straighten it some, when you feel well enough. You also dislocated two fingers on your left hand, but we have fixed those although they will have to stay taped together for a while."

"Oh, by the way," he added as though reeling off the last couple of minor items on a shopping list, "you also took a couple of chunks out of your left shin and we had to put some stitches into your scalp. Apart from that you're just fine. I'll come back and check you over later." And with that Ronald could hear the click of a clipboard being slipped back onto the end of the bed and then the doctor moved away, giving orders as he went.

A gentler voice requested politely, with due reverence to his rank, that he lie still while she removed the bandages. Doing as he was told, and to his enormous relief, he felt practised fingers deftly unwinding the shroud of bandage that encircled his head.

With the bandages finally removed he kept his eyes shut, afraid of what he might see, until the nurse said, "It's alright, you can open your eyes now – it's not so very bad."

Still he kept his eyes firmly shut, terrified of disfigurement, until she said, "Do please look, I promise you have not been burnt," and with these words she pressed a hand mirror into his grip.

Raising it slowly to his face, he opened one eye and, as the reflected image came into focus, he gasped involuntarily and dropped the mirror to his chest.

"Don't be silly," said the nurse, "you must look," and made him take hold of the mirror again. This time he managed to open both eyes and stared in horror at his reflection. The whole of his face was swollen like a melon, his skin was every shade of black and blue, green and yellow that could be imagined, and somewhere in the middle of it all was his nose, but certainly not where it used to be. A line of stitches ran diagonally from the centre of his forehead and disappeared into his hairline.

An agonised gasp escaped his lips and the nurse spoke to him again, this time quite sharply, chiding him.

"You know we've had men in here, much worse than you, some with half their faces burnt away, so just be thankful and stop being such a baby."

He was so shocked by what she had said, but knowing the truth of it, he burst into uncontrollable tears. The nurse shushed him saying "There, there," and fussed round him, passing him a handkerchief to dry his eyes.

He wanted to say sorry, to apologise for being so emotional. He guessed it was the relief at knowing he had survived relatively unscathed, but the only words that came out were "Water, Drink."

A glass duly arrived in front of him and he drank deeply. "Slow down, sir," said the nurse, "or you're going to want the toilet." That reminded him and he made to get out of bed.

"You can stay put – because you were under for so long we put in a catheter. Another nurse will be along shortly to remove it. You might not want to watch," said Nurse Clarke as she walked away down the ward, her shoes squeaking on the polished floorboards – the sounds of mice.

The nurse arrived shortly after. He did not care to watch, blushing at the perceived indignity.

Hutch came to visit, bringing best wishes from Keith, now promoted from Pilot Officer to Flight Lieutenant, as well as cigarettes – they smoked largely in silence, Hutch afraid to discuss his injuries and Ronald unwilling to revisit the moment of the crash – a magazine to read, and the latest news from the squadron. The Red Cross had confirmed that Teddy Jones had survived and been taken prisoner almost immediately; no hope of escape having been shot down so close to the Luftwaffe airfield. The doctors would not let Hutch stay long, and although he promised he would visit again, they both knew there was little chance of that.

The days drifted by in a haze of cigarette smoke as his injuries slowly healed. There was a short operation to sort out his nose. He was terrified of the anaesthetic, reliving the last seconds of the crash while he was under, in that dreadful slow-motion of inescapability, but when he came round at least his nose was back where he expected it to be and still roughly the same profile. Yet more bruising. A livid scar across the top of his forehead would be a permanent reminder of the violence of his crash.

Then came the day when the doctor pronounced him fit enough to be discharged, and brought the unexpected news that his father would be driving down to take him home for his period of convalescence.

The drive from the hospital to his parents' home in Thorlby on the edge of the Lincolnshire Wolds was very long and tiring.

There were innumerable hold-ups for military convoys; troops, vehicles of every description, munitions and aircraft with their wings strapped to the fuselage sides on long loaders, half hidden under grey/green tarpaulins. At first he did not recognise them, but then he saw the white-on-blue star of the United States Army Air Force and realised they were a mixture Republican P47 Thunderbolts and North American P51 Mustangs, single seat fighters on shipment from Liverpool to any one of the dozens of bases that had been hastily constructed on the flat, open fields of Norfolk and Suffolk.

He already knew that, re-engined with a Rolls Royce Merlin instead of the original lacklustre Packard, the Mustang had been transformed into the finest long range fighter, a match for anything the Germans could put up and capable of going all the way across Northern Europe to Germany's capital city, Berlin. How he wished that they could have had that sort of endurance with the Spitfire. Every sortie over France had been made with one eye very firmly on the fuel-gauge.

At the start of the drive, his father had tried to engage him in conversation, but he was not in the mood and particularly he did not want to talk about the crash. He still wondered whether, despite what

Hutch had said, there was something more or different that he could or should have done which might have made the difference between the Spit being written off (as it was) to be broken up and carted away for scrap and spares or being classed as repairable to fight again another day. The "ifs and buts" continued to rumble through his head and distracted him from anything but the most trivial of conversation with his father, who eventually gave up trying.

Thus, apart from perking up a bit to look at the transport convoys and craning his neck to see out of the window every time the sound of an aero engine passed overhead, he sat slumped, silent, hugging himself in his overcoat, staring out of the side window of the car or with his eyes closed as they moved slowly up the A1 trunk road, through the drab bomb-damaged outskirts of north London, completely ignoring his father's suggestion that he might like to visit their old house. He had only vaguely heard his father, but at that moment his mind was in another place at another time.

Eventually his father broke into his consciousness by saying that it was time for a comfort break. His actual words were that he needed a Jimmy, using the shortened version of the Cockney rhyming slang, and as it was nearly lunch time (had they really been on the road for more than four hours?) and there was a pub ahead on the left, they might as well stop and get a bite to eat at the same time.

The pub, called the Checkerboard and featuring a picture of a partly played game of chess on its sign, was the typical old English pub so favoured by the recently arrived Americans, but built in the mock-Tudor style of the early 30s, painted a creamy yellow with black "timbers" above the ground floor going up to the eaves to complete the Elizabethan look.

Tall, leaded windows complimented the design, although the effect was temporarily spoilt and compromised by the spider's web of criss-crossed sticky tape applied to the glass to minimise blast damage from an exploding bomb. Ronald wondered whether anyone had actually tested to see whether it made any difference whatsoever. From what he had seen during a visit to the fighter base at Manston, it had not made a jot, but the destruction there had been caused by direct hits; whether there had been flying glass was largely academic. A bit of sticky paper was not going to do much good when a 500lb bomb had your name on it, he thought moodily.

By now his father was out of the car shouting to him to hurry up, before disappearing inside at some speed. He walked slowly and stiffly, limping slightly, through the front door with its brass ringed porthole, and then into the bar. To his surprise, it was light and airy (despite the sticky tape) and occupied by a dozen or so people, mostly elderly men, who as one, turned to gaze at this stranger in his long RAF overcoat. Games of dominoes went on hold.

With his footsteps echoing off the polished wooden parquet floor, he wandered over to the chrome topped bar. He debated whether to try and sit on one of the high bar stools, but the injuries to his legs made this difficult and so instead he slipped off his overcoat, laid it beside him on the stool to wait for his father and leaned back, propping himself as comfortably as he could against the bar top.

Subconsciously, he reached into his tunic pocket, took out a packet of cigarettes – he had not smoked in the car – found the silver Dunhill lighter that his mother had given him when he was commissioned, tapped both ends of the cigarette on the packet to compact the tobacco, then lit up, drawing the smoke deeply into his lungs.

Before he had chance to exhale, he realised there was a rather elderly gentleman standing in front of him, apparently studying him intently from head to toe. Thinking the man was about to remonstrate with him for smoking, he blew the smoke up to the ceiling in a long plume. Instead the man, with his gaze fixed firmly on the small violet and white diagonally striped ribbon of the DFC awarded for his five confirmed 'kills' (which he had sewn with immense pride over the left breast pocket of his uniform jacket) stuck out his hand and shook his own firmly saying just two words, "Good man." With that, the man turned away and went back to his table and conversation around the room resumed.

What was that all about? Ronald wondered. Had it been his imagination, or there had been complete silence since he walked into the room?

As he watched his father returning from the toilet at the far corner of the room, a voice from behind startled him.

"Don't worry about old Tom, he's quite harmless, but he was in the last war and tells everyone that he was the best turned out soldier and he can't abide to see sloppy dressing. Apparently you met with his approval, which is something of a compliment."

Turning round to meet the voice, Ronald saw a young man about his own age, behind the bar. Most strikingly, the man wore a black patch over his left eye and where his left arm should have been, the empty sleeve of his jacket was neatly pinned to the side.

To Ronald's apparently enquiring expression he said, "Dunkirk. Not all of us got back in one piece." Trying not to appear too inquisitive, Ronald noticed the scarring on his face and that part of the barman's left ear was also missing.

"Could have been worse. At least I can still pull a pint, but cutting your meat is a bit of a bugger," the barman added without rancour.

"Drink?"

Ronald felt the heat of shame coursing through his veins. Shame at his own reaction in the hospital when the bandages were removed and he made to turn away, unable to meet the barman's gaze. Just at that moment, his father was at his side saying, "Yes, thank you, two pints of mild." The barman turned and walked down the bar to pull the pints, saving Ronald any further embarrassment. He realised that it was highly likely that the injuries he had seen might just be the tip of the iceberg.

His father led him away from the bar to a comfortable corner seat next to one of the big windows, before going back to collect the beers and order sandwiches. He was under strict instructions from Mother that they were not to spoil their appetites as she was going to cook a special welcome home meal.

The beers were at least wet, but the alcohol on an empty stomach, after at least three weeks abstinence, went straight to Ronald's head. The sandwiches were filling even though the ingredients were of dubious origin and quality, but at the end of their meal he felt more human than he had done for quite some time. The old gentleman had left the bar as they were eating, pausing momentarily to snap to attention, saluting smartly before continuing on his way. Ronald had not known how to respond properly, so he just smiled, touched his finger to his forehead in a mock salute and had been rewarded with another, "Good", perhaps with a half whispered, "luck", which lifted his spirits enormously.

For the first time since leaving the hospital, he and his father chatted as they always had, about nothing of consequence and in the process simply enjoyed each other's company. He learned with pleasure that his younger sister Torrie should be able to get home before his sick leave finished, but unfortunately the ship on which his older brother Stan was serving was still somewhere in the Mediterranean, presumed to be on its way to Malta.

But once again, when his father turned the conversation to his crash, he was gripped by the need to fend him off, firmly saying "Not yet, Dad, not yet. I'll tell you when I'm ready." Thankfully his father had not persisted.

Just as he was finishing his second cigarette at the table, his father suggested that it was time to go, stood up and went over to pay the bill. While he watched his father chatting to the barman and heard the clink of coins on the bar top, his thoughts of how normal, how peace-time the scene was, were completely shattered by the sudden on-rush overhead of many aero engines, growing instantly to a thunderous crescendo, drinks glasses chattering. Everyone looked up at the ceiling; conversation froze in the cacophony.

Leaning over, he strained to follow the sound from his vantage point. Looking up through the window he saw a tight formation of six (or was it eight?) American four-engined B17 Flying Fortress bombers disappear low over the roof tops of the row of houses on the opposite side of the road. Then they were gone and silence returned to the room.

He heard someone mutter, "Bloody Yanks – can't they do their low flying somewhere else?" as the hubbub of conversation resumed.

Then, at the moment he and his father left the pub and were walking out to the car, a second formation of bombers flew directly above, perhaps only a hundred feet up. It caught them completely unawares and they both ducked involuntarily as the roar assaulted them. So low were the aircraft, the wash from the two dozen or more propellers swished in the air past their ears and spun some fallen leaves into miniature whirlpools.

Grinning with embarrassment, they climbed into the car with Alfred echoing the "Bloody Yanks" sentiment as he started the engine.

"Hopefully, another three hours and we should be home, provided there are no more delays," said his father, adding, "If we are late, Mother will be less than happy. She has been planning this meal from the moment we heard that you were recovering in hospital."

He went on, "I don't suppose you really gave it much of a thought, but I had the devil's own game stopping her jumping on the first train and going down to see you. It took me an age to persuade her to put all her energy into doing something special for your return."

Mortified, Ronald suddenly realised that he hadn't given anyone or anything else any thought at all, so wrapped up had he been in his own problems. Truth to tell, he really had believed that he was going to burn alive in the cockpit of his doomed Spitfire as it self-destructed on the runway at Shoreham, and he had been terrified at the prospect of living with the extent of his disfigurement. The guilt and shame of the relief he had felt on learning his almost miraculous escape had burnt deep into his soul, far deeper than the friction burns around his shoulders.

"Whatever happens when we get home," his father warned, "leave your mother be if she cries, and make sure that you tell her that the meal is the best you have ever tasted. She has been saving all our ration cards, cadging food off friends, and she's spent ages raiding the hedgerows for blackberries to make a pudding. And you will eat every morsel that is put in front of you, or else!" he concluded with mock sternness.

After this, they continued in a more companionable frame until the effects of his beers at lunchtime finally overcame Ronald and he fell soundly asleep. The remainder of the trip was blessedly uneventful, and so deep was his sleep that he did not even waken when his father stopped to fill the car with petrol, using the ration coupons that he had borrowed from friends and neighbours in order to make the 400 mile round trip. Without their generosity, such a long journey would have been impossible, but his father had been determined that he should not be put through the stress of an extended train journey from the south coast. Passenger trains were hardly able to keep to timetable when priority was given to the movement of war materials.

A gentle, but persistent pulling at his shoulder roused Ronald from his slumber. To his great relief he saw that they were home. Dusk was falling and chinks of light were showing through the front room curtains. The blackout seemed not to be so rigorously enforced these days.

The house, a detached double-fronted built in late Victorian times using the local soft yellow sandstone, appeared almost luminous in the growing darkness. As soon as the car tyres crunched on the gravel of the drive that led up to the front door then back to the roadside in a tight curve, encompassing a small half-moon of grass and a strip of flowerbeds, the light over the front porch flicked on. His father tutted with annoyance.

"Don't worry Dad," he said as the stepped gingerly out of the car, balancing for a moment on his good leg, "I don't suppose Jerry is after us tonight." His father was about to reply something along the lines of national security, when the front door was flung open and his mother ran out, apron flapping at her waist, and enfolded Ronald in her arms, before bursting into tears. She continued to hug him, crying with relief, until he prised her arms loose and held her at bay.

When his mother had calmed a little, they all went indoors. His father insisted that he carry his battered suitcase, which he took upstairs, not to his old room, but to the guest bedroom because, as his mother put it, the room faced west for the light and he would be more comfortable in the double bed. His father carefully adjusted the blackout so that not a chink of light showed through.

He unpacked slowly, placing his few items in the chest of drawers that his mother had freshened with scented liners – not quite to his taste, but he appreciated the thought. His mother had also brought in some of his old casual clothes which he changed into, even though they smelled faintly of camphor.

At length, his father called him down and did him the honour of pouring him a glass of dry sherry from the glass decanter on the sideboard, although in truth he really would have preferred a large slug of scotch. There never seemed to be a shortage in the Officers' Mess.

Over dinner, which was excellent by anyone's standards in these days of shortage, and despite the 'chicken' being rabbit, the talk was of family and friends, the ever-present rationing which seemed to get more restrictive by the day and, briefly, the progress of the war. His mother had obviously been forewarned not to raise the question of his crash even though she cast long, concerned glances at the bruising that was still evident on his face. He touched the scar on his forehead self-consciously. His mother gave him a sympathetic, encouraging smile in response.

Dessert, more to his liking, was the fruit picked by his mother while foraging along the hedgerows and which she served with wartime custard. It was piping hot and had some real sharpness, in the absence of any sugar for cooking, which he found deeply satisfying. Wartime food seemed generally to have become so bland.

Under his mother's somewhat disapproving eye, he sat back replete and lit a cigarette, although she was mollified a little as she saw he still had the Dunhill lighter which she had presented to him when he had won his RAF wings.

Excusing herself to do the washing up, so that her "boys" could be alone to talk (had they not been thus all day?) Ronald found there was not a great deal that they could say to each other without getting onto the subject of the war. His father did ask the same question as the MO had asked at the hospital and he had given exactly the same answer. What else could he say? He was only a foot soldier doing one tiny task at a time in the greater picture, clinging to the belief that if he did his bit right, and everyone else did theirs, then the outcome, the defeat of Germany, was inevitable – sooner or later, but which of these and at what cost was quite beyond him.

Mention of his sister Torrie lifted the mood. He was so very fond of her and she had always doted on her "big bro" as she sometimes called him. Not able to face going into the Land Army or the FANY's, the Nursing Yeomanry – she had a morbid fear of anything to do with hospitals or farming, she joked, and so she had volunteered for the Women's Army Corps, to 'do her bit'. On her home leave had quietly told her father, against all the rules, that she would possibly be going to an anti-aircraft battery once she had completed her training.

The prospect of his sister coming home gave him something to look forward to because, when he admitted it to himself, he was not sure how he was going to cope. In fact, he really wanted to get back to the Officers' Mess to be in familiar surroundings and with people who understood – what his parents could or would not; the fear, the excitement, the sense of bereavement (or lack of it), the disgust at the continual killing.

Perhaps he resented his father for trying to understand. His killing war during the Great War had been second-hand, but he did not want to offend his father by saying this, although secretly he feared he might let his feelings slip out in an unguarded moment.

For a few minutes before bedtime, they ended the evening as a family, speculating about Ronald's older brother on the Mediterranean convoys.

For a long time Ronald lay awake, eyes wide open, listening to the insistent rumble of hundreds of Lancaster and Halifax bombers forming up and streaming eastwards to unload their lethal cargoes of high-explosive and incendiaries somewhere over the industrial heartland of the German Ruhr. Temporarily, with the eyes of a civilian, Ronald found he had some sympathy for those non-combatants on the receiving end. It was inevitable that Berlin would become *the target for tonight*, as much for its symbolic value as for its strategic worth, but he knew he would always have mixed feelings about that particular target.

Later in the night, he vaguely heard the bombers returning and much later, in the early light of dawn, the discordant note of a damaged bomber limping home with one or perhaps two engines silenced. Death, his or theirs, was a constant shadow.

Eventually sleep claimed him, but the dreams about his crash continued and he woke the next morning with a crushing headache which only added to the feeling of lethargy that had settled over him like a damp blanket. He stayed in bed all morning, but by the time his mother coaxed him downstairs, he was in a truly black mood and they found it impossible to make any conversation with him at all.

It was, if anything, worse the next day. He could hear tense exchanges between his parents as they tried to work out how to lift his spirits. His father was all for letting nature take its course, but this clearly did not satisfy his mother. The day ground its way to its almost inevitable conclusion of mutual hostility, mother and father completely frustrated by what they saw as his lack of motivation and he, wishing they would leave him in peace, unable to cope with their well-intentioned concern.

He retired early to bed, as soon as dinner was finished, barely able to wish his parents goodnight. As he climbed wearily up the stairs, he heard his mother crying and his father saying that they would have to find something to cheer him up.

Briefly he considered going back down to apologise for his lack of manners, but concluded that he had probably done enough damage for one day, so he continued up to his room. Whisky and cigarettes were his only companions until he fell asleep. He was oblivious to the phone calls made by his parents as he lay wallowing in his melancholy.

CHAPTER 8

The following morning, when his parents appeared in his bedroom with his breakfast tray, his mother announced, "We thought you might like a visitor today."

She was clearly not in the mood to allow him the slightest chance to disagree as she continued, "You will remember the Davis's from Rissington. Well, their daughter Elisabeth, Libby, has called to say she will pop over and see you later this afternoon. I'll fix tea and see if I can find some biscuits, so do try and make a bit of an effort, Ronald."

The use of his full name instead of her pet name of Ronnie, indicated that she was extremely cross with him, but dear God, Libby! All teeth and pigtails! As his father left the room, dutifully following Mother, Ronald could have sworn that he turned back just for a split second and gave the faintest of winks. What could that mean?

His mood, one of apathy tinged with a touch of childish petulance, continued unabated through the morning and into the early afternoon, until around 3 pm when, still languishing in his bed, he heard the doorbell and voices downstairs. Promising himself that he would try to be on his best behaviour, to make some effort to be civil, he realised that he should have shaved at the very least, but then found it was too late as he heard footsteps coming lightly up the stairs. He hurriedly put a comb through his hair and straightened the bedclothes as best he could – no point in looking a complete wreck if the girl had the decency to pay him a visit. He owed her that much.

His mother entered the room first, obscuring his view of the doorway, carrying a tea tray set for two, and biscuits, which she set down on the ottoman at the foot of the bed.

"You remember Libby, don't you Ronald?" (another warning) as she stepped aside to reveal his visitor.

His jaw dropped. She was absolutely, bloody stunning. No longer aged fourteen as he foolishly remembered, but grown to a twenty-year-old blonde. Her shoulder length hair was swept up and back in the current Lana Turner style. She was dressed in a black wool skirt, white blouse, open at the neck to reveal a small gold cross. A close-fitting yellow jacket was trimmed with black piping to the collar and pockets. A tiny black hat with a single feather was pinned to the crown of her head and the ensemble was finished off by coffee coloured high heeled suede shoes. She looked every inch a film star.

Without removing her pale yellow kid gloves, she walked to the side of the bed and offered her hand, saying, "Hello Ronnie, it's been a long time. It's lovely to see you again."

Ronald took her hand, slack jawed, until he managed to find his voice and he responded in kind. Over her shoulder, Ronald glimpsed his mother leaving the room with the biggest grin on her face.

Perching on the edge of the bed, Libby crossed her legs.

"Not quite the outfit for cycling," she continued with a smile. "But I thought it might brighten things up for you. Got it from my sister, Susan, who would ask to be remembered to you. She had it from her days before the war with that fashion house in London. I'm surprised you can't smell the lavender bags from there. Shall I pour?"

An hour and a half passed it seemed as a minute, and then she announced she had to leave before it got too late, but not before he had extracted a promise from her to meet him without fail the next day. Although she tried to keep the tone of the conversation light and carefree, there was no missing the cloud of concern that had crossed her face as she saw his injuries. Standing beside the bed she again offered him her hand. He felt the soft smoothness of her touch as she leaned forward to place the gentlest of kisses on the scar on his forehead.

"All better now," she murmured as though comforting an injured child. For a moment he inhaled her perfume – expensive French, probably Molinard, a gift from Susan – as the nearness of her body stirred him.

"I'll remember to shave next time," he said with a laugh, to cover the blush that he could feel rising to his cheeks.

Over dinner it was inescapable that his mood had lifted. His parents exchanged knowing glances. The day ended on an entirely happier note, and that night, perhaps for the first time since his crash, his sleep was deep and dreamless.

The next morning, before he was properly awake, he sensed that someone had entered his room and instinctively braced himself as he, or she, took a flying leap onto the bed.

Torrie landed beside him with a thump that left him entirely awake as she threw an arm around him and squeezed him as hard as she could.

"Hello, Flight Lieutenant Wallace," she growled playfully into his hair, "I've missed you so much and then, when I heard about the crash, I was worried sick. It is so good to see you in one piece."

"Only got a day's leave here, so out of bed now, sleepy head."

Then she bounced off the bed, but before she left the room she paused and said, "I hear Libby visited yesterday," adding, to his barely suppressed smile, "you look like the cat that got the cream!" She ran off down the stairs laughing.

Over a very late breakfast, they discussed Ronald's plans for the day; Torrie made it very clear to him that in her self-imposed role of chaperone she was coming along too. At first he was opposed to the idea because he wanted to have Libby all to himself, but in the end, the day went well and Torrie succeeded in taking away all the gauche awkwardness that might have existed between them.

He borrowed his father's car and drove over to Rissington. The three of them spent the day walking and talking, laughing and joking, tipsy on their own company. Libby and Torrie, of similar age, renewed their friendship which had been interrupted by the war. Libby let it slip that she was working in the meteorology section at Coningsby and her leave from the base would be ending in three days. Ronald's heart lurched at the thought he would lose her so soon.

Far too quickly, the day, remarkable for the few times they had mentioned the war, came to an end, with Ronald taking Libby home before waiting with Torrie at the bus stop after a tearful farewell with their parents.

Hugging him tight as the bus drew near, Torrie whispered in his ear in a conspiratorial manner, "Don't waste it, dearest brother; she's lovely," and then she was gone up the steps of the bus and disappearing from sight, waving wildly and blowing kisses through the back window like a mischievous school child. Long after the bus had gone, Ronald stood rooted to the spot, contemplating what had happened in just twenty-four hours.

Arriving home, he found his parents in deep discussion, so he left them to it and settled in the lounge to smoke and read a magazine. Snatches of conversation drifted through with his father seeming to argue that if Ronald was old enough to fight for king and country then he was old enough to organise his own life in other ways. His mother apparently did not agree – Ronnie was still her baby.

Moments later however, his father came into the room to inform him that they both needed to go away for a couple of days despite the end of Ronald's leave already being on the horizon. Mother's sister in Lincoln was unwell so they would go to help out. They would go by bus so that they could leave the car for him, provided he did not drive too far. His father reminded him that it was still ten days until the next set of petrol ration coupons became available.

Surprised by this news, he expressed sympathy for his aunt's sudden illness, which had not been mentioned since his arrival, but Ronald said that he was perfectly happy to cater for himself during their absence. While they went off to pack a few things, he telephoned Libby to explain this unexpected turn of events and, with a flutter in his chest, arranged to pick her up for a picnic tea the next day.

Collecting Libby from her parents' house shortly after lunch, he found her dressed in a sharply-tailored hounds-tooth suit, black buttoned gloves, with a cream silk scarf tied loosely at her throat. Her golden hair was piled on top of her head and held in place with a silver clip. Her handbag, he noticed, had been substituted with a small mock-crocodile valise. She was, he thought, out with the intention of making a good impression and so far, without a doubt, she was succeeding.

Stretching his culinary skills to the limit by cooking two hard boiled eggs, a further in-road on his parents' rations, he had already prepared a simple picnic. They drove just a few miles up into the Lincolnshire Wolds and found a shaded spot looking east over the coastal plain towards the distant sea.

They spread a blanket against the trunk of an ancient tree in the shade of its dappled canopy. The air was redolent with the sounds and scents of late summer, a woodpigeon cooed softly in the branches high above, a skylark rose chittering nearby, although there was the ever present rumble of aero engines under test at the nearby bomber bases. In fact it was almost impossible to escape this sound anywhere in Lincolnshire and so numerous were the airfields that it had been nicknamed "Bomber County".

Time passed slowly, even though, as his convalescence was inevitably reaching its end, he had that unpleasant hollow feeling in the pit of his stomach that he used to associate with the countdown to the end of a family holiday.

Their picnic comprised a few sandwiches, the boiled eggs, a few biscuits and a thermos of tea, which was hardly the food of love, even though he felt he was slowly but surely beginning to fall in love with her.

They talked about everything and anything, avoiding, for fear that it might spoil the atmosphere between them, any mention of the war. Libby was worried about her sister, who she had not heard from for several months. On her last visit home Susan had made a point of giving her most of the couturier clothes that she had acquired before the war during her time in the fashion business. Her flair for languages, especially French and German had given her extended visits to Paris where she had worked, albeit briefly, with Coco Chanel.

On that last occasion, as they parted, Susan had hugged Libby, closing her in an embrace that somehow said they might not see each other again for a long time. Susan had made a joke about having to go away – "en vacances" was her phrase, but Libby wondered if this was a hint that she might be going over to France to work with the Resistance. Libby was only too aware that her own section in Coningsby was regularly asked to predict weather patterns for remote areas in France, which were so remote that they could have no military significance except as a clandestine landing or drop zone for secret agents.

After they finished eating, he learnt that smoking was not a habit in which Libby either indulged or approved, but having made her point she said no more. It was not in her nature to nag, but to please her, he refrained from lighting another cigarette

As the afternoon drifted into early evening, the warmth of the sun, the sounds of the countryside, and the distant drone of engines lulled his senses and he drifted off to sleep, his head resting on his rolled up jacket, dreaming of a night in Berlin where scantily clad showgirls danced under spotlights around his father, while his mother looked on wagging an admonishing finger. A drum-roll grew and swelled to fill his head.

He woke with a start as a squadron of Spitfires roared overhead in a choir of Merlin engines and, as his head cleared, he found Libby leaning back against the trunk of the tree, sketchpad and pencil in hand. Reaching toward her, to hold and turn the pad so that he could look at her work, she teased him, holding it high above her head. The more he reached, the more she stretched up, laughing and keeping him gently at bay with the other hand. At last, with their eyes only inches apart, Ronald's right hand gently holding her left wrist to retrieve the pad, they kissed, the softest touch of lips, then as her arm relaxed above him, kissing more firmly, their mouths opening slightly, tongues touching and tasting. Ronald sensed the sketchpad falling onto the blanket as her arms folded around him.

The embrace seemed to go on for an eternity, but at last they parted, swimming back from the pool of passion into which they had plunged.

Reaching down for the upturned pad, and finding no more resistance from Libby, he flipped it over to reveal, not a portrait of himself deep in sleep as he expected, but a marvellous caricature of him sitting astride a miniature Spitfire, tennis racquet in hand swatting away a swarm of bees or wasps, each one adorned with a tiny swastika.

The likeness was so good that he kissed her again and begged her to sign and date the masterpiece, which she did, carefully pencilling her signature and the date 27-09-1943 and then, after a moment's hesitation, added the words "with love".

The best of the day was now over, so they packed the picnic case and rug into the car. For a while they walked along a green lane bounded by tall hedgerows; a robin sang its soft lament for the passing of summer and they stood hand in hand, while he told her about the crash. The more he told her, the tighter she gripped his hand and all the while looking anxiously at him, but he reassured her that he was fully recovered from the memory of the moment when he hung upside down in the seat harness, believing he was about to die.

Since she looked so distraught by his description of the Spitfire's final seconds he grabbed her by the waist and spun her round and round until she did not know whether she was laughing or crying. He kissed her again, tenderly, then they walked arm in arm back to the car, watching the motes dance in the shafts of sunlight as the shadows lengthened. Dusk was creeping upon them by the time they arrived back at his parents' house.

For the second time that day, Ronald stretched his culinary skills to the limit as he attempted to prepare what he considered might be a romantic dinner for two. His mother had thoughtfully left soup in the larder, which he thought he might be able to reheat. He found his mother had also left him a rabbit stew which he thought he might also be able to reheat, to be served with some of his father's freshly dug potatoes and a boiling of fresh picked peas. The once ornamental and lawned garden had largely been given over to food cultivation as his father, in common with anyone who had a patch of ground, followed the Government's exhortation to "Dig for Victory".

His father's skills in the garden were infinitely greater than his own in the kitchen, and in the end it took Libby to come to the rescue as saucepan lids rattled like a pressure cooker about to explode and she regulated the temperature of the oven to prevent the stew being cremated.

Ronald smiled his gratitude, left Libby in charge, and went off to lay the dining table. At least here, wartime shortages did not impinge and it gave him pleasure to set the table with some of the family silver. He raided his mother's secret store of decorative candles, carefully hoarded from the earliest days of the war, and set two of them into crystal candlesticks, promising himself that he would repay from the squadron mess as soon as he returned to active service.

Lighting them with his Dunhill, he checked that there were no chinks in the blackout curtains before extinguishing the ceiling light to leave the room softly lit by two table lamps, while the candles flickered to enhance the romantic ambiance he was working so hard to create.

Having confirmed that Libby was completely in charge of events in the kitchen – she shooed him away – he went off in search of a bottle of his father's homemade elderflower wine, vintage 1942. This had been prepared the previous autumn, to supplement the steadily dwindling "house cellar" for which there was little hope of replenishment until the war's end. His father had warned him several times that the wine was, in his words, experimental and unpredictable, and to be treated with extreme caution. There was no sherry in the rack and for a moment Ronald felt a twinge of guilt for his lack of appreciation for the glass his father had poured the night he arrived home.

Ronald uncorked the bottle with all the care that would attend a bomb disposal expert defusing an unexploded bomb. He took a sip and found it to be surprisingly palatable; not too sweet and with a hint of fizz. He poured generous measures carefully into a pair of his father's best hock glasses as Libby came into the dining room, carrying a tray with two bowls of steaming soup and a smaller bowl of croutons. Even stale bread had to find its place on the dinner table – waste not, want not was his mother's guiding rule.

"His" meal was an outstanding success and they chatted amiably while the elderflower wine warmed their souls. They pushed any thought of the war from their minds, from the room, from their lives, if only for a few hours.

With dinner finished, and as they drained the last of the wine, Ronald reached across the table and held her hand lightly by the fingertips. She did not draw back, but held his gaze with an amused smile about her lips.

The romance barely evaporated as they stood together at the kitchen sink to do the washing up. Then they retired to the lounge, enjoying the warmth of their company. Their world was complete.

As the evening drew to a close, Libby stood up from his side on the sofa where they had been sitting since their dinner, listening to the radio. Ronald watched her through the doorway, walking down the hall to the front door where she bent down to pick up her valise. Thinking she was ready to go home, he left the lounge and walked slowly, reluctantly down the hallway towards her, intending to pick up the car keys, unwilling to let her go.

But before he could say anything, to ask her to change her mind, to please stay, she reached out, took his hand and without hesitation led him up the stairs and into his bedroom. His pulses began to race.

Without a word Libby went to the mantelpiece, turned on the gas supply at the side and lit the gas fire. Kissing him lightly as she returned to the doorway where he had remained rooted to the spot, she switched off the ceiling light so that the room was illuminated by the rose-coloured glow from the gas fire, gradually growing brighter, hissing and popping as the elements heated up.

Slipping off her jacket and dropping it to the floor Libby drew him to the bedside where they stood toe to toe hardly breathing, until Libby took hold of his hand once again and pressed it gently to her breast.

As she closed her eyes, a sigh escaped her lips and she put her arms around his neck pulling him close. With fumbling fingers, he unbuttoned her blouse, her skirt and let them fall to the floor as she removed his shirt, unbuckled his trouser belt and slid his trousers from him. They stood together, silent, barely touching, breathing deeply.

Sliding the straps of her camisole top to the side he lifted it over her head and with her arms still uplifted lowered his lips to her nipple. Removing her silk knickers to leave her dressed only in a garter belt and silk stockings, he held her tight and she felt the growing hardness between his legs.

For moments they clung to each other, and then fell to the bed, kissing and touching, caressing and licking as their passion grew. He looked in wonderment at her beautiful body tracing a fine line from her neck down between her breasts, down across her flat belly and then further into the soft curls of hair between her legs and then further to where she was moist with her anticipation.

Naked together in the dim light, he made to roll on top of her, but she put a hand to his shoulder and, pressing him back moved astride him, pressing her body to his. Sitting up, she reached behind her neck and removed the silver clip to let her hair cascade free in a halo around her face.

He reached up to cup her breasts in his hands smiling inwardly as he remembered something his mother had once said in an unguarded slightly tipsy moment – what did not fit in a champagne glass was wasted. Here was just a little more, he thought, as he caressed her nipples until they became hard and erect with her passion.

Looking up at her, bathed in the light from the fire he knew he never had, and never would, see anything again so beautiful. He pulled her head down to his lips to kiss her deeply.

At this, she rose up on her knees, reached down between her legs, took hold of his erection which was now throbbing with urgency and lowered herself onto him with a throaty groan. Realising that she was not a virgin, but then nor was he, he pushed back against her body to increase her pleasure as she began to move rhythmically with him. To his horror, he felt himself burst inside her and found he was mumbling an apology over and over again as she shushed him and told him the next time it would be OK. It was.

During the night, as he drifted in a dreamless sleep, he felt her stir beside him, then her hand sliding down his body to his groin and as his senses stirred he felt her, touching, caressing, teasing, exciting him wildly. Taking her head gently in his hands he pulled her to his chest then rolled her onto her back; she parted her legs. He entered her and lay for a moment drowning in her kisses until she wrapped her legs around his waist. Then they made love, the bed creaking and groaning from their exertions, until they came to a climax together, to lie panting and shuddering together from the height and depth of their experience.

Later, still in the light of the old gas fire they fell asleep, Libby taking a firm grip on his arm as it wrapped around her, her bottom snuggled into the curve of his body.

It was late when they woke and Ronald went naked from the room to run her a bath, laced with some of his mother's precious bath crystals, deep and hot in complete disregard of Government regulations, and then padded down in bare feet to the kitchen to make a cup of tea.

By the time he got back upstairs, Libby was already in the bath, her hair pinned back up, luxuriating in the foam.

Responding to her call, he went into the bathroom and she motioned for him to get into the bath behind her. Laughing at her suggestion he nevertheless did as he was bid, and nestled in behind her. Taking a soft natural sponge from the windowsill he began to wash her. First her back then her neck and then, pulling her gently back onto his chest, he began to soap her breasts. It was not long before she began to move against him, until leaning forward, slipping and sliding, she moved over him, engulfed him and made love to him uncaring about the water slopping from the bath onto the linoleum floor. Afterwards, as she lay wrapped in his arms, she told him that she loved him.

The remainder of that day passed far too quickly. Just after lunch they heard the sound of tyres scrunching on the gravel drive. Thinking that it was his parents returning early, Ronald opened the front door, only to find a motorcycle courier on the doorstep, ready to knock.

Taking the small brown envelope, he tore it open with a sinking heart. As he feared it would, the telegram contained his orders to report in three days time to the RAF station at Hornchurch in Essex. He would undergo a full medical examination which would establish whether he was fit to return to flying duties.

To avoid spoiling the moment, he folded the envelope and hid it in his trouser pocket while telling Libby that it was a telegram from his father reporting on his aunt's steady recovery. He was sure she would forgive him the little white lie whenever he found the right moment to tell her of his recall to duty.

Later that afternoon, sitting with Libby in the lounge reading one of his father's journals, while Libby embroidered the border of a delicate silk handkerchief as a birthday present for her sister, it occurred to him that in less than forty-eight hours they had gone from being acquaintances, to friends, to lovers and now to behaving like an old married couple. In these difficult times that seemed to him to be no bad thing.

Still with the telegram at the back of his mind, he went over to his father's old gramophone and leafed through the small collection of dance records stacked by its side.

Seeing one that was designated as a slow foxtrot, which he thought he could just about manage, he removed the shiny black disc from its brown card sleeve and read the burgundy coloured centre label: "Until – Jan Wildeman and his Quintet", the gold lettering informed him.

Winding the mechanism, he carefully placed the disc on the felt cover of the turntable, set the disc in motion and gently lowered the playing head with its steel needle onto the surface. After a second or two of hiss and crackle, the opening bars from a clarinet and accordion filled the room, attracting Libby's attention. Holding out his hands, she came into his arms and they stepped away into the sensuous rhythm of the foxtrot, as the vocalist sang.

Until there are no stars to shine,
There's no such thing as time,
I'll love but you.

Burying his head into the nape of her neck, breathing in her perfume they danced on into the second verse.

Until there are no songs to sing,
There's no such thing as spring,
I'll love but you.

On they danced, now looking into each other's eyes, hers sparkling and moist with the emotion of the moment.

Until there is no moon above,
There's no such thing as love,

I'll love but you, sang the vocalist to complete the third verse and, as the music swept into the final refrain, Ronald knew he had made an important decision, perhaps the most important of his life.

When the music stopped, they stood together in the centre of the room, deaf to the hiss of the record in its final groove. After a second or two, he held her slightly away from him, caressed her cheek, and said simply, "Will you marry me?"

Without a moment's hesitation Libby replied, "Of course, darling! I was beginning to wonder what was taking you so long to get around to asking!"

He swept her up into his arms, and they both collapsed onto the sofa in a fit of laughter.

CHAPTER 9

The morning after his conversation with Keith, having gone to his bed fearful that old memories would trigger another of his nightmares, he woke somewhat surprised that he had had a dreamless night. Not having anything better to do after breakfast, and to keep his mind occupied as he anticipated what might be about to land in his lap, he copied out the code from the solicitor's letter so that Keith could take it away if he wanted to.

His former Squadron colleague arrived at 11.00am sharp, turning on to the drive in a rather elderly, but immaculately kept maroon coloured Jaguar XJ8, blipping the throttle to clear the plugs as he switched off the engine. Old habits, it seemed, died hard. Keith gave Ronald a cheery wave as he slipped easily from behind the steering wheel and appeared to be quite sprightly for his age, even though he was only a year or so younger than Ronald. Slim of build, he was dressed in light grey slacks and a dark blue blazer with a RAF squadron badge sewn onto the left breast pocket. A maroon coloured, paisley-patterned cravat was tied carefully at the open collar of his shirt. A neatly trimmed goatee beard gave him a slightly artistic air.

Ronald recognised him instantly, despite the gap of so many years, and they shook hands warmly in greeting. Despite having been away from his home county for some years, Keith retained the soft burr in his accent of the Norfolk/Suffolk border. Later that day, they joked about how 'sniffy' some of the old RAF regulars had been about his *rural* accent.

Over coffee, they began to bring each other up to date on their personal histories. Keith, a widower for some years, had two sons, each contemplating early retirement, and a younger daughter. He sympathised with Ronald over the untimely loss of his wife so long ago.

Ronald thanked him profusely for, as he put it, "saving my arse" that day, but Keith waved the gratitude away, saying that Ronald would have done no less if the tables had been reversed. Their reminiscences took them through to lunchtime, so they walked to the pub nearby for a snack.

During lunch, they began to talk about the events that had brought them together. Following his visit to Farrell in London, Keith had hoped that the solicitor's trick with the dice had been a hint, directing him to Ronald's squadron nickname and call-sign of Lucky 6, but it had still been something of a shot in the dark when he made the phone call. As he had mentioned previously, there was no identifying name on the slip of paper.

Ronald took a few minutes to bring Keith up to date on the details of his own trip to London and then he handed Keith the copy of the code which he had prepared for him. Keith looked at it and read it with mounting astonishment.

Unlike Ronald, Keith had remained active in RAF circles and was still a fundraiser, despite his years, for the RAF's charities. These two connections gave him an extensive overview of the wartime survivors. From their conversation they concluded that, in all probability, Keith was one of perhaps only two or three pilots still surviving who would have known both Ronald and Hutch, even though Keith had hardly seen Ronald since the day they parted company over the south coast. Clearly, they agreed, Hutch had gone to great lengths to bring the two of them together to unlock and solve his puzzle.

They debated the words, "BLACK KNIGHT", at length, but could only conclude that either it was a further code in itself, or it was misspelled or just conceivably, it could be an oblique reference to a chess piece for some purpose yet to be discovered. In the end they decided to put that on one side and to concentrate initially on the puzzle, hoping that the two words might find their proper place as the picture unfolded.

Back at the house, Ronald laid out on the dining table the solicitor's letter with Keith's copy of the code, and Hutch's log book for 1945 at the side of his own, both open at the same page. They sat together in silence reading and re-reading each document, looking for anything, a discrepancy, a deliberate mistake, some obvious clue that could begin to point them in the right direction. In the end, after more than an hour's close scrutiny, they were forced to the inescapable conclusion that there was nothing in Hutch's log book either before May 1st or after May 4th that threw any light on the three missing days.

To all intents and purposes, both logs recorded the same events leading up to the day of the Grossenbrode raid and any discrepancies afterwards they considered to be irrelevant as, by then, peace had been declared. Keith even tried heating the blank pages to see if perhaps there was some form of schoolboy's invisible writing involving the use of lemon juice, but the pages obstinately refused to give up their secrets.

At length, Keith reached into his jacket and took out a square of paper, a silver propelling pencil and proceeded to jot down a few notes. After staring at the letter for what seemed an eternity, Keith grunted as though a thought had struck him and asked, "Do you mind if I make a phone call? Can I use your house phone? I don't get on too well with mobiles."

"Help yourself," replied Ronald, motioning him toward the rather ancient phone which was perched on a pile of phone books on a small stand in the hall.

While Ronald continued reading, he could hear the mechanical whirring of the phone's chrome dialling ring and then Keith speaking for perhaps two minutes. After Keith came back into the room, he sat for a moment holding the original letter and Ronald's copy side by side, comparing them minutely and then said slowly, as though he were still processing the information he had just received.

"I noticed something, but I wanted to check before I said anything."

Pointing at the letter, then at the copy, he continued.

"What I noticed is that the number eight, here, at the very centre of the grid," he tapped the letter lightly with the tip of his silver pencil, "is coloured red on the solicitor's letter, but it's black on your copy and so I wondered if there was a typing error on the letter or whether it was an exact copy from the original will. I've just phoned Mr. Farrell. Thankfully he was in and took my call straight away. He said how pleased he was that we had met up. He was very clear that it was going to take the two of us working together to find the answer. He assured me that it was all just as much of a mystery to him. Hutch had not given him the answer, but he immediately confirmed that the red colour was correct. He particularly remembered Hutch had insisted he must check every element of his code before he would sign. So," he concluded with a satisfied look on his face, "we proceed on the basis that it's a red and not a black eight."

"I never considered the point," admitted Ronald, "I just made sure I got it right; letter for letter, number for number and all the proper symbols when I copied it for you."

"OK," said Keith, deep in thought, "the eight being red in colour must have real, possibly great significance, being right at the centre of the grid. I think it must be a key, a starting point for our thoughts, if nothing else. Why red and not black? Or green or any other colour for that matter?"

They both fell silent while Keith made more notes or doodles – Ronald could not tell which – then he turned to writing eights over and over again so that they flowed across the page like tiny interlinked whirlpools, before overwriting one in particular in his concentration, as though willing it to give up its secret. Then his hand slowed and came to a halt, pressing the point into the page for several seconds until he said slowly but very deliberately,

"I know it's a hell of a long shot, but do you remember that the Jerries used different colours – black or white, red and yellow come to mind – to number their fighters? What if... what if a red eight means a German fighter – perhaps one in particular?"

Ronald grunted an acknowledgement. "Could be. I guess we could go with that, at least for the time being and see where it gets us. But, then, what about these two letters 'PQ'? They keep appearing all over the grid."

Stretching and yawning loudly Keith commented, "The only thing I associate the letters PQ during the war is that they were the code letters used to designate the shipping convoys, the Russian convoys, going from west to east, up through the Arctic Circle, into places like Murmansk. Then they were changed round to QP for the convoys coming back. Never went to the Russian ports, did you?"

"No, of course not," Ronald replied with a laugh, "too bloody cold, but *convoy*, that rings a bell somehow," and he kept repeating the word over and over, wrestling with some distant memory. For a moment the cotton wool drifted back like the flotsam on an incoming tide, but then just as suddenly it cleared and the understanding struck him so forcefully that he leapt to his feet, startling Keith.

"*Baltic* Convoy, that's it, that was our call sign on the Grossenbrode raid." The excitement began to run through his body.

Then, leaning over the table, "Look," he said, "look here," jabbing his finger at the code. "Look at these letters. They have been frustrating me for ages and I just could not put my finger on what it was. Look at the letters PQ on the top line next to the first set of numbers – they could be fuselage letters from a British fighter."

With his voice breaking from the realisation, he sank slowly back to his chair saying, "Oh Christ, it's The Prussian Queen; PQ – they're Hutch's letters!"

Over a glass of beer, Ronald described the events as they had unfolded on 1st May 1945 during that fateful last mission of the war in Europe.

Ronald had been dreaming in a not unpleasant way about Libby when a hand shook him roughly at the shoulder. His attempts to snuggle back down were to no avail. A flashlight was held close to his eyes to force him awake.

"Sorry sir," said the orderly, "there's a bit of a panic. Briefing at 05.00."

Squinting at his watch, he says that it's 4.30 am and still dark, an hour or more from the first glimmer of dawn.

To his enquiring face, the orderly responded, "Sorry, I can't tell you anything but I've been ordered to get everyone up. Maximum effort. The planes are being armoured and fuelled."

At this point, Ronald became aware of the underlying rumble of more than a dozen Napier Sabre engines warming up.

Thrusting a chunky cheese sandwich into his hand to keep him going, and leaving a mug of hot sweet tea on the packing case that served as his bedside table, the orderly dashed from the room to waken another pilot.

Rubbing the sleep from his eyes and dressing as rapidly as he could, against a background of shouted orders and people running to and fro, Ronald made his way to the partially demolished hangar that was serving as their temporary headquarters. They had been on the captured airfield for less than a week.

With his watch showing nearly 5am, the footsteps of one or two latecomers could be heard running across the broken glass and the other debris that littered the ground. No time or point in clearing up: they might be on a different airfield by nightfall, so quickly was the front line moving east and north across the German landscape.

With everyone in attendance, Hutch rolled out a map and taped it to the rear fuselage of a partly dismantled Me109. He switched on a small lamp to highlight a length of bright red tape, blood red, leading north-east from their base to the Baltic coast, then turning sharply due west to their destination.

Without any pleasantries or introduction he said, "Hitler is dead." Gasps and ironic cheers.

"Intelligence believes that German High Command is going to try to escape to Sweden. The Russians have, we are told, still not completely closed the ring round Berlin and there is a narrow corridor open to the north-west, still held by what is left of their Sixth Army. The belief is that they are going to make a run for the Grossenbrode sea plane base at the southern end of the Kiel Bight. As you can see, the base occupies the neck of land that gives access to the island of Fehmarn so it should be reasonably easy to identify from the air even though we will be at zero feet."

Feet shuffled in the dust. Cigarettes glowed in the early light.

"As you may know, the Allied forces have been forbidden to cross the Elbe river and the Russians say they are too busy in the east, and up to their necks supporting their troops in Berlin, to get involved – so it's down to us. Study the map and recce photos carefully before you go. We will come in over the sea from the east, out of the sun, which will just have risen by the time we get there. The attack must be pressed home," he stressed, "irrespective of cost. We must not fail." There was no escaping his meaning.

Sounds like a bloody suicide mission, thought Ronald. Why now? Why now?

"I will lead as Red One; Ronno you will be my number two." (why, thought Ronald) "Choose your own targets – one pass only. Do not go back and don't fart about on the approach trying to put off the gunners. You will waste speed and give them a better chance of hitting you. Four waves thirty seconds apart. Go straight over the peninsula, turn north, then loop around the top of the island, stay away from the coast for two minutes then turn in and fly back on a reverse bearing. Call sign will be *Baltic Convoy*. Any questions?"

Apart from wanting to know why Hutch was leading rather than himself, Ronald asked about flak cover. In reply he was told that they were trying to co-ordinate a squadron of American Mustangs to come in from the south to deal with the defences, but they were not to wait and would have to manage one way or another. The target had been given top priority.

One way ticket, thought Ronald, as he began to regret eating anything at all.

"Right gentlemen, take off at 07.00. We go all the way on the deck – do not fire under any circumstances, unless directly threatened by another aircraft and select targets of opportunity on the way back, but for God's sake don't shoot any Russians. We don't need to start another war before we finish this one." Nervous laughter rang out in response. More cigarettes.

Stepping to the side while the squadron's pilots gathered in a semi-circle round the map to make brief mental notes, Hutch took

Ronald by the arm and said quietly, "If I can't get back, you pick up all the strays and bring them home. Keep a beer cold for me and we'll share it shortly."

Ronald had the feeling that Hutch was talking nonsense, but time did not permit further enquiry as Hutch turned on his heel and strode quickly away towards his waiting aircraft. In passing, Ronald noticed Hutch tying a red white and blue silk scarf around his neck as he went.

From behind, the voice of Peter Smith said in a tone that betrayed his nervousness, "Roll the dice Ronno."

Unable and unwilling to resist, he did as he was bid and the dice tumbled from his hand onto the top of a discarded ammunition case. Double six. Sighs of relief. Smiles, weary and strained. Cigarette stubs ground into the floor.

As he ran to Miss Faithful, he could see Hutch climbing into the Prussian Queen, turning for a second to send him a mock salute, and, as Ronald held up six fingers, Hutch threw his head back in laughter, but there was no merriment in his eyes.

His fitter was waiting at the plane, and dragged the parachute off the wing, slipping it over his shoulders then dropping it into the well of his seat, clipping it across his chest as he settled into the cockpit. With the Sutton safety harness loosely laid around him, he shouted over the roar of the engine and the rush of the slipstream, "Tight, tight as you can, pray God this is the last time." The fitter duly obliged – in the belief that it would be the only time that he would be permitted to cause pain to an officer – patted him on the shoulder, mouthed a "good luck" and slipped down from the wing.

After checking the dancing dials on the instrument panel, Ronald closed his eyes, focused on an image of Libby, said his usual prayer for deliverance and opened the throttle as Hutch led the squadron away.

Forming up over the airfield under the watchful eye of the recently reinforced RAF Regiment with its multiple Bofors anti-aircraft guns (goodness knows what the German Luftwaffe might have up its sleeve even at this late stage), fourteen Tempests in three flights of four with a final pair headed slightly east of north toward the Baltic coast. Ronald took station just behind Hutch's port wing. Red Three and Four were echeloned out to Hutch's right, adopting a conventional finger-four formation, to complete the first line of attack. Blue, Yellow and Green sections tucked in close behind.

Hugging the contours of the landscape the formation hurtled north at speed, fields, farms, villages and churches flashing beneath them. Ronald hardly dared look down at the panorama unrolling below, fearful of missing the danger of on-rushing power lines. Twice Hutch called for emergency climb and as one the flight rose and fell back over these lethal barriers.

Infrequent bursts of anti-aircraft fire peppered the sky around them but nothing to cause any problems. Ahead, oblivious of Armageddon hurtling toward it, Ronald spotted the gangly outline of a Fiesler Storch light reconnaissance plane, but even as he released the safety catch a single word in his headphones stopped his hand. "Ignore," came Hutch's command and the flight roared less than twenty feet over the top of the Storch. Ronald glimpsed the pilot, open-mouthed, fighting to retain control of his aircraft as it was tossed in the turbulent wake of their passage.

Ronald wondered what the man could have been doing, bumbling across the sky as if without a care in the world, or was it a last minute desperate attempt at an escape, but he would never know because the white sands of the Baltic Coast lay immediately ahead. On the eastern horizon the sun was breaking through a layer of low cloud casting long shadows, pointing like signposts towards their destination, thirty miles to the west.

As they crossed the shoreline, Ronald was amazed to see it dotted with small groups of civilians apparently encamped round hand carts, baby prams, or an occasional horse with cart. These wretched, frightened refugees had reached the end of their world in their flight from the relentless oncoming tide of Russian armour.

Faces turned up, some fearful, some raising hands in a half-hearted greeting, perhaps expecting the never-to-come salvation. Others, realising in the last instant that these aircraft bore not the black and white crosses of their Luftwaffe, threw themselves flat to the sand. They could only expect the worst.

A lone soldier raised a rifle, but then thought better of it and Ronald watched him turn and hurl it, like an Olympic hammer thrower holding it two-handed by the muzzle, into the sea. A memory of another place in another time, 1936, went fleetingly through his mind.

"Baltic Convoy, 90 degrees port," came Hutch's calm instruction just as though he were talking at the Air Pageant that they had both so enjoyed. Was that, like the Olympics, less than ten years ago? As one, fourteen aircraft wheeled to their left over the sparkling surface of the Baltic, which was broken only by the sweeping white wavelets being driven on by the stiff, northerly breeze.

"Increasing to 360 – take out any advance defences as you find them. Looks as though we are going to have to manage without the Mustangs. We can't hang around waiting for them. Good luck gentlemen and remember – one pass only."

With these words Hutch committed them to the attack, but at the same moment a worried voice broke the air, "Red Four to Convoy Leader, I think I'm losing coolant – pressure's dropping. Compass seems to be off, too."

Twisting as much as his harness would permit, Ronald looked back over his right shoulder until he could focus on Red Four, a young Australian pilot called Maguire. A telltale ribbon of vapour could be seen streaming back from the port side of the engine cowling.

Having a clearer view than Hutch, Ronald put his hand to his facemask, switched his microphone to transmit and ordered, "Red Four, Red Two, break off and return to base. You are definitely losing fluid. Sorry we can't spare any cover. Good luck. Out." and looking back again he saw Maguire's plane pulling up out of formation, perfectly silhouetted against the morning sky before turning south and diving back to the deck, with the escape of coolant already looking a little worse.

Ronald said a prayer that the lad – Christ, he was only three years younger than himself – would make it back safely. Like any piston engine, the Sabre would not run for very long without coolant. He looked across at Hutch and shook his head. Hutch responded with a shrug of the shoulders as if to say "That's the way it goes – on with the show".

At 360 miles per hour, thirteen aircraft dipped, until they were no more than fifty feet above the waves breaking against the north German coast.

At 360 miles per hour, covering a mile every ten seconds, Ronald calculated that he, they, had possibly, indeed probably, only five or six minutes to live. His throat tightened, his pulse rate increased and he felt more frightened than at any time since the war had begun. Surely, he implored, he must survive this one last mission.

Onward they thundered, passing yet more refugees on their left who had also reached their journey's end, at the shore of the Baltic, to await their uncertain fate.

Four minutes:

Ronald hunkered down in his seat if only to give himself the semblance of greater protection, but knowing in his heart that it was more psychological than real. He found himself humming snatches of Vera Lynne's "We'll meet again", but it brought him little comfort as he contemplated his slim chances of survival.

Three minutes:

As the sun rose slowly into the sky behind them, Ronald armed the eight sixty pound rockets and twisted the outer ring to the firing button from safe to fire for the four cannon. The die was cast. He switched the oxygen flow to maximum to give his mind a temporary boost. He switched to main fuel tanks. The Napier Sabre did not miss a beat.

Two minutes:

"Discard drop tanks – increase to three eighty," came Hutch's final instruction and twenty four empty tanks fluttered down into the sea. Freed of the extra drag, the flight accelerated to nearly 400 miles per hour, climbing to one hundred feet and preparing to attack.

Sixty seconds – six and one half miles.

A hundred yards to his right, Ronald looked across to Hutch, who raised his hand in salute. His drop tanks had not released.

A hundred yards further away Hutch's remaining wingman began to drift out to starboard, seeking his targets.

Four thousand yards astern Baz was leading the first group of four, Blue section. A similar distance further back, Peter Smith led three more, Yellow section. Finally,- bringing up the rear, 'the tail-end charlies', the remaining pair of relatively new pilots, Green Section, who it was hoped would have an easier ride by being the last to arrive at the target and at the same time be available to break away and deal with any enemy fighter cover. Inevitably they were drifting further and further astern. Green by name, green by nature – so horribly inexperienced, but no time left to fret for their safety.

Forty five seconds:

To his left, as his view of the sea plane base started to clear with the low-lying island of Fehmarn emerging out of the mists to the north, Ronald could see a large, heavily armed picket boat anchored broadsides to their approach, red and black naval pennants fluttering at stem and stern. Even as his hand moved to the release for the rockets, he saw muzzle flashes from multiple anti-aircraft units fore and aft of the funnel, and, as he banked and raced toward the gun boat, twenty millimetre and thirty millimetre flak began curving up and towards him, as though to strike him between the eyes.

Without further thought, he jabbed his left thumb onto the button located in the centre of the throttle lever to fire two salvos of rockets at the gunboat and watched their four exhaust trails being drawn like magnets to their target. He was too close to miss and immediately switched the selector adjacent to the throttle to arm the guns and gave the mid-section of the boat a short burst of canon fire for good measure, briefly seeing the shells churn the water and march into the hull, upwards and across the deck mowing down sailors before the rockets impacted. The resulting fireball and force of the explosion threw his plane off course momentarily. As he came through the clouds of upward billowing smoke, as though parting a curtain, he was thrust into a vision of impending hell which would test his nerve to its limit.

Further to his left, at the southern end of the bay, a thirty metre high concrete flak tower was pouring fire into the air, red, green, yellow, angry black puffs of 88 mm and on top of the tower, a small radar array, controlling some of the automated gunfire. How he wished they'd had the Mustangs to draw the teeth of the gunners' fire.

At anchor, or about to move, were three giant six-engined Blom & Voss seaplanes, each one bigger than a Lancaster bomber and each with its engines tuning. A fourth was moving away from its moorings under what seemed to be full power. Several small naval cutters were scurrying to and from the shore.

"My God, it's true," Ronald thought in the split-second before he opened fire.

To his right, he could see Hutch launch his rockets, before firing at a Blom & Voss twin engined sea plane sitting on its cradle above the concrete apron, his cannon shells running onward and into a cluster of buildings as he passed. Further to his right, he could see Hutch's wingman, Red Three, peeling away to pour fire into the fourth Blom & Voss which was attempting to take off, exhaust smoke from its diesel engines streaming back as the pilot desperately held the throttles open wide.

A long burst of cannon fire caught the giant sea plane in the starboard wing. Two engines burst into flames, trailing smoke and debris in their wake before the wing dipped and the plane cartwheeled into the surface of the bay, disappearing in a cloud of spray and fire.

Realising that the flak tower had to be silenced if possible, Ronald fired his four remaining rockets, but although he saw four solid strikes around the centre of the tower, at that moment there seemed to be no noticeable reduction in the lethal streams pouring from it. Racing toward the top of the tower he let it have a long burst from the four cannon, hoping to knock out the radar and array of aerials that adorned the top levels, but again with no obvious result – hot glowing coals continued to pursue him as he swept through the column of smoke and dust rising from the base.

Crossing the peninsular, he scanned the sky for the members of the second wave coming in thirty seconds behind. Of Hutch there was no sign, but half a mile away he could see the wingman, turning away toward the north. As he turned to follow, a blinding flash startled him and he was horrified to find a Tempest, either number two or number four from Blue Section, disintegrating in front of him, having gone straight into the concrete apron in a ball of flame, a victim of the intense flak.

Over his right shoulder he saw with relief Baz emerge from the inferno, but still pursued by the German gunners.

Calling to him, "Baz, I can't see Hutch, did they get him?" to which came the reply, in a voice laden with fear, "Christ Ronno, I don't know, but we've got to do something, or the others are going to get slaughtered."

Thinking quickly about Hutch's orders, but realising that he had no choice but to disobey, Ronald responded, "All Baltic Convoy rendezvous fifteen miles south. Return to base if no sign of me and Blue One in ten minutes. Do not, I repeat, do not wait any longer." He knew he was teetering on the edge of panic like a beast waiting to go to slaughter.

"Come on Baz, we'll make one pass from the north – pray God it helps. On my port wing – go," so saying Baz slid his Tempest onto Ronald's left and as they cleared the north tip of the peninsula, gaining height, they turned to see the third wave engaging and the fourth still three miles out.

What Ronald saw next shook him to the core. Yellow Two of the third wave was caught in cross fire, shaken by hammer blows, before exploding from a direct hit. An 88mm battery had found its target and the burning remnants cascaded onto the shoreline. Yellow Four seemed to be out of control, rolling onto its side, just feet above the waves, its pilot dead or dying, Yellow Three firing its rockets, but of Yellow one, Smithie, there was no sign.

Knowing they had only seconds, Ronald shouted "Full throttle, find the guns, find the bloody guns," and back they sped, wingtip to wingtip.

Ahead, the base, alight with outgoing light, medium and heavy flak, was already engaging Green flight. For a split second the picture froze, a montage of death. To his left the picket boat blazed furiously. Ahead, columns of smoke billowed from shattered aircraft and buildings. Yellow Two's wingtip catching the wave tops and cartwheeling toward the land, a flock of gulls dropping like blooded snowflakes, people running for their lives, but still the guns pouring out their lethal rivers of death. One, no two, of the giant seaplanes on fire and sinking by their moorings.

Would they not give up? he thought, as he pressed the firing button, seeking out the anti-aircraft guns and walking the cannon fire from side to side, watching his shell-fire chew its way through a 30mm multiple barrel unit and another beyond, flinging body parts hither and thither in a charnel house of destruction. In his headphones, he could hear Baz yelling obscenities and out the corner of his eye saw a hand's-breadth of his own wingtip disappear as a burst of radar controlled gunfire found him.

Just ten seconds, live or die and it would all be over. He would not, could not, go round again. He was grinding his teeth incessantly.

More sounds, like hail on a tin roof assailed him and he knew that the gunners had his range.

Eight seconds; still not breathing, his chest bursting, his neck aching from the effort of forcing himself to hold the line of attack and watching, always, for enemy fighters. His heart stopped momentarily as a shadow, a darkness from above, forced into his consciousness. Glancing up, there, just fifteen feet above him was Yellow One, on its back, canopy shattered and her pilot hanging lifeless in his harness, so close he could almost touch him, his hands resting against the shattered glass as though to push it clear, but Smithie, poor Smithie was dead, his fiancée a widow before marriage.

Two seconds: One last burst from his cannon, perhaps a few shells saved for the homeward leg, and he was through, Baz still at his wingtip, obscenities still pouring from his lips, but alive, undeniably alive. To his left, the final pair was attacking, rockets streaking into buildings, cannon-fire ripping through aircraft at their moorings, churning water and land.

Smithie's shattered Tempest plunged into the base of the flak-tower, cremating anyone in the vicinity as its fuel tanks exploded in a fireball. Under the weight of the onslaught, the flak had finally been reduced to a shadow of its initial intensity, so that both aircraft of Green section emerged through the rising columns of flame and smoke, unscathed.

Zero seconds, and Ronald let out his breath, gulping greedily on the flow of oxygen like a drowning soul.

"Red Two to Baltic Convoy," he gasped, pulling back on the control column to gain height. "Rendezvous as instructed two thousand feet – watch for fighters. Anyone seen Red One, Hutch?"

For long moments there was only the crackle of static filling his headphones, but then the voice of Baz came through, weak with relief.

"Lost sight of him, Ronno, after you hit that picket boat. How many did we lose?"

As the two pilots from Green section reported in, Ronald hardly dared think of their losses – he was certain that the whole of Yellow section was gone, plus at least one from Blue and then Hutch – six, possibly more out of thirteen, a fifty percent casualty rate in return for the four large transports, a destroyed seaplane base and half a dozen small, insignificant float planes. Then he remembered Maguire; yet another potential loss.

With a bitter knot in his stomach, Ronald wondered if the destruction of the whole of the German High Command, not just the chosen few, would have been worth the price they had just paid.

Ronald sat back in his chair, finding he was short of breath and his fists were clenched tight from the tension, the stress of the memory. He had led them away to the south, just four in number, to the rendezvous point where they circled for agonising minutes, ever fearful of the dreaded flak, waiting for the stragglers. Blue Three, Kelsey, joined them en route, crabbing across the sky, tail plane and port wing almost shredded by flak so he had sent Kelsey ahead with Green One and Two – he could not even remember their names now, try as he might – as escort.

He and Baz had continued to circle, hearts in mouths, then Baz had given a cry, not of warning, but of relief, as he spotted one more Tempest, the last of the few, Red Three, Archie Evans, he remembered now. Of Blue Four, Jones, Evans' buddy, the pair of Welsh pilot officers, inseparable in battle, but not now spared the separation of death, and Blue Two, Wojec, another of the brave Poles, there had been no sign,

Ronald had delayed as long as he dared, longer than he should, but finally with Evans reporting increasing engine temperature and no response to his calls over the R/T, he had led the survivors home, turning away from the columns of smoke rising and drifting away on the wind, the pyre of their endeavours. For Wojec and Jones there would be no marker of their passing, save "missing – believed killed".

Over their own airfield, he had held off until all the others had landed. Kelsey, Blue Three, he could see had elected for a wheels up landing and as he made his final approach he could see Geoff sitting on the wing, just behind the shattered propeller, lighting a cigarette. Now that he was down in one piece, the risk of fire seemed not to concern him in the slightest. Geoff gave him a cheerful, relieved wave as he taxied by.

Opening the throttle to clear the plugs, he had rested his head against the crash pad of the seat, closed his eyes and said, he hoped for the very last time, his thank you prayer and he listened, like a condemned man reprieved, to the silence which was broken only by the sound of the cooling of the Napier Sabre engine, a parting whisper from Miss Faithful.

It had seemed to take all his strength to wind back the canopy even a fraction. He felt utterly drained. Then his fitter was on the wing, helping him to move the canopy, because, as he had pointed out, the side-runner had been damaged by a piece of flak. Yet again, of such small things was a life spared or taken.

He could remember how he needed the support of his fitter to get out of the cockpit, and again, as he slipped down off the wing. His legs had gone to rubber, in the realisation that he had survived. For a few moments he was super sensitive to his immediate environment, drawing in the spring scent of pine from the nearby forest as it mingled with the aromas of hot oil, burnt fuel and the residue wafting from the gun muzzles. In the same moment he saw himself as his father almost twenty years before and said another quiet offering for his deliverance.

The fitter, almost old enough to be his father, had helped him light a cigarette to steady his shaking hands, and had looked at him in a kindly way, perhaps to acknowledge that the fighting, and the dying was done by the young for the most part – Ronald was an old man at twenty-four – and held out his hand to grip Ronald's firmly, saying "Job done, sir, it's all finished."

And indeed it was.

He never flew again in anger. That night they all met in what stood for the mess. Someone produced a couple of bottles of Scotch and they drank the lot in muted recognition of the departed and their own random survival. Even Geoff, who professed a profound dislike of the stuff, found that the occasion demanded that he should overcome his aversion, and he downed his fair share.

Before retiring to his bed, with his mind having that extreme, but sometimes dangerous clarity of a body that is drunkenly sober, he had carried out two tasks. Firstly he wrote a citation for every member of the attack and then, with a growing sense of despair, he drafted the letters to the families of those who would not be returning home.

Of Maguire, the young Australian, who he had sent back unescorted, there was no trace. Vanished into thin air. Yet another letter.

With a final enquiry to the Duty Officer, his last act before passing out from the effects of the alcohol and sheer exhaustion was to write the letter for Hutch.

For the next forty-eight hours they had flown protective patrols, just in pairs, as news of the surrender negotiations began to leak out. The Luftwaffe had undertaken not to fly, so a patrol was a better way of doing nothing – it was hard to give up the habits of half a decade at war.

On the third day he flew one last patrol with Baz Bajkowski and Geoff Kelsey, somewhat against orders. No one had defined how far a patrol should extend, so they flew back to Grossenbrode, perhaps in the hope they might find some evidence of Hutch, but of course there was nothing.

As they flew north, white flags of surrender were everywhere, hanging from homes and official buildings, such as were still standing, where once the red, black and white of the German Swastika had flown with such arrogance.

At Grossenbrode they were stunned by the damage they had caused. The flak tower had collapsed almost entirely, the seaplane base was virtually razed to the ground. What they had not blown up, fire had burnt down. From the air, circling at minimum throttle, they identified the charred remains of at least four Tempests.

Baz broke formation and rose into a perfect victory roll in final tribute. Geoff followed suit, but Ronald, unable to fully comprehend that he was no longer at risk, maintained the patrol and watched as the first of the tide of refugees, still moving west along the coast, reached the outskirts of the base. One low pass, on silent wings, scattered their vanguard, but Ronald had no doubt that it would take stronger measures to deter the inevitable looting. He could only hope that the forward units of Montgomery's 8th Army, the Desert Rats, would quickly occupy the base and give some final dignity to the earthly residue, however little, of his colleagues.

Of the giant seaplanes, only the tip of a tailfin jutting out of the calm waters of the Baltic now remained. The graves of the others were marked by the stain of oil or diesel escaping to the surface. But of Hutch there was still no sign. Ronald said a prayer for those who had paid the ultimate price.

Turning once again to the south, heading warily back to base, Germany and its Luftwaffe held just one last surprise for them. With only a split second's shout of warning from Geoff, Ronald for once lost in a daydream, a lone German fighter met them head-on. It was a rare beast, a Dornier "Arrow" – the Luftwaffe's last and fastest piston-engined fighter, unique in having one engine with a propeller at the front and a second in the fuselage behind the pilot, driving a pusher propeller at the rear. It was fully capable of outrunning any Allied fighter over Germany at the time.

Ronald recognised it instantly, but even as his finger moved instinctively to release the safety for the guns, Geoff's voice broke in, "Let the bugger go – what's one, more or less."

And so they had watched the craft pass below them, the pilot peering up and, seeing that they would not fire, raised his hand in salute and then he was gone to God knows where in his solo bid for freedom. Ronald wondered if perhaps it was Max, the test pilot he had met in '36, but for sure he would never know.

In a strange way, having only just finished with killing the enemy, Ronald had wished him good luck and hoped, one pilot as to another, that the man might find a safe haven.

That night, with the sound of Keith snoring gently in the guest bedroom, and now separated by almost sixty years from that day, Ronald found that, as he drifted off to sleep, his personal sentiment had not changed.

CHAPTER 10

Keith had sat quietly through Ronald's dramatic telling of the raid, listening intently, but then offered up his glass for a refill, commenting, "We heard that it was bad, but I never realised – and all a complete waste as you found out later."

Whilst they both continued to absorb the possibility that the letters were indeed the identification from the Tempest flown by Hutch, Keith made more notes on his piece of paper as though he was still trying to work out the puzzle as a mathematical or algebraic formula.

"You know, when I first saw this," he said, again pointing at the letter, "I too thought it was just a form of bid at bridge or the record of a game of chess, or even a joke perhaps on Hutch's part, especially after you showed me those blank pages. I know only a bit about bridge and rather less about chess, but even so, I am sure it's neither, at least in the conventional sense. I mean, look at the compass points. They are completely the wrong way round for bridge. Then on the other hand, the apparent chess moves are all wrong too, but on balance I do still think it is a puzzle to be solved, and not just a bad joke. God help us if it is."

He took another long swig from his glass and sighed contentedly as the liquor warmed his throat.

Another bell began to ring faintly in Ronald's subconscious, but whatever it was it remained beyond his reach, an annoying niggle that he could not put to rest.

Realising it was getting late, Ronald suggested that he prepare them a simple supper, to which Keith readily agreed, and then added, with some certainty that Keith might no longer be fit to drive,

"Why don't you stay over? I get the feeling we need to stick at this until we crack it. I've got spare toiletries and pyjamas and the guest room is already made up." To his surprise, Keith agreed, joking that they had better be careful as they would get a certain reputation if they made a habit of it.

As it turned out, the evening, whilst not being a complete waste of time, produced nothing but continuing frustration, although the more they talked about it, the more they were convinced that the jumble of letters and numbers told a tale.

In the end they gave up trying, and returned to their reminiscences.

Ronald was particularly interested to hear about Keith's time in Berlin shortly after the Allies were allowed access to the ruined city by the Russians in the mid-summer of 1945.

Keith, who had been in Berlin as part of an RAF inspection team looking at and assessing captured Luftwaffe aircraft, recalled that even though there was real tension between the Western Allies and the Russians on the political level, there was still genuine camaraderie between the soldiers and airmen on both sides as they celebrated the victory over the common enemy.

On one memorable occasion, he had met up with two Russians, one an army major and the other with the equivalent rank to a Squadron Leader. They both had a remarkable command of English so there had been little problem with making himself understood.

At the end of the rather stiff and very formal function, a victory celebration filled with tedious speeches of self-congratulation, the two men had offered him a tour of what was about to become the Russian zone. The devastation was unbelievable – not a roof was intact, barely a pane of glass had survived unbroken. Bulldozers had carved rough alleyways through the rubble and the surviving residents of Berlin, old men, women and children, had been forced to complete the process by hand so that, on foot, he seemed to be walking along endless corridors. But even that was not enough to sanitise the city; the smell of death was everywhere, rising like an evil vapour from the countless bodies, still buried under the rubble.

They had taken him over to the Tiergarten, Berlin's one time zoological garden from which the caged animals had long since gone, eaten, killed or escaped. The once luxuriant, neatly tended park with its large areas of wooded coverts and fine, mature specimen trees was reduced to a wasteland. Brutally shattered stumps were all that remained, bringing back images of the battlefields of the Western Front during the Great War, which he had seen in the picture books of his childhood. Any loose lying timber had been quickly swept up by the surviving residents of Berlin –winter lay ahead and there would be no coal.

There, on the very western edge of the park, they showed him the *Flakturm,* the notorious flak tower, one of three built at great speed in '43 to protect Berlin. A forty metre high reinforced concrete defence point, it had been built around four circular towers, bristling with anti-aircraft guns of all calibres, some radar controlled. It had proved to be so formidable and impregnable that it had withstood every aerial bombardment and continued to be so effective, that the Russians had declared it to be a no-fly zone. Too many of their pilots had died in the mistaken belief that they could take it out.

The garrison and the several hundred civilians who had sought sanctuary there, had only yielded in the last days before the surrender when their commandant accepted that annihilation was inevitable. They were besieged and surrounded on all sides by Russian heavy guns, which were able to fire at point-blank range across what had once been the lush landscape of the park, now reduced to a cratered desert. In fact, the Russian major also told Keith that, for the time being, they had decided it was too much trouble to knock it down.

Later they had taken him to the Reichschancel Building, which was in ruins from the continuous artillery bombardment, but still flying the Russian's red hammer-and-sickle flag raised in the first week of May, symbolic of Germany's utter defeat. Just a couple of hundred yards away he was given privileged access to Hitler's bunker. Going outside into what was once the secluded garden, they pointed to the very place where, they said, the burned remains of Adolf Hitler and Eva Braun had been found. The garden was just a sea of craters, but still stacked in a corner nearby, was a pile of jerry cans, which they said had contained the petrol that had been used to incinerate their bodies. Even though these events had taken place only a few weeks previously, he admitted to Ronald that he had struggled to understand how anyone could have lived, let alone survived, in Berlin in those last, desperate days.

Keith had been stunned by the extent of the bunker which had many corridors, was on at least three different levels underground with countless rooms for accommodation, recreation, Hitler's personal private quarters (which he was not permitted to visit) as well as a once fully-equipped operating theatre. Everything, in fact, required to sustain a substantial community underground, although the surgical equipment had long since been removed, sent back to Mother Russia as a tiny part of the reparations Germany was to pay. There was, in addition, a sophisticated air purification and pumping system designed to insulate the occupants from a possible chemical or gas attack, but completely ineffective against the sheer weight of manpower the Russians threw at, and sacrificed, to take the symbolic heart of fascism.

Although largely ransacked, there were still lots of papers, the spindrift of German bureaucracy, lying around in the debris of battle.

However, as he could not read German, these were of no interest to him, although he did find a rather fine Weiss gold inlaid Pelikan fountain pen lying in a corner and had slipped it surreptitiously into his pocket, as a souvenir.

Later that day, he had been invited to an evening party being organised to celebrate – quite what he could no longer remember. But the Russians, by repute, seemed willing to celebrate at the drop of a hat. He had managed to scrounge a bottle of scotch as his entry ticket and when he got to the venue the party was in full swing. The Russians seemed partial to Glenn Miller's music, which was coming full blast out of a speaker system, interspersed with traditional Russian melodies and songs. Everyone who was in uniform was wearing their medals, many of which seemed to have been only recently awarded.

What had surprised him most was the number of women there – frankly he had not expected any at all. They were of all ages, some probably only fourteen years old and plastered with make-up to look as grown-up as possible, while others were very, very much older. As the evening wore on it became clear that for the women, the young or not so young, just about anything and everything they had was on offer, either then or later, in return for money, food, or cigarettes – preferably the latter. Cigarettes had become the currency of exchange. Reich marks had become worthless. Sex, that other currency, was not even a close second. The Russian conquerors had not come to barter.

The quantity of food for the party was unlike anything he had seen for a very long time, which he found almost shocking after the strict rationing back home, and then there was the endless supply of Schnapps, presumably 'liberated' from a nearby German warehouse. And Vodka, gallons of the stuff, with which they toasted each other, their leaders, their mothers, fathers, brothers, sisters, sweethearts (no mention of wives it seemed) in fact almost anyone and anything, in a kind of euphoric mania that only the victors, or those who know they are about to die, can hope to achieve.

He heard stories of similar times in Hitler's bunker in the last days of the war, especially after the Führer's death. These details came from a very attractive, raven haired girl, about twenty years old, who claimed to have been there, almost to the very end. However, as Keith repeatedly pointed out to Ronald, at that particular time she and he were involved in a pretty heavy petting session after she had already "frisked" him thoroughly, to remove his cigarettes, lighter and most, but not quite all of the money in his wallet. This was in return for the most serious kissing he had ever experienced. In the telling, Keith had a real twinkle in his eye and a quite lecherous chuckle in his voice. He had thought at the time that she might have been prepared to say and do anything to earn his favours, but declined to throw any more light on how their evening had ended, and left Ronald to reach his own conclusions.

Ronald was fascinated to hear of Keith's experiences in Berlin and carefully sidestepped the invitation to expand on his own life in the immediate aftermath of VE day (even though they had been less than 200 miles apart.) For the time being, he satisfied Keith's curiosity by saying that he had taken the first opportunity to get home to see his wife, Libby.

At this point, they were just finishing their third whisky nightcap, so Ronald seized the moment to persuade Keith to call it a day, which suggestion Keith took without too much resistance saying that he too with age had become more of an early riser. It was not long before Ronald could hear Keith's snoring, but he lay awake for a while, still trying to puzzle away at Hutch's riddle.

The next morning, shaved and showered, he had been in the kitchen laying the breakfast table and making tea when he heard the floorboards creaking overhead. However, rather than the footsteps going on toward the bathroom, he heard Keith suddenly run along the landing and come rushing downstairs, to appear, a moment later, through the doorway, barefoot and still in his pyjamas, breathless and agitated, hair awry.

"Ron," he exclaimed, without even saying good morning.

"I've just remembered something and I don't know if it might be important." Without pausing for breath he dashed on, "You remember I mentioned the Russian major and his pal who took me to the party, well they told me this really odd story, which he said he had been told by a soldier who had been holding a position to the west of Berlin, about half way across between the outskirts of the city and the River Elbe."

Pausing to catch his breath, he continued, "Anyway, so the story went, this soldier was on duty just west of a small forest which, they thought might contain a hidden German airfield, when they saw a ME109 flying toward it slowly and rather quietly, *na-tseep-ach-ki*, 'on tiptoes' as the major put it over and over again." Keith conjured up an image of a drunken Russian officer in his tunic and soft calf-length boots, arms outstretched, up on his toes twirling slowly, like the aircraft seeking its refuge.

"God knows where it could have come from, but of course they fired on it, even though it was really out of range of their small calibre weapons. Then, just a short time later, they saw an English single-engined plane, definitely not a Spitfire, fly over and so they gave it a loud cheer, thinking it was going to shoot down the German. Both aircraft disappeared from view."

"Apparently no more than half an hour elapsed, when they heard the sound of aero engines at full throttle flying very fast in their direction. To their complete surprise, a German plane and the English plane came directly toward them, flat out at tree top height, flying literally wingtip to wingtip. The planes were over them and gone in a second, so that they only had time to get off a couple of bursts of ack-ack."

Keith stopped again to catch his breath, but before Ronald could say anything in reply, Keith ploughed on,"Wait, that's not all. There's something even more curious. The major said that this soldier had been told by another soldier stationed at the banks of the Elbe that he too had seen two fighters going like bats out of hell toward the northwest, in formation and, wait for it, when a third, an American Mustang tried to intercept, the British fighter had fired on it until it backed off!"

"Well, by that time of night, we were all really drunk and the Russians fell about laughing at the idea that, not content with shooting at the Germans, the Allies had taken to shooting at each other. They thought it was a real hoot; they didn't believe it anyway, but we drank several toasts on the strength."

Ronald tried to speak but Keith held up his hand.

"No don't stop me, I've got to get this out or I'll burst – there's a bit more. A few weeks later, I bumped into Hutch at Tempelhof, Berlin's civilian airfield, where I had gone to look at some captured German planes including the first Me262 jet fighter I had ever seen in the flesh. I even sat in it – fantastic for its time. He was sorting, filtering German Luftwaffe paperwork, looking for their secret projects.

When I saw him, Hutch was with an older man, English, not in the military, Jimmy… no, Jimmy Gillard I remember now. Dressed like a tramp. At the time, I thought they seemed as thick as thieves, strange bedfellows, but it was none of my business.

Anyway I digress. We got to chatting about Russian "hospitality" which was getting a bit thin by then, when I remembered the major's story and related it to Hutch. At the time, Hutch laughed it off, and, as though he wanted desperately to change the subject, he said something along the lines that he'd seen Hitler standing at the American PX the day before. I'm certain he was hiding something, but I tell you I saw something in his eyes, I know I did."

Keith paused for a moment to draw breath, smoothing down his hair, before speculating, "It didn't mean anything then, but what if the British fighter was Hutch's – it could tie in with the three days he was missing. And perhaps that's why Hutch selected me – with my information I might be able to help you interpret the code. What do you think?" Having unburdened himself, Keith flopped down onto a kitchen chair and looked up at Ronald for an inspired response.

Ronald did not know what to think – it all seemed too fantastic. He could imagine that anyone looking in from the outside would see two old codgers, well into their dotage, behaving like a pair of over-excited teenagers trying to unravel a mystery that was nearly sixty years old with some bits and pieces that might just fit together. It would be so much easier to go away quietly, but that would mean they had failed, failed Hutch as much as themselves. He needed desperately to give himself a little breathing space.

"What I think," said Ronald, "is that we need a decent breakfast, so you go and shower while I lash up a full English, then we'll talk some more, OK?" By then he was talking to himself as he heard Keith heading upstairs.

However, moments later he heard Keith coming back downstairs, again at some speed and once again he appeared in the kitchen as fast as his ageing legs would carry him. *Here we go again – not even the chance to draw breath.*

"I've remembered something else, or at least I think I do. It's all a bit hazy now."

"Go on," encouraged Ronald as he stood at the cooker, frying the bacon, "but do hurry up or your bacon will be done to a crisp!"

"Well," said Keith, taking another deep breath, "you remember, of course, the Russian major and the first soldier, near the airfield." Ronald nodded. "The major told me that, although they had virtually encircled Berlin by that time, they had encountered some pockets of particularly fierce resistance. In the last days they found that the greatest resistance, tenacious to the end, came from a sort of Foreign Legion in reverse – S.S. units that had been raised in the occupied countries. No one liked to talk about it very much at the time and, even now, it's not well documented because it's so sensitive for the countries involved.

Apparently the Germans tried to recruit amongst our own lads being held as Prisoners of War – something along the lines that fascism was the only and last defence against the terror of communism. It got nowhere with our lot, but with the Cold War and the Iron Curtain that followed... well, anyway, the major recalled that the reason they had not attacked that particular airfield was that it was defended by one of these S.S. regiments. The death of Hitler had been announced and, as they had taken so many casualties, disproportionately high even for the Russians, they had rather left the defenders to stew on the assumption that the formal German surrender was only a matter of hours, a couple of days at most, away. I had never heard of these regiments, so out of curiosity I asked if he knew what nationality – he said he was fairly sure they were Danish."

At the word Danish, a connection was made in Ronald's mind, and more pieces of the jigsaw started to tumble into place. "Sweet Jesus!" Ronald exclaimed. "No, surely not, it can't be possible," but he was more talking to himself, rather than Keith, as he tried to come to terms with his extraordinary conclusion.

Then, noticing that the bacon was close to being cremated, Ronald ordered Keith out of the kitchen to make himself ready for the day, saying that they would look at the code closely after eating breakfast. Keith disappeared with a cheery, "Right ho, Skipper."

Later, with the breakfast pots pushed to the side of the dining table, Ronald placed the code between them and began by saying, "We need to break this code into manageable pieces, but I've been doing some serious thinking overnight, in fact I've done little else. I don't seem to want that much sleep these days.

"I think we are going to start with the assumption that the story you heard in Berlin from the Russians is at least in part true, if not entirely so. On that basis and bearing in mind that Hutch put May 1st into your note we could start to look at whether we can identify two aircraft within the code."

"Hang on," Keith interrupted, "we have already done that, haven't we. Last night you mentioned the Prussian Queen. That was Hutch's ship – he always insisted on that set of code letters and we think that the red eight might refer to a German plane, so that's the two."

"Possibly," admitted Ronald without much conviction. "It's as good a start as any, but what about these chess moves? Where do they get us?"

"Well," replied Keith, "let's assume for another moment that any similarity to chess is purely a smokescreen or a even deliberate red herring to confuse or deter anyone who got hold of the code that Hutch did not want to see it. We, on the other hand, and only we, are supposed to find the answer and therefore, between us, we must already have the answers in our pasts. In fact I'm fairly sure you have all the answers, even though you may not know it yet. I think all I am supposed to do is help you find them."

"Think, Ron, think back to what could be the connections between you and Hutch and something in your joint past."

Ronald sat for a few moments in silence. "Well. I have thought long and hard about your comment just now that the S.S. regiment outside Berlin was Danish, and I've come to the conclusion, clutching at straws perhaps, that it has real significance. Give me a moment, and I'll try to explain." Keith settled back in his chair and folded his arms, awaiting enlightenment.

"Before the war, in 1936, I was in Berlin for about a month with my father and Hutch. We stayed with an old friend of my father's from the Great War. I found out much later, years after the war, that my father was probably a bit of an amateur spy for our government, but to coincide with our visit, our host put together a big family party. He invited his in-laws from Denmark, his wife's sister and her two children. He also invited his own sister and her daughter from the east of Germany, which was then known as Prussia. It's now part of Poland. His nephew, Max, was already serving in Berlin as a test pilot with the Luftwaffe. It was a real family get-together.

"I remember that Hutch was infatuated by the German niece from the moment he met her. She was really pretty and the same age as Hutch. She was called Regina so Hutch teasingly called her his Prussian Queen. I think he carried a torch for her despite being on opposite sides and don't forget he carried her letters on his plane throughout the war. Maybe he was in Berlin to find out if he could contact her again after the war ended."

"Little chance of that," Keith scoffed. "From what I heard, unless they got out before the Russian advance in the autumn of '44, they were all gonners."

"Be that as it may," conceded Ronald, "but there was another element. All the visitors were cousins, and as they say, blood is thicker than water, so perhaps there is something in the code to link them all."

Pausing to collect his thoughts he went on, "At the time, I was not yet sixteen remember. I formed a good friendship with the Danish girl, Karin, but I found her brother Svenn too intense, too committed to fascism, although I was really too young to fully appreciate what it all meant."

"Anyway, after we got back from Germany, Karin and I wrote to each other right up to the outbreak of the war, but after that the letters ceased. I was never able to get back in touch with her after the war, but I remember her letters had become increasingly concerned about her brother's commitment to fighting the communists. She was so cross with him that I am sure she once wrote describing him, much as she loved him, as her 'Black Knight'." Keith mouthed a triumphant "Yes!"

He paused as the mental cogs ground forward a notch. "So, there you have it; there's the connection to the note from our solicitor," he concluded with the feeling that yet another piece of the puzzle had just fallen into place

At this point, Keith held up his hand to silence Ronald and said, "Before we go any further there's something I want to get, so I need to pop into Lincoln to a decent stationers. Just bear with me – I should be back within the hour."

Keith was gone five minutes later, the Jaguar purring down the drive and out of sight. While he was gone, Ronald sat staring at the code trying to accept he was on the point of breaking through the mental barriers he had constructed, and so strongly reinforced like the wartime concrete to protect his sanity. For the most part, in the daytime, over the intervening years, he had been largely successful, but in the nights, those hours before the dawn, so dreaded by soldiers from time immemorial, it was a very different story. Demons to be held at bay, terrors to be endured.

He was still in this reflective mood, verging on melancholy when he heard Keith's car coming back up the drive. He welcomed the interruption to his depressing train of thought.

Once back in the house, Keith delved into a plastic carrier bag and took out a motorists map for part of Europe, covering Denmark and northern Germany.

"I felt we could not go much further without one of these," he explained as he unfolded the map and spread it across the far end of the dining table.

"Let's try and look at this code, line by line, and see if it tells us anything, putting in what we know already," said Keith, hoping to put some order in to their deliberations. "Otherwise, we're at risk of rushing around like headless chickens."

"OK," said Ronald, "where do we start?"

"At the top, at the beginning."

"With that circle in the top left hand corner?" queried Ronald. "And, if you look, there's one at the end as well. Are they just for fun, for decoration, for symmetry or do you think they really have some significance?"

"I don't think anything about this is random or trivial. Hutch checked everything, every tiny detail with his solicitor before it was printed, so every detail must be deliberate."

"What is a circle?" continued Keith. "It's something complete, a beginning and an end in itself; a nought or a zero mathematically. Or it could be the start of a sequence, nought, one, two, three etcetera," he mused, stroking his beard thoughtfully.

"Let's suppose that it's a start, a starting point, then the end, the last zero might mean the same place. Look at the dates, assuming that's what they are, around the "4" and the "5". This must be the Grossenbrode raid, the zero is your base and there on the last line is Hutch flying back to base – perhaps the ">>>180" is the direction – due south, on the day he reappeared."

"I think you're right. Look there! That must be me in Miss Faithful!" Ronald cried out in excitement, pointing to the letters MF, "and there's the other eleven who made the attack. What was his name… Maguire? He had to turn back with engine problems, so there were only thirteen of us, unlucky for him. We never saw him again. He mentioned his compass was on the blink and the suspicion grew that he had strayed too far to the east on the way back to our own base and was shot down over the Russian lines. They weren't too fussy who they fired at. '07.30' must be the time –look, see my log. We only had thirty minutes flight time, and we left at 7 am, so the sun would be at our backs, just above the horizon on the run in."

"The next numbers must be a map reference," said Keith as he began to pore over the open map of northern Germany. "It may only be a current road map, but, unusually, it does have longitude and latitude, so if we work from the lines, North and then counting East, we get… Grossenbrode," he exclaimed triumphantly.

"You said you all made one pass on the seaplane base, but after Hutch disappeared you went back, contrary to orders, with Baz Bajkowski to try and draw the fire from the third and fourth waves."

"Bloody silly thing to do," scoffed Ronald, "but I knew I had no choice. The boys behind me were getting blown out of the sky and we just had to do something. It was too late in the war to sacrifice pilots like that."

"Got you your DSO though, didn't it!" said Keith.

"I would have given the damn thing back if I thought I could have saved another of those boys. What a sodding waste," said Ronald, his eyes glazing at the memories of flak, tons of it and exploding aircraft. He wiped, subconsciously, at his eyes and blew his nose on a freshly laundered handkerchief.

"But look at the next line –"PQO!" The zero surely can't mean your base, so it must mean something different. Perhaps it means 'only' or 'alone' which would make some sense and, as the next set of numbers have no letters, let's assume, as before, that it's a map reference."

Again, Keith traced his finger across the map, this time further to the south as he worked through the numbers. "So, if we put that in we get... nothing, well at least nothing concrete. The map is too small scale, just a road, although it's not very far to the northwest of Berlin, which might be a good sign."

"A long straight one?" queried Ronald.

"Yes possibly."

"An autobahn, one of Hitler's pet projects?"

"Yes, possibly. There's a modern motorway to the west, but this could be one of the originals. It's road number is 'five', so with such a low number it might have been important enough." Keith agreed.

"The Jerries flew off their motorways later in the war, didn't they?"

"And," interrupted Keith, "the map indicates that there is a small forest alongside the road."

"Bingo! We've got a match for the Russians' story!" Ronald shouted, thumping on the table in excitement.

Trying to calm him, Keith said, "Slow down a minute. Let's not jump to too many conclusions, but I do think it looks fairly convincing. If we take the next line, we have the Prussian Queen with the red eight, which we think might be, could be another fighter, but what about the "Bf". Forget about the chess connection. The further we go, the more I am convinced anything to do with chess is a complete red herring. How about, instead, reading the letters as Bayerische Flugzeugfabrik? – maybe a Messerschmitt 109 with a red identifying eight?"

By this time Ronald was quite agitated. "You know, I'm sure you are right. We always used the designation "Me", but all those years ago when Hutch and I were both in Berlin I vaguely remember Otto Hecker saying that they used the designation "Bf" and, I think this is Hutch's way of telling me."

"Telling you what – just that it's a Messerschmitt? We got that already. Is there more?"

"Oh, yes," Ronald replied, "I think it tells me also who the pilot might be."

"Are you serious; how can you tell from those two letters?"

With a catch in his throat Ronald replied "I think Hutch is telling me that the pilot was one of Otto's sons, Wolfgang or Dieter, but in fact I know it can only be Wolfgang, because my father established after the war that Dieter was killed in 1944, shot down in the retreat from Russia."

"Wolfgang, on the other hand, was only reported as missing in April 1945 by my father, but I remember, although I never really thought it had any significance, that my father also told me that Wolfgang had been posted to the west of Berlin in January '45."

"Bloody hell," breathed Keith, "if you are right then Hutch put a lot more thought into this code than we realised. He really wanted to get you hooked. That must also explain why Hutch decided to send you his logs with the three important pages sealed together, even though there was nothing written there. He just wanted to annoy the hell out of you and keep you concentrating on the code."

"And he certainly succeeded," Ronald nodded in agreement. "So let's crack on and see if we can finish the rest of it. Look, he's having a joke with us, but it tells us we are on the right track. He put Black Knight on your letter whereas in chess the symbol Bk is sufficient, so he added the N to make a bit of a pun. Always the joker. Then he puts Black Knight in square brackets with Red Eight to symbolise the two travelling together and with Hutch – two planes, three people heading north over the Russian lines as fast as they can go with Hutch acting as escort."

"But where?" said Keith. "And do you reckon you could get two in a 109?"

"You might have to take the seat out. I sat in one once, in Berlin. It was a tight squeeze for one; cosy shall we say, but just about possible for two. No parachutes, of course, but this was the last roll of the dice for both of them, so I guess it didn't matter too much. They would be flying too low to use them anyway.

"But to try and answer your question... if I were Hutch I would try to get out to the sea, away from the flak, maybe back over the Grossenbrode base – it had been knocked flat only a couple of hours previously, or around it anyway, then..." Ronald traced a line over the map, "then north-west over the Baltic sea – but well away from Kiel and its defences. Then into Denmark, perhaps over the Kiel Bight, then up the Flensburg Fjord and across Jutland, praying that the Germans were too concerned with their own survival to bother. And I guess that the combination of the German and English planes would still have served to confuse, just as it had done all along."

"Then they had to find the place to land and, just as importantly, to hide the 109 in some way." He left the thought hanging in the air.

Keith did not demur, but then insisted on persevering with the final part of the code. "We've started, so we'll finish," he mimicked, "But, seriously, what about these numbers on line three. I doubt they can be a time, like it is in the second line down, unless Hutch had a clock that ran backwards, or do you think it might be referring to the next day?"

"No, I don't think so either," Ronald agreed, "and anyway I think this code all relates to the same day, until it shows him on the way back."

"OK, on that basis, let's assume, just like they appear in lines seven and six, the numbers at the end of the line are a map reference, even though they seem to be deliberately kept incomplete." Keith ran his finger up the map... "Well, with what we've been given I suppose that makes sense," he muttered to himself, "but all I get is the middle of bloody nowhere in west Denmark, Jutland, somewhere to the north of a town called Ribe. I guess the 'Dk' at the end of the line confirms it."

"And the 318 followed by the 110 at the beginning?"

"I'm guessing that might be a compass bearing and then distance. It's just too fantastic to think there's a twin-engined Messerschmitt 110 bomber somewhere in this equation. Next thing you know, we'll be looking for a whole squadron!" Keith joked, tongue firmly in cheek.

"If it's distance, then we could check with a school compass – or a piece of string would do." A moment later, Ronald went out to the kitchen to find some string. Taking a pencil, Keith carefully drew a line from the Grossenbrode base, 318 degrees, roughly northwest, up across the Danish peninsula, until it met the North Sea coast. "Doubt they gave it a burial at sea," he muttered under his breath.

From the ball produced by Ronald, Keith measured out a length, as accurately as he could, equivalent to 110 miles according to the scale on the map.

"So, if we put one end roughly on the third reference point – hold it steady Ronnie," he stretched it to its fullest extent and curved it in an arc across northern Germany. It neatly bisected the seaplane base at Grossenbrode.

"Well, would you believe it!" exclaimed Ronald, "only one hundred and ten miles. Would have thought it much further. But it's some proof that they went back over the seaplane base, and then, at full speed it was only twenty minutes flying time into Denmark.

"You know," said Keith thoughtfully, as he began to tick the timetable off on his fingers, "if we allow thirty minutes to get over to the airfield on the A5, maybe another forty or so on the ground, and twenty more back to Grossenbrode, that's only an hour and a half since you lost contact with him – give or take – and then another twenty or thirty getting into Denmark," Keith shook his head in disbelief, "Hutch was probably there, on the ground in Denmark, before you had your debrief!"

Ronald ran his finger back and forth across the code, the silence disturbed only by the grandfather clock as it ticked irresistibly toward their destiny. He let out a resigned sigh. "And that's just what it says, there at the beginning of line four. He was in Denmark at 10.15 – long before we even began to think he might be really missing. Bastard!" The word was torn from his lips in an uncharacteristic flash of his anger, but which encapsulated everything that had been brewing since the day he saw *that* photograph. But then, just as quickly, he realised he did not actually mean it. He could not turn the clock back.

"But a crafty one at that. Took some balls to fly into Russian territory, alone, even if you don't agree with what he did, but then I guess, afterwards, he had his own cross to bear. Can't help but respect the man for that, can you?"

Ronald was in two minds as to whether he agreed, but a rumbling from his stomach reminded him that lunch time might be approaching. When he looked at the grandfather clock, he was surprised to see that the whole morning had passed and it was nearing 2 pm. Keith, ever mindful of 'keeping the tank topped up', suggested they go back to the pub they had visited the previous day for a liquid lunch – his treat – which Ronald readily accepted.

There, they continued their discussions while Keith kept the drinks flowing. As their imagination ran riot, they found all sorts of implausible explanations, some bordering on pure fantasy, until they reached the point where Ronald declared a halt to the intake, for Keith's sake as much as his own, when they concluded, finally, that they had a workable solution to Hutch's code. The only real problem remaining was that they had only an approximate location of an airstrip which could be anywhere along the line of the bearing.

"So is that it? Do you think we've really cracked it, despite neither of us having the faintest idea what 'DH82' in the last line might mean?" Keith asked, after their slightly unsteady walk back home, stretching and scratching the back of his head, but being careful not to disarrange his thinning hair.

"Yes, I think so," Ronald replied slowly as he scanned the notes they had both made, "or at least as good as we can, without Hutch writing it out in plain English for us. Perhaps the 'DH82' bit will sort itself out when we get there."

"What's next?" Keith asked yawning loudly and giving a passable impression of the dormouse from *Alice Through the Looking Glass*, about to fall asleep, and entirely missing the point of what Ronald had said.

"You mean, apart from a couple of large whiskies, or would you prefer a large brandy. We go, of course." Perhaps it was the drink talking, but he felt sure of what needed to be done.

Keith was about to ask for a very large brandy on the assumption that he could stay another night, when the full implication of Ronald's words finally sank in. His mouth opened and closed, like a fish out of water, before he found his voice.

"Seriously, you want to go over to Denmark? It's a bloody long way."

"We'll fly, to Billund in the centre of Jutland, or Aarhus in the north."

"Then what?" asked Keith, in a tone that implied that Ronald really had not thought things through.

"We hire a car and drive."

"No can do," replied Keith, before taking a deep breath as though about to deliver a lecture, which in part he was. "Can't hire a car over the age of eighty, and neither of us are going to pass for less, even if we lied on the application form. Someone might just notice when we go to pick the car up."

"Oh rats, I'd forgotten that," sighed Ronald at the frustration of his master-plan, then he brightened, "maybe one of your lads could drive us?"

Keith thought for a moment or two. "No, I really do not want to get them involved. They would think we were both crazy, going off on some half-baked wild goose chase and I really would like to retain a little of their respect."

"Sally, maybe." Referring to his daughter. "She would be up for anything, but now is not a really good time for her in our business. She has just had a holiday in the Maldives, to celebrate her silver wedding, and I know she will not want to be away from the office for the next few weeks."

"You know, when she was small, she occasionally flew with me when I went away on business. She was always on at me to do aerobatics in my little Cessna, and got cross with me when I had to tell her the plane could not do them."

Keith then realised that Ronald really was not listening properly to what he was saying. Leaning across he prodded Ronald gently on the forearm.

"Penny for your thoughts!" he said lightly.

Ronald was visibly startled by Keith's touch and apologised, explaining: "Sorry about that, but I drifted off when you mentioned aerobatics. I was back in Berlin in Otto's personal plane, a four seat Messerschmitt 108. I was fifteen going on sixteen and it was my first flight, well not really because we had flown out to Germany, but it was my first flight at the sharp end, so to speak."

Keith nodded.

"Anyway he took me up for a little leisure flight, just for the experience so he told my father, and then he proceeded to throw me across the sky. I loved every second of it. It seemed that I had no nerve endings in my stomach at all. He did the same for Hutch, but he threw up, much to his embarrassment. Didn't much like to be reminded of it, either!

"It's odd, but I could say that Otto saved my life that day."

"How so?" asked Keith. "By not killing you, there and then?" he added with a laugh.

"You might think so, but no. In fact, it all happened that day off Brighton, the day you and Hutch got me home. I was dead and I knew it. I had screwed up and that Focke-Wulf 190 was going to finish me off. Then Otto's voice came to me, clear as a bell; I swear it was as though he was sitting next to me. He had said 'If you can take a spin it may save your life'. Eighteen turns he put me through that day. We even came out of the cloud upside down and scared the hell out of my dad, but I loved it. Never really thought about it after that, until that patrol in 43."

"The 190's last attack had knocked off the rear-view mirror and messed the Spit up really badly – he was better than me and I knew it – but with Otto's words I sensed rather than saw the next attack. There were bits coming off the wingtip, so it was stick back, full left rudder – you know the drill – close the throttle and over she went, portside onto her back, into a flat spin.

"Round and round we went," Keith watched Ronald's hands and feet flying the manoeuvre, knowing Ronald was back in the cockpit fighting for his life, "and I counted them, just like Otto, in German. Vierzehn, funfzehn, sechszehn, sixteen of them, the Spit's engine popping and banging, praying that it would not quit. The silence was eerie, almost like being in a glider, apart from the creaking and groaning of the wings and the airframe. I hoped the Jerry would think he had finished me off and not follow me down."

With a good-natured laugh, as he recovered himself, he added, "You have no idea how much rubbish there was on the floor of that Spit, despite the best efforts of the mechanics and fitters to tidy up. There were screws and washers, a couple of pieces of pencil and some other bits and bobs, all rolling around on the underside of the canopy above my head as we came down. I remember saying a little prayer, that they would all behave themselves and go back to wherever they had come from, without jamming anything up – if I was ever given the chance to finish the spin!"

"Well, the rest you know, but that day I told Otto that I owed him one, even though it was one of his Luftwaffe chums who was trying to bring my career to a premature and very permanent end."

"All the more reason to go to Denmark and sort this out," he said, with a note of finality in his voice.

"I've been thinking," said Keith to relieve the tension in the air. "What if we take the ferry from Harwich with one of our cars; surely we could manage that between us, don't you reckon."

Keith stayed another night. Now that they had reached the point where they thought they had cracked the code and that what lay ahead was the proving or disproving of their deliberations, the thread, that had bound them together in friendship over the last forty-eight hours, seemed to snap.

Throughout the evening their conversation was stilted. Ronald found that Keith was just as reluctant to discuss much of his own wartime service. They drank and chatted, rather than engaging in any meaningful form of exchange. The gulf of fifty years was not to be bridged so easily and it was Keith who suggested an early night, although by then, the level on a newly opened bottle of scotch had sunk well below half.

The next morning at a breakfast table once again laid for two – how he had enjoyed that particular change to his unending daily routine – Ronald was pleasantly surprised to find that the camaraderie of the last couple of days had returned.

Keith was in a bright, jovial mood and regaled him with some of the funnier incidents of his business life, so that they ended up parting on the best of terms with Keith saying that he would "clear his diary" of his many and varied social engagements – his voice laden with irony – to give Ronald a free hand at arranging the sea crossing with the ferry company.

Keith had just finished putting a duster over the car before driving home – got to keep the old girl at her best – when Ronald sauntered through the front door and gave the Jaguar an admiring glance.

"Mary loved this car," Keith said with a catch in his voice, "and I can't bear to part with it. Drinks petrol, pollutes the atmosphere, but at least it does it with style!" he joked, but Ronald could tell that Keith had not entirely come to terms with the loss of his wife.

"Right," he said, holding out his hand, "I'm ready to be off."

"Before you go," Ronald replied with a twinkle in his eye, "there's something more I'd like to show you – in the code."

Keith raised his eyebrows in surprise.

"But we got it all sorted last night, didn't we?"

"Well," said Ronald, "humour me for one minute, will you? It's just that we said that everything in the code had to be important, so I would really like you to take one more look."

Intrigued, Keith followed Ronald back into the house and through to the dining room, where the code still lay on the table.

Keith stared at the code for a moment or two, scratching thoughtfully behind his ear. "No, I still don't see anything more. Are you pulling my leg?"

"No, Hutch wouldn't do that to us."

Keith snorted his disbelief.

"Seriously – it came to me during the night. It was so simple, staring us in the face all the time!"

Clearly enjoying himself, Ronald paused for effect, before continuing, "Look again at the Bridge compass points. You said they were all muddled up."

"That's right. Just a red herring to put others off the scent."

"Well, in a way, yes, but not entirely," said Ronald. "Look at the letters and tell me what you see."

Starting at the top, Keith read out, clockwise: "North-South-West-East," and looked at Ronald with a shrug of his shoulders. "So?"

"Try again," Ronald encouraged him, "but start with the S."

With a resigned sigh, knowing that he was having to be led by the nose, he read out "South, West, East and North."

"Not the directions, just the letters."

"S – W – E – N," Keith intoned.

"No, not like that. Now try saying the W the German way."

"S – V – E – N," he said, in a flat monotone – and then the penny dropped.

"Would you bloody believe it!" Keith exploded, shaking his head in amazement.

"Good old Hutch; he thought of everything, didn't he."

Keith was still chuckling to himself as he fired up the Jaguar, wound down the passenger window, leaned across and gave Ronald a thumbs-up.

"Won't be long now, Skipper, and we'll have it sorted."

No, I guess it won't, thought Ronald, as the butterflies began to gnaw at his stomach once again.

After Keith had gone, his Jaguar drifting silently down the drive, Ronald changed into walking clothes, putting a stout pair of boots into the luggage compartment of his old estate car. He thought a walk in the Wolds would do him the world of good.

He felt in need of some time to himself, to review what had happened in such a brief period and to decide, finally, whether or not he wanted to continue, despite what he had agreed the previous night. He suspected that Keith was having similar doubts, but at least, unlike Keith, he had no family ties to worry about.

Torrie would, as usual, tell him not to be so silly at his age, going off on some wild goose chase, but then she would laugh, send her love and tell him to get on with it. Her love and support had been without qualification through the good times and, more importantly, the bad. In the very worst of all times, when he had believed he was looking into the abyss, she had saved his life and given him the reason for going on.

He set off in his car in no particular direction, other than knowing he was heading up into the Wolds, and although he avoided turning into the village of Thorlby where his parents had lived during the war and for so many years afterwards, he realised that fate, if there were such a thing, had brought him on to a road, where sixty years previously events had come together like links in a chain, drawing him inescapably into love – a love that had endured.

He walked purposefully for an hour, while his mind gradually cleared of the doubts that had assailed him for so many days. He stood for a long time staring out across the soft folds of the Lincolnshire countryside, watching the light and shade change with the passing clouds, standing next to a tree – he was sure, he wanted to believe it was *the* tree where his journey into love had begun.

He could still hear the constant rumble of the bomber engines and for a moment he thought he could hear, once more, that choir of Merlins. Then straining his eyes and ears, he realised it was not a trick of his mind, but the sound of the Battle of Britain Memorial Flight coming up from Coningsby. Spitfire, Hurricane and Lancaster, six Merlins, in close formation low over the distant hills, flying majestically straight toward him, reawakening the excitement, the enthusiasm, the passion that had been born in him in 1936. As best he could, standing out from the edge of the field, he waved wildly, his walking stick held high in the air, remembering his time, his place, his right to be called a Spitfire pilot.

To his utter delight, he was rewarded with a waggle of wings from the Spitfire, which then, completely against regulations he was sure, pulled up into a graceful victory roll before dropping back neatly into formation. Unable to resist the temptation Ronald threw his hat into the air, laughing as he had done at Hendon all those years ago, before looking round for fear that someone might have observed him make a complete fool of himself – but, as so often, he was entirely alone.

Nevertheless, an omen or not, his mind was now made up. He would turn the pages, he would revisit that one, so brief episode in his life and he would not be afraid of it, or the steps that he and Keith would shortly take.

CHAPTER 11

Back at home, weary, but reinvigorated, he went into the dining room where Hutch's log books still lay on the table. Although they were of genuine historical interest, they were going to tell him nothing more than he knew already. If Hutch had family, then tracing them was quite beyond his resources and so he re-parcelled them in the plastic envelope in which they had been received, and re-addressed them to the archive officer of the RAF Museum at Hendon.

That done, he made himself a simple supper and then telephoned Keith to tell him of his decision. Keith welcomed the news, admitting that he had similar reservations, but somewhat to Ronald's dismay then proceeded to give him a long list of dates when he would not be available. In the end, after comparing diaries, they concluded that their trip was going to have to take place in the late summer, rather than any earlier, as he had originally hoped. He realised that, now their decision was made, he had become impatient to find the answers and chafed at the thought of the delay.

Briefly he had considered going on his own, but no sooner had the thought occurred, he dismissed it. He recognised it had taken the two of them to get this far – Keith's input had been invaluable and so it would be completely unfair to rob him, at this late stage, of the chance to be party to the solution – if there should be one. Or perhaps it was more likely that he preferred not to fail alone. A week or two more would surely not make any difference.

He broke the connection with the promise that he would get back to Keith as soon as he had made the booking within Keith's timetable and then, with the shadows lengthening, Ronald went through to the lounge to begin the last phase of his reading.

Making himself comfortable, with glass and bottle of scotch at his side he flipped steadily through the pages of his log book for the early summer of 1944 – the days and weeks before the D-Day landings on the coast of Normandy. A note attached to the entry for the 3rd of May caught his eye.

B 17 Flying Fort crash-landed on base. Only 3 engines, wing half eaten away by fire on 4th. No ammo, no guns, everything unnecessary thrown overboard to lighten the ship. 2 dead – pilot and co-pilot – bombardier at the controls – belly and tail gunners *wounded. Hit by flak over target and again over coast (FW 190). Crew looked as though they had been to hell and back. Asked where they had been – "BERLIN"*

With an inward sigh, Ronald delved once more into his de-mob suitcase until his hand lit upon the small, dog-eared school exercise book on the cover of which was written, by his own juvenile hand, in rather grand manner: "*Expedition to Germany 1936*".

He smiled at his own innocence of youth, but at that time, when flying across the Atlantic to America was a technical challenge, fraught with danger, and package-holidays by jet-plane were still the stuff of science fiction, "*Expedition*" was a fair word to describe the trip he had undertaken and the events he had witnessed. A heavily creased black and white photograph he left in its place, slipped inside the back cover. He did not need to look at it to remember the image.

Resting his head against the support of his wing chair, diary in hand, his mind flew back sixty, no almost seventy years to his long dead father, his first meeting with Hutch and their extraordinary visit to Germany's capital city.

Some months short of his sixteenth birthday, Ronald arrived back from school to their new semi-detached home in Finchley one afternoon late in April 1936. He intended to have a good moan over dinner about the course subjects and his teachers, but he found his father already waiting for him in the parlour. Quickly reviewing recent events, he could not recall any particular misdemeanour and so, from the sombre look on his father's face, he feared news of some family tragedy. His mother, however, offered him a slight smile which gave him a grain of comfort.

He noticed a newspaper at his father's side and, reading the headlines upside down, saw the account of Germany's open support for the Nationalist side of the civil war that had recently broken out in Spain.

When his father spoke, it was in a tone and a manner tinged with sadness.

"I have told you very little about my time during the Great War. I was one of the lucky ones and came home without a scratch. So many families were torn apart by that terrible conflict, but your mother and I were blessed with our three children, although I now begin to fear we may only have brought you all into the world, only to face the same problems once again."

Ronald had the distinct impression that his father had rehearsed the speech because in truth it all sounded rather pompous and he really did not understand what his father was trying to tell him.

But his father continued, "Under their new leader, Mr. Hitler, Germany seems set to rise again. There is much in the newspapers about secret armies and new armament factories. With what we have already seen in Spain and from my own contacts through my job at Hendon, it's clear that the German airline, Deutsche Lufthansa, has been used for some time as a training facility to get round the terms of the Versailles Treaty which, as you may know, forbids Germany to have an armed air force."

For a moment he paused, but, despite seeing the blank look on Ronald's face, he went on, "I know I am probably boring you with this talk of politics, but your mother and I are very afraid that one day, perhaps sooner than we are ready for, you may face the same enemy as we did. I want you to try to understand that."

Ronald's mother attempted to intervene, to stop Alfred "frightening the boy", even though Ronald had enough difficulty in understanding his school work, let alone the possibility of another war with Germany, but Alfred continued, ignoring her protest:

"What you will not know is that I still have a contact or two in Germany." Ronald raised his eyebrows in surprise.

"In the late summer of 1918, before the Armistice, a German pilot, Otto Hecker, was brought as a prisoner of war to our headquarters, after he had been shot down by one of our pilots. He was only my age and from a good family; I got to know him really quite well in the days before he was taken away. Perhaps it was because we were so remarkably alike, even though he was an officer and I was only an NCO. The difference in rank meant nothing. We were just two young men, hoping we would survive the war.

"Otto had just learnt his wife was pregnant, expecting their first child, just like your mother, and there were other similarities that gave us so much in common, even though we were supposed to be enemies. Despite this, we formed a friendship, a bond in the short time before he was sent off to a P.O.W camp

"We agreed to keep in touch after the war ended, although I did think I would never hear from him again, but to my great surprise, in the middle of 1919 a letter arrived from him. He told me of the birth of his son Wolfgang and his hopes for Germany in the aftermath of the war."

"We have managed to keep in touch ever since and now your mother and I feel it would be good for you to see the Heckers and get to know Wolfgang and his younger brother Dieter – he's about your age. Maybe your generation can continue the friendship."

Seeing that Ronald was not overly impressed with this suggestion, his father added, "I thought we might be away for about a month; I've been given a special leave from work. I also thought it might be better if you had a companion. Stan can't take the time off from his job, so I've spoken to one of my colleagues, Eddie Hutchinson, and he has agreed that his son Richard can come with us. You'll be good company for each other."

At this Ronald brightened a little. He had met Richard, ("call me Hutch") a year or so older than him, two or three times briefly and they had got on well. Hutch had shown a genuine interest in Ronald's hobby of building balsa wood model aircraft. Perhaps the trip would not be so bad after all.

But his father was not finished. "Through my contacts at work I have managed to get tickets for the Deutsche Lufthansa service on the latest version of their Junkers 52 airliner."

Now Ronald was paying attention properly; he was fascinated by anything to do with flying and had already told his parents that he wanted to become an airline pilot when he left school. The three-engined, all-metal Junkers was the newest model in the Lufthansa fleet – the height of luxury despite its rather utilitarian exterior.

"We will fly out from Croydon to Frankfurt-am-Main, south-west Germany where we will probably have to change planes and then fly on to Berlin. Otto will meet us at their new airport, Tempelhof."

"I know you don't speak any German, so I've bought you a Berlitz phrase book. I'll show you a few simple things to try and learn and I can help you with the pronunciation. Richard has some German so he will be able to help as interpreter if you get stuck."

Ronald was surprised to learn that his father spoke any German, but there was much he was learning about his father as he grew up.

A few days later, the two families met up to discuss the travel arrangements.

Richard's mother Flora was petite and quiet, as though to compensate for his father, Edward, who was rather overweight. He smoked incessantly on an old briar pipe, which was stained yellow with use. He seemed to have great difficulty in getting the pipe lit, using match after match, prodding the tobacco with a small pen knife and tamping it back down to get a satisfactory draw, punctuating his conversation with either pipe or knife, by way of emphasis as he spoke. Just occasionally Edward would drift off into deep thought, puffing away contentedly on the pipe, surrounded by a haze of blue pungent smoke.

On one thing he was very clear: he had a profound mistrust of their Mr. Hitler "and that Nazi Party of his".

Hutch was not so reticent as he looked forward to the holiday.

"You know, Ronno," said Hutch, "we are going to have such a good time in Germany. My father says he thinks your father may be able to get us flights with one of their gliding clubs that are so popular nowadays over there."

Looking back over the years, Ronald could not suppress a smile. Hutch was about to get rather more than he had bargained for.

A couple of weeks before their trip to Germany, Ronald's father sprang another surprise.

While they were working together outside to finish the covering of Ronald's glider in readiness for a model aircraft competition to be held at Hendon that autumn, the pair of them coughing from the strong acetone vapours, his father said, "I thought you might like to have a day at this year's Air Pageant – I have arranged tickets for the two of us plus Richard, if he would like to come too. As well as the flying displays there is also the New Types section –there should be some interesting new models and prototypes on display. There's something I want you to see."

On the 27th June 1936 in company with Hutch, Alfred and Ronald rode out on the recently completed underground line to Hendon Central and then walked the short distance to the airfield. It was turning out to be a warm sunny day with only light broken cloud. The conditions for flying were perfect.

Even as they arrived, the air was filled with the sounds of aircraft engines being warmed up and the public address system announcing the programme for the afternoon.

Away in one corner, a fun-fair was in full swing with an automated fairground organ thundering out popular tunes from its pipes, drums and cymbals. All the rides, the big wheel, the chair-o-plane, the cake walk, the waltzers and the traditional merry-go-rounds were busy with customers, young and old, enjoying a day's relaxation and entertainment.

Ronald and Hutch tried their hands at the shooting gallery, using air rifles to knock down painted silhouettes of ducks and skittles. Ronald beat Hutch who blamed a faulty sight on his gun – at least, that was his excuse, although, as he confessed later, his aim was more than a little distracted by the attractive young lady who was firing next to him. Alfred pulled his leg mercilessly, reminding him to concentrate on the job in hand and not as he put it "the bird by the hand".

Hutch had taken it all in good part, and so they continued shooting until they had enough tokens for a glass vase for Ronald's mother, Cissy, and a pretty bracelet for Hutch's current, if temporary, girlfriend. He readily admitted he liked to play the field – lots of fish in the sea he said, with a glint in his eye.

Mother had packed them a picnic of sandwiches, hard boiled eggs and some salad with a flask of sweet tea, but before they sat down to eat, Ronald's father suggested that they should both go with him over to a specially designated area, called the New Types Park. There, on static display, in pride of place was the brand new, R.J. Mitchell designed, Supermarine Spitfire, still bearing its prototype registration letters on its silver painted fuselage.

Both Richard and Ronald stared at it open mouthed.

"Go on lads," said Ronald's father, "I've got special clearance for you," as he held up the perimeter rope over their heads.

"Sorry, the cockpit is out of bounds – but it's OK to go right round."

For ten long minutes they walked round and round, running their hands over the sleek surfaces of the elliptical wings, noting where, one day, two or three machine guns would be mounted in each wing.

Ronald stood at the front, gazing up at the polished boss which housed the two-bladed wooden propeller, and behind, the twelve stub exhausts for the newly developed Rolls Royce Merlin engine – all supported on the narrow, almost delicate undercarriage. Hutch stood completely motionless at the back of the wing, one hand resting, caressing the fuselage. In his fertile imagination, he was already in the cockpit, dreaming of dog-fights or romancing a girlfriend with daring displays.

It took no little urging from his father to move Ronald and Hutch out to the front of the enclosure, where they found a man from Supermarine erecting a small information board. It gave them brief details of weight, dimensions, rate of climb and, most importantly, speed – 325 mph at 15,000 feet. As they were discussing these performance figures, the engineer turned and said, "Well, we don't want to tell them everything do we?" with a broad wink. Hutch almost had to be dragged away to lunch.

Over their lunch, Hutch announced that he was going to join the RAF as soon as he was old enough and, if they were not recruiting, then he would join the Air Squadron if he went up to university. He knew that getting into the RAF would not be easy. Despite the growing signs of militancy that they had all seen reported from Germany, and the war in Spain, there were currently no signs that the peacetime level of recruitment into the RAF was being expanded. Not even Mr. Hitler's often stated plans to restore Germany's dignity by tearing up the Versailles Treaty seemed to be lending any urgency. Indeed, as Alfred explained, the Spitfire was a private venture, yet to receive any orders for the RAF, but he was full of confidence that the government must eventually see sense.

There were still plenty of pilots around from the Great War, who were not yet beyond their early forties, upon whom the government could call in an emergency. Hutch might well have a long wait, the thought of which he found intensely frustrating.

For Ronald, being that little bit younger, such thoughts were further at bay. For him, university beckoned, but only if he could obtain satisfactory results in his final matriculation exams. Then, and only then, would there be any possibility of joining a university's Air Squadron.

The show began promptly at 3 pm. under broken cloud. It opened with the playing of the National Anthem, for which everyone stood bare-headed, and sang the words, but rather raggedly, as the delays in the public address system rolled around the airfield.

Then to a great roar from the crowd, the show was opened by the RAF display squadron – three Hawker Furies, frontline biplane fighters, not just flying in tight formation, but actually tied wing-tip to wing-tip. Their display started with a high speed fly-past and their performance, to everyone's amazement, concluded with the formation, still tied together, carrying out a wide barrel roll, which was met with even greater applause.

To follow, a huge Handley Page Heyford, the RAF's largest bi-plane bomber with a sixty feet wingspan, lumbered across the sky, the pilot and gunner waving from their open cockpit and gun turret.

To cap his display the pilot gained height over the far end of the field, dived in and then pulled up over the centre line, climbing, climbing ever more steeply to curl gracefully over the top in a perfect loop, the largest aircraft, the commentator informed them, ever to have achieved the feat at a public display. The enthusiastic crowd went wild with applause as the pilot made a final pass, standing to attention and saluting from the cockpit.

Part way through the afternoon, the crowd was treated to a mock aerial battle, between teams of fighters, the Red and the Blue, recalling the scenes over the Western Front less than twenty years previously. The sounds of racing engines and machine-gun fire peppered the air as the Red team defended their airship, in reality a war surplus observation balloon, which was to be attacked by the Blues. At length, the Blues prevailed and the airship descended in flames to burn itself out on the far side of the field. Friend and foe departed in tight formation to leave the field of battle.

The show continued with numerous different attractions, a trio of Siskin biplanes spinning down in unison, round and round, fifteen or twenty times before breaking away to reform and repeat the show. Hutch thought the pilots must have had cast-iron stomachs. Little did he know that he was only weeks away from his own, first-hand experience.

Later, the crowd was directed to watch a small passenger plane high overhead, from which a young lady, clad in a white flying suit, performed a parachute jump under a multicoloured canopy. She drifted down, waving happily to the crowd, as though it was the most natural thing in the world, to land accurately and lightly on a blue fabric cross laid on the grass. She was carried from the field still waving to the crowd in an open-top yellow Rolls Royce – such was the novelty of a parachute descent, especially by a woman. Ronald commented jokingly that it would be bad enough to leap out of a perfectly good aeroplane at the best of times, while Hutch wondered what it might be like to try to get out of a stricken aeroplane if his life depended on it. Alfred suggested that, at an appropriate moment, they might be able to ask Otto Hecker for a first-hand account.

The finale was a fly-past of all the RAF's aircraft that had participated during the day, the combined roar of their engines filling the sky with sound, slowly fading away. As the strains of the National Anthem once again echoed across the field, the commentator announced "God Save the King" to close the pageant.

The crowds began to drift homewards, but as Ronald turned to leave his father said simply, "No, let's wait a few minutes." And he promptly sat down on the grass, amongst the sea of discarded papers, ice cream wrappers, and abandoned programmes without explaining why, until he pointed over to the New Types Park.

There, they saw the ground crew come out to the Spitfire to make it ready for departure, when it would return to Supermarine's home airfield at Eastleigh in Hampshire, barely a few minutes flight time away.

By now the massive crowd was reduced to just a few dozen who had gathered at the perimeter rope, waiting patiently. Their reward was not long in coming.

A battery cart was wheeled out by a mechanic and parked under the starboard wing. The thick, black power cable was plugged into a socket just to the rear of the engine.

As one of the ground crew primed the engine, turning the propeller by hand a couple of times, another member of the ground crew climbed up onto the left wing, slid back the canopy, opened the half door and stepped gingerly into the cockpit, lowering himself on to the seat, taking a firm grip at the top of the windscreen surround.

A moment or two later Ronald heard the distinctive whine of the starter motor being initiated. Within seconds, the propeller turning only very slowly, there came the sound of ignition. With a bang and a puff of blue smoke from one or two of the stub exhausts ranged along either side of the engine cowling, the 27 litre Rolls Royce Merlin engine gradually sprang into life, the propeller spinning faster and faster until it became a transparent disc and the engine settled to a steady rumble. The wash from the propeller ruffled the grass, scattering a whirlwind of rubbish.

Unannounced, Supermarine's chief test pilot, dressed in a light blue flying suit and matching leather helmet, spoke briefly to the senior mechanic, before climbing onto the wing to take his place at the controls.

He was strapped securely into his seat and after making himself comfortable and carrying out a few final checks in the cockpit, he opened the throttle and ran the Merlin up to full power, the plane straining at the wheel chocks. For the first time they heard the cry of the Merlin, a sound which would become such an icon, sounding down the following decades.

Satisfied with everything, the pilot signalled for the chocks to be removed and with a crewman at each wingtip eased the Spitfire forward and away for take-off, swinging the nose from side to side in order to obtain a clear view ahead. As the Spitfire turned, Ronald and Hutch revelled in the gale of wind in the face, which carried the pungent smell of Castrol oil from the exhausts.

Turning round into wind, the pilot again ran the engine up to full power, then released the brakes and they all held their breath when the Spitfire leapt forward as though eager to claim its place in the sky. After only fifty yards the tail was up, the wheels pattering over the grass, then it lifted clear and, rising effortlessly into the early evening sun, the Spitfire climbed steadily, until it was just a speck against the setting sun. Hutch gave an audible sigh.

Then someone nearby, perhaps with the keenest eyesight, shouted and pointed. Following his lead, they saw the Spitfire, higher now, turning and diving back toward them, the Merlin snarling its song, hurling the airframe back to earth, almost caressing the grass, then up, up and rolling over to its side, exposing the graceful silhouette of its elliptical wings, then further, onto its back, still climbing and finally all the way over in a perfect roll. They heard pilot throttling back and with a final waggle of the wings, the Spitfire departed steadily to the south west, the Merlin whispering its goodbye.

Ronald and Hutch stood for a moment rooted to the spot, enthralled, then cheered and hollered, throwing their caps into the air and dancing about each other with excitement. Even Alfred joined in saying, "There you are, lads. That's why I brought you. God willing, you've just seen the future of the RAF," and so, carrying with them the unmistakable and unforgettable sound and sight of the Spitfire, they packed their things and made their way home, talking as much with their hands as they relived, time and time again those few glorious moments.

The sound of the telephone, yet another cold-caller, roused Ronald from his thoughts. Perhaps they had been too naive, too romantic, but they had been just a couple of teenagers, with all their lives ahead of them, full of promise, largely unaware of the gathering shadows. They had witnessed, been part of, in some small way, a moment of history, which had put into their bellies a fire, a desire to be willing, active participants.

From that day they had both believed that there could be nothing better than to be a Spitfire pilot, even though they had both known, by the time they got back from Germany, that possibly, maybe probably, if they were skilful enough, flying Spitfires might involve them in rather more than flamboyant displays at an air show.

Smiling to himself at his one-time naïveté, Ronald reflected for the umpteenth time in his long and sometimes very lonely life, the random and capricious ways of war that had kept him alive, flying more than 250 combat missions while others...... His eyes misted with the memories.

CHAPTER 12

On the 14th July 1936 they travelled down to Croydon Airport by coach and reported to the departures desk for Deutsche Lufthansa where each passenger and their bags were carefully weighed and checked.

After a brief half-hour wait in the small but comfortable departure lounge, their names were called. Once their passports and travel documents, including a visa issued by the German Embassy in London, had been verified against the passenger list, they were instructed to board their flight. An airport courier escorted them across the tarmac apron toward the waiting Junkers 52 Trimotor, which stood ready in its silver and blue livery, to receive its sixteen passengers.

Five small steps gave access to the entry and when it came to Ronald's turn he paused briefly in the doorway to run his fingers over the tightly corrugated surface of the light, but exceptionally strong, aluminium-manganese alloy skin that clothed the whole of the fuselage and the wings. Once inside, he was surprised by the steep incline of the passenger cabin.

While the outside was spartan and utilitarian, everything in the interior was a complete contrast. Curtains at every window, a moiré silk effect "wallpaper" in eau de nil, and luxurious seats in red leather with white piping. There were eight on either side of the gangway which led between the door and the cockpit. To the rear of the fuselage, there was a small galley from which food could be served during the flight.

Two air stewards, white jacketed, black shoes highly polished, gradually settled the passengers into specifically allocated seats, thus ensuring the proper balance of the aircraft, which, they explained, was the reason for all passengers and their luggage being weighed on arrival.

The senior steward, his status confirmed by the swastika armband around his left sleeve, enquired politely, in excellent English, whether Ronald required anything for the first leg of the flight, which would last roughly three and a half hours, but which might be longer if there was a strong head-wind. The steward suggested he might like something to read or perhaps a sweet to help him cope with the effects of altitude. Ronald already knew that they would be flying at only four thousand feet, but responded that he would appreciate some sweets, which were delivered to him on a silver salver a couple of minutes later.

As the passenger compartment gradually filled, Hutch being seated on the opposite side of the gangway and Ronald's father immediately behind, Ronald took further stock of his surroundings. The large rectangular window afforded him an excellent view down behind the left wing. He had a small Kodak camera with which he hoped to take a few photos on the flight. In front, fixed to the bulkhead that gave access to the cockpit he noticed a framed photograph and realised it was of Germany's elected leader, Adolf Hitler.

Moments later the pilot and co-pilot, dressed in dark uniforms and peaked caps bearing the Winged Crane insignia of the airline, entered the cabin, flight bags in hand and made their way quickly up the gangway and into the cockpit. Before the door was firmly closed Ronald caught a glimpse of the control yoke for the co-pilot and the extensive array of dials and levers in front of the co-pilot's seat.

A minute or two later, one by one, the three engines coughed into life with spouts of flame and smoke belching from the exhaust ports and Ronald felt for the first time the thrill of an aircraft coming to life, a thrill that never left him even through the long days of the war.

The sounds and smells of that very first flight would be forever etched on his memory and in a nostalgic, romantic way every piston engine aircraft would "come alive" for him in the same way as a steam train. The jets would do it better, faster, but without a personality, without a soul.

With all the engines at maximum power, the Junkers rolled slowly down the grass runway, gathering speed at what seemed to be a leisurely pace until the tail wheel lifted off, the cabin righted itself to the level and at last, with a final gentle bump, the plane became airborne and began banking in a shallow curve away to the southeast heading for the south coast and onward to Germany.

Ronald was fascinated by his first aerial view, leaning forward in his seat and craning his neck to watch as the towns, villages and green fields, the patchwork quilt of the English countryside, slipped steadily by.

At their cruising height of 4,000 feet the pilot throttled all three engines back so that the level of noise became more tolerable and conversation with his neighbour reasonably possible. But in many ways Ronald preferred to be cocooned in his own world by the constant drumming of the engines as he watched the passing cloud formations, some towering many thousands of feet above, as he dreamed of when, or if, he might become a pilot in his own right.

Eventually, he realised they had crossed the Kent coast and were heading out over the English Channel. As he watched small coasters butting their way through the choppy seas, north towards the Thames estuary, he was reminded of the words of the poem *Cargoes* by the Poet Laureate John Masefield, which he enjoyed so much.

Within just minutes they were over the coast of France still heading south east, then over the flat farmland of northern France where his father had been stationed less than twenty years previously.

Twisting in his seat, he turned to his father who seemed instinctively to understand his unspoken enquiry and pointed out of the right hand window away to the south.

Occasionally Hutch, sitting on the opposite side of the aisle tried to engage him in conversation, but the drumming of the engines made this inconvenient and he so was content to watch the fields pass by, especially when they passed over the great defences that formed France's eastern defence against any future attack by Germany – The Maginot Line.

During the twenties the French government had determined that there should not in future be the easy passage onto French soil that the German army had achieved in 1914 and so it had spent millions upon millions of francs constructing the extended defences, which the military of the day were confident would hold France safe against any attack. From the air, the connecting trenches, fortifications and massive gun emplacements were clearly visible.

Shortly afterwards, the senior steward passed through the cabin to announce that they were over German territory and would be landing at Frankfurt within the hour. During the flight they had been served with strong coffee and small open sandwiches on tasty black bread, which Ronald quite liked, as opposed to the coffee which, taken without milk or cream, he found too bitter for his taste. The remaining passengers all appeared to be German citizens, and talked loudly to each other to be heard above the noise of the engines and fortified their coffees with something taken from a leather bound hip flask.

Shortly afterwards, the Junkers began a gradual descent and, passing through a layer of cloud, Ronald saw for the first time the ancient town of Frankfurt-am-Main with its tight packed houses and narrow cobbled streets. Even from the air, Ronald could see many horse drawn carts and carriages, which surprised him. This ancient form of transport contrasted sharply with the new four lane highway which seemed to be still under construction leading away to the north-east in the direction of Berlin. Ronald noted the large number of lorries using the road. At the time, he thought nothing further of it.

Once they had landed and come to a halt outside the airport terminus building, recently extended and improved by all appearances, they were asked to disembark in order to go through the formalities of German customs and border control, which would record their entry into Germany, even though they were advised they would re-board the same aircraft for the second leg of their flight to Berlin, once the Junkers had been refuelled.

The immigration process was, in Ronald's eyes, very formal if not a little daunting. The flight steward led them personally, as the only non-Germans, to a large, imposing desk where they were to be interviewed – at some length. To one side of the desk was a small bronze bust of *Der Führer* next to a small swastika flag mounted on a twelve inch high silver pole. In the centre of the desk were two carousels of rubber stamps, one either side of a black inking pad. Ronald could see that their fate would depend on which of the stamps was applied to their papers.

Each of their passports was carefully inspected by a black uniformed official whose only insignia was a small badge worn on the left breast pocket and which featured a German swastika, a hooked black cross on a white background. The visas from the German embassy in London were inspected minutely.

With the paperwork largely completed, he deferred to another official also dressed in a black uniform, but with a high collared jacket which sported twin lightning flashes embroidered onto each wing of the collar under the neck. Ronald assumed this gave him the status of an officer.

The second official continued the enquiry:

"Who is this?" pointing at Hutch.

"A family friend."

"Parents' permission?"

Alfred smiled indulgently and reached into his jacket pocket to produce a letter signed by Hutch's father – 'just in case'.

"Purpose of visit?"

"To renew a friendship." The official looked at Alfred suspiciously as though no English person could or should have a friend in Germany.

At this point, Ronald realised that the conversation between his father and the first official had been conducted entirely in German in which, again to Ronald's surprise, his father seemed to be virtually fluent. Ronald could see that his father was starting to become more than a little annoyed at the persistent nature of the enquiries.

As the official consulted a sheaf of documents on a clipboard, Alfred began to drum his fingers on the counter top. Ronald recognised the warning signs of his father's growing impatience and irritation. The drumbeat of *Rule Britannia* continued a little more loudly as the official leafed punctiliously through his papers.

"Your occupation?"

"Aeronautical engineer," replied Alfred, after a moment's hesitation.

"Name of your host in Germany?"

"Herr Otto Hecker and Frau Elise Hecker of Charlottenburg, Berlin," Alfred said slowly and deliberately, hissing it through his teeth.

Ronald, who had not understood the exchange, looked across at Hutch who raised an eyebrow in reply, but then he heard his father mention their German hosts' names in person.

Immediately the attitude and demeanour of the second official changed and, as he snapped to attention, he said in perfect English, "Haupsturmführer Evers at your service. On behalf of the German Reich and the German people I welcome you all to our country as the honoured guests of the respected General der Flieger. We will ensure that you have a safe and comfortable onward flight. Heil Hitler!" and so saying he saluted, thrusting his right arm forward and upwards, fingers extended. Taking Ronald completely unawares, the first official then also leapt to attention, saluting similarly.

Within moments the carousels had been spun, like a Russian roulette and the appropriate stamps selected and applied to their passports and their visas, allowing them to remain within the Greater German Reich for a maximum of twenty-eight days. Each time the junior official selected a stamp he did so with exaggerated care, as though to make the point that they were privileged to be allowed entry, carefully rolling the stamp across the pad, turning the stamp toward his face to check it was perfectly coated and then pressing it to the surface of each document with a deliberate and calculated precision that seemed to suggest a condescending superiority.

Hauptsturmführer Evers cautioned that they should be vigilant in ensuring that they did not forget the closing date on their visa, but Alfred assured him, with a heavy irony, which was not entirely lost on the captain, that they had no intention of outstaying their welcome. There was only a curt nod of the head, before they were issued with a special travel pass and Evers escorted them back to their waiting aircraft. He told them that the flight had been cleared of, as he put it, all unnecessary passengers and he wished them an agreeable onward journey to Berlin, There, he assured them, the General de Flieger would welcome them personally, having just been informed by telephone of their arrival in Frankfurt.

Once inside the Junkers they found that they were the only passengers apart from a solitary gentleman, dressed in a dark suit and carrying a raincoat, who sat next to the door, but he did not speak or even acknowledge their presence. Ronald thought, but was not sure, that the man had been among the passengers on board when they left Croydon.

Since the flight to Berlin would take little over an hour, the assistant steward had apparently been dispensed with and only the senior steward remained. His attitude was markedly changed as he fussed round his remaining three British passengers, ensuring they were seated comfortably for the next phase of their flight. As soon as they were airborne, he reappeared with coffee, biscuits and Schnapps for them alone.

This time, with his father sitting opposite, rather than behind, Ronald was able to enquire about what had just happened at the airport. His father explained that the Hauptsturmführer had become increasingly inquisitive about the purpose of their visit and, although he had been sorely tempted to tell him to "mind his own bloody business", he had decided that candour was the best answer.

"But what does General de Flieger mean?" asked Ronald.

"I don't really know," replied his father, continuing, "I already knew that Otto is fairly senior in the German Air Ministry these days, but I thought he had retired long ago from anything military, although the title of "General of the Aircrew" would seem to suggest otherwise. Anyway, just the mention of his name brought the Captain to his senses. It will be interesting to see what sort of reception we get in Berlin."

Three-quarters of an hour later, and still thinking about what had happened at Frankfurt, Ronald felt the aircraft beginning to descend.

The steward announced that they would be landing at Berlin's newest airport, the Tempelhof, in ten minutes and requested they ensure their personal possessions were secure for landing. Then he went aft and spoke at some length to the gentleman by the door. Ronald noticed that he looked in their direction several times during the conversation. By now Ronald's imagination was beginning to work overtime as he wondered whether they were being followed and watched.

The approach to Tempelhof brought them in over the centre of Berlin so that they had a grandstand view of the city, gleaming in the late afternoon sunshine. Everywhere he looked there seemed to be new building on an impressive scale, dwarfing what he thought must be the old town. In a style reminiscent of the Roman, new official looking buildings lined and defined new wide avenues along which mature trees had been planted to soften the stark vertical and horizontal lines of the buildings. As the Junkers dropped lower over the centre of the city he could see couples walking arm in arm, mothers or nannies pushing perambulators and streams of traffic, cars, trolley-buses and just a few lorries pressing down the avenues. Here and there, an open horse-drawn landau progressed at a leisurely pace, the passengers gazing up to observe the Junkers passing slowly overhead.

Moments later they passed, not once, but twice over the main terminal building, which had been built for the country's prestige, as the largest, most imposing, in the whole of Europe. The pilot clearly intended to afford his special passengers the opportunity to be thoroughly impressed by its sheer scale. Its construction was in the form of a crescent, more than a kilometre long, reminiscent of the open wings of an eagle and at the centre, pointing straight at the heart of Berlin, the entrance concourse was flanked by rows of flagpoles each topped with a national flag or a swastika fluttering in the gentle breeze.

Then it was gone from view as the Junkers banked to starboard, completed a sharp turn and dropped on to the newly laid concrete runway with a slight thud and squeal of tyres.

Once again Ronald was canted back in his seat as the tail wheel dropped to the ground and so he propped himself upright to continue his view of the airport. At last, the main terminus came into sight. It was colossal, awesome and growing larger by the second as the Junkers taxied in closer and closer still, as though to enter the building itself.

Then, with a final surge of power from the port engine the plane made a sharp right turn and came to a rest, its wingtip only feet from the glazed frontage, so that the whole aircraft was entirely sheltered by the great curving canopy which stretched for hundreds of metres on either side. Switches cut, the engines slowed. The one on the wing next to Ronald backfired as it stopped, surprising him momentarily. He turned to Hutch who grinned at his startled expression.

Immediately, the steward reappeared to open the cabin door. From one side, two uniformed porters appeared, pushing a short set of steps on wheels which they fixed at the cabin door. As he collected his thoughts, Ronald turned to discover that the man in the suit was already gone, but then briefly, he caught sight of him striding towards a door set a little away from the main entrance. There, he was met by an officer in uniform. German salutes were exchanged and, shaking hands, they disappeared quickly inside with, Ronald noticed, a final backward glance at their aircraft, as the three of them began to descend the steps.

While they gathered at the foot of the steps uncertain quite which door to select, Ronald looked up and up and then further up at the façade of the terminus which towered fully fifty feet above them and could not help but make a comparison with the pleasant, almost cosy, departure lounge at Croydon. If the architect's intention was to make a statement about the renewal, the revival of Germany then, thought Ronald, he had certainly succeeded.

"Welcome to Berlin," said the steward breaking into Ronald's thoughts. "Please follow me. Your baggage will be brought to you shortly." And so saying, he set off quickly towards the imposing entry with its great glazed doors. Alfred, Ronald and Hutch struggled to keep up.

Inside, in the cool shade of the marbled and mirrored arrivals area, Ronald was immediately struck by the vertical drapes hanging everywhere, bright red, each emblazoned with a black swastika on a white circular background. At the exit from the arrivals hall, the doorway was flanked, on either side, by a free standing drape hanging from a twenty foot high gilded pole surmounted by a similarly gilded eagle, wings outstretched, holding in its talons a gilded laurel wreath encircling the same hooked cross. In the background, military marching music was playing quietly, interrupted only by loudspeaker announcements of flights about to arrive or depart.

"Freddy!" A booming voice behind him made him jump and he turned quickly to find himself looking into the smiling face of a great bear of a man, dark hair combed back and slicked with brilliantine, dressed in a beautifully cut three-piece camel coloured suit, red silk spotted tie and two-tone brown and cream brogues. A light-coloured fedora was clasped in his left hand.

"Freddy," he said again, "so bloody good to see you," addressing his father who seemed to be in a slight state of shock, before Alfred recovered and held out his hand in greeting, but Otto Hecker was having none of that. Instead he threw his arms around Alfred and gave him a great hug, clapping him on the back.

"Yes, I know, I've put on a bit of weight since you last saw me, but it's still the same old Otto."

Recovering further, and disentangling himself from Otto's clutch, Alfred shook him properly by the hand, at which Otto bowed slightly, and then Alfred introduced Ronald and his good friend Hutch. Taking each in turn with a firm handshake, Otto continued:

"Welcome to each of you, welcome to Germany, welcome to Tempelhof. What do you boys think of our newest airport, opened by our Chancellor just a few weeks ago? Very impressive, ja? It is the new gateway into Germany to welcome all the contestants and the national leaders, including perhaps your Mr. Chamberlain, who may be attending the Olympic Games in a couple of weeks' time." There was no doubting Otto's pride and enthusiasm.

As they all nodded in agreement, Ronald replied politely, "Yes, Herr Hecker it's so big – so much marble. It reminds me so much of my studies of the Roman Empire."

Otto laughed, deep and throaty, and replied, "Please, boys, you may call me Otto, but I thank you for the courtesy." Then he continued, "We Germans have a great liking for the organisation and discipline offered by the Romans, but enough of that for now. It's time we got you all home, so that you can unpack, maybe take a little rest, and then get ready for dinner. Elise has prepared a special welcome for you," and with that he turned on his heel and led the way out of the arrivals building, past crowds of people, elegantly dressed, and accompanied by porters in uniform, pushing piles of expensive luggage on wheeled trolleys.

Without a doubt, Ronald thought, Berlin's Tempelhof was reserved for the elite of Germany's and Europe's society.

Once outside, Otto, who had not paused for a moment in chatting to his father, suddenly stopped in his tracks, raised his left arm and waved his hat in a beckoning gesture. Out of the corner of his eye, Ronald noticed a large saloon ease its way out of a long line of similar looking cars, the majority of which were painted in black and each flying a pennant from its front mudguard.

From their right, a porter arrived with a trolley bearing their luggage. As his father began to pat the pockets of his jacket to find a tip for the porter Otto shook his head. "Nein, not necessary, in our new Reich everyone has a job and is properly paid –not like the bad old days after the war."

Looking a little sheepish at the rejection of his gratuity, Alfred began again patting his pockets, this time for the comfort of his cigarettes. "We have so much to talk about, later," he added, with a meaningful look at his old friend.

The large Mercedes 504 Tourer drew up in front of them and the driver, a small, thin-faced, wiry man dressed in a tight fitting dark uniform leapt out, saluted in the old fashioned military style to the peak of his cap and then quickly loaded all the bags into the cavernous boot of the car.

Ronald stared with astonishment at the car. It put his father's recently acquired Vauxhall Light Six firmly in the shade. In two-tone red and cream the sleek lines of the body were accentuated by the front mudguards sweeping back from the massive, circular, chromed headlights and then downwards gracefully to form the running boards. The three-pointed star of the Mercedes motor company was mounted almost as a mascot to the radiator cap which topped off the massive chromed radiator. To Ronald it resembled a gunsight, sitting at the end of the unbelievably long bonnet. Whitewall tyres were set on wire-spoked wheels, and a spare was lashed with a broad leather strap to the coachwork on either side ahead of the front door hinges. The car seemed to ooze luxury and to mirror Otto's flamboyant style.

"Top up or down?" asked Otto, but before anyone could answer he continued. "Top down I think," with a wave of his hand and the driver immediately set about folding back the black pram-style hood. "This is my driver Werner Fischer." The driver came smartly to attention, before opening the passenger doors.

"This way you can see my beautiful Berlin at its best and today it really is warm enough. Don't go too fast, Werner," he advised, speaking to the driver, "we don't want to get blown away." He translated for them.

Jokingly, he added for their benefit, "I don't want to get my hair messed up, which Ronald thought highly unlikely in any event, given the amount of brilliantine Otto seemed to have used.

"OK," Otto continued, "Freddy, you go in the front and I will sit in the back between the two boys and try my best to give you all a guided tour." Speaking directly to Alfred he added, "You might just remember Werner, at least by name. He was my, how would you say it?" He paused for a moment to find the right word. "Yes, that's the right word; he was my batman in the Geschwader during '17 and '18, until your lot got hold of me." He poked Alfred gently in the side.

"He had always promised that if anything happened to me, he would try to keep an eye on Elise for me. He was true to his word and made sure that she and little Wolfgang were safe through the turmoil after the Armistice until I was repatriated. He said to me *Befehl ist Befehl*, but this was not a military duty, just one of comradeship. Never-the-less," Otto spoke the word slowly as though savouring his use of English, "I felt I owed him so much in return. We rather lost touch in the twenties, but then when Herman appointed me to my current post – what a grand title I have for such a little job – I was told I needed a driver. I thought I had found a way of repaying the debt – the pay is good and the hours not too long, so I had some enquiries made, rather than take one of the drivers offered to me."

Otto continued. "I discovered that Werner had fallen on hard times. He was on his own, his wife having been killed in a tragic accident and he had just about gone to pieces. He's been with me for almost two years now and it's just like the old times. Thankfully his service with me in the war was sufficient warranty of his character for the Party, but he's under no immediate pressure to join."

So saying, he translated quickly to Werner who immediately offered his hand to Alfred and then turned to Ronald and Hutch with a wide smile saying, "OK guys, lets hit the trail," mimicking the popular cowboy films of the day, before firing up the big V8 engine of the Mercedes and engaging the clutch, so that the car drew away with a purr from the kerbside. Phrases from the movies seemed to be the extent of Werner's grasp of English.

Ronald settled comfortably into the opulence of the cream leather upholstery as Hutch took the driver's side, behind Werner. Even with Otto's substantial frame, there was ample room for the three of them on the back seat. On the front mudguard a pennant fluttered in the passing breeze. With a red border and quartered in black and white, it featured a golden eagle, wings outstretched with a gold swastika in its talons. Noticing Ronald's interest, Otto leaned close and whispered, "It goes with the job. It's a great way of getting through traffic." He gave Ronald a broad wink.

Hutch, who up to this point had been remarkable by his silence, interrupted by starting to address a question to their host: "Herr Hecker," he began but he was immediately stopped by Otto, who again insisted that formalities were not necessary. He also indicated that, later, when they met his wife, Elise, they might address her as Frau Hecker as a courtesy when they were introduced, but thereafter it would be perfectly acceptable to call her Elise.

Hutch then remembered his question and asked why Tempelhof was so massive. Otto thought for a moment, then went on to explain that it was not just a question of trying to make a good impression; it was also all about the future.

"The German aircraft industry has great plans for the development of air travel and we see Berlin as the natural centre of travel across the whole of Europe, perhaps the world. Today you flew in a Junkers 52, less than twenty seats, but already we have the new Junkers 200 coming into service which can carry almost 50 passengers in comfort, far more than the Ford Tri-motor or even the Douglas DC2 or its replacement the DC3."

He continued, obviously intent on making a point to his audience: "Already our designers have plans for airliners that could carry up to 100 passengers in complete safety and comfort right across the Atlantic to New York, and, although these are still on the drawing board, the design work is well advanced. Provided there are no interruptions," he paused, looking meaningfully at Alfred, "we could see the prototypes flying within two or three years."

"We all know," he continued, almost with a conspiratorial air, "that the combustion engine, diesel or petrol, with pistons driving a propeller –or even two – is not going to be enough. Already we are beginning to experience problems with propellers reaching the limits of their performance. They just cannot go round fast enough, no matter how big we make them – even three metres across if you can imagine such a thing."

"But across the world scientists, including ours, are working on a new form of propulsion – a method by which air is drawn in at the front of a tube, compressed by fans Inside, and then mixed with fuel so that it is expelled, under tremendous pressure, to give all the power you could possibly need to fly higher and faster. And Germany, I am proud to say, is close to putting such an engine into production. Then the world will have to sit up and take notice."

"You have them in England, but they keep exploding. You ask your father – he knows!" he concluded with a broad wink. Alfred held up his hands as though to express his ignorance, but Otto insisted, repeating, "Certainly, he knows!"

"Maybe one day, everyone will have their own little jet plane, just as we are planning a little reliable car for everyone – a Volkswagen, a people's car which will be on the roads very soon to race up and down the autobahns, our new four lane highways." Otto was unable to keep a note of superior smugness out of his voice as he extolled Germany's recent achievements.

"But that's enough shop-talk from me for now. Let's just sit back and enjoy the ride. It's only going to take just over an hour and I'll try to point out a few of the places of interest as we go."

The Mercedes proceeded at a modest pace northwards towards the centre of the city along the Mehringdamm, threading serenely through the traffic which, from time to time at an intersection, was stopped by a uniformed traffic policeman to allow the Mercedes a smooth and interrupted passage. Otto waved his thanks, as he pointed at this new building on one side or that historic building on the other.

At length, after crossing the Landwehr Canal, they came onto the Wilhelmstrasse which Otto explained would take them into the heart of the City, the Alexanderplatz, with the intention of showing them a few more of the sights. As they drew nearer to the centre, Otto became more animated and at one point stood up , arms spread wide as he indicated the new neo-classical building of the Reichsluftfartministerium (what a mouthful thought Ronald) the German Aviation Ministry – "my other home" – according to Otto. Next came the new Reich Chancellery still under construction in the same neo-classical style, and then, on Prinz Albrechtstrasse a brief, but very brief mention of "Police Headquarters" which Ronald came to realise, years later, meant the offices of the dreaded secret police, the Geheime Staatspolizei, the Gestapo.

Shortly afterwards, with a turn to the right they drove onto the Unter den Linden avenue, heading eastwards amongst the slow moving traffic, bumping sedately over the tracks for the trolley-buses. Ronald in particular was fascinated by the broad tree lined boulevard, crowded with families promenading in the late afternoon sunshine, such a contrast to anything he had experienced at home in the suburbs of London. Equally fascinating to him was the number of men in uniforms of all different hues; brown, blue, grey and black, and everywhere he could see the hanging drapes of red and black, all sporting the black swastika so that the gathered throng resembled, it seemed to him, more of a military parade than a snapshot of domestic life.

Then they circulated slowly anti-clockwise round the Alexanderplatz and back onto Unter den Linden this time westward with the Brandenburg Gate in full view before them. Like so many of the buildings they had passed, it too was decorated with red swastika banners, but here these were alternated with white flags bearing the five Olympic rings.

At this time, Ronald remembered his camera and asked if they might stop for a photograph. Otto instructed Werner to bring the car to a halt on the Pariserplatz, and they all climbed out and huddled together so that Werner could frame them against the backdrop of the Brandenburg Gate with its columns and high arches. The gate was topped by a bronze statue of Eirene, the winged goddess of peace riding in a chariot pulled by four charging horses. When he looked at the photograph years later, the irony of the iconic image was not lost on him.

For a moment, it seemed a policeman would move them on, but then he appeared to recognise the official nature of the car and its high-ranking occupant, so he saluted smartly in the German way, turned on his heel and walked away. "You see, rank really does have its privileges, Freddy." Alfred rolled his eyes.

Getting back into the car, they rejoined the slow moving traffic, passed through the Brandenburg Gate, whose stonework was being cleaned, in readiness, Otto reminded them, for the forthcoming Olympics which was a matter of great national pride. On the far side of the gate, he pointed out the Reichstag, the parliament building, still in process of being rebuilt to repair the damage caused by a disastrous fire three years earlier. He seemed to ignore the question from Hutch as to how the fire had started.

Then they motored along the Charlottenburger Chausee and drove slowly into the lush grounds of the Tiergarten park with its famous zoo where the sounds of a military band playing march music drifted toward them through the trees. Skirting round the zoo they drove past a large open area where they could see a hundred or more boys, all dressed in white shirts and black shorts, practising parade ground drill, marching smartly back and forth to the orders of a young man in grey military uniform. Ronald thought it all a bit odd, and said so to Otto. He smiled indulgently and explained that this was a unit of the Hitler Jugend, the Hitler Youth, in Berlin and that drill was only a very small part of a regime for *all* young people, designed to improve their health and fitness. When Hutch commented that an occasional game of footie in the local park was enough for him, Otto roared with laughter and offered him a day or two with Wolfgang when he next turned out with his unit. Hutch declined with as much tact as he could manage. Otto let it go at that, but from the look on his face he clearly felt that British youth were somewhat lacking by comparison.

Next, instead of taking the direct route home, Otto diverted the car through the park for a little detour to the north, until they were driving along the south bank of the River Spree which was dotted with leisure craft mingling with commercial steamers and barges. It was a hive of activity. Crossing over one of the many bridges that spanned the Spree they followed its curve westward so that they had a good view of the Schloss Charlottenburg, Berlin's largest palace built in the early 18th century on the Spree's south bank. Otto promised them a visit to view its magnificent painted ceilings and frescoes if time permitted during their stay. Once again Otto proved to be the perfect tour guide, and perhaps it was just as well he could not foresee that the palace would be completely destroyed in just seven years' time.

Finally they turned south once again, driving back over the Spree and onto one of Berlin's main thoroughfares, the Siegessaule before diverting off on to another area of parkland where the housing development appeared to have taken place only quite recently. The street sign read "Goethepark/Charlottenburg". It was evidently an up-market, exclusive part of town. Hutch summed it up in one word: "Posh!"

As he sat listening and trying to take it all in, Ronald's mind raced – Hermann – was that *the* Hermann Goring; what was Otto's role that it merited an official car and driver; how did his father know about this new form of propulsion, which he had never mentioned? Was it just pure coincidence that Ronald had seen the man from the flight, seated in the back of another official Mercedes a couple of junctions previously, despite him leaving the airport well before them?

Were they being followed, he wondered, or was it just his overactive imagination fired by his recent reading of John Buchan's

The 39 Steps and all that it implied about dark forces being abroad for Germany during the Great War?

He was still mulling over these thoughts when they turned on to the newly constructed, broad avenue of Geothe Park, lined with young plane trees and Otto announced their arrival at "our little house". Ahead lay a pair of large wrought iron gates, hung on tall white pillars each topped by a gold eagle. One gate bore the house number 7, the other an entwined E and O.

"Our dream house," said Otto, adding, "perhaps it should have had a good historical German name in keeping with Goethe Park, but Elise so loved the way you English like to combine your Christian names, so we came up with Elisto. Sounds good, Ja?"

Then he paused for a moment and began to chuckle. "Not so easy for you Freddy," and then as he worked out some of the less romantic combinations of Alfred and Cissy in his head, he laughed so much the tears ran down his cheeks.

"Sorry old friend," he apologised, realising his gaff. "No offence intended."

"None taken," said Alfred, good naturedly with a wry smile. "We did try, but not for very long.'' Otto visibly relaxed.

Sweeping through, the Mercedes proceeded up a long winding drive, lined with recently planted almond trees, passing immaculately tended lawns and flower beds, and coming to a halt moments later at the foot of a broad flight of marble steps. These led up to the front door of a house, which was quite unlike anything they had ever seen.

Firstly, the house was big, not high, but wide and flat topped, on two floors only.

Secondly it was white, startlingly so. Together the two factors combined to give it the look of a sleek liner at anchor, an impression enhanced by the presence of the occasional circular window like a porthole. The main windows, wide but not particularly high were framed in green painted steel, with horizontal glazing bars of the same colour. There was a raised band of concrete, also painted green, that ran all around the house, just below the parapet to further emphasise the sense of length and spaciousness.

Above the front double doors, themselves of glass with an intricate abstract design inlaid in black ebonised rosewood, suggesting deer leaping toward each other, stood a half-round, almost fully glazed tower a further two storeys in height enclosing a circular staircase which Ronald learned shortly gave access to the bedrooms on the first floor, as well as to a superb sun terrace above. This was sheltered from the adverse effects of wind by frosted glass screens held in place by chromium-plated brackets Half a dozen comfortable sun-loungers were shaded by a colourful fixed awning.

Within moments, Werner had unloaded their bags and driven the Mercedes away to be housed in the large underground garage along with Otto's other vehicles. Werner, Otto explained, had a small self-contained flat in one wing of the house, and in his duties doubled up as a butler, valet, gardener and general factotum, as and when the need arose.

As they stood outside gazing up and around this incredible house, Otto cleared his throat and said with obvious pride in his voice "Welcome to our new home. You are our first guests to stay with us. We only moved in four months ago." With that the front door swung open and a tall, elegant, very attractive woman dressed in a pale blue skirt and white embroidered blouse stepped lightly out onto the porch.

"Freddy, boys, may I present my darling Elise," and introduced them each in turn.

"Frau Hecker," said Alfred. "It is a pleasure to meet you at last and to be welcomed to your beautiful home," speaking in his best and most formal German. She coloured slightly, perhaps at the formality of the greeting, then she took a step closer and kissed him lightly on each cheek, insisting they all call her Elise.

When Werner reappeared from the garage to bring in their bags, Otto ushered them indoors, where more surprises awaited them. The hallway was large, disappearing from view around a curve on which there was mounted a large clock fixed into the wall itself with plain black hour and minute hands and just the quarter hours marked out in black bands.

"Very minimalist," muttered Ronald's father.

As they progressed in to the house, passing double doors on the left, they found that the curve of the hall held the main staircase winding in a spiral up to the first floor. Although the wooden floor of the hallway was laid as highly-polished parquet with an intricate geometric design, the stair carpet was deep red, with black edging, not the full width of the tread, the exposed band on either side being painted in cream to contrast with the salmon pink on the walls. Vaguely it crossed Ronald's mind that the colours on the staircase were similar to the drapes he had first seen in Tempelhof, but he thought no more of it as Otto led them through a pair of double doors to the right into a vast, bow-fronted lounge, This, in turn, overlooked a large expanse of lawn with gravel paths leading away from the house towards an encircling beech hedge which obscured the remainder of the garden.

Beyond the lounge, through a wall of folding doors lay the dining room. Otto explained that the doors could be folded back completely so that the two rooms could be combined to create a banqueting hall or a ballroom. What amazed Ronald was that the whole of the bay was made of glass which gave the effect of the room being part of the garden.

"Come," said Otto, "please sit for a few minutes before you go up to your rooms. It has been such a long day for you and we have some coffee and cake to revive you, plus a little something else, if you would like."

Elise served coffee in delicate, beautifully decorated porcelain cups, to be taken with cream or milk as they pleased. The cake, more like tasty pastries were eaten with a teaspoon following the example set by Otto. As it turned out, Otto would ever be the perfect host, leading by example to show them the nuances of German society. The 'something else' turned out to be a peach flavoured schnapps – better for the afternoon – which was poured for everyone, despite protests from his father that Ronald was too young.

"In a year or two," said Otto, rebuffing his father, "young Ronald will be old enough to fight for his country even if he cannot vote for its leaders so I think he must be old enough to handle just a little drink. To put your mind at rest, Freddy, I shall put Werner on guard duty to make sure Ronald does not sneak down in the night for a top up." They all laughed, Ronald's father did appear reassured and Ronald enjoyed his snifter, plus just a small top-up when his father was not looking.

The conversation continued always in English which was a great relief, but Ronald found the long, low sofa in pale green leather so comfortable that he began to drift to the edge of falling asleep.

Seeing this, Otto said it was time for everyone either to go to their rooms, to have a moment to freshen up, or catch forty winks, (looking pleased with himself that he remembered the vernacular), or they were free to wander the gardens until dinner, which would be served at 8.00 pm sharp.

Otto explained that his older son Wolfgang would not be joining them as he was away on a flying course – "Like father like son," he quipped – but their younger son Dieter, who was just a few months older than Ronald, would make himself known as soon as he got back from his after-school class.

The bedrooms proved to be somewhat more conventional. Ronald and Hutch were to share a twin bedded room, both beds having ash head and footboards and which were made up with a lightweight form of quilt rather than the sheets and blankets they were accustomed to at home. Each bed had a matching cabinet with its own chrome and glass bedside lamp. It appeared, certainly, that the Hecker family was devoted to contemporary German design. It was all so very different.

CHAPTER 13

A couple of days after they arrived in Berlin, following a dinner carefully prepared by Elise and served by Werner in his role as butler, and washed down with a couple of bottles of Hochheimer Riesling '28 just as carefully chilled by Werner, they sat lingering over coffee in an atmosphere of enjoyable friendship. Then Alfred broke the spell by asking the one question that perhaps everyone had been dreading.

"What, Otto, is happening about the Jews?"

Otto's bonhomie visibly evaporated; Elise's face fell as she took an audible, involuntary, intake of breath. For a moment Ronald thought Otto might explode in a fit of temper, but instead Otto exhaled slowly, making a visible effort to remain calm and spread his hands flat on the table in front of him before responding.

"You know, Freddy, I could answer you by saying that our Führer has issued a *Fuhrerbefehl*, a Führer Order, forbidding any discussion of the Jewish question in this month before the Olympic Games; or I could say to you that the Jews are part of an international conspiracy to undermine Germany; or I could refer you to the Propaganda Ministry for an official response, but I will instead tell you, my friend, what I, no, what we, think." As he spoke, he looked directly at Elise, who blushed and seemed close to tears.

Again he drew breath, before continuing, seeming to measure each word with great care, "Almost a quarter of a century ago our two countries fought a war, the war you call the Great War, which everyone said was the war to end all wars. It was a terrible time and I pray that there will never be another one, even though it, by chance, brought our friendship. We Germans fought as one army, protestant and catholic, non-believer and Jew, many Jews in fact."

"Religion or personal background was not an issue. Bravery or cowardice was not dependent on such matters. We had Jews in our squadron, but all that mattered to me was, and still does for that matter, that they did the job for which they were trained. If they failed they went to prison, or, in the worst cases, of which there were thankfully very few, they were executed by firing squad for their cowardice. To my knowledge all Jews in our squadron performed their duties to the highest standard; they did their duty as loyal Germans. Werner was one of those who were completely loyal. My personal opinion has not changed." Alfred looked visibly surprised to hear that Werner was Jewish.

He paused for a moment as if weighing the consequences of what he had just inadvertently revealed, shot a warning glance at Elise, and then continued in a guarded tone, "My friends, we take you into our trust" – he stressed the *we*, "when I tell you that Werner is one quarter Jewish which brings him under the current regulations. Strictly I should dismiss him and employ a pure German, but I have a certain status and for now, so nothing changes. I owe him my life from the time he pulled me out of my crashed triplane in '17, and I'm not about to forget that. There may be dark days ahead for those with Jewish ancestry and thus there is some risk to us."

As he spoke, he had risen from his chair, walked round the table until he was standing directly behind Elise. Then he leaned over, placed his arms lovingly around her and, nuzzling his face into the nape of her neck so that when he spoke again, squeezing her tight, his voice was muffled – but there was no mistaking the emotion running through him:

"Werner, as I have already told you, is absolutely devoted to Elise, and as you know, I trust him implicitly, but our boys know nothing and it's better that they don't. Wolfgang and Dieter are both in the Hitler Jugend, which some say is a bit like your Boy Scouts, but there is more to it than that and the boys could, shall we say, come under some pressure to talk about private things in their family and friends. So it is better that they know nothing. My position is not a cast iron guarantee that the situation will not change."

With that, he kissed Elise tenderly on her neck and finished by saying, "So there you have it, Freddy. I beg of you as a friend, no more questions on this troublesome subject."

Later that night in discussion with Hutch, they realised that Otto, ever the diplomat, had not actually answered Alfred's question. But perhaps he had, in a way that would not compromise him. They could not help but feel, from what Otto had said, that he was not entirely wedded to the party line which declared that all Jews were to be excluded, in one way or another, from German society.

As he lay in the darkness, listening to Hutch's steady breathing, Ronald wondered if his father was still downstairs, deep in conversation with Otto and perhaps Elise to divine their true beliefs on the subject. But whatever the outcome, Alfred never broke the confidence, never mentioned it again during their time in Germany and carried whatever he had learned to his grave.

How many fifteen year olds, he wondered, British or German, could say that they had once, in 1936, met the future head of the German Luftwaffe (albeit briefly) and the then Leader of the Third Reich, Adolf Hitler (albeit only fleetingly)? Like it or not now, he had been flattered, at the time, that he had been granted such a privilege. Hutch, being older and perhaps more critical had speculated whether they had been set up for some sort of propaganda coup, but as far as they could tell there was only ever one report of that chance meeting in the German press and certainly no mention of it was ever made in the papers back at home.

The 22nd July 1936, that special extraordinary day had started unexceptionally, quite routinely, with Otto announcing that he had to go, as he put it, "into the office", but nevertheless they were all invited to join him. Perhaps there was something in his tone of voice which suggested that this might be no ordinary visit or no ordinary office and so they all accepted.

With the benefit of hindsight, long after the war, Ronald understood that he and Hutch were just incidental players that day, and that the invitation was aimed directly at his father. Otto's intention was, undeniably, to persuade him that Germany's technical superiority was such that it could not and should not be matched.

Once again, they had piled into the Mercedes with Werner at the wheel. They set off heading north and west out of the city, rather than towards the city's centre, to Otto's room in the Air Ministry as they had expected.

Otto was yet again in a genial, jovial mood, still acting as their tour guide, pointing out places of interest and the many buildings in the final stages of construction for the forthcoming Olympic Games. To their left, they could clearly see the bell tower rising above the main stadium; the bell would toll each time a gold medal was won, Otto explained.

In twenty minutes they were cruising along one of the new autobahns – four lanes, straight as a die, heading at speed, northwards out into the open, rather flat German countryside. The buffeting from the airflow inhibited any real conversation, but after a further thirty minutes in light traffic, the Mercedes slowed and Otto announced that they were nearly there.

By now, it seemed obvious that they were not going to an office in any conventional sense and shortly afterwards, when they arrived at the gates of an airfield, which was military in nature judging by the uniformed guards at the barrier, Otto spread his arms wide like a circus ringmaster and declaimed, "My office!"

The guards, recognising the visitors' car, began to come to attention when Otto waved down their salutes saying, "No formalities necessary gentlemen." They immediately raised the red and white striped barrier and Werner drove the Mercedes slowly through as Otto reported to the senior officer, "My special friends are my guests today – I will vouch for their good conduct."

A few minutes later, their papers duly stamped, and, after following a perimeter road around the edge of the airfield for perhaps half a mile, Werner brought the car to a halt a little to one side of a large, recently constructed hangar, parking neatly at the far edge of the concrete apron which was laid out in a wide semi-circle. The doors were open just a fraction, inviting closer inspection, but it was impossible to see inside, to see what secrets it might contain.

For a while, as the temperature of the day built slowly, they waited patiently by the car, Otto and Alfred smoking and chatting, Ronald and Hutch idly observing the comings and goings of several light aircraft as well as one sturdy biplane, painted in military colours, with a powerful, rasping engine.

After a couple of passes it landed, taxied round the perimeter track and parked near their car, the pilot blipping the throttle "to clear the plugs" as Otto explained later.

The cockpit hood was pushed slowly back and two men climbed out, the older from the rear seat onto the left wing who Ronald concluded was probably the instructor and onto the right wing, from the front seat, went the younger – the pupil. They checked the plane together, shook hands and exchanged a few words, before the younger man saluted smartly and walked away.

The older man, tall and slim, who appeared to be in his mid to late twenties, then turned and walked towards them, pulling off his flying helmet to reveal a shock of blond hair over the bluest eyes Ronald had ever seen. As he came near, he held out his hand in greeting, saying in perfect, but heavily accented English,

"Hello, you must be our visitors from England. Permit me to introduce myself. I am Max, Otto's nephew. Well, actually it is Graf Maximillian von Lehdendorff, but Max is enough. My mother married into old family from just outside Königsburg, which is a couple of hundred miles north-east of here in East Prussia."

He bowed slightly from the waist before continuing, "I know you are going to meet my mother and my little sister who will be arriving tomorrow to attend the Olympic Games. My aunt, Elise's sister, and her family from Denmark will be arriving later in the week."

"My sister, Regina, is an enthusiastic and skilful horse-woman, but to her great disappointment was not selected for the German equestrian team. Nevertheless she is good friends with all of the team members and is coming to give her support. She speaks a little English, but she is also almost fluent in Russian."

Changing the subject, he continued, "I think Uncle Otto is arranging a big party for us all – it is not often that both sides of the family can get together. I am sure we will all get on just fine."

Ronald enquired politely whether Max's father would be attending, but Max explained that his father, as an officer in the cavalry, had been severely injured during the latter part of the Great War and died of the long term effects of those injuries some ten years later. After his father's death Max had inherited the title on his twenty-first birthday, some six years previously. His mother had never remarried, devoting all her energies into bringing up the two children and managing her late husband's small estate. Ronald later learned that the term *small* was relative, as the family estate extended in total to some three thousand acres.

"I believe Otto has a surprise for you today," and as he spoke, while introductions were made all round, they heard the deep rumbling sounds of the hangar doors starting to open, moving steadily sideways on well-oiled tracks.

As the light began to flood inwards through the widening gap, they could see the outline of a single-seat, low-winged aircraft, which a group of mechanics were now making ready to push out onto the concrete apron.

Once again, in his somewhat theatrical way, Otto opened his arms wide and said simply, "my baby," but then, realising that there were others present who had far greater claim to its fatherhood, corrected himself, adding, "our baby," with the emphasis on the "Our". Then he continued "I thought you might like to see the latest version of our new single seat fighter – only for the defence of the Reich of course." Just as much as our Spitfire, Ronald thought instantly, recognising the trace of irony in Otto's voice. Hutch was straining at the leash to get close while Alfred looked on with apparent disinterest, but Ronald could tell that his father was taking in every little detail. Ronald was about to take a photograph, but a look from Otto and a restraining hand from his father deterred him.

Warming to his subject, Otto explained, "This is the Bayerische Flugzeugwerke 109, or as you will perhaps know it, the ME109 from its close association to its designer, Willy Messerschmitt. It only flew for the first time last year, and already it has broken all speed records here in Germany. Soon we hope to take the outright airspeed record from our friends, the Italians, who have it with a float plane of all things!" and he roared with laughter.

"Today, I thought you might like to watch a test flight. We have just fitted a new three blade propeller with variable pitch. Your father will explain, I am sure, what that means for improving the performance of the aircraft, but it leaves your new Supermarine Spitfire in the shade, we think," and he finished with a broad conspiratorial wink, which left Ronald wondering if Otto could have been at Hendon.

"Anyway," Otto continued, "I have some paperwork to attend to so Max, who is going to make the test flight after lunch, will show you round the aircraft. You can get in if you want, but just don't touch anything, and don't steal it," he concluded jokingly.

With that, he walked away into the hangar leaving them with Max who took them on a tour round the plane, and answered their many questions as best he could.

The plane, Ronald noted, was slightly smaller than the Spitfire which gave it an almost delicate appearance, standing on a narrow undercarriage and only eight feet tall. Unlike the Spitfire, with its smooth almost bubble-like enclosure, this cockpit canopy was very angular and hinged over to the right side.

He could see the flared scoops for the air intake on either side of the engine cowl and then he noticed a large hole in the centre of the propeller boss.

Seeing the direction of his gaze Max explained, "We have taken a different direction from you in England, where it comes to putting guns in our aeroplane. You are putting two or three in each wing, but we think it's better to put the guns where the pilot is looking – right down the line of the engine, so we will have a small cannon or machine gun on either side on top of the engine ahead of the cockpit and a much bigger one, perhaps thirty millimetres firing through the centre of the propeller – it will have a big punch like our Mr. Schmelling." He chuckled at his own joke as he made a light hearted reference to Germany's recent heavy weight boxing champion of the world.

"Would you like to get in?" asked Max, "Uncle Otto says it's OK, and he's the boss!"

The words were hardly out of his mouth before Hutch was on his way, reaching up to pull himself onto the left wing, but Max restrained him gently, signalling to a mechanic to bring a small set of steps.

Following Max's instruction, Hutch stepped onto the wing then swung his right leg over the cockpit side and, grasping onto the top edge of the windscreen, lowered himself onto the pilot's seat. Ronald heard his voice protesting that he could not see out. Max replied that if he were really flying he would be sitting on his parachute bag which would raise him to the proper height.

As the conversation continued above, Ronald walked with his father observing the dark, mottled green colour scheme, the yellow propeller boss, and the black and white rectangular cross painted halfway down the fuselage below which was stencilled a short serial number and the inscription "V4A". His father suggested that this might mean this plane was the fourth version of the A series prototype. Ronald thought his father remarkably well informed and began to wonder whether there might be another side to their holiday.

Soon, it was Ronald's turn to climb into the cockpit, but to give himself some idea of what it would be like to sit as a pilot he squatted on the seat, peering down the line of the top of the engine, before sitting properly with his feet barely able to touch the rudder pedals, set on either side of a large tubular hump which ran the length of the cockpit floor. This, Max explained, would house the big thirty millimetre cannon when fitted, but Ronald found it impossible to imagine what it would be like to use, never having fired anything bigger than an air rifle at the local fairground.

The cockpit was almost unbearably small with hardly room for even his narrow shoulders. The right wall of the cockpit was dominated by a bank of switches, making the space even more cramped. As best he could, he followed Max's lead as he explained all the controls, moving the control stick tentatively from side to side to operate the ailerons. Max assured him that this was the best of German engineering and there was no chance he could damage it.

All too soon, it seemed, it was time to get out and, as he stood up in the cockpit, he turned to see Hutch talking excitedly to his father and Otto, who was now dressed in a flying suit and carrying what appeared to be a spare set of dark green overalls.

"Now, boys," he boomed as Ronald joined them, "shall we lunch or shall we fly," but before they had chance to answer he continued, "I think we fly first, otherwise maybe we have lunch twice!" He laughed out loud and punched Hutch lightly on the shoulder.

"So, I think you first Ronald, then Hutch, as he got into the Messerschmitt first. Here, slip these on over your clothes." He handed Ronald the overalls.

"Max will help you in on the right side," he instructed, as they headed off toward a small four-seater monoplane, which had already been started and warmed up by the mechanics. Painted silver with a red tail plane which was embellished with a small swastika high up on the fin, and polished overall to a glossy finish, it sparkled in the strong summer sunlight. Moments later Ronald was strapped securely, very securely into the right hand seat as Max closed the door, giving him an encouraging smile. The cockpit was very compact and was fitted with dual controls. Ronald, sweeping his eyes across the bank of dials, where understanding was yet beyond his reach, rested his hand lightly on the control stick which jutted up out of the floor between his thighs.

"All in good time, young Ronald." Tapping the side of his nose, and with a grin, Otto added, as he pulled on a pair of cream silk gloves, "Let's see if you can be a good passenger, before you become a pilot!" Ronald swallowed hard as his heart began to patter.

"This is my little run-about, a roadster of the skies, a Messerschmitt 108, the most advanced four-seat tourer in the world and I will have the honour to be demonstrating it at the Olympics. It has a couple of special modifications, as you will see.

"Once upon a time, you know, I used to be a damn fine pilot, and although I don't fly so much these days – Elise says it's bad for my digestion – I still like to keep my hand in occasionally. Oh, by the way, maybe you should keep this nearby," and so saying he reached into an inside pocket of his flying suit and handed Ronald a stout brown paper bag. "Just in case!" he added with a twinkle in his eye.

"Hold on tight," he advised, showing Ronald a grab handle on the cockpit side and another fixed below the edge of his seat. The far end of the airfield shimmered in the heat-haze and Ronald experienced a tingle of anticipation in his stomach. Then they were off, bumping across the grass alongside the tarmac runway.

The last words Ronald clearly heard were, "This is how we did it in '17," as Otto thrust the throttle open wide, the engine roaring and the plane reaching for the sky, the undercarriage retracting into the wheelwells with a solid clunk. But only seconds after take-off Ronald was staring up at the ground as Otto inverted the plane and flew the length of the airfield upside down, before flipping the craft level and pulling up at full throttle, aiming for the heavens.

Holding the throttle open, Otto kept the plane climbing almost vertically, hanging on its propeller until it could lift no more and they slid gracefully earthwards tail-first. "Would look damn good with some smoke, don't you think. I'll have some fitted for the demonstration next week."

For the next fifteen minutes Ronald's world was filled with climbing and diving, loops and turns as Otto effortlessly recreated his flying of almost twenty years before. To his surprise, Ronald found that his stomach stayed with him and not even once did he think he might need the paper bag. He was loving every second of the flight, thrilled by all the sensations of speed and the pressures, the G-force, on his body during the aerobatics.

Finally, Otto climbed the little plane higher and higher until they were above the white fluffy clouds that dotted the sky. When Otto leaned toward him, giving a thumbs-up, Ronald nodded enthusiastically in response – he could think of no other place in the world he would rather be at that particular moment.

Otto then shouted, "OK, it's your turn, now!" Ronald gaped in surprise, but he was not going to be one to let the opportunity slip and so, with Otto's gentle coaching he managed to fly reasonably straight and level, his heart beating wildly, sensing the movement of the craft as it rose and fell in the slight turbulence. He was in heaven. With a little help from Otto he managed a couple of wide turns before Otto signalled that the lesson was over.

Once he had handed back control, Otto said, "Let's land on that nice flat cloud over there." He was pointing to a large flat topped cumulonimbus nearby and without waiting for Ronald to answer, he veered the plane to the right and lined up to make a gentle landing on the cotton wool surface, cutting back the throttle until the engine was barely turning.

As the plane's belly touched the upper tendrils of cloud, Otto shouted, "Hold on for landing," then he cut the throttle completely, pulled back slightly on the control stick and the plane sank into the cloud, like a paper dart into a bath of milk.

In the next instant, with the wings denied the speed of the airflow to keep them aloft, the plane stalled, and, with a sickening shudder rolled onto its back and fell earthward like a stone, spinning round and round. Emerging through the base of the cloud as the ground reappeared below them, Ronald could feel his gorge beginning to rise while he could hear Otto, completely relaxed, hands folded lightly across his chest, counting "dreizehn, vierzehn, funfzehn" as the turns continued and the ground came ever closer.

In the eerie, wind-filled, upside-down silence, Ronald looked expectantly at Otto who smiled, winked and said, "Siebzehn, Achtzehn, eighteen, I think that's enough, don't you". Ronald heartily agreed, with the thought that if his grip on the hand-holds were any tighter he would surely crush them. In the next moment, Otto's hands and feet blended in perfect harmony to bring the tourer back into level flight at the edge of the airfield, while he carefully smoothed his hair back into place, before dropping the craft gently down, this time onto the smooth tarmac, saying, "This way is much more comfortable, don't you think," to Ronald's rather pale face. Ronald managed a weak smile and a nervous little laugh as his digestion settled and the colour returned to his knuckles.

"Your father tells me you want to be in your Royal Air Force like him, but as a pilot, so let me tell you this: Learn how to take a spin – it may save your life. It did mine in the last war and it might yet save yours," and at this he gave Ronald a long and knowing look.

"Always remember that as a fighter pilot your first duty is to survive. Survival is paramount. You can always get a new plane." How these words would come to echo down the years.

"You did really well. You have a natural touch. You will make a fine pilot, if that is what life brings to you. Shall we see how Hutch copes?" He had a mischievous grin on his face.

Once they were back at the hangar Ronald climbed out, stripped off the overalls, just slightly damp, and handed them to Hutch who by now was filled with trepidation, knowing what fate awaited him. He took the paper bag with a look on his face that suggested he feared he might be going to need it.

At this point Ronald realised that his legs were not working too well and so he flopped down onto the grass at the edge of the apron until he felt his strength returning. His father sauntered over, smiling, and knelt beside him, putting a fatherly hand on his shoulder.

"Sorry for not letting you in on the possibility that you might be having a flight with Otto, but he had wanted it to be a surprise provided the weather conditions were right. Although I have to admit that I had no idea Otto was going to indulge in such a display of aerobatics. He told me he usually keeps his plane at a small private airfield set in the Grunewald forest a few miles from home, but he transferred it here a couple of days ago just for you and Hutch. Mind you, I got the feeling that airfield is very private – perhaps for Party members only. Might explain…" He did not finish his thought.

Unsure why his father had gone off at such a tangent, but suitably impressed by the apparent honour, Ronald said faintly, "It's OK, Dad, it's fine." Alfred settled himself comfortably on the grass and they sat together watching intently while Otto repeated the routine for Hutch. Actually, Ronald felt worse for seeing the plane spinning down out of the underbelly of a cloud, and far worse when he saw just how close to the ground they had been before Otto pulled out of the spin. Moments later, Hutch was tumbling out of the passenger side, evidently trying to hide the fact that his paper bag was not entirely empty. "I swear to God I'll never do more than ten spins," was all he said, sheepishly. Since Hutch made no mention of being allowed to take the control, Ronald thought it prudent not to mention Otto's treat; he had no wish to upset his friend.

Otto then took them all to lunch in a small mess room inside the hangar, where he insisted that they all had a small Schnapps "to settle their tummies" before they ate. Ronald found his appetite remarkably robust and Hutch soon perked up and ate heartily. Otto was once again at his expansive best, regaling them with tales of combat from the Great War, "flying" the scenes of great aerial dog-fights in his mind's eye and with his hands as he talked. He talked of the loss of comrades and respect for those he had vanquished.

He talked openly of his own fear on realising that he was, in that final moment of his last sortie, outnumbered, outgunned, outflown and outmanoeuvred. He talked movingly of praying for a swift, pain-free end and then of his lesser, but different fear of being a prisoner of war, but out of which had come his enduring friendship with Alfred.

Then with lunch over and the table cleared by the mess orderlies, Otto took cigars from a humidor, which Alfred declined, lit one, and invited them outside to watch the test flight. Max promptly excused himself from the table and went off to change, returning ten minutes later dressed in a white flying suit and white leather flying helmet with a pair of goggles attached.

They waited patiently with Otto, as the engineers and mechanics fussed round the fighter, topping up the fuel from a bowser, coupling up a starter trolley and were in process of strapping Max into his seat, when, perhaps alerted by a distant sound, Otto suddenly whirled round and stared intently in the direction of the entrance gates almost a half mile distant. Without explanation, but with what sounded like an anguished cry, Otto ran from their side, dashed into the office nearby and returned moments later with a pair of powerful binoculars.

Speaking rapidly in German under his breath, he trained the binoculars on the entrance, then exclaimed, "My God! He's here! But he's not supposed to visit until tomorrow! If they had told me, I would not have brought any of you today. Do nothing, say nothing and stay over there by the car with Werner!" he ordered, pushing them all forcibly in Werner's direction as he spoke.

"The Führer is here!" were his parting words.

By now it was clear that a motorcade, led by three large black Mercedes, the first flying an official standard, was rapidly approaching. It was flanked by motorcycle outriders and two accompanying, open-backed trucks carrying, what appeared to be armed soldiers, the Führer's SS bodyguard.

The motorcade swept past and came to a halt near the fighter. The soldiers alighted, and, from the first truck, one ran forward to open the rear door of the leading Mercedes. Standing rigidly to attention, he saluted with arm raised as a man of medium build, dressed in uniform, stepped out and returned the salute with his hand, not outstretched, but held back as though he were taking an oath in court. His dark hair and small moustache were clearly visible.

To a resounding chorus of "Heil Hitler," the Führer strode away from the car and spoke briefly to the technicians, before addressing some comments to Otto, who responded with a small bow. Without a backward glance over his shoulder toward his English guests, Otto invited the Führer to accompany him to a row of chairs that had been hastily brought out from the hangar and set out on the far side of the fighter.

(Ronald still recalled vividly the jet black uniforms of the soldiers of the bodyguard and how, standing motionless at the rear of the row of chairs they formed a dark, and to Ronald even at fifteen, a foreboding backcloth to the Führer and his entourage.)

"Who's the top brass with Hitler?" Hutch asked Alfred, who thought for a few moments before replying.

"The portly one on the left of Mister Hitler is the head of the German Air Ministry, Herman Goering. The thin gentleman on Mr. Hitler's right is Joseph Goebels who is the head of Germany's Propaganda Ministry. Another one I think I recognise is the officer on Goering's left. Of course he doesn't officially exist since Germany doesn't officially have an Air Force, but that's Erhard Milch, head of the Luftwaffe."

Pointing discretely, Alfred drew their attention to the only man not in uniform and, speaking almost in a whisper, he added, "That's Mr Willy Messerschmitt, the designer of this aeroplane. Reginald Mitchell says he's absolutely brilliant. It looks as though they are planning to make some publicity out of today, especially with what is going on in Spain where the Luftwaffe is using the civil war as something of a proving ground."

Clearing his throat, he continued, "All of this is of course highly irregular and completely in breach of the Versailles Treaty, but we seem to have gone way beyond doing anything about it. More likely, this is about showing the world just how far they have come in restoring their military status. I think Germany has already made her intentions clear when she moved into the Rhineland earlier this year and the League of Nations said hardly a word against it." With that, he lapsed into silence. He was not renowned for long speeches.

Over to the left, one group of photographers was unloading and setting up cine equipment to record the occasion, while another photographer took pictures of the plane with its pilot from every angle.

Before long, the pre-flight checks were completed, the photographers were moved away while Max, who had been waiting all the while impatiently in the cockpit, received some last-minute instruction from a senior technician.

Once the starter trolley was connected, Ronald heard the rising whine of the starter motor, driving the propeller to turn slowly at first and then, to the accompaniment of blue smoke from the exhausts, the engine caught and settled to a steady beat. With the cockpit canopy securely closed, Max opened the throttle and taxied the fighter slowly away from the apron, whipping up a cloud of dust. The Führer shielded his eyes with a gloved hand.

Completing the run out to the main runway, the fighter paused as Max carried out final checks, then he was off at full throttle, getting airborne in less than two hundred and fifty yards and climbing steeply away to the south while he carried out a number of manoeuvres according to – as Otto confirmed later – a specially designed test programme. However, in view of the unexpected visit of the German leader, Otto also explained that programme had, of necessity, been simplified so that only the high speed flypasts were to be featured.

In fact, Max only made two runs at speed, one from the west and the other from the east, so as to give the photographers both profiles of the Messerschmitt. Everyone was completely taken aback by the speed at which Max brought the plane over the airfield at no more than thirty feet of altitude. He was reported to be travelling at over 400 miles per hour. The cine cameras whirred at high speed, tracking the aircraft as it roared past. On the second pass, the Führer stood abruptly and applauded enthusiastically, joined immediately by all the members of his party. Goering slapped one of his aides heartily on the back in celebration.

Reaching the end of the airfield, Max pulled up sharply, cut the throttle, using the steep climb to reduce his speed, and for good measure, he put in a couple of flick rolls as though to emphasise the agility of the aircraft, before turning to glide back, side-slipping the Messerschmitt into a perfect three point landing. He taxied round to the hangar where Otto stood, waiting nervously, to welcome him back.

As Max descended from the plane there was lively applause from the excited audience, once again led by the Führer. There was a general air amongst the dignitaries and Otto's staff of a job well done. Despite the warning glance from his father, Ronald took the opportunity to sneak a snapshot of the occasion.

Otto then introduced Max to the Führer, who nodded his head from time to time as Max described the test flight, with animated gestures. At one point in their conversation, Max fluttered his hand and pointed to the rear of the fighter. The Führer listened intently, head cocked slightly to one side, completely absorbed in the detail. Then, after making some observation for which an aide made an immediate written note, he shook Max by the hand, before moving back to allow Max to salute. The Führer acknowledged in his own manner.

As the Führer turned to walk back to his limousine, he appeared to notice, for the first time, the small group of civilian onlookers standing to one side and immediately headed in their direction. Striding purposefully, he had the look of a man intent on speaking to them, and left his staff trailing in his wake.

"Christ!" said Hutch. "Get rid of the camera!" said Alfred, so Ronald reached discretely over the side of the car and gently placed the camera on the rear seat, praying it was out of sight. By the driver's door, Werner stood rigidly to attention, eyes fixed on a point in the far distance.

The Führer's simple light brown tunic was unadorned except for an Iron Cross medal clipped to the left breast pocket. Ronald noted that his plain, unpatterned tie was held neatly in place by a small gold pin, fashioned as an eagle, open winged, gripping a circular wreath in its talon, which was fixed just below the knot. His left sleeve bore a swastika arm-band above the elbow. His high-peaked cap, with red cap band, cast his eyes into deep shadow.

"Let me do any talking," insisted Ronald's father, but it soon became evident that they were not expected to speak. In the background, Ronald could see Goering wagging his finger at Otto, although any reprimand did not seem to be too severe. In fact, Goering seemed to point directly at Alfred and nodded slowly as Otto responded. Ronald thought he appeared satisfied with Otto's explanation, because the exchange concluded with Goering shaking Otto firmly by the hand before a formal salute.

In the meantime, the Führer had removed his cap, which he tucked under his left arm, and came to each of them in turn to shake their hand. Speaking through an interpreter, said in a deep voice which seemed to come from the back of his throat, "Welcome to Germany, welcome to the Greater German Reich. We welcome all our visitors from abroad, especially our friends from England."

Ronald was particularly struck by his intense, unwavering gaze and, as the Führer shook his hand, he dipped into his limited knowledge of the German language and said hesitantly, "Danke Schon". The Führer smiled broadly and responded with the faintest nod of his head, "Bitte Schon, mein junge", patting him lightly on the shoulder in a paternal way, before placing himself between Ronald and his father to pose for a publicity photograph. The photographer duly obliged, working quickly so as not to delay the Führer unnecessarily.

Then, without a further word or a glance, The Führer left them, brushing his hair back with his hand as he replaced his cap. Flanked by his bodyguard, re-entered his Mercedes. The driver had already erected the black canvas roof for the journey back to the Reich Chancellery in the heart of Berlin. The convoy departed at once, to leave them alone once more with Otto, who seemed to be having some difficulty in breathing.

Eventually he calmed and gasped, "I had some explaining to do, but, thank goodness, our Führer has a reputation for admiring young people, else I could have had a lot more explaining to do," and he smiled weakly in an effort to restore his normally urbane manner.

Then he continued, "As I said, he was not supposed to be here until tomorrow, but I was not told of any change to his schedule. What I had not told you was that we are also experimenting with an additive to the aviation fuel which can give a power boost. Today was supposed to be a rehearsal for tomorrow's official test."

Seeing Alfred's raised eyebrow, Otto added, "We are trying a mixture of water and methanol which is injected into the cylinders with the petrol. No it doesn't make the engine go rusty inside," he added, noticing Ronald's puzzled look, "but it does help cool the cylinders, so we can get more power."

"In fact," he added, lowering his voice in a conspiratorial way "just today, Max reported that the boost had pushed the speed, for a few seconds, to over 680 kilometres per hour, that's 425 miles per hour, but he thought there might be a little problem with the tail plane at these high speeds, so we may have to add some bracing. Nevertheless, it's nearly a hundred of your miles per hour faster than your Spitfire, Freddy," he concluded, looking directly at Ronald's father as though trying to send him a message.

Alfred, who appeared to look not in the least interested, merely said, "Oh, really, Otto, I wouldn't know." Otto gave him a most sceptical look in return and seemed to be about to make a comment, but then his face cleared, and, with a broad smile on his face, he shouted to Max, who was still standing by the aeroplane, that they would be returning home. Max responded, "See you at the party," with a cheery wave as he turned to supervise the Messerschmitt being taken back into its hangar.

Otto ushered them all back into the car saying, "Home James," to Werner who clearly did not understand the joke and looked a little offended when everyone laughed, and was only mollified when Otto explained at some length in German.

As they left the airfield, and noticing Ronald's and Hutch's backward glances, Otto nudged each of them in the ribs saying, "I will keep an eye on the papers – you might be famous."

Much to their surprise, two days later, on the second page of the Berliner Zeitung, there was their photograph under the caption "Our

Führer welcomes visitors from England" with a short article describing the technical achievements of the special flight programme. It went on to say that the Führer was looking forward to welcoming many more visitors from around the world when he attended the opening ceremony for the forthcoming Olympic Games.

Even more surprising was the arrival at the house, late the following day by special courier, of an official envelope, bearing the seal of the Reichs Informations Ministerium, the Propaganda Ministry. Addressed personally to Herr Alfred Wallace, it contained half a dozen glossy copies of the photograph at the airfield, each signed on the back "Adolf Hitler 25 Juli 1936".

Alfred doubted that the signature was really the Führer's, and suggested it was probably a good facsimile done by a secretary, but Ronald naturally preferred to think otherwise. Ronald tucked his copy into the back of his travel diary, a small school exercise book rather grandly titled 'Expedition to Germany', in which he was carefully recording the details of their holiday. The events of the 22nd July occupied three full pages.

CHAPTER 14

As Max had said, Otto's sister, Margheritta, and her daughter Regina arrived by train the next day July 23rd from their home in East Prussia. Werner collected them from the Bornholmer Station in the north of the city with the open topped Mercedes. The weather was so warm there was no thought of erecting the hood.

Margheritta was tall and slim, her hair prematurely greying and she looked as though she was over-burdened with the cares of her life, following the death of her husband.

Regina was, by contrast, nearly as tall, but with a beautiful complexion, long flowing brown hair and a vivacious personality. Her deep set brown eyes, long eyelashes and sensuous, full lips gave her an appearance which reminded everyone of the popular film actress Greta Garbo. Max persistently pulled his sister's leg, suggesting that she should be going into films rather, as he put it, teasing her as only a brother may, than wasting her time messing around with horses. Films, he insisted, were the new entertainment medium for the German people. Regina merely blushed at the suggestion that she was pretty enough to be a film actress, and said that he was just being fanciful, but everyone could see that a small part of her was flattered by the notion as she stretched her arms up into an exaggerated film star pose.

Hutch for his part, was instantly smitten by her beauty and seemed to find any excuse to be in her company. She too appeared to find his attentions acceptable as the days went by, and they chatted in the limited vocabulary of each other's language. Ronald's father tutted, muttering something about holiday romances usually being doomed to fail.

The Danish side of the family, the Iversens, arrived the next day, Werner meeting them at the main station on the east of the Alexanderplatz and conveying them home in the Mercedes. Still the weather held fair.

Elise had prepared another of her special meals to celebrate the occasion and spent most of the morning fussing round the house, rearranging a chair, plumping up a cushion, arranging fresh flowers until everything was to her satisfaction.

Wolfgang and Dieter were under strict instruction not to be late home from their activities with the Hitler Jugend and Otto was placed under a sentence akin to the pain of death if he were late. Nothing was to spoil the plans for Elise's reunion with her sister, whom she had not seen for almost two years.

In fact, Otto was as good as his word and personally provided an escort to the Mercedes as he drove home in his small yellow two-seater Opel roadster. A great tooting of car-horns announced their arrival in the late afternoon.

Elise, who had been checking the driveway through the glazed hall door, it seemed every two minutes since lunch time, whilst trying to retain an air of cool detachment, flew out of the door and down the steps and into her sister's arms, hardly had the wheels of the Mercedes stopped turning. The two women hugged and kissed, laughing and crying in the pleasure of their meeting, while the English boys and the German boys gathered at the top of the steps in nervous anticipation.

Anna Iversen, Elise's sister could have been her twin, tall and blonde, her hair worn long and tied back in a brightly coloured silk scarf. Her husband Peder had not been able to accompany them because it was approaching harvest time on their farm. Her daughter, Karin, a brunette, was petite with sparkling eyes and gave Ronald a shy smile as they were introduced.

Svenn, her older brother, was equally as blonde as his mother, with an athletic build, but to Ronald's way of thinking, Svenn had an intensity of manner that he found slightly unsettling. Svenn, on the other hand, hit it off immediately with Wolfgang and Dieter after he complimented them on their Hitler Jugend uniforms.

With the introductions completed, Elise and Otto ushered everyone indoors, allocated the newcomers to their rooms and bade everyone be ready to assemble for dinner within the hour.

The evening proved to be a huge success, except for one event which cast a shadow that could not quite be erased.

Elise had excelled herself in the kitchen to honour her sister's visit, producing a range of Danish dishes including pickled herrings as an entrée, and for the main course, a large silverside of beef with pickled cabbage and caramelised potatoes. Otto matched her step for step with wines to complement the courses – a 1921 Niersteiner

Oelberg Orleans Spatlese for the starter, followed by a magnificent Burgundy, a 1920 Chateau Mouton Rothchild for the main.

Bottles of champagne, a Krug 1928, stood on the sideboard, chilling slowly on ice, in readiness for the toasts at the end of the meal.

Werner was in his element, fussing round the guests to ensure their glasses were kept topped up, chivvying the two maids who had been enrolled for the night to serve the courses, smiling ever more broadly as the evening progressed. From where he was seated, Ronald could just see that Werner had his own supply of liquid refreshment, from which he kept himself topped up whenever he had the need or opportunity to leave the room. At one point Werner caught Ronald's glance and gave him a broad wink to buy his silence.

At the far end of the table, Svenn, sitting with Wolfgang and Dieter, spent most of the evening deep in conversation with them almost to the point of rudeness, completely ignoring his other cousins. Wolfgang on the other hand did his best to engage in conversation with Hutch, and as the evening wore on seemed to relish his newly formed role as a go-between for Hutch and Regina, even though it appeared to Ronald that Hutch was managing quite nicely on his own.

Otto was the perfect host, taking Ronald under his wing, interpreting as much of the flow of conversation as he could so that Ronald felt not the least bit isolated or left out. The sense of family was very strong. Elise, whose knowledge of English was limited to a few phrases, devoted much of her attention to Alfred, grateful that his use of German was almost fluent, even though, in his words, he was still a bit rusty. Her favourite phrase seemed to be that Alfred was 'her perfect English Gentleman' and Ronald thought that there was just the tiniest bit of flirting as she steadily drew him out of the typical English reserve. Gradually Alfred's German was unlocked and Ronald found himself in the odd position of looking to Otto for an interpretation of what his own father was saying.

Once Otto appreciated the irony he roared with laughter, slapping his hand onto the table to attract Alfred's attention and telling him that he, Otto, now appointed himself personal Dollmetsch – Interpreter – between father and son! Alfred blushed, realising how deeply he had been in conversation with Elise to the exclusion of all others, but he took the leg-pulling in good spirit. Otto then interpreted for Elise, who laughed happily and again the sense of family washed over Ronald.

Seeing that everyone had finished eating, Otto signalled to Werner to open the champagne. With a practised hand Werner carefully removed the foil cap before releasing the wire cage that held the cork in place. Wrapping a white napkin round the body of the bottle, he deftly twisted the bottle against the cork until the cork slipped from the bottle with a soft pop and then poured just a drop into each glass. This way stops the glass overflowing, Otto explained, so that not a drop of the precious liquid should be wasted as Werner filled each glass almost to the brim. It was after all, a Krug 28 – as though that put it into the premier class – and Otto put the tips of his right hand together, pressed them to his lips and blew a kiss, opening his hand to emphasise the superb quality.

The toasts began to flow, "Skal" from Denmark, "Cheers" from Ronald's father, each time everyone standing to hold their glasses aloft, the golden, bubbling liquid and the crystal flutes flashing in the light from the silver candelabra on the table and the teardrop chandeliers above. Hutch followed Otto's "Prost" with a cheeky "Bottoms up", which he had to explain, much to the amusement of all. Regina, sitting across the table from Hutch, giggled and blushed. Ronald was pondering what might be his choice of toast when Svenn stood stiffly, a little drunkenly, raised his glass and said, "Heil Hitler."

For a second there was a stunned silence, hands and glasses stilled in mid air, a frozen tableau, before Otto rescued the situation, speaking quietly, "No, Svenn, this is not a formal occasion for a Führer toast – this is just family and friends together, so I think, don't you that we should all stand together and drink to Freunden und Familie, Family and Friends."

Rising from the table, he went to the door and shouted a request to Werner who appeared shortly bearing a small silver tray laden with shot glasses ranged around the edge. Balanced in the centre, was a tall bottle filled with a clear liquid which it appeared had only that instant been removed from an ice cabinet, as the exterior was rapidly condensing to frost.

Werner placed a glass in front of each guest without exception and filled each glass to the brim with the viscous liquid.

Then with a broad smile breaking the tension, Otto invited them all to stand. Glasses raised, each family spoke the toast in their own language, then downed the shot in one gulp to Otto's accompanying cry of, "Down the hatch."

"Wow!" said Hutch in a hoarse voice as the cold of the Schnapps turned to fire in his throat. "Double wow!" said Ronald, not to be outdone and the ladies giggled. Any embarrassment at Svenn's faux pas evaporated like the fumes from the alcohol and the friendly, intimate atmosphere was restored.

Next, Otto, with tears in his eyes, walked once more round the table and kissed each person, man and boy, woman and girl, as a father might kiss a child, even Ronald's father, who looked completely taken aback, saying, his voice breaking with emotion, "I want us all to remember this special evening, whatever happens."

Later, years later, Ronald came to realise that Otto had a very clear view of what was to happen in the ensuing four or five years, and that for all his bonhomie, Otto's status within the Nazi Party was very much more senior than he had lead everyone to believe.

Equally, it appeared, with the benefit of hindsight, that Otto had done everything he could that night to link them all with a bond of friendship which might survive the oncoming tide of war. In part, as they were to discover long beyond his lifetime, Otto had perhaps, succeeded beyond his wildest dreams.

On July 28th, with only three days to go to the opening of the Olympics, Otto announced over breakfast that he and Elise had arranged to hold a party for the whole family and some special friends and guests at the house that night. He gave strict instructions that everyone should stay well clear of the lounge and dining room, which were to be laid up in readiness for dinner.

Shortly afterwards, a coach arrived at the house, disgorging two dozen boys from the Hitler Jugend who set about, under Werner's instruction, removing all unnecessary furniture and then setting up an extended rectangle of tables which were covered with white damask cloths. Still under Werner's instruction, they laid the tables with the finest crockery, cutlery and glassware, fit for the banquet.

Much to their surprise, Otto returned during the afternoon with dinner jackets for Hutch, Ronald and Alfred, explaining that he had taken the liberty of obtaining measurements for their clothes, so that their evening attire could be in keeping with the other guests.

As the day wore on, catering vans arrived and delivered supplies for the kitchen, under the watchful eye of Elise and the watchful tongue of Werner such that by late afternoon preparations for the party were all complete. Werner had excelled himself with all the arrangements and, at one point, had been seen adjusting the lay-up of the table with a measuring stick to ensure absolute perfection. The doors in the glass wall to the garden were thrown open to admit the warm, mid-summer evening air.

Job done, Werner wandered the house with a look of triumph on his face and invited, no, insisted that anyone who had a moment to spare, should inspect his handiwork. The glassware for wine, red, white and champagne gleamed, the cutlery shone, the napkins were tied in blue ribbon and four elegant candelabra were evenly spaced down the centre of the table. His finishing touch was the setting of miniature, silver flagpoles, each no more than twelve inches high, one flying the red and white for Denmark, then the red white and blue of the Union Flag in honour of the English guests, but at the centre of the table he had placed a double staff, flying, on one side the black red and yellow of the historic German flag while on the other side flew the swastika. "Die neue," – the new one, Werner said to Ronald with obvious pride in his voice.

With an hour to go, Otto banished everyone to their rooms to dress. Ronald struggled with the unfamiliar starched shirt and its pearl studs, almost failed to attach the stiff wing collar, but his father came to his rescue with the tying of the formal black bow-tie. Hutch required similar assistance with the tie, but later, as they waited nervously downstairs, Regina took more than a couple of moments to straighten Hutch's tie. Ronald was fairly sure he had seen Hutch surreptitiously twist it out of position as they walked downstairs. Any excuse, it seemed, to be close to Regina. She kissed him playfully on the tip of his nose once she was satisfied with the result. Hutch grinned with pleasure.

At the due hour, Otto and Elise positioned themselves in the hallway near the front door to welcome their guests, who would be formally announced by Werner. Although dressed in a stylishly cut evening suit with full tails, Otto wore, at his throat under a high wing collar his Iron Cross on its black silk ribbon, edged in white. The beam on his face could not have been broader.

Gradually the guests began to arrive, the first being Max accompanied by his girlfriend, a beautiful blonde film actress in a fabulous black and silver full length gown with a plunging neckline, which attracted everyone's attention throughout the evening. Max brought with him the formal apologies of Reichsmarshall Hermann Goering and his wife Emmy – affairs of state sadly had to take precedence, but in return there was an invitation for Otto and Alfred to visit him at his country manor *Carinhall* which was set in the forests some twenty miles north-east of Berlin if time permitted during Alfred's stay. Otto beamed and Alfred, while looking flustered, asked Max to convey his thanks to the Reichsmarshall. It was all very formal and again Ronald was surprised by his father's fluency. Werner, thinking he might be about to drive to the country home of the head of the Luftwaffe, already renowned for its elegance and the opulence of its fittings, looked fit to burst.

Then, realising the implication as to the guest list for the night, he quickly instructed two of the oldest boys from the Hitler Jugend to remove the two settings on the dining table at the end next to where Elise would sit and to rearrange the entire table. Elise could barely hide her disappointment, but just before they sat down to dinner, Ronald again saw Werner with his stick meticulously checking the revised placings. Elise's face visibly brightened when she saw the results of Werner's attention to detail, presuming perhaps a little prematurely that she was included in the Reichmashall's invitation.

Other guests arrived: a banker, an industrialist, two from Otto's Air Ministry, the head of a construction company, an exotic dancer (or actress as she preferred to be called), a film maker – all accompanied by their wives, or partners. All were attired in evening wear and all were brought from their homes to the house by a fleet of official chauffeur-driven limousines, ordered at great expense by Otto on his business account at the Air Ministry. A complement of forty-six sat down to dinner with Elise at the head of the table.

Alfred was seated halfway down. Ronald had the impression that the seating plan was not entirely random as he noticed that the two gentlemen from the Air Ministry were seated opposite, and next to his father was a large, somewhat overweight industrialist who talked loudly the whole evening.

Hutch, although expressing disappointment at not being next to Regina, found that he was opposite Max's girlfriend and, as the night wore on, it appeared he did not mind too much.

Ronald's companions were Karin to his left and Max to his right so that he was a couple of places down the table from Hutch, but he was still able to converse.

At one point, Max leaned over to Ronald and whispered, "You thought my name was a bit of a mouthful, but how about the gentleman sitting near my uncle?" He nodded towards the far end of the table. "He is, to give him his full title, Claus Phillip Maria Schenk Graf von Stauffenberg. That's his wife Nina sitting opposite." Ronald looked down the table to see a man of medium build in his late twenties, dark haired with fine features, dressed in an evening suit of a military cut, and deep in conversation with Otto. The Grafin, Nina, an attractive blonde haired lady of a similar age was listening intently.

Max continued. "He is a brilliant officer and Uncle Otto expects great things of him. He is going up to the Military Academy here in Berlin this autumn. He is from a very old German family, part of the aristocracy. I'm only very minor," he added with a laugh.

Ronald wanted to tell his father, but Alfred was too far away to engage in conversation and Ronald felt he looked rather isolated, but as the drinks flowed and the evening wore on, he could see that his father was becoming quite animated.

Max was kind enough to interpret some of the exchanges that were flowing round the table which were mostly about the state of the economy or the forthcoming Olympics, which a small man near Ronald pronounced the best thing to have happened to his business – ever. Max explained that this gentleman owned a building company that had the contract to build the Olympic village to house the competitors and was faring very well from the project financially.

From time to time comments were expressed, aimed apparently at Alfred's ears, applauding Germany's progress since the National Socialist party came to power and it was as this point Ronald realised that almost without exception the men around the table wore a badge in their lapel to indicate their membership of the Party. Universally, they acclaimed the election of Adolf Hitler as the country's leader to be a very good thing.

Ronald found some of this very hard to absorb and was thankful he was excluded from most of this conversation. Hutch, however, when pressed about his future plans, declared that he intended to join the Royal Air Force.

"Ah yes," came a sneering put-you-down comment. "Those little biplanes with such silly romantic names." It was intended to embarrass him, but Max came to his rescue saying, "Not at all, the RAF has its Hurricane fighter, a bit slower than our 109, and now it has its Spitfire, which one day might be a match, so that's two to one of ours". Then he added, "We are doing our best to keep ahead, as our Führer saw last week." There was much nodding of heads around the table as he repeated himself in German.

From the head of the table, Elise, who looked radiant in a blue off-the-shoulder ball gown, a pearl choker set with diamonds at her throat, clapped her hands and said, "No more politics – this is a very special night with very special guests," indicating all the visitors, "so I want you to talk about beautiful things, holidays, travel, and, of course, the weather for our English friends," laughter round the table, "but no more politics. I insist," as she flashed her most charming smile.

"Yes, of course, my darling," came Otto's voice obediently from the far end of the table.

For this night at least, the word of Elise was law. Gradually the direction of the conversation changed to lighter topics. In a bizarre twist, as the night wore on and the champagne started to have its effect, Ronald found himself being pressed to provide an explanation of that most English of sports, cricket.

The more he tried to explain, with Max struggling to translate, indeed even to find appropriate German words to reflect the nuances of the game, the more unintelligible it all became. Eventually Max had to admit defeat as he failed to comprehend Ronald's description of who was in and who was out, or why. But the guests were still not satisfied and to a shouted chorus of "Show us", Ronald found himself bowling the length of the dining-room with a bread roll to Hutch, who stood in front of a set of stumps created from a candelabra and newly lit long-stem candles. He improvised by batting with a coal shovel hastily located by Werner, while Alfred acted as wicketkeeper.

For the next half hour, chaos ensued as bread rolls were batted the length and breadth of the room with everyone clamouring to bat or bowl. Even Elise hitched up her voluminous skirt when it became her turn at the stumps and screamed with hilarity when she struck her "ball" straight into the lap of the overweight industrialist, who promptly ate it.

With the midnight hour approaching, and carriages due, Elise announced that it had been the best evening of her life and had then proceeded to give Alfred a long and lingering kiss for being, as she put it, a real sport and gentleman. Actually, Ronald saw a completely different side to his father that night, almost flirtatious, extraordinarily sociable and who was about to spring the biggest surprise of Ronald's short life.

As the last of the guests departed, save for Max, his girlfriend and the "actress", Ronald was about to head off to his bedroom when Otto called him back and next thing, still in their evening attire, they were all seated in the limousines and on their way for, as Otto insisted on calling it, a bit of adult fun.

The "fun", after a half hour drive into the city centre, the warmth of the day still lingering, was a visit to the Friedrichstadtpalast, a music hall akin to the Folies Bergere of Paris with a nude review, singers and dancers, where Marlene Dietrich had once been the featured vocalist. The resident chanteuse entranced the audience with Marlene's signature song – Lili Marlene.

As if that were not enough, and by this time his father was more inebriated than Ronald had ever seen, Otto and Alfred went up on stage at the very end of the show. Surrounded by some of the loveliest girls, they sang, both of them passable tenors, arm in arm, a selection of wartime ballads from the trenches, two former enemies once again, if only temporarily, linked in friendship.

The audience, many of them old enough to have sung for real in the squalor of the trenches twenty years before, hummed the tunes from the heart, gently, with a deeply-felt emotion. As the final notes faded away, Otto and Alfred took their bow and embraced while the audience, nearly three thousand strong roared their approval, pounding on the tables and stamping on the floor.

However, it was not quite over. As the uproar subsided and the audience began to think about leaving, from the gods of the theatre came a single voice, a fine baritone striking out with the words of a song which went to the psyche of both nations: Stille Nacht, Heilige Nacht – Silent Night, Holy Night. One by one other voices, all male, perhaps those who had sung in the trenches, Christmas after Christmas to make contact with their loved ones, melded together so that the ensemble became a wave of emotion swelling and filling the auditorium. The ladies remained silent; it was not their time. At the end, there was complete silence while the audience filed quietly away.

Ronald knew he would never see the like ever again.

The next morning it was obvious that Alfred had a monumental headache. He sat at the dining table, in a dining room only partly tidied from the excesses of the previous evening, head in hands, groaning quietly. His condition was not helped when Otto, fresh as a daisy, thumped him on the back by way of a good morning greeting.

Ronald and Hutch tried to coax him into drinking some coffee and eating a little food, but he resisted and instead pulled both of them toward him by the scruff of the neck, holding them close and saying in a voice reduced to a hoarse whisper, "Last night never happened. It is our secret. Mother must never know. Promise!"

Only once during his time in Berlin did Ronald see Otto in uniform. It occurred a night or so before the opening ceremony for the Olympics. Ronald heard the sound of the Opel Coupe being started in the underground garage by Werner, the car's tuned exhaust rumbling and reverberating through the house.

Thinking he might get a short ride in the car, Ronald wandered out of the lounge and was heading toward the front door along the curved hallway when he came across Otto, who was standing in front of a full length mirror, part of a chromium-plated hat-stand, next to the door.

Otto was dressed in a jet black uniform, black Sam Brown belt, highly polished calf length boots and an officer's peaked cap with silver braiding. Above the peak, on the band, was fixed a silver cap badge in the form of a death's head skull surmounted by a winged eagle. The high collar of his jacket was embroidered with twin lightning flashes and hanging at his throat, on a blue and red ribbon was a black iron cross topped with a small sprig of oak leaves. Fastened to his left hip was a small black and silver ceremonial dagger.

Realising that he was being observed, Otto turned slowly to face him and with a broad smile on his face, bowed slightly from the waist and said, "What do you think, young Ronald? Smart, eh?" as he continued to straighten his tunic. "I was awarded this for my service... last time," he added, fingering the iron cross.

Somewhat nonplussed, and finding the blackness of the uniform rather oppressive, uncertain of what reply to make, Ronald responded, "Otto, are you a Nazi?"

"If by that, you mean am I a member of the NSDAP, the National Socialist Party of Germany, then, yes, of course. We all are – to show our solidarity with our leader who is giving us back our pride, our respect. I even have a badge of membership," pointing to a small enamel badge pinned to the left breast pocket. "Mine was given to me personally by our Führer many years ago," he added, beaming with obvious pride. "S.S. Obergruppenfuhrer Otto Hecker at your service, young Ronald."

The conversation went no further. Ronald heard a soft footfall behind him, and turning slightly, could see out of the corner of his eye, his father hidden from Otto's view by the curve of the hall.

Ronald was about to speak, but his father silenced him with a finger to his lips, before turning on his heel and walking quietly away, shaking his head.

With a click of his heels and a barely perceptible nod of his head, Otto was gone, striding down the front steps to jump into his roadster, spinning the wheels just a little as he drove away – ever the showman. They never spoke of his membership of the Nazi party or his war service medal again, but on that point, Ronald was left wondering whether, when Otto referred to the 'last time' he had in mind that there might be a 'next time'.

Ronald sighed. Berlin at its best or at its worst, but either way there never was another night like it. Despite the events that unfolded over the next few years, he treasured the memories of that night, a time when he probably felt closer to his father than at any other, and closer too, if he dare admit it, in a confusing conflict of emotion to the spirit of the German people.

He remembered how, during the cricket match, Claus von Stauffenberg had introduced himself, bowing stiffly from the waist, bringing his heels together with the faintest of clicks. Ronald had noticed that he was not wearing a Party badge and had been about to ask if he were a Party member, when the drift of conversation took them in different directions. As it turned out, in the coming years, these were different directions which led, eventually, to the same end.

But ultimately, the injunction, *Befehl ist Befehl had* applied on both sides of the divide.

Then, as he held the diary gently trying not to damage the pages, while he reflected on the events of more than half a lifetime ago, another thought struck him. He, his father and Hutch had been together for the whole of the holiday, except that is, he now remembered, one afternoon, (was it the day before he saw Otto in uniform? – he could not quite remember and his diary was no help) when Otto offered to take Alfred out for a spin in his Opel roadster. In his limited experience at the time, a spin meant half an hour, an hour at the most, but they were gone for the best part of half a day. And not a word of explanation on their return, save that Alfred looked troubled and preoccupied for the rest of the day. Had they indeed gone to *Carinhall*? And if they had, what then? Another secret carried to the grave? Thinking back, although nothing was said, perhaps a clue lay in Elise's demeanour at dinner that night. It was, after all, the only time he had seen any tension between Otto and

Elise, but that night she was definitely miffed about something and made her feelings quite plain. Otto had done his best to placate her and the next day a very large bouquet of flowers had been specially delivered to the house. A peace offering? He would never know.

CHAPTER 15

On Saturday August 1st, just as they were finishing an early lunch, Otto levered himself up from his chair at the head of the extended dining table, clapped his hands, and announced, with a big smile on his face,

"Right, children, time to get ready, I think. Will you please be ready and assemble not a minute later than 1.45 pm at the front door. The cars will arrive at precisely that moment and anyone late will not be taken to the Stadium. It's only a ten minute drive and we need to be in our seats by 3.00 pm Now, off you go," and so saying he shooed everyone from the dining room, overriding the protests of the one or two that had not finished their coffee.

Ronald and Hutch both changed into white flannel trousers, in fact their cricketing trousers, but smart enough for the occasion, blue blazers with silver buttons for Ronald and gold coloured for Hutch. They debated about wearing ties but in the end settled for leaving their shirts open-necked. When Ronald commented that they looked like Tweedle Dum and Tweedle Dee, Hutch fetched out a dark red cravat and tied it skilfully at his throat.

"There," he declared, "at least we will know who is Dum and who is Dee," looking straight at Ronald with a laugh.

As they left their room to go downstairs they bumped into Ronald's father who was formally attired in a dark suit, white shirt, dark blue spotted tie and a matching kerchief in his breast pocket. His one concession to informality was a cream panama hat, carried in his left hand and which he had borrowed from Otto to protect his bald patch.

"Goodness, Dad," said Ronald, "you'll be boiled in that," for indeed it held the promise a very warm afternoon once the morning's drizzle cleared away.

"I know," Alfred responded in a resigned tone, "but we must keep up standards. At least the hat will help keep a cool head." There was something in the way he said it that made Ronald suspect that he was not referring only to his own personal comfort.

Downstairs, they found they were the last to be ready. Otto was in another of his smart, pale lounge suits and all of the ladies had opted for lightweight colourful summer dresses with broad brimmed hats to keep them cool. Regina looked more beautiful than ever, so Hutch said later, and had completed her ensemble with a pair of white silk gloves and a delicate red, white and blue foulard tied as a bandana around the brim of her hat; the colours of England, which Hutch was convinced were a subtle message, directed at him personally.

Both Wolfgang and Dieter were dressed in the uniform of the Hitler Jugend – grey full length socks, black trousers and white shirt with a black scarf. Each wore an enamel badge for the youth movement.

Elise also wore a small enamelled badge, triangular in shape, which featured, on a black background, a white cross with a tiny red swastika at its centre, for the League of National Socialist Women and she pinned a similar badge on to her sister-in-law's blouse saying, "There, Margheritta. That's better. You ladies from the east are yet to catch up with the fashion, so this makes you an honorary member." Ronald's father raised an eyebrow.

It took three large Mercedes limousines, each with its Swastika pennant on the front mudguard, to transport the fourteen that made up their party. Ronald travelled with Otto, Elise and his father. Hutch very niftily edged into the group which included Karin and Regina, sitting between them on the back seat grinning from ear to ear. Karin's mother Anna sat as chaperone to ensure no hanky-panky on the way to the stadium, laughing happily at her use of the English vernacular.

They set off in high spirits, away down the long winding drive, Otto standing up in the front passenger seat of the leading car shouting "Wagons Roll" at the top of his voice and patting Werner on the head as he did so. Werner looked not the least bit amused, but led the convoy off at a steady pace out onto the Heerstrasse and westwards toward the Olympic Stadium.

True to Otto's word, the drive took barely fifteen minutes and hardly ruffled the dresses and hairdos of the ladies, Werner being under strict instruction not to exceed thirty kilometres per hour at any time "for their greater comfort".

Driving into the stadium complex, they were immediately directed by a uniformed official to a large parking area and Otto instructed Werner to drive through to a cordoned-off area for the "V.I.P's" as he put it.

Ronald stared up in amazement at the recently completed stadium. Otto explained with some relish, that although Germany had not been awarded the 11th Summer Olympiad until 1931 and the building programme had immediately become mired in the bureaucratic maze of the old government, as soon as the Führer had become Chancellor in 1933, he had personally cut through all the red tape which seemed to be choking the project. He ordered that the one hundred thousand seat stadium be completed on time, irrespective of budget.

Germany was just recovering from the Depression Years. The Führer had championed the games as a vehicle for the country's re-generation, for increased employment and for national pride. He also expected, demanded, that the cream of German athletes must excel in all areas against international competition.

Flourishing a sheaf of official passes held high in his hand, Otto shepherded his little flock quickly through the admission formalities at the spectators' entrance on the southern side of the huge three storey amphitheatre.

Ronald continued to be surprised at the number of times that Otto was officially recognised and acknowledged with a German salute, but it was beginning to become increasingly obvious to him that Otto's status within the German political and military hierarchy was rather more than he had originally indicated. For his part Otto responded to the salutes with a brief half-raising of his right arm and a dismissive, "Yes, yes, that will do for now."

As they travelled through the internal corridors of the stadium, being swept slowly along with the tide of spectators, and ascending two levels toward their seats, they passed rows of souvenir stands, all of which were selling memorabilia for the Olympic Games. For a few pfennigs less than one Reich mark, Ronald bought himself a small, silvered, rectangular badge featuring the five Olympic rings highlighted in coloured enamels. The year, 1936, was split to either end of the bar, between raised oak leaves. When he pinned it to his lapel, Otto gave him a thumbs-up, which rather pleased him, especially as his own father had pooh-poohed the expense.

A minute later, he found that Hutch had bought a similar badge and watched with amusement as Hutch presented it to Regina as a gift. She smiled shyly, but when Hutch pinned carefully it to her blouse, she thanked him with a kiss planted lightly on his cheek, though her lips seemed to linger for just a fraction longer. Hutch was left with the softest grin on his face, and he too was rewarded with a discrete thumbs-up from Otto, who was now thoroughly enjoying his role of patron, tour-guide and benevolent uncle to all.

Much later, Hutch had confided that, just before they returned home from Berlin, he had used a penknife to scratch a linked H and R on to the back of the badge, to symbolise their love.

Still leading the way, Otto took them up one more flight of stairs, while the sounds from the crowd, competing with announcements over the loudspeaker system, grew ever greater.

Then they were ushered through a rectangular archway, stepping out on to a broad deck from which gangways led down to the seating area. Only at that moment did Ronald fully appreciate that their seats were immediately adjacent and just behind the section which was reserved for the Olympic dignitaries. A uniformed steward stepped forward and, after checking the remaining documents still held by Otto, he led them down to their reserved seats, which were in a block, not fifty feet from the podium with its battery of microphones, grouped around a lectern at the front.

"Good seats, don't you think?" said Otto as he settled himself between Ronald, on his left, and his father on the front row. Ronald turned to find Regina in the seat immediately behind him with Hutch making himself comfortable next to her. He gave Ronald a broad wink. In the row behind, Elise was in animated conversation with Regina's mother.

"Yes, fantastic," replied Ronald as he struggled to make himself heard. In fact, he hardly knew what to say, so overwhelmed was he by the spectacle. The stadium was almost filled to its capacity – he had never seen so many people in one place, so many dressed in uniforms, both military and as part of the country's administration. He could not help but contrast the spectacle, which now surrounded him, with the air show at Hendon just a month previously, where uniforms had hardly been in evidence at all.

And then there were the banners, by the dozen, perhaps by the hundred, all around the stadium, twenty and thirty feet tall, row upon row, regimented like a crimson-red forest to aggrandise the swastika. Here and there, seemingly by way only of a reminder, a concession to its honourable origins, flew the white flag of the Olympics with its five colourful rings.

Overhead, a huge Zeppelin airship hovered, tailfin emblazoned with the swastika, its six engines holding it on station, their drone adding to the general level of noise. For a time, it was so low over the stadium that Ronald had a clear view of the passenger car slung under its belly and could easily see a film crew recording the event, as newsreel, for distribution to the cinemas across the world.

A tap on his right shoulder attracted his attention, and he turned to find his father, leaning over behind Otto's back to whisper, "Those things used to give me the creeps last time. They went so high and so quietly that we rarely knew they were coming." Ronald could only smile in response for fear that any reply might be heard by Otto or cause offence.

Instead, he continued to gaze around the stadium, taking in the sights and sounds as best he could. To his far left, looking to the west, the stadium was open, almost down to ground level, whereas to his right, to the east, it was fully built up with a flight of steps leading through the centre of the seating up to a high platform on which stood an ornate metal cauldron. To the rear of the platform was a device which, when he first saw it, he thought must be cine equipment – it looked similar with its tripod legs – but he realised it was markedly different to the equipment he had seen out at the test fight of the 109 he had witnessed a couple of days previously. Intrigued, he asked Otto for an explanation.

Beaming with pride he said, "I am glad you asked, young Ronald." Ronald recognised he was being patronised, but thought it polite to let it go. "This," Otto continued, "is our great invention for the Olympic games. Fernseeapparat, seeing across distance, or television as I think you will call it in England when you have it one day."

"We already have it," interjected Ronald's father, not to be outdone.

"Yes, perhaps," Otto responded, as though speaking to a child. Ronald could feel an edge of tension between them.

"But this will send pictures of the games live, as it happens, to shops and theatres all across Berlin where the people," he stressed the word," the people will be able to watch the games for free. Not like in England, where only a few rich people can watch in their own homes." Otto had a rather triumphant smile on his face and Alfred had no means of reply as he had to admit that in general terms Otto was right. Fortunately at that moment a fanfare of music blared out through the loudspeaker system which prevented, at least temporarily, any further sparring between the two.

"Look down there," said Otto, pointing down to their left at the dais which Ronald now saw had largely filled with its complement of special guests, high ranking officials and officers in full military uniform, "The Führer is about to arrive."

As he spoke, there was a ripple of excitement in the crowd and Ronald watched as Adolf Hitler, the Chancellor and Führer of Germany walked slowly down a long flight of stairs, accompanied by Joseph Goebels with a host of minor officials, and out onto the floor of the arena. The crowd rose to its feet and erupted into thunderous applause. Chants of "Heil Hitler!" echoed round the stadium. The Führer, dressed in a uniform and peaked cap similar to the outfit he had worn at the airfield, acknowledged the accolade briefly, before crossing the running track to stand for a moment on the infield. Then a little girl, dressed in a pretty summer frock and carrying a bunch of flowers, stepped hesitantly forward, curtsied and offered the bouquet to her country's leader. The Führer smiled broadly in accepting her tribute and ruffled her hair affectionately. The crowd roared its approval.

Turning once again to acknowledge the greeting, the Führer ascended the staircase, moving out on to the front of the dais to take up his allotted position at its centre. All the while the crowd chanted his name, still standing, still with arms raised in the German salute.

Then, at an unseen signal, the crowd on the far side of the arena directly facing the Führer seemed to still, to become quiet just for a moment in anticipation of what might follow. Ronald had the impression that the arena was holding its breath as, one by one, black dots, black squares began to appear, cards held aloft over the heads of selected spectators. Swiftly the squares melded to form three words each fully fifty feet in height, inclined across the seating tier, until Ronald could clearly read: WIR GEHOREN DIR.

Not understanding, Ronald looked to his father for an explanation. Against a swelling tide of the crowd's chanting of these words, and with a look of utter disapproval in his eyes, Alfred mouthed, "We belong to you," and he pointed directly at the Führer. "It's a very personal message, a pledge of loyalty for all the world to see." Ronald could just make out his words as his father struggled to make himself heard above the continuing waves of sound. To Ronald, they seemed to say: Lead us and we will follow you wherever you go. He was just too young to fully appreciate the implications and the effect they would have on his life in a very few years.

Ronald looked around him – all faces were turned towards the Führer who raised a hand to acknowledge the accolade. In the row behind him, Margheritta's face bore a look akin to adoration; Elise gave Ronald an encouraging smile while Wolfgang and Dieter cheered and stamped their feet. Only Karin seemed not to be party to the euphoria as she stood quietly, looking rather bewildered, cast adrift on the tsunami of emotion that was engulfing the stadium. Ronald winked at her and she gave a little giggle. Hutch was trying to look bored by the whole affair, but Ronald could see that he was bemused by Regina's apparent enthusiasm for the moment. He held Ronald's gaze and shook his head slowly as though he could not quite believe what he was seeing and hearing.

As for Otto, he was standing arm outstretched in common with everyone else, but his lips were still and his face bore a troubled, faraway look as though his mind was absorbed in other issues. Then, realising that he was being studied intently by the teenager at his side, he dropped his arm and began to applaud enthusiastically. Not wishing to appear rude or ungrateful of the honour of being a guest at the ceremony, Ronald began to applaud politely and was rewarded with an appreciative squeeze of his shoulder from Otto.

Even though Otto had explained earlier that flying would form part of the Olympic competition, but not actually taking place until after their return to England, Ronald was still surprised to see three small sport planes parked on the infield away to his left. They were, of course, marked with the German swastika.

Ronald was about to ask Otto if the planes had been flown in when he noticed that the Zeppelin airship had withdrawn to one side. For this he was thankful as he had begun to find the continuous drone of the engines rather irritating, but then Otto drew his attention to two small aircraft that were approaching, one from the east and one from the west, along the centre line of the stadium. Ronald recognised that they were the same type as he had flown with Otto and to his questioning look Otto responded.

"Not me this time. My turn comes later this week. Today it is my friend Ernst Udet and one of his pupils from the Luft…" he checked and corrected himself, "from one of our sports flying clubs. Their display will have a special feature. Watch."

Ronald followed the line of his finger and sat entranced as the two Me108s put on a brief display of aerobatics. "Not as good as mine," said Otto as he nudged Ronald, but then the display concluded with the two planes putting on smoke and flying five perfect circles, three over two, which began to drift across the stadium on the gentle breeze. The crowd roared its approval.

After that, events began to move quite quickly. Mr Goebels spoke at some length, lifting the crowd with his enthusiasm to new heights of applause as he extolled, according to Otto, the new German way, but then he deferred to another official, who began the opening ceremony proper.

Through the open west gate came streams of uniformed stewards bearing banners to line the edge of the athletics running track and shortly after came the parade of the competing teams, Greece leading the way, in acknowledgment of its place in the modern Olympics, resurrected only thirty years previously. Country by country, its athletes followed in alphabetical order, progressing past the dais on which the Führer stood at the forefront, some teams waving and some, Austria being the first, offering the German salute.

Alfred tutted and said he hoped 'our lot' would do the right thing. He was not disappointed when the team from Great Britain walked past the Führer waving, as did the large team from the United States of America with its small band of black athletes.

Last to enter, as the host nation and to an even greater roar from the spectators, was the team from Germany. Without exception, man and woman, they gave the German salute as they passed the dais and then took their place, with almost military precision – perhaps not surprising as many of their competitors were wearing full military uniform – alongside the other forty-eight competing nations on the green expanse of the infield.

Next, the huge Olympic flag, carried by six competitors, was escorted into the stadium and brought before the dais where another competitor, a weightlifter, spoke the Olympic oath of fair competition on behalf of all those taking part. So far, the Führer had said not a word.

As the flag was carried away to be installed on a pole adjacent to the cauldron at the east end of the stadium, Otto said in a rather theatrical manner, "There is just one more thing; an inspired idea from our Führer," and he pointed again toward the west gate where they could see a runner approaching, holding high a burning torch.

"It was the Führer's idea to have the Olympic torch lit at Olympia in Greece a couple of months ago by the power of the sun's rays, and then for it to be carried across Greece via Athens, by a continuous relay of runners, and then overland all the way northwards, day by day, across Europe to arrive in the stadium today. This, the Führer believes, will symbolise the unity of the world in the ideals of international understanding and sporting friendship."

He sat back, looking rather pleased with himself before quipping, "But we have to win everything!"

"Just joking!" he added in response to the agonised look on Alfred's face. "I'm only pulling your leg, Freddy. It's only sport, after all!" Alfred managed to force a thin smile, but it was, of course, so very much more than just sport.

As Ronald turned to look at Hutch, he saw that Hutch was holding Regina's hand and, so as not to intrude on their intimacy, he looked quickly away to see that the torch had paused briefly in front of the Führer, to acknowledge his status as national leader, before proceeding around the track to the far end. There the athlete began to climb the steps in the direction of the cauldron. When he topped the last step, he paused, raised the torch on high, strode over to the cauldron, stepped up on to a small plinth and held the torch, which seemed to burn even more brightly, over the bowl.

At that moment, the Führer's voice rang out, booming through the loudspeaker system in his characteristic timbre, just one simple sentence to open formally the Eleventh Olympiad. As the Führer stepped back from the microphone, at the far end of the stadium, the runner tossed the torch into the bowl and a column of flame burst skywards. "Seig Heil, Heil Hitler!" roared the crowd, time and time again, the waves of sound reverberating round the stadium.

While the Führer and his entourage left the platform, Ronald sat stunned by what he had just experienced. Turning round to Hutch with a quizzical expression, Hutch seemed only to be able to respond with an enigmatic shrug of his shoulders, blowing out his cheeks and gave a slight shake of his head to express his own bemusement.

In the meantime, Otto was clapping Alfred on the back, saying, "There you are, Freddy. That's how to run an event properly. It takes good German organisation; none of your English laisser-faire." Alfred looked rather crestfallen for, as he felt obliged to concede in discussion with Ronald later that night, it had been a marvellously orchestrated ceremony and it would, he thought, have been completely enjoyable, if it had not been for the permanent military overtone, which, he believed, had brought in an altogether darker flavour.

As they began to return to their cars, Ronald saw that Margheritta had insisted on placing herself strategically between Hutch and Regina, another chaperone to prevent any monkey business, as Otto put it, but that evening, when Ronald tried to discuss the day's events with Hutch, it was soon obvious that the focus of his thoughts lay just a couple of doors away, down the corridor.

"God help me," Hutch had said, the anguish plain in his voice. "I've fallen in love with Regina and I know she feels the same about me. What on earth am I going to do?"

For all of his fifteen years, Ronald did not have the answer and Hutch forbade him to discuss it with his father. All he knew, in the months that lay ahead, as the world hurtled toward war, was that Hutch and Regina had continued to correspond, like he and Karin, just as pen-friends – or so he believed.

Ronald remembered that he had persisted in trying to engage Hutch in discussion that night after the visit to the Olympic Stadium until, with the irritation sounding loud in his voice just before they fell asleep, Hutch burst out, "Oh, do give it a rest, Ronno. It's as plain as the nose on your face that *we* are going to have to do it all over again."

Well, of course, he was right, but perhaps Hutch would not have been quite so enthusiastic, so cavalier in his opinion, if, that night, he could have foreseen that, in less than five years, both his parents, Flora and Edward, would be dead in the London Blitz while he struggled to find his feet in the RAF in the aftermath of the Battle of Britain.

The Morrison shelter in the family kitchen had done its job as they crouched under its shelter leaving them virtually unscathed as the house collapsed about them, but the blast wave from the five hundred kilogramme ariel mine sucked the life from them. At least Hutch would be able to pay his last respects. As the destruction of London continued unabated, so many would only have a box of rubble and perhaps a few fragments to lower into the ground.

Parting is such sweet sorrow they say, but for one it was more sorrow than sweet, Ronald remembered with a trace of sadness.

When it came time to leave, Otto sent Werner to collect their bags, which he loaded into the Mercedes, while the whole family gathered in the lounge where Elise had coffee waiting with *kusskage*, little sweet biscuits.

At first, Ronald thought that Otto was going to make one of his grand speeches, but he remained silent and seemed genuinely overcome by the moment of parting.

He shook Ronald formally by the hand, but as he released his grip he wrapped his arms around Ronald, hugging him tight saying, "Auf Wiedersehen, young Ronald. Whatever happens in your life, do your duty, do your best. Make your parents proud of you – just as my boys will. Befehl ist befehl." Ronald thanked him, unsure what reply to make.

Otto spoke similarly to Hutch, but when they talked about it later, they concluded that Otto's words to Hutch were (prophetically as events were to show) slightly different. Otto had ended by saying, "Make our family proud."

While Elise handed round the coffees, Otto took Alfred off to one side and was deep in conversation with him for several minutes, both animated in their expressions until Otto roared with laughter, grabbed Alfred in a bear-hug, then apologised – "You English are far too reserved" – and finished with a stiff bow of the head.

Goodbyes were said all round until Margheritta pointed out that Hutch, who must have slipped unnoticed from the room, and Regina were missing. Ronald volunteered to go in search and moments later found them tucked away, out of sight, in the lobby to Werner's quarters, locked in an embrace, which was definitely not of the brother and sister kind.

As they parted, fingertips lingering, at the sound of Ronald's discrete cough, Regina ran through to the main building racked by floods of tears while Hutch turned to Ronald, his face contorted with anguish, "What am I going to do? She's the girl for me."

Again Ronald had no answer and, as is the way of such things having a momentum of their own, within ten minutes they were all seated in the Mercedes with Werner at the wheel, Otto having pleaded another commitment. Looking back from the car, Ronald could see the family Hecker tightly grouped at the top of the steps and chanced one last photograph, for the record, as the car began to roll down the drive.

At the very last second, Regina appeared at the side of the group and ran quickly down the steps. Hutch shouted to Werner to stop the car. Even he could understand the pain in Hutch's voice and the Mercedes stopped instantly. Then she was at their side, leaning into the car to tie the coloured foulard from her sunhat, loosely around Hutch's neck. She kissed him full on the lips, to Alfred's half-hearted disapproval. Hutch held her for a moment longer, but then she was gone, utterly distraught, crying once more.

How he wished, with the benefit of hindsight, that he could have understood more of what he had seen and experienced, but as he reminded himself incessantly he had been only fifteen years old at the time and hardly worldly-wise. And it seemed to him that, even at two years older than himself, Hutch had been no more able to divine the dark secrets that that time had unfolded.

How could he have failed to have been impressed by the quality of life in Otto's family, the respect they showed for each other, the cleanliness and orderliness of the German society, that he experienced at the time? Of course he had seen nothing of the darkness that was being unleashed, and all that had been found later, which served only to prove the rightness of their cause in bringing Nazism to an end.

But when he listened to Otto talk about Germany in the 1920's and the terrible times they had been through, as communism fought to gain the upper hand, he had felt some sympathy, even with only a partial insight to what the German people were trying to achieve in restoring their country from the ravages of war and what, shortly afterwards had almost been a civil war. But the circumvention of the restrictions imposed by the Treaty of Versailles, the Spanish Civil War then ongoing and the significance of the extension of German rule into the Sudetenland and Austria, had been lost on him, although apparently not on his father.

As the political climate worsened after their return to England, his father hardly ever mentioned Otto and by 1938, a war with Germany was no longer a question of if, but when.

Befehl ist Befehl, he thought ironically. They had all done their duty, some with blind conviction, some with reasoned commitment, some with regret, but for all their possible faults, he personally had been saddened by the passing of the Hecker family into the dustbin of history.

From his own father's research in the immediate post-war period, he knew that their beautiful house in the suburbs of Berlin had probably been destroyed along with all its wonderful contents by the Allied bomber raids in 1945.

Alfred and Otto may have ended up political enemies for a second time, but his father had been keen to honour the worth of their friendship by trying to discover their fate.

Otto was recorded by Alfred as having been killed in the defence of Berlin in March or April 1945.

Of Elise, nothing was known. If she had survived the surrender, then as a woman in Berlin she cannot have hoped to escape the almost universal rape of German women as the Red Army took control of the city both during the battle from January 1945 and in the subsequent occupation. Many had chosen to take their own lives rather than suffer such humiliation.

All that he had discovered about Wolfgang was that his squadron had been assigned to an airfield to the west of Berlin in January 1945, tasked with attempting to stem the floods of American daylight bombers. He might as well have been King Canute trying to hold back the tide. Beyond this posting, nothing was known and so he was recorded as being 'missing in action'.

Dieter who had also enlisted in the Luftwaffe had been posted missing over western Russia during the general retreat in the summer of 1944.

Nor was anything known of the fate of Max, his mother or his lovely sister Regina, with whom Hutch had been so enamoured. They were just three amongst the countless thousands who had simply vanished in the maelstrom of the war.

CHAPTER 16

In the years after the Second World War, as he tried to recover from the traumatic and harrowing combat actions he had experienced, as well as his own personal tragedy, Ronald began hesitantly to revisit some of the events that led up to the outbreak of hostilities, including his own involvement and what had been, or might have been the role played by his father.

At the beginning of the war in September 1939, his father, having been born in the mid 1880's, was precluded by age from active service, despite volunteering to re-enlist. Not even the Royal Air Force in its darkest days had need of a former Royal Flying Corps master armourer (retired) who had been on reserve for the best part of twenty years – or so it had seemed.

During the war, in any discussion between the two of them, whenever Ronald had tried to investigate his father's contribution to the war effort, he had been gently and politely rebuffed with his father quoting the Official Secrets Act as a cloak, a shield never to be breached. And so Ronald had been obliged to let it go. As a consequence, he never gained anything more than a vague understanding that his father was something to do with photo reconnaissance and strategic planning.

In the paranoia of secrecy that was part and parcel of total war, not even father and son were exempt from the maxim that "Careless Talk Costs Lives".

In the years after the war, his father insisted on maintaining his dignified, but unbreakable silence to the very end, which came suddenly and unexpectedly, shortly after his seventy fifth birthday. A severe stroke stopped Alfred in his tracks, robbing him of movement and much of his speech. He lingered for only a few days before passing away, surrounded by three generations of his family at his bedside.

At the funeral, held in the local parish church, an oasis of coolness in what was otherwise a stiflingly hot summer's day, Ronald declined to give the eulogy. This was a burden that he passed to his younger sister Torrie, being unsure of whether he had really known his father at all. Torrie, however, had no such reservations and spoke movingly of a loving and caring father and grandfather, husband of forty-eight years to Cissy and then of his service to his country in two world wars – but even she had to skate over what had been his actual role from 1939 to 1945 – merely recording his post-war service as a respected senior civil servant within the Ministry of Defence. A large wreath from the Royal Air Force and a condolence card bearing a suitable sentiment, signed on behalf of an Air Vice Marshal, perhaps hinted at something greater.

Standing at the graveside, slowly cooking in the heavy black suit he had selected for the occasion, he felt his mother's hand slip into his, squeezing it tight, and he took comfort from her as the final words of the vicar washed over him, and he watched with aching sadness as the pale oak coffin sank into the freshly dug earth. He despaired that he seemed unable to bring the support to his mother, but as the handful of soil from each passing mourner pattered onto the coffin lid, he felt a frustration that he would never get to know what secrets his father had taken with him into eternity.

Yet only an hour later, at the funeral tea, his mother, managing her grief with great dignity, reopened that curtain when she drew him to one side and, enfolding him in her arms as she had not done for so very many years, whispered into his ear, "Ronnie, dear, you know he was a spy, don't you. You were part of it!"

As she released him from her embrace she looked at him, smiled with tears in her eyes, and, holding her hands to his face said, "Think about it – your Dad was so proud of you, and what you did to help him and our country, and he was especially proud of what you did during the war." Before he could think of a way to respond to such a revelation, she disappeared into the crowd of well-wishers who had come into the local Conservative Club from the graveside to converse in hushed tones at the funeral tea.

And think he did, of little else, for days and weeks afterwards until piece by piece, the penny began to drop. It had after all been a huge game of cat and mouse between two countries preparing for war. With the benefit of hindsight he realised that his father's connection to Otto Hecker had been used to engineer their visit to Germany so that he might establish the extent of Germany's technical advances. Perhaps equally, Otto had been tasked to invite his father in order to make such a potent demonstration of Germany's growing airpower. From that point onwards, the possibilities were endless and he realised he had been, for the most part, an unwitting player as part of his father's "cover".

It had not, after all, been his imagination that they had been followed day by day, during the whole of their time in Germany. Perhaps even the performance of the customs officer at Frankfurt on the day they landed had been a carefully orchestrated charade intended to convince them all that there was no ulterior motive, and that their visit to Germany had no special significance beyond the pleasant renewal of an old friendship.

It even occurred to him that possibly the announcement by Mr. Chamberlain of "Peace in our Time" by means of the treaty signed with Germany in 1938, had not been just the political weakness for which he was so reviled in later years, but a calculated gamble to buy time to enable Great Britain to re-arm. As 1940 was to prove, it was a close run thing.

In the following months, whenever he tried to confirm his conclusions with his mother, she merely laughed, saying it was "all too long ago to bother with". His sister also laughed at him, calling him a silly old fool for his overactive imagination, and so, when Cissy followed her husband into the graveyard a couple of years later, apparently unable to face life without him, the window on Berlin was closed for all time.

Until, that is, it came to the time when it was necessary to clear their parent's house, prior to sale. While Torrie worked quietly upstairs, often in tears, sorting her mother's clothes to go to a charity shop, Ronald went through the painful process of clearing his father's old oak fall-front bureau.

As he opened the front flap and gently lowered it onto its supporting rails, he was assailed by the overpowering smell of stale smoke.

The process of emptying the bureau, drawer by drawer, compartment by compartment became a journey through time of all the insignificant trivia that make up lives gone by. Dozens of old bills, bank statements, correspondence and faded newspaper articles were interspersed with cancelled passports, old driving licences and one or two documents of vaguely historical interest which he earmarked for one of the local societies interested in such things.

All this detritus of his father's past went, sheaf by sheaf, into a black plastic bag for delivery to the local refuse tip, but at the back of the top drawer he found a selection of red leatherette, velvet-lined boxes containing his father's Great War service medals which included, to his surprise, an Order of the British Empire – something else which his father had never mentioned. The rose pink ribbon had a narrow central stripe of pearl grey, which denoted that it was of the military, rather than the civilian division. This made yet another small mystery to be investigated, so he put the medals back in their cases and slipped them safely into his overcoat pocket.

At last the task was done, and all that remained were a scattering of paperclips, perished rubber bands and the accumulated dust of time.

Because the drawer under the writing flap was set in its own sleeve, he pulled it out fully and got down onto his knees to peer into the darkness of the void. Initially he thought the cavity was clear, but then he fancied he could see something hanging down at the very back. Fetching a torch, he saw what seemed to be part of a letter, wedged up behind the back board of the top compartments.

Intrigued, he teased the document, yellowing with age, from its hiding place and what he read on the torn half-sheet of paper of the finest quality, caused his heart to skip a beat.

Addressed from *Elisto, Goethepark 7, Charlottenburg, Berlin,* but with an embossed German eagle and swastika heading the page, and dated 16th April 1936 it began:

Dear Freddy,

At the insistence of our Führer, it gives me great pleasure to invite you and your family to visit us in Berlin in July so that we may renew our friendship. In recognition of your kindness to me personally, our Führer asks that your son Ronald and a friend of similar age should accompany you so that they may meet our sons as representatives of German...

The remainder of the page was missing, but for Ronald it was enough: Bluff and double bluff.

CHAPTER 17

He slipped another log book from the pile, this time for 1944. It was a time when he said goodbye to his Spitfire, as the squadron was tasked to convert to the Hawker Tempest in readiness for the assault on Fortress Europe. His days at twenty-five thousand feet, skipping amongst the clouds were over. Now it was going to get close-up and personal – ground attack in support of the advancing troops. He read on and remembered.

Tuesday 25th May 1944
Test flight 35 minutes.
Tempest Mk V

He gazed up in awe at the six and a half tons of fighter, designed for ground attack by Hawkers, as a worthy successor to the Hurricane.

God, it was big, he thought as he contemplated the fourteeen foot diameter, four bladed propeller fronting the cowl which enclosed the massive 35 litre Napier Sabre engine, capable of producing more than two thousand horsepower and which, if he had the nerve, would propel the plane at over 430 miles per hour in level flight and five or even six hundred (if he was completely without nerves) in a dive.

There was even talk of the plane approaching the speed of sound in a dive from altitude. To satisfy the engine's thirst for air, a huge oval shaped air intake had been sculpted under the nose, immediately behind the propeller which helped to compress and ram the air through to the cylinder heads.

The undercarriage was wide set, thank goodness, with massive brakes set inside the wheel hubs, essential to bring the monster to a halt. It had the highest landing speed he had ever encountered, far exceeding the Spitfire's.

He reached up and ran the palm of his hand across the front edge of the wing. It was cold and polished like glass. It was of a new and revolutionary design, much thinner, and with new Hispano cannon especially developed to fit inside the wing.

He gulped, and gulped again before moving round the wing, checking the aileron movement before going to the tail and testing the elevators and the nine foot high blade of the rudder.

Returning to the trailing edge of the wing on the right side, he stood trying to remember the instructions he had received in the classroom that morning. At this moment, he rather wished he had not eaten lunch, or breakfast for that matter. His stomach was doing things normally reserved for being profoundly sick, and he prayed he was not about to disgrace himself.

A polite cough just behind him brought him to his senses, as a fitter suggested, without a trace of irony, "It goes better with you up there, sir," pointing up at the cockpit almost ten feet above, but the look on his face enquired whether Ronald had the guts to do it. He was beginning to wonder.

Now or never, he thought; so without further delay, he put his foot into a stirrup which the fitter had pulled down from the belly of the aircraft and opened a tiny spring loaded panel, set flush into the mid-side of the fuselage, which gave him a hand grip.

Hauling himself up, he put his right foot onto a spring-loaded panel on the trailing edge of the wing, opened a second spring-loaded flange which opened to give him a platform for his left; then, with both hands on the top of the cockpit screen he stepped over the sill, lowered himself inside and settled into the seat, shuffling his bottom to make himself moderately comfortable on his parachute pack. God knows, he thought, how was he going to manage all that in an emergency. Getting into the Spit was a doddle by comparison.

As the fitter connected the shoulder harness and thigh straps onto the central quick release box, tugging them uncomfortably tight, Ronald pulled on his silk flying gloves and surveyed the cockpit. It was a fairly conventional layout, throttle and trim wheel on his immediate left, undercarriage control and radio on his right. The arrangement of the various dials on the instrument panel, each white on black, was slightly different to the Spit, but familiar enough, as he tried desperately to remember everything he had read the night before in the pilot's notes.

"Time to go, sir. Good luck! Try to bring her back in one piece. Oh, by the way watch out for her pulling to the left on take-off," came the helpful advice from the fitter, and with that he was gone leaving Ronald alone – alone with the doubts and fears that any novice has for their first flight in a new plane.

Unlike the Spitfire which could be started by the ground crew from the outside, the Tempest was started by the pilot by the use of a cartridge, not unlike a thirty millimetre cannon shell, from within the plane's engine bay, which would fire hot gasses directly into a small but powerful turbine which would start the engine turning with sufficient force to initiate complete ignition. Reaching for the dial to his right just below the instrument panel, he selected the first cartridge and heard the faint clunk of the shell moving into the mouth of the firing tube, just ahead of him on the other side of the firewall.

After priming the engine and carburettor with its diet of high octane aviation fuel, he opened the cooling flaps on the engine cowl to their fullest extent, closed his eyes momentarily, before pressing down on the firing button. There was an ear shattering bang which startled him as he watched the propeller in front of him begin to move, but only half a turn.

Turning the selector to move from the first spent cartridge to the second live cartridge, he took another deep breath. Out of the corner of his eye he could see the anxious look on the faces of the ground crew. Was he going to make a mess of it all?

He had been warned that if the second failed to start the engine, he must not try a third cartridge until the ground crew had vented the engine of the excess fuel, or a fire in the engine compartment was almost certain.

Saying a fervent prayer, he pressed the starter for the second time. This time the bang of the starter cartridge was followed by the distinct sound of a detonation in a couple of cylinders, then more, as the great propeller began to revolve.

A moment later, as blue smoke belched back from the exhaust stubs, threatening to fill the cockpit with choking fumes, all the cylinders caught and the propeller whirled into a translucent silver disk. The plane shook from stem to stern with the brute force of the engine, blurring his vision, so he adjusted the throttle until the vibrations settled to something reasonably acceptable.

Having been cautioned that the engine would over-heat quite quickly, he cranked the blister canopy closed, locked it and released the brakes. The plane lurched forward as soon as the ground crew removed the triangular chock from the front of each wheel. Next time, he thought, chocks first, brakes second.

At this point, realising that he would not be able to see where he was going, so steep was the angle of the fuselage, he released the canopy and slid it fully back, poking his head out into the slipstream to left and right, as the plane crabbed its way forward around the perimeter track until he reached the main runway.

Lining the plane up on the centre of the tarmac, which stretched away into the distance, shimmering with the heat-haze, he requested and was granted clearance to take off.

Closing the hood once again, and with a noticeable shake in his left hand he pushed the throttle lever forward a couple of inches, less than a third of the travel available.

The result was electric – the plane leapt forward, immediately veering to the left, so he corrected the swing with the pedals and as the Tempest rapidly gathered speed, he felt the tail-wheel come up and at that point he blessed the manufacturers for the teardrop shaped canopy; when the fuselage came level, the visibility was fantastic – not a single blind spot.

Checking his speed indicator, he could feel the plane going light so he gave it a touch more throttle, the engine responding instantly, pulled gently on the stick and the Tempest lifted into the air. Clearing the perimeter fence by fifty feet, he raised the wheels and sensed the air flow settling over the highly polished airframe.

Right, he thought, let's see what you can do, opening the throttle and pulling on the stick. The vertical acceleration was stunning – he put in a couple of slow rolls on the way up and, within what seemed only seconds, he was at fifteen thousand feet, scampering amongst the clouds.

From then on it was, once again, a big kid at play, loops, spins, barrel-rolls; an outside loop presented no problem. Then he tried a simulated ground attack dive, and frightened himself more than he cared to admit. Without even using full throttle, he was doing nearly 600 mph in seconds, as two thousand horses dragged the great weight of the Tempest earthwards.

Finally he chickened out, and, with wings shuddering from the aerodynamic stresses, he pulled out of the dive and allowed the sheer momentum of the aircraft to take him back almost to his original height.

All too soon, his allocated thirty minutes were over and, having obtained a return bearing from the control tower, he let the Tempest drift down through the layers of thin cloud with the engine at little more than tick over. Soon enough, he would have to take a beast like this to war, but for now he enjoyed that moment of peace as his heartbeat settled.

Shortly after, he was over the threshold of the runway and again had cause to be thankful for the blister canopy – although he lost the forward view, at least he could see down over the wing to judge his height. The runway sped under the wing at an incredible rate so it seemed, even with full flaps breaking up the airflow, but the landing itself was reasonable, he thought; only a couple of bounces, although he needed almost all of the runway to bring the Tempest to a halt, the brakes screeching in protest. She was quite a handful.

Back on the apron in front of the hangar he switched off, watching the silver disc of the propeller disintegrate into the individual blades, turning, slowing and stopping, the engine cracking and ticking as it cooled.

Sliding back the canopy after disconnecting the oxygen supply and radio, he breathed deeply to take in the fresh air, while he climbed out and down onto the wing. Having unclipped his parachute he slid on his bottom and dropped to the ground.

The same fitter was waiting for him.

"Well done, sir, I guess you enjoyed that," as he saw the big grin on Ronald's face, despite the beads of sweat that covered it. Ronald pulled off his silk scarf to wipe the perspiration away as the fitter continued, "Good landing too, for your first effort. Don't worry," he said jokingly, "you'll get worse, but we've had a couple that bounced thirty to forty feet as they touched down. Last week we had a write-off when the plane stalled after the bounce. We got the pilot out in one piece, but he was shaken up pretty badly, and swore he would never fly a Tempest again. You did OK."

Ronald certainly hoped so. Training was one thing, but combat was another. At least, he thought, he would have live firing and ground attack practice before his squadron would be reassigned to combat, which might help build up his confidence.

Date 28th May 1944
Gunnery / Rocket practice
Briefing 09.30
"Take off 11.00, flying in formation northeast to The Wash then follow the coast until you pick up Skegness on your left"

"The bombing range at Donna Nook is at map reference 53 85' N 0 15'E"

"Reference points are the town of Mablethorpe and then the windmill and watchtower a dozen miles further north at Saltfleet"

"Identify the targets as you go up – they are clearly set out on the beach. Establish contact with Donna Nook control and then make a circuit anti-clockwise from there to come back southward onto the range."

"Your aircraft have been loaded with full ammunition and a full set of live rockets. You will have enough for three passes – half your ammunition and then half your rockets – the final pass with rockets is to be made at maximum speed four hundred and fifty knots to simulate battle attack, so start at five thousand feet and watch for over shoot. Observe a minimum safety margin of four hundred yards between aircraft. Those of you that are converting from Spitfires seem to be having a particular problem with the extra speed. Good luck."

As Hutch prepared to roll up the map from which he had been explaining the run he added, tapping the map as he did so, "Oh, by the way, a word of warning. Do not under any circumstances, except in an absolute emergency approach North Cotes airfield which is only five miles to the north along the coast. A couple of ME 410's sneaked in there the day before yesterday and shot the field up pretty badly. We lost three Beaufighters and their crews which were lined up for take-off – just one pass from each and the RAF Regiment hardly got in a shot, so they are very sensitive and likely to be trigger happy. In an emergency, Gopshill further to the north will take you, but in a real emergency and you have no alternative, then North Cotes must be approached wheels down, otherwise they are certain to shoot first and ask questions afterwards."

His words hung in the air like the stale cigarette smoke – everyone seemed to be smoking more these days. Ronald looked round at the others in the room. Their squadron was now complete. Hutch had been made up to Wing Commander, himself to Squadron Leader, then Digger Jones a very likeable Australian, Geoff Kelsey who he knew from Manston, dependable, always talking about going into teaching afterwards, Freddy Grewcock, Taffy Williams who was just back from weeks in hospital following a mid-air collision. In addition there was Jon "Baz" Bajkowski, a Pole who was reticent about his passage from Poland to England, but who talked about little else than avenging his homeland's defeat in '39 and Peter Lawson who had overcome the loss of his left hand in action over Belgium late the previous year, but managed to persuade the board that he was still fit to fly.

As for the others, they were all new boys, fresh in from advance training after completing basic training courses in the relative safety of Canada, or Texas. Not one of them had yet seen combat and not one of them had more than a dozen hours on Tempests – nor did he for that matter, but their lack of flying experience was really worrying.

To be fair, they did listen when he and any of the other experienced, long-served, pilots tried to explain what combat flying was like; advice given in the hope that their experience would somehow rub off. But when he took the young (well he was only twenty-two) Archie Madeley up on a mock combat training flight, the lad's performance had been woeful. Only once did he get into a good firing position behind Ronald and not once did he manage to evade Ronald's attacks.

He had even got the Tempest into a flat spin on its back and it took all Ronald's skill to calm him and talk him out of it. Archie's voice had been full of fear and panic as the controls of the inverted Tempest failed to respond, and afterwards he had come, ashen faced, to Ronald full of apology and gratitude, in equal measure.

Ronald could only pray that Archie's first combat would be up against an equally inexperienced opponent. If he met one of the German pilots posted back from the Eastern Front, where they had scored literally hundreds of victories against poorly trained Russian pilots, then Archie's life-expectation might be very short indeed.

However, he kept that thought to himself, not wanting to worry the lad too much (why did he feel so much like a father talking when he was only two years older); but instead he encouraged Archie to pester Hutch for as much time in the air as possible.

A brilliant sun in an azure blue sky beat down on the Perspex canopy, making it almost unbearably hot. For this training sortie, Ronald had chosen to fly in shirtsleeves and was glad that he had. He could imagine the discomfort of others who had worn their flight jackets – no cooling air flow for them until they were in flight.

With a final check of his instruments, he lined up on the runway to the left of Hutch with Baz on the right and Peter Lawson on the far right.

By flights of four, sixteen Tempests thundered down the runway, fully fuelled and armoured so that the exercise was as realistic as possible. In fingers of four, they roared over the roof tops, climbing steadily away from their base, Hutch steering them northeast toward Grantham.

Within moments, one of the new boys reported that he had a partial electrical failure with his fuel gauge, airspeed indicator and reflector gunsight ceasing to work, so he was ordered back.

Fifteen aircraft continued, gaining height, under a crystal blue sky, broken only by bands of high cirrus, the mare's tail clouds. Higher still and Ronald began to feel the chill of the altitude, and turned on the cockpit heater.

The steady thrum of the Napier engine gave Ronald a sense of peace, but when he looked up and to his right he could see, like scratches on a dirty window pane, the unmistakable marks of condensation trails streaming back from dozens of American Flying Fortresses, heading eastward into the heart of Germany.

Silently, he wished them Godspeed knowing that many, far too many by some reports, would not return. The American idea of the box formation of bombers, armed with dozens of machine guns being able to defend themselves against fighter attack simply had not worked. The German fighters had cut them to shreds, too small and too fast for the airborne gunners. The losses had been so great that operations had been scaled back (he had heard) until the Mustang fighter had been brought into an escort role, having the flying range, manoeuvrability and firepower to match the latest German fighters.

He had once tried to get into the belly ball turret of a B17, but found he was simply too big. He could barely imagine the courage needed to spend six or seven hours cooped up in the turret, with, as a Yank had put it, "Your butt hanging out". He had even heard of turrets being completely shot away leaving the gunner dangling in the slip stream like a hooked fish, dead or wounded, secured to the plane only by his safety harness. Whether the rest of the crew had the time to open the top hatch while in the thick of combat, before the lack of oxygen rendered the gunner unconscious or asphyxiated, was another matter altogether.

The command "Echelon right" broke into his thoughts, and the fifteen aircraft gradually shuffled themselves into an extended line, each plane to the side and slightly to the rear of the next, like a skein of geese in migration. In the turbulence of the air, the line of aircraft rose and fell in rhythm. Ronald was third in the pattern. To his left, bathed in sunlight he could see the rectangular towers of Lincoln cathedral atop the hill overlooking the city. Not long now.

Another five minutes, then there was the steely blue-grey of the North Sea and the formation wheeled left and north over Skegness, to begin a gradual descent through clear skies, sliding past Mablethorpe until Ronald could clearly see the soft, white sands of the bombing range and the watchtower at Saltfleet. A red range flag, fluttering in the stiff easterly breeze, gave an indication of wind direction. He could see a solitary figure climbing the open staircase of the thirty feet high tower, from which the fall of their munitions would be reported and recorded.

"Line Astern," came the command, and thus aligned they thundered at two hundred feet past the control tower three miles further up the coast.

Hutch then led them away from the coast, eastwards, then turning round to the north, climbing again rapidly.

"Remember, minimum spacing four hundred yards – take different targets alternately."

"Full throttle, attacking, go," and with these words Hutch's Tempest reared up, dipping its left wing to complete the turn, followed by Baz, Ronald and the others. As the g-forces pulled at his body and the earth and sea spun below him under his cockpit, Ronald was reminded of the trip to Hendon years before to watch the RAF display team, the Black Arrows, in their single engined biplanes.

Rolling level, Ronald pushed forward on the stick going over the top and down steeply like the biggest Big Dipper ride ever invented. Ahead he could see firstly Hutch, and then Baz, lining up on their targets – for Hutch a great black canvas square with a large red circle at its centre, for Baz a mock-up of a tank constructed of old scaffolding poles and canvas. Choosing to follow Hutch, with their number four in line behind Baz he watched, a quarter of a mile ahead, the fire of cannon from the Tempest, spent shells fluttering down from the waste chutes, sand spraying up from the surface of the beach, tearing through the canvas. Out of the corner of his eye he saw Baz firing, but he was too late and fired high.

Then it was his turn.

With the black square of the target occupying the top third of the reflector site he pressed the firing button. Even as an experienced pilot, the immense recoil of the four 20mm cannon firing together took him by surprise. Cannon shells chewed up the sand at the approach of the target, then using the rudder pedals he rocked the plane slightly from side to side to maximise the strike, then pulling back on the stick in a stomach-churning climb, trails of vapour streaming from his wingtips.

Turning in for the first time with the rockets, he followed the pattern of the previous pass, and, bracing for the recoil pressed the firing button. But there was none, and he watched as the four solid fuel rockets sped away from his wing trailing smoke, to explode well short of the target. He had fired too early. He cursed himself for his lack of thought, but hoped it was a lesson well learnt. Around him the bursts of rocket fire from the following aircraft were a salutary reminder of the destructive power of each missile.

The third pass went without a hitch, but then Hutch took them up to almost five thousand feet for the final run. At maximum boost, the Napier engine hurled the Tempest to 500 mph in seconds. With the airframe shuddering from the acceleration, he had only moments to select the target, arm the rockets, fire and pull away. He was lower than he had intended and was over the top of his rockets before they exploded inside one of the mock tank targets. The plane lifted slightly from the shock wave of the explosions.

"Christ! Ronno," came the heavily accented voice of Baz, "that was a bit bloody close. You're supposed to knock them out with the rockets, not scare them to death with your prop!"

"OK lads," came Hutch's voice, "that's it for today. Not so bad for a first attempt, but we'll get the full de-brief tomorrow. Form up on me and lets go home." So saying he led the squadron around in one more circuit in echelon past the Donna Nook control tower, Hutch dipping his wings in salute, then as one they climbed back into the deep blue sky. Ronald hoped that the man in the watch tower at the end of the range had judged them well.

The next day, the debrief, whilst detailed, could be summed up as "could do better". On average the more veteran pilots had done a bit better than the new boys, but everyone agreed that there was no substitute for experience. The debate continued long into the night as tactics and aiming points of their forthcoming ground attack role were discussed over and over again.

Ronald put down the flight log with a deep sigh. That day had been almost carefree, but the opportunity for further range practice never came. Too few pilots and too many battles to be fought.

He remembered that, within three months of his return to active duty in Germany, half the squadron were dead. Two of the new ones – he could not even remember their names and wondered if he ever knew – were picked off by 190's on their very first operational sortie. One had managed to get enough height to bale out, but the plane was on fire at the time, and Ronald was too occupied at that moment and he did not see if there was a parachute canopy – missing believed killed was, once again, the official record.

As for the other, his end had been quick and violent. A cannon shell from a Flakpanzer, striking the wing root, snapped the wing off at only a hundred feet of altitude. Ronald doubted the youngster even had time to realise what had happened before the stricken Tempest hit the ground at more than 300 mph. Ronald flew straight through the fireball and his Miss Faithful was hit several times by the ground fire. He had a narrow escape.

As for Taffy, he remembered, his loss was all the more tragic. Flying in formation just after take-off his engine had stopped completely without warning. Ronald could distinctly remember the burly Welshman saying, "Oh shit! Too low to bale – I'll try to get her down," but with two 500 pound bombs slung underwing the Tempest flew like a brick and Taffy had barely finished speaking when the Tempest hit the ground, bounced and exploded.

Peter Lawson had already been shot down in the support of the airborne landings to take the bridge over the Rhine at Arnhem, but despite the lack of a hand, he had successfully deployed his parachute and spent the remaining months of the war in captivity. In a way, he had been one of the lucky ones.

Ronald could no longer remember how the others went, but like every other pilot he began to feel the odds running against him even though one of the more learned members of the squadron had demonstrated mathematically (so he claimed) that the odds reset after every mission. Nevertheless Ronald still continued to roll his little yellow dice before each mission. New pilots came and went with alarming regularity.

CHAPTER 18

Ronald dropped the log book into his lap as he felt tears trickling down his cheeks. How could any sort of loving God be so cruel, had been his abiding thought for more than half a century.

They had told his parents the next day, as soon as they walked through the front door, so great was their excitement at being able to tell someone, anyone about their engagement. His father raised an eyebrow, blew out his cheeks while his mother clapped her hand to her mouth, let out a shriek, wiped her tears and hugged Libby until she begged for mercy.

Later that night they told Libby's parents. They reacted with less enthusiasm, but her father eventually gave his blessing, although he insisted they wait until she had turned twenty-one.

Thus it was, that in an all too brief break between training with his new Tempest (to be named Miss Faithful) and being scheduled to return to active duties, they were married on the day after Libby's twenty-first birthday in her parish church, both of them in uniform, on a fine, sunny day in late May. Hutch had been his best man – he only pretended to lose the ring. Torrie acted as her bridesmaid in the continued absence of her sister, Susan. When Ronald was invited to kiss his bride, the embrace raised more than a few cheers among the congregation. They left the church to a guard of honour, under crossed swords provided by six of his squadron. Both mothers cried into their handkerchiefs.

A family friend snapped the newly-weds at the church door, using half a roll of his carefully hoarded film and presented one of the prints, fixed into a small, engine-turned, silver frame, as his wedding gift.

The reception was held in the village hall where friends and relatives had donated food for the wedding breakfast. The father of the bride spoke movingly of faith and commitment, welcoming Ronald into their family. For an hour the war was banished. The wedding cake was a fruitcake with a cardboard cover, painted and decorated to look like sugar icing – wartime shortages were everywhere. Hutch, ever the prankster, produced a saw, before handing the happy couple his officer's sword to make the first cut.

The guests laughed and cheered. Ronald's speech was not memorable, but Libby's eyes shone with the sort of adoration which said that he could have been speaking in Chinese for all she cared. The perfect couple.

The honeymoon suite was one night in a hotel in Horncastle, then they both went back to their service duties and had not met again for nearly two months. Libby was given compassionate leave to visit him in hospital.

Four years later, almost to the day his beloved, beautiful Libby was dead – complications in childbirth, eclampsia they called it, and, to make his pain and despair almost unbearable, the baby was stillborn. It was so unspeakably unfair. The funeral under leaden skies had torn the heart from him and left an ache that fifty, sixty years had not dimmed or assuaged.

He did not spend the rest of his life alone. Some years later, after a certain amount of matchmaking by his friends, he married a charming lady. She made it abundantly clear that she was not interested in hearing about any of his wartime experiences, so he buried them deeper in his mind. There was sex, initially tender and caring but as time went by it became mechanical, intermittent and brief, such that from time to time she accused him of being disinterested. Sometime later, was it months or years, after another bout of unsatisfying lovemaking, he found himself unable to deny that it was Libby's face, not hers, he was seeing.

She ejected him without protest from the bedroom. When he returned from work that day she was gone, packed her bags, leaving a note that he would be hearing from her lawyers. The divorce papers eventually arrived – he signed without bothering to read them. He never saw her again and that door to his emotions was locked for all time.

Ronald wiped his eyes, cleared his throat self-consciously and looked at his watch and saw that it was nearly 2am. He was beginning to wonder if he really could open all the closed doors to his past. If he was to answer Hutch, then it seemed he would be left with no choice.

CHAPTER 19

He had chafed at the bit to get into battle, but D-Day came and went. He and others from his squadron – just the ones with sufficient air combat experience – were held back to deal with a new and potentially devastating weapon, the creation of Germany's top aviation scientists. It was said to be one of a series of wonder weapons, which could, which should, which must turn the direction of the war, belatedly back in Germany's favour.

18th July 1944
V1 Patrol Hastings 2 hours

Briefing had been simple – shoot down as many of these pilotless flying bombs as possible. Easy enough to say, but the real trick was how to do it and not get yourself blown up in the process.

The flying bomb itself was a masterpiece of simplicity, a triumph of German ingenuity – build a teardrop shaped tube twenty-six feet long and no more than thirty inches wide; stick a ton of high explosive at the front, some elementary guidance stuff at the back in the narrow end and put the fuel in the middle. Then mount a crude, but oh-so-effective ram-jet engine on top at the back supported on a rudimentary tail plane with a tiny rudder and elevators and finish off with stubby wings no more than eighteen feet in span to give it lift.

The engine was the clever bit – just a grid of flaps at the front of a ten feet long tube, a spark plug in the middle and an open tail pipe at the back to expel the gases. Although the craft required a form of rocket-assisted catapult to get it flying, the in-rush of air through the mouth of the entry port created the right mix with the fuel, to be ignited explosively by the spark plug – a small proportion of the resulting shock wave rushing forward in the tube to force the flaps closed, but so that the vast amount of the shock wave was sent backwards blasting out of the rear exhaust. Ronald imagined it like a frog pushing and resting, pushing and resting, but so many times a second that there was a stream of energy pouring out of the exhaust, enough to drive the bomb forward at almost four hundred miles per hour. The staccato rasp of the engine once airborne, gave it the characteristic off-key buzzing sound so that it came to be nicknamed the buzz bomb.

Connect all this to a basic clock or timer, work out that one hundred and fifty miles to the heart of London from the coast of northern France is twenty minutes flying time – give or take, with a bit of adjustment for wind direction, especially a head wind – clock runs out, engine stops and down goes the bomb somewhere, anywhere over London. How the Londoners had grown to hate and fear those moments of silence as the bomb descended, arming its warhead on the way down, to explode entirely at random, on a home, factory or school, spreading death and destruction.

Seeing and hearing was infinitely preferable to hearing and not seeing, which was a heart-stopping eternity while you waited to see if you heard the bang. In many ways it was worse than the Blitz when there was some warning and time to get to a shelter. If Germany could put enough of these missiles into the air for long enough, a ton at a time and no loss of pilot, then the flying bombs could possibly change the course of the war.

Photo-reconnaissance had discovered dozens, then hundreds of catapult launch sites – ski slopes they were called – all along the Pas de Calais and further to the south, all aimed more or less directly at the heart of London. The bomber boys had been blasting them for weeks, but shortly after D-day the flying bombs had arrived in London to wreak their damage, just one or two initially, as though they were a test run for what was to follow. Then, within a couple of days, came a steady stream, gradually increasing and now running at dozens a day. The people of London, who had begun to believe their war was over following the invasion of France, were beginning to get into a panic – the government was getting worried by the rising death toll.

In France, the Allied invasion troops were stuck in Normandy. Getting inland, off the beaches after the 6th of June had been achieved, at some cost; every death was a life not lived and fulfilled, but the casualties had been "acceptable". Now they were bogged down in the 'bocage' of Normandy, the spider's web of small fields and sunken roads that had made attack a nightmare and defence a tactical dream. The V1's were proving to be a major distraction.

So here he was, stooging around at quarter throttle looking for a little speck coming in below him at close to, but not quite at his maximum speed. The Spits had tried, but with limited success; the new jets – the Meteors – were the best hope (he had not even seen one yet), but they were still some weeks from being worked up to combat readiness.

So it was down to the Typhoons and Tempests with their extra grunt to try to stop the bombs before they got too far inland. South of London an arc of anti-aircraft guns were hastily being rushed into place – the last line of defence before the buzz became bomb.

Looking round from his blister canopy, Ronald could see the coastal town of Hastings off to his right, and the outline of the French coast lost in the blue grey haze, on his left. Apart from anything else, he and the others, stationed at ten mile intervals, were sitting ducks for any marauding German fighter. It was almost impossible to scan the sky above for an attacker, whilst keeping a continuous watch over the sea below, eyes peeled for that tiny fleeting cross that would reveal the approach of his quarry.

There, a speck, surely, or was it something in his eye? He blinked, and blinked again to clear his vision. Yes, yes, there was one, batting towards him getting bigger every second.

Opening the throttle, he called it in to control, "Tango five attacking now." Christ, it was fast, steady, but bloody fast!

Hard over on the port wing, the speed building rapidly, he circled down round behind the bomb which was leaving the faintest trail of exhaust gas as it rocketed in toward the coast. Levelling off so that he was in the bomb's slipstream, he opened the throttle to close the range down to fifty yards. From directly behind, the cross section the diminutive craft was tiny, making it a very difficult and dangerous target.

The conventional wisdom was that it was safest to attack from the rear. A beam attack, although offering a much bigger target, risked hitting the warhead with very real danger to the attacking aircraft. Thus far, in the few days since the onslaught began, no safer tactic had been developed, so he followed the advice.

Now at a speed in excess of 400 indicated air speed, he flipped off the safety cover on the firing button and, centring the body of the bomb in his reflector sight, gave it an initial short burst, but with no obvious result. Frustratingly, the recoil from the few shells fired had checked his own speed, making him fall further back, out of effective range.

Feeding in more throttle he closed the gap again. Flying towards the nation's capital at more than seven miles per minute, time was not on his side. Hastings was already far behind and the anti-aircraft guns lay ahead. They would put up a barrage ahead of the bomb; their bursts of lethal shrapnel would not differentiate between target and pursuer. Being shot down by his own side was not an appealing thought.

Inching closer, he opened fire, a longer burst this time and had the satisfaction of seeing bits starting to come off the left stubby wing. Keeping his finger on the firing button and pushing the throttle to its maximum he used the rudder pedals to "walk" the nose of the Tempest back and forth across the stern of the target.

Instantly, he could see flashes of light as his shells struck all over the target, but before he could move a muscle, the engine pod separated from the body, lifting up and hurtling straight toward him as the body, trailing flame, dropped from sight below the nose of the Tempest. In a flash, the engine, tumbling like a drum-majors baton, flew back inches over his canopy and, twisting round, he watched it narrowly miss the tail fin. Strike one, he thought as the Americans were prone to say, but it had been too close for comfort.

Taking a deep breath to try and calm his racing pulses, he throttled back, turning tightly and reversed his course to resume his patrol off Hastings.

Twenty minutes later another bomb came his way from a different angle, black in colour this time rather than the olive green of his first, so perhaps it was from a different launch site.

Announcing the attack, he followed the same procedure as previously and fired a long burst at the silhouette – no apparent result, so he fired again walking the fire pattern, but still no result until the firing ceased and he heard the hiss of gas and clanking of empty breaches; out of ammunition.

Angered and cursing, he opened the throttle wide and drew alongside the bomb as it flew serenely along. Even above the roar of the straining Napier engine he could detect the howl of the ram-jet engine. It was so bloody frustrating that its wingtip was only an arm's width away from his, but he could do nothing about it.

Just as he was giving thought as to whether he could chew bits out of it with the Tempest's propeller, a warning light flashed up on the instrument panel which told him he was down to minimum fuel.

With the ache of being thwarted in his heart, he cut the throttle and watched the craft pull steadily ahead to meet its destiny with the gunners outside London. Turning east, he pointed an imaginary pistol with his fingers at the fast disappearing speck, but it was going to take more than an imaginary cowboy's bullet to protect London and its millions of frightened citizens.

Returning to base, he found that the other pilots had had the same mixed degree of success. Possibly because their very small silhouette, these flying bombs were proving a real problem to deal with. The anti-aircraft batteries were having a little more success, but the amount of shells being put into the air were also causing problems of their own for the people on the ground because of the amount of shrapnel raining down on the surrounding villages and countryside. For the moment, until the bombs could be stopped, it was a small price that had to be paid.

As they all sat around in the mess that night discussing tactics for dealing with the bombs, mention was made of another squadron claiming success, not by shooting but by the simple, but arguably dangerous method of flying alongside the bomb wing to wing. The idea was that the airflow over the fighter's wing would disturb the airflow under and over the bomb's wing, which, it was thought, would make it unstable. This should result in the bomb rolling beyond the control of its inbuilt stabilisers and then it would plunge to the ground, hopefully, before the warhead had been fused.

The debate continued long into the evening without any conclusion being reached, save that in the absence of anything else, the attack from astern still seemed to be the preferred option.

20th July 1944
Patrol Hasting 2 hours

No patrol on the 19th due to the impossible flying conditions, very low cloud and driving rain made finding, let alone attacking the flying bombs impossible, but for a pilotless craft, weather conditions were largely irrelevant and so they had come hour after hour, more than two hundred in the day, homing in on a defenceless London.

Here we go again, he thought. The low pressure area had cleared away to the east, leaving the sky for the most part clear, with broken cumulus cloud at about ten thousand feet which gave plenty of height for his patrol and also for those pilots in their designated sectors to the north and south of him.

After ten minutes on patrol, he spotted his first flying bomb of the day. Reporting his attack he plunged down through a thin layer of mist taking station behind the speeding craft.

This time, a short burst of fire clipped a couple of feet off the left wing and the bomb rapidly rolled over to its left side and plunged from his sight.

As he reported the kill, excited voices broke into his earphones. It seemed that a major assault was underway across the whole of the south coast. Saturation of the coastal defences had always been the German High Command's intention and it looked as though this was what they were trying to achieve.

Gaining height, Ronald saw another bomb coming his way a little further to the south so he gave chase, his ears popping from the rapid decompression.

As he lined up behind the bomb he could not help but be fascinated by the technology that was needed to put and keep such a device in the air. Speculating whether, one day, there might be at some time in the future pilotless aircraft as well as pilotless missiles, he opened fire. The first burst seemed to do little, but the second burst clearly had some effect because the bomb started to climb. He gave it a third burst and had the satisfaction of seeing it rear up, stall and tumble away past his right wing. Again he could only hope the warhead would not arm on the way down.

Climbing for a third time, he was soon on the tail of yet another rocket. A prolonged burst from his guns, and flame poured from the sides of its engine. It stuttered in its course and began to drop away.

As he turned to look at the stricken missile he saw another, his fourth of the day, coming straight at him.

There was no time to gain height, his fuel was rapidly becoming exhausted and as he had no real idea of how much ammunition he had left, he decided to let the bomb overtake him.

As the craft rapidly came up from astern, he opened the throttle with the intention of matching its speed and pulling in behind, but then realised that as it drew level with him it was also drifting quite steadily toward him until it was no more than ten feet away, the black and white swastika on its tailfin catching the mid-morning sun.

Why not? he thought. Why not give it a try?

Closer and closer the two wings came; the stubby eight foot starboard wing of the bomb dwarfed by the wing of the Tempest. Closer still, until he had eighteen inches of the tip of his wing under the wing of the bomb, but disappointingly there was no appreciable effect – certainly not the instant destabilisation he had been assured would be induced.

It struck him how incongruous they must look to anyone watching on the ground, almost like a mother and child, hand in hand, hurtling across the sky.

Enough of this, he thought and slapped the control stick on the Tempest to the right. In response, the left wing lifted, contacting the flying bomb with a perceptible thud. For the bomb, however it was the end. The contact with the Tempest raised its wing by more than forty-five degrees then over it went, rolling onto its back, smoke belching from the exhaust as it plummeted from sight.

The warning light on the instrument panel once again alerted him of low fuel and so he returned to base, where to his surprise and to the annoyance of the fitter, he found that the impact with the bomb had put quite a noticeable dent in the left wing tip of his Tempest, but it was, thankfully, not enough to warrant taking Miss Faithful out of service for repair.

Ronald paused in his reading and reflected ruefully that, if only he had known what lay in store in the days ahead, he would not have worried too much about such a minor knock.

For the next two or three days a series of small things, gremlins in the works or his aim had been off, had conspired to deprive him of success despite there being no shortage of targets as the intensity of the aerial assault increased. Too many flying bombs were saturating the defences and getting through to London, where the numbers of dead and injured were rising alarmingly. There was mounting criticism in the press about the failure of the RAF to stop the bombs in their tracks. The criticisms hurt – they were all flying at least two and sometimes three sorties in a day and the nervous tension of these very high speed chases was exhausting.

There was talk of the Meteors being thrown into the fray to help bolster the lines of defence even though they had not fully completed their work up to combat readiness. If the piston-engined fighters could hold on another few days then the jets with their vastly superior speed could help stem the onslaught. More than three thousand missiles had so far been launched from France, with no sign of the launch rate abating. Dealing with this menace had become a major distraction from the planned conduct of the air war against Germany, such that the RAF's heavy bombers had been moved over to daylight attacks to try and knock out the launch sites.

The Prime Minister, Winston Churchill had ordered the change of priorities personally because of the threat to the country's morale. Ronald and his colleagues had taken it as a personal request from Winston to try just that little bit harder.

Only once in the fifty plus years since the war had Ronald thought in any detail about his part in stopping the barrage of flying bombs. This had occurred in 1993 during the first Gulf War. He had watched a piece of film reportage from Baghdad. It had shown an American cruise missile, caught on film flying down a city centre street and then making a right turn around a large building at an intersection, as though following an internal map. Watching this brought back all the memories of his involvement with their forefathers. He thanked his lucky stars that his targets had only the simplest of instruments to guide them, without any ability to take evasive action, but they had still packed just as devastating a punch.

28th, July 1944
Patrol Hastings   1 hour 5 minutes

Second patrol of the day, the first concluding with one buzz bomb shot down, bringing his total so far to six.

There was no let up to the intensity of the bombardment, but at least the Meteors would be entering the fray in the next twenty-four hours, their final training having been expedited in order to rush them into the struggle to contain the growing menace. He had little doubt that all the pilots needed to be rested. They were all beginning to make unnecessary mistakes, particularly when landing, which was a sure sign that they were reaching the limits of their endurance.

Whether it was his own tiredness, bad luck, or just carelessness he would never know, but he had just finished an attack at the southern edge of his sector – a successful attack, his seventh kill, but one which had used up far too much of his ammunition – when he spotted a second rocket hard on the heels of the first, so close that he had no time to line up a proper approach.

Hauling the Tempest round toward the target, his vision greying from the centrifugal force, he allowed the fullest deflection, aiming well ahead. More in hope than expectation he fired a tentative burst and watched his tracers homing in on his prey.

As his speed brought the Tempest round behind the bomb, closing rapidly for a second burst, the sky in front of him exploded;

angry, boiling, a heavy orange centre tinged with black oily smoke. His plane, before he could react, plunged into the centre of the storm. Instantly the Tempest was engulfed in hot screaming metal. Something big and heavy slammed into the propeller boss shaking the Tempest to its core.

At the same time, before he could utter the obscenity that was forming on his lips, more debris hit the screen, canopy and wings. Glancing to left and right he could see chunks flaking off his wings as a horrendous shudder assailed the aircraft.

At his left shoulder, he sensed rather than saw the cockpit's Plexiglas canopy start to disintegrate and a hammer blow struck his upper arm making him shout with the pain. Minute shards peppered his face, but his goggles saved his eyes.

The vibration from the engine was increasing alarmingly, and instinctively he pulled hard on the stick in the hope that he could gain some height. On the radio he called a Mayday, as he fought to suppress the panic flooding through his veins. At least he was over land.

One of the propeller blades sheared off, intensifying the vibration.

It was time to go. The plane was not going to last much longer and as if to prove the point, the engine stopped dead and, with a sickening screech, the momentum of the propeller snapped the drive shaft; the boss with the remaining three blades crashed into the port wing and careened away.

Ripping off the radio and oxygen connections, he lifted his feet up off the rudder pedals, and pulled with all his might on bright red handle jutting out of the instrument panel to jettison the remains of the canopy, As the canopy disintegrated and spun away into the slipstream together with the large emergency escape panel on the right side of the cockpit, everything loose inside the cockpit whirled about his face in the gale of wind.

Half blinded by his map, he thumped the emergency release box on his chest for the Sutton harness, hauled the control column back into his lap then slammed it as hard as he could toward the instrument panel.

Instead of being ejected from the cockpit like a cork from a bottle as the manual, the Pilot's Notes, said he should be, he found that he floated away with agonising slowness, curling himself into a ball to watch the disintegration of his plane as though in slow motion, and praying that he would not hit the tail-fin as it sliced past him. He expected to be ripped away into the slipstream, but it was not so and he had the frightening experience of watching the left wing break off and come fluttering toward him.

Still counting; and eight, and nine, and ten, he reached for and took a grip of death on the hand-sized D shaped metal ring secured to the front of the parachute harness. Pulling with all his strength he waited for the canopy to open – waited an eternity it seemed as his eyes followed the shattered remains of his Tempest spiralling down. Moments later, like a broken butterfly, it impacted in a field of cows, the explosion scything through the herd.

A violent jerk around his groin took his breath away and he was spun forcibly round as the risers, the thick webbing straps to which the canopy cords were attached unwound themselves and, to his great relief, he saw the white silk of his parachute opening, undamaged, above him.

The roar of the airstream faded from his ears.

Remembering his parachute training, he went to reach up for the toggles in order to have some control over the direction he was facing and only at this point did he realise that he could not move his left arm. There was a jagged tear in the fabric of his flying jacket and looking down he could see blood beginning to drip from the tips of his glove. Then the pain hit him.

Three minutes later and only half conscious and shivering with shock from the loss of blood, he thumped into a cornfield just to the west of Godalming. Vaguely he heard people running, voices, and the sound of an ambulance bell. The smell of damp earth and a lark singing were the last sensations before he passed out.

As he closed the log book, Ronald recalled that later that day they had removed a large piece of Perspex from his left arm which had been broken by the impact. Distracted by the thought, he found himself rubbing gently on the scarred depression at the top of his left arm above the bicep. He had been offered the Perspex shrapnel by the surgeon as a souvenir and although he accepted it initially, he soon tired of its reminder, sitting as a silent witness to his pain on the bedside unit and so he had consigned it to the waste bin a couple of days later.

He had taken no further part in the battle against the flying bombs. A combination of defence methods finally turned the tables – until the arrival of the V2 rockets for which there was no possible defence. On balance he concluded that he preferred a quarry that fired back.

The second period of hospitalisation in a year and the loss of his first "Miss Faithful" had depressed him enormously, but his morale had been quickly restored by two unexpected visitors to his bedside.

Firstly, there was the arrival on compassionate leave of Libby, whose suggestion of "kissing everything better" was wholly welcome. Secondly, there was a fleeting visit by Torrie, who had managed to persuade her battery commander to give her a few hours leave so that she could see her big brother.

Hitching a lift the short distance to the hospital, she brought with her all her usual enthusiasm and, perhaps more importantly, a large bar of American chocolate. Assuring him that acquiring such a rare treat had not required her to do anything illegal, although she refused to elaborate on whether anything even slightly immoral was involved, she left him with the further assurance that his injury was nothing more than just a scratch. Mischievously, she suggested that his face had had a close encounter with a hedgehog, but he was grateful they had taken such care to cleanse his wounds.

She also told him, swearing him to absolute secrecy in the process, that her anti-aircraft battery had just been issued with new, top-secret, proximity fuses for their shells. A near miss was now enough to knock the buzz bombs out of the sky. The first conscious sound he had heard on coming round from the anaesthetic had been the continued discordant drone of the flying bombs and so he had been relieved to know that another, more effective weapon had finally been deployed.

Then she had gone, clattering down the wooden floor of the ward, waving over her shoulder and shouting her goodbyes to all. How he loved her then – and still did.

Reaching into the leather case that held the key to so many of his memories his fingers came upon a small brown jeweller's box. Inside, though he had not looked at it for sixty years, was a small enamel badge in the shape of a caterpillar. It was a tribute to the art of the silkworm that had produced the fabric of his parachute and a tribute to him from the Irving Parachute Company that his life had been saved by their product. That the caterpillar was set with green rather than red eyes was an acknowledgment that his plane was not on fire at the time he jumped. For that small mercy he would be eternally grateful.

He had spent three weeks in hospital while his injuries began to mend. There were numerous other nicks and cuts from the shattered canopy which healed steadily to leave little scarring; the bruising from the opening of the parachute was only a minor irritation. His popularity among the nurses increased immediately upon the arrival of the chocolate so that he received the *best* of care, although he had to remind one especially pretty nurse that he was a very happily married man. Another brief visit from Libby set that particular record straight and then it was time to leave, arm plastered and in a sling, the sleeve of his jacket pinned neatly to the side.

Petrol rationing, even more severe now, to protect supplies for the invasion forces in France, meant that his father could not collect him this time, so the Station Adjutant took him to the train, mentioning quite casually, en route, that Ronald had been recommended for a Bar to his Distinguished Flying Cross in recognition of his contribution to the battle against the V1s.

The journey to his parents' home railway station had taken ages, with frequent interruptions and not helped by his broken arm which continued to trouble him. He was at least travelling light with little more than the clothes he stood up in, so that he was freed of the burden of trying to cope with a suitcase.

His need to light a succession of cigarettes was met by a Petty Officer from the Royal Navy travelling home on his first leave since D-Day. Notwithstanding the longstanding warning that "careless talk costs lives" the Petty Officer told Ronald of his time on an unnamed cruiser which took part in the pre-dawn barrage on the 6th of June and how they had gone on firing hour after hour, only breaking off for long enough to allow the gun barrels to cool.

He had listened intently to Ronald's description of chasing down the buzz bombs, told him of his own family's loss in London in the early days of the Blitz and, as the train pulled in to Lincoln thanked Ronald profusely, to his embarrassment, for what he had done. As the Petty Officer left the train, Ronald realised that he did not even know the man's name and reflected on the comradeship of strangers thrown together in adversity.

One station further along the line, Ronald alighted from the train into the concerned arms of his mother who dedicated the next month to making his convalescence as comfortable as possible.

Truth to tell, nothing she did could match the tender loving care that Libby lavished upon him when she came home on leave a week or so later. He remembered with a smile, that when the care became more loving than tender, his parents had made themselves scarce – discreetly.

By the middle of October and with the aid of some physiotherapy he was declared fit to return to his squadron, to return to combat, not from a base in England, but from a forward airfield in northern France, recaptured from its former occupiers as the push to harass the German forces within their own borders intensified.

He did not return home for the next six months and the memory of Libby and that last night in her arms after their passion was spent, were his comfort and companion while he and his comrades carried the war to an enemy whose tenacity would continue to amaze and disconcert until that very last day at Grossenbrode.

CHAPTER 20

With all their plans completed, Ronald had little difficulty making the on-line booking for the ferry crossing to Denmark; in fact he was quite proud of himself as a silver-surfer even though at his age the silver was getting somewhat tarnished. Muttering to himself almost constantly, it had taken him nearly an hour to navigate his way through the various screens; payment using his credit card was quite straightforward, although he had to phone a neighbour to ask where to find the security code on his card, bemoaning the fact that once upon a time the promise of a cheque in the post used to be considered good enough.

He supposed that gradually he was finding himself increasingly at odds with the encroaching world of technology. The internet however he had regarded as the last of the great challenges of his long life and, still having vague thoughts that he should one day record his life history for his nephews and nieces, he had undertaken a course of classes at the local adult education centre. He was not interested in the finer points of computing and so he took only sufficient classes to become familiar with surfing the internet, setting up an e-mail address for himself and learning the rudiments of using the word-processing package that the shop installed on the basic laptop he had chosen – once he had persuaded the very young salesman that, despite the enthusiasm of his generation for watching videos and gaming, such toys were surplus to his requirements.

Memories of German interference with radio transmissions during his wartime flying convinced him that he should have an anti-virus package, but the offer of an extended warranty he politely declined, largely on the basis that the end of the warranty and the end of his earthly time might be a close run thing.

Both he and Keith had agreed that, curtailing their lifestyles for the sake of preserving the bank balances to be available for their heirs, was quite unnecessary and so he had reserved the best twin cabin on the ferry – which came with the benefit a balcony, even though he doubted he would have the courage to use it.

It had always struck him as odd that aerobatics, whether in training or combat, had no virtually adverse effects on his body and usually left him thrilled by the rush of adrenalin, whereas boating of any description produced a distinctly queasy sensation from the moment he set foot on board.

Despite unending reassurances from his friends – *don't worry, one little jab from the ship's MO and you'll be fine for the duration* – he had always declined the world of cruising, despite the torrent of glossy brochures that seemed to pour through his letter box every autumn. Even the "promise" of guaranteed shipboard romances had never been enough to make him change his mind.

He had done love once, which had been denied to him in any lasting way, he had done the sex thing which proved unsatisfactory. In the end, he had concluded that he was better off in his own company, although, for all that, he found himself looking forward to Keith's companionship on the journey.

Ideally he would have preferred a shorter sea crossing, but as they had agreed that Keith would do all of the driving, it was unfair to ask that he should drive all the way from either the Hook of Holland or Cuxhaven in north-west Germany. By sailing direct to Esbjerg on the west coast of Denmark they would reduce the continental driving to tens rather than hundreds of miles.

Keith also pointed out that apart from the personal effort of driving great distances on the wrong side of the road, the longer sea voyage would be kinder to the "old girl", as he referred to his elderly Jaguar. "Might as well do it in a bit of comfort" was his comment, but it was his way of saying, politely, that the thought of being in Ronald's ancient estate car – a relic from the days when he kept a couple of Golden Retrievers for company – was less than attractive. Ronald thought this was a fair trade, but deep down he prayed for a smooth crossing.

Keith might have been less enthusiastic if he had realised he would be sharing a cabin with someone who might be throwing up every ten minutes, even in the gentlest of swells

From their calculations they believed that their quarry lay within a ninety minute drive from the port and with the ferry arriving at lunch time they felt this would give them a fairly full afternoon to begin their investigations, but because of the uncertainty of their quest they decided not to try and pre-book a room for the first night.

Using his newly acquired skills on the internet, Ronald used a search engine to download a list of suitable pubs in the locality, all of which seemed to offer a high standard of cuisine. In any event they only planned to stay three nights in Denmark with the intention of catching the return ferry on the fourth afternoon. If they could not answer Hutch's riddle in almost four days of searching then, as far as they were concerned, they were going to have to admit defeat and accept, reluctantly, that it was going to remain unsolved for all time.

Of course, thought Ronald, there still remained the distinct possibility that this was an elaborate hoax – in which case what was the point to it all? Then again, and perhaps more worryingly, there was the risk that his secret had been discovered in the mean time.

However, from his discussions with the London solicitor Colin Farrell, it appeared that, even though Hutch had put his plans in train some considerable time prior to his death, and the fact that Hutch had not signed his will until just a few days before he died, had lead them to the inescapable conclusion that Hutch must have been able to verify that his secret had remained secure and undiscovered for more than fifty years.

At this point in their debate a further thought had struck Ronald. What if Hutch could have checked his security without ever going to Denmark? What if there was someone still alive in Denmark who could give him that comfort, just a phone call away? That raised other possibilities that would only be answered, if at all, by their visit.

Letters from Denmark had ceased with the German occupation and his letters to Karin had gone unanswered, but was it significant, with the benefit of hindsight, that they were never returned marked undelivered? He did not know whether such things happened in post-war Europe which was in such turmoil for so long.

Eventually he had given up trying to contact Karin and, never having visited the country either before or after the war, the ongoing silence dissuaded him from enquiring further. He had concluded that his Danish family no longer existed as had been the fate of so many millions of unfortunate souls across the breadth of Europe. The loss of Stan, his handsome older brother, however painful personally, had somehow paled in significance as he became aware of the extent of human loss during those war years.

But what if he were wrong; what if there were another reason for the silence from Denmark? Was this what Hutch was trying to tell him? One way or another, God willing, they should know within a few days.

When Keith called to collect him a week later Ronald had packed a light suitcase for the journey. Tucked amongst the folds of a clean shirt, he had included a sheet of aluminium approximately eight inches square and an electronic gadget he had purchased from a hardware shop. It had taken him an age to make himself familiar with its operating procedures. Something he had seen at the air museum had given him an idea how they might have hidden the 109, but until the time came to put his theory to the test, he preferred to keep it under wraps, and did not tell Keith about it.

Keith had, as agreed, equipped the Jaguar with a couple of simple tools. A stout pair of tyre levers and a small, but robust military-surplus folding shovel were stored carefully out of sight in the spare wheel well under the boot carpet. When Ronald enquired what was wrapped in a canvas bag strapped up against the rear-seat back under the parcel shelf, Keith merely tapped the side of his nose, saying that one never knew when a metal detector might come in useful.

Ronald loaded his suitcase into the boot next to Keith's, fervently hoping they would not be called upon to explain their cargo. As far as he could tell, metal detecting in Denmark required no more official sanction than it did in England, but the crime of breaking and entering was frowned on equally in both countries, and perhaps especially so if the perpetrators were found to be a pair of geriatric octogenarians.

Settled comfortably into the soft cream leather of the Jaguar's passenger seat as Keith drove steadily south on the A1, Ronald felt that old feeling of butterflies in the tummy, but whether this was from the thought of the sea crossing or from the anticipation of their venture he could not say. He remained optimistic that there really was something to be discovered on the west coast of Denmark. He realised that Keith continued to be sceptical, but then, as Keith had pointed out, perhaps his role was to be a catalyst. Whatever, Keith had been wholly supportive and, as he drifted on the edge of sleep, he knew that Keith was a full partner and if they should fail, pray God they did not, then he would share the disappointment.

He dozed briefly as they progressed in companiable silence and woke from a dream about Libby, feeling disappointed and disoriented as Keith switched from the A1 to the A14 heading east and then south toward Harwich.

Keith then suggested that, as they had more than enough time in hand, they should take a break for lunch. Looking at the roadmap Ronald suggested they continue the twenty odd miles to Bury St Edmonds. Twenty-five minutes later Keith parked the Jaguar outside an old coaching inn which advertised home cooked food and had a welcoming look about it. The façade was decorated with flower boxes and hanging baskets all in full bloom.

"Looks OK," grunted Keith. "Got to have a pee – see you in the bar," as he headed off in search of the toilets.

Inside, Ronald selected a corner seat, already laid for two and was about to go to the bar when a young waitress came over to the table, laid a menu at each place and asked for his drinks order. Scanning the bar, he could see a pump for the locally brewed pale ale and ordered two half pints – just to keep them going.

By the time Keith came to the table the drinks were served and half emptied in seconds. "I'll have another of those – Cheers," said Keith with a small belch as he reviewed the menu.

Having made their selections, Ronald signalled the waitress who took their orders; steak and chips for Ronald, plaice and potatoes for Keith, bringing refills for their glasses. The food, when it came a few minutes later matched up to Ronald's expectations – the steak, medium-rare and cooked to perfection, melted in his mouth – and so they ate in quiet contemplation until Keith suddenly blurted out:

"We must be absolutely bonkers. Here we are, two old farts setting off like Indiana Jones on what might be a complete wild goose chase, except that he was forty years younger than us and had a magical 'get out of jail free' card. We must be absolutely bloody bonkers," he said again with a laugh, shaking his head.

Putting his knife and fork down with studied care, Ronald looked Keith in the eye and asked, "Seriously, do you want to back out now? It's not too late, you know. I wouldn't blame you. But isn't there a small corner inside you that still wants to know if it was the drink talking in that Russian, or did he really see something quite extraordinary? I know I do, and I'm too old to worry about the consequences."

Keith hesitated only for a moment, before replying. "Yes, no, of course I do – find out, I mean. But promise me this," pointing his fork at Ronald for emphasis, "that if I end up in jail you will come and visit me every day while I am there... And explain to my kids how the hell I got there. I didn't dare tell them before we left because I knew they would do their damnedest to stop me. Have my driving licence suspended or something. They think this is some form of 'old codgers' road trip – a last fling before they finally clip our wings, so to speak."

Ronald smiled wearily, offered Keith his hand across the table and said, "Deal!" as they shook on the bargain.

"Mind you," said Keith, "if it's you that ends up in jail the only thing you will get from me is the squeal off the Jag's tyres. I don't know you, never met you before and I'll be on that ferry home before your cell door clangs shut. Deal?" holding out his hand to Ronald who accepted it as they both roared with laughter, much to the amusement of the waitress.

They completed their meal in more relaxed mood with Ronald insisting that he settle the bill after coffee, with a generous tip to the waitress, who by then had concluded that these two elderly gentlemen were not entirely safe to be out on the road.

With nature's call attended to, they set off south at a sedate pace toward Harwich, still finding time for a cup of tea in Colchester before joining the check-in queue for documentation and passports at the port gates. While Keith busied himself with applying a GB sticker to the rear window – not on the newly waxed paintwork thank you – Ronald checked his map of Denmark and the download of the best route out of Esbjerg, placing it carefully in the map pocket by his right knee so that it would be readily available the next day.

Within minutes Keith was back in the car, firing up the four litre engine as the queue began to move. "Too late to back out now," he said with a grin as he selected Drive and eased the car forwards toward the cavernous entrance of the ferry's roll-on roll-off deck. "But God help you if you puke all over me tonight."

As one of the largest cars making the crossing, they were thankfully not directed on to the steep steel ramp of the upper parking deck, but instead circled the interior of the main loading deck until they were once again facing the bow doors, parking in a forest of trucks and continental lorries.

"Let's hope we are off first," said Keith as he removed their cases from the boot, locked the car and headed off in the direction of one of the stairwells. Ronald noted that many of the passengers were heading down, not up and heaved a great sigh of relief that they had reserved first class accommodation. Making the trip by boat was bad enough, but the thought of spending the night in the bowels of the ship, in a windowless cabin, possibly below the waterline, was the stuff of nightmares

Their tickets required that they report to the ship's purser and a few minutes later, having completed a check-in formality they were escorted to their cabin by a smartly dressed Danish steward who informed them that if they had any other requirements, such as champagne, they should contact him immediately. Wishing them

"Godt tour", and handing them the coded card for the door, he withdrew to let them settle in.

"Blimey," said Ronald as he surveyed the comfortable twin beds, a pair of easy chairs, coffee table with fresh fruit, a writing desk and art prints on the walls.

"This is a bit posh," as he sat on the edge of one of the beds before stretching out full length. "Beats a Spit cockpit any day," he added, "but I'd rather take that against this, if it's going to be rough tonight."

"I had forgotten that you have never cruised, but as staterooms go it's not too bad for one night. That last cruise Mary and I took on the QE, our suite was out of this world. She loved the big boats and we were so fortunate to have that time for our ruby anniversary – damn good job we can't see into the future."

With his eyes watering, Keith cleared his throat, adding, "I don't think you need have any worries about the weather; the forecast was really good. It will be like a mill pond and these boats have really good stabilisers."

"Hmmph," Ronald responded, "I'll be the judge of that," muttering under his breath as he started to unpack a few things for the night.

Still muttering to himself, he set a fold-up alarm clock and a couple of pill bottles on the side table between the beds, before hesitating, apparently in two minds. Then, delving into his sponge bag he extracted a small yellow cube which he placed carefully next to the clock.

Keith, who was just stepping out of the bathroom spotted it immediately and exclaimed, "Jesus, Ronno, is that it, is that really it?" as he picked up the little yellow die and held it almost reverently in the palm of his hand.

"Sixty years and you still have it."

"Yes, that's the one. I don't really know why I brought it, but somehow it seemed the right thing to do."

Seeing the look of amazement on Keith's face, he continued, "Go on, roll it. You know, we know, we all knew that it is loaded – a tiny fault in manufacture – but it meant so much to all of us at the time even though it was a load of old hokum."

As Keith hesitated, Ronald repeated, "Go on, give it a roll, but do you realise you just called me Ronno for the first time. Since we met again you have called me Ron or Ronald, but never my old squadron nickname – only the family, Libby and," he hesitated, "Karin ever called me Ronnie. I think we are going back, don't you. Go on, roll it," he said for the third time.

Keith, who seemed to have been holding his breath, rolled the die round in the cup of his hand, closed his eyes tight and tossed the die onto the table. When he opened them, there sat the six.

"Oh bloody hell."

Contrary to Ronald's initial fears, the crossing to Denmark proved to be a most enjoyable experience. A little after 5pm, the ferry slipped its moorings and headed slowly and sedately downriver, out into the North Sea following the Suffolk and Norfolk coasts then heading north-east toward the distant Danish waters.

Once it became clear that Keith's predictions for the weather were coming true Ronald began to relax, helped by Keith as they visited the ship's bars, then on to the casino, where they lost hopelessly, and finally to the premier restaurant where they both dined on reindeer steaks and other Scandinavian delicacies, which they washed down with a couple of bottles of decent French burgundy – at Keith's insistence.

Later Ronald concluded that, despite his age, Keith had a prodigious capacity for alcohol, so after an extended visit to the ship's nightclub (where Keith loudly expressed the view that he wished he were sixty years younger as he watched some of the young ladies on the dance floor) Ronald ensured that they took a long walk round the promenade deck, hoping that the onrush of cold sea air would help Keith to sober up.

By this time, Keith was talking largely to himself, and the only time he made much sense was when they stood at the ship's rail watching the moonlight across the near-flat sea and he said, "Thank Christ, I wasn't on night fighters."

For a few moments he was silent, perhaps lost in his own unspoken memories, then he put an arm round Ronald's shoulders, looking at him through unfocused eyes before saying, his voice betraying the effects of the alcohol, "Come on Ronno, old lad, time for bed. Haven't had a blow-out like that for years. Bloody good mate you are, always were."

Actually Ronald was not sure he was that much more sober than Keith and so, leaning on each other they returned unsteadily to their cabin where Ronald managed to persuade Keith to drink a large black coffee before tipping him into bed.

Lying in the dark, listening to the rumble of the ship's engines and the hum of the air-conditioning while he waited for his heart rhythm to settle, he was taken completely by surprise when Keith, whom he thought to be deeply asleep, said in the clearest voice as though he had not had a drink all night, "We think we know what he did, we think we know how he did it, but how the hell did he set it up?"

A moment's pause, then, "In the middle of the bloody war!" as he fell silent and began to snore loudly.

With that thought hanging in the air, which puzzled Ronald just as much, he drifted off to sleep, rocked as a baby by the gentle movement of the ship, dreaming once again of Libby, a full life with her and their grandchildren, lots of them.

Unusually, for this was an often repeated dream, he awoke not with a sense of profound loss, but feeling refreshed and looking forward with eager anticipation to the days ahead.

Keith was already up, shaved and showered and greeted Ronald cheerily as he dressed, not showing the slightest effect from the previous evening's indulgence.

"See you at breakfast," he said as he disappeared out of the cabin door, but half an hour later as he met Keith in the buffet restaurant, Ronald was not so sure that his stomach was up to it.

"Nonsense," said Keith in response to Ronald's expressed reluctance. "You stay there and I'll fetch you a decent Danish breakfast." Shortly he was back with coffee, bread rolls and a selection of meats, cheeses and jams.

"Eat."

"Yes mother," said Ronald dutifully in a tone of doubt, but was pleasantly surprised that his appetite perked up at the first taste of a freshly baked bread roll with its poppy seed topping, and eventually he cleared his plate.

Keith's appetite seemed to have been stimulated by all the alcohol and he cleared a second plate of food including marinated herring on rye bread. "All it needs is a good glass of ice cold schnapps to wash it down."

Instantly his comment reminded Ronald of the occasion sixty years before in Berlin when chilled schnapps first passed his lips. Involuntarily he shivered as more memories crowded in, causing Keith to comment, "Someone walk across your grave?"

"Something like that," replied Ronald. "I feel there are quite a few ghosts riding with us just now."

"Me too," Keith nodded.

After taking a breath of fresh air, they returned to their cabin and packed their things, but not before Keith had again fallen prey to the temptation of the die. He picked it up, weighing in the palm of his hand as though to try and feel the bias, then he flipped it onto the table where it spun on a corner, chattering across the surface, coming slowly to rest – three. Keith looked at Ronald with a raised eyebrow, who only shook his head in response, smiled tolerantly and with an indulgent shake of his head, popped the die into his jacket pocket. "We might need this later," he said.

Back on deck they came across a pair of lounger chairs sheltered from the cool sea breeze where they settled to await the end of the voyage in comfort. Their conversation ranged widely, but mostly about Keith and his wartime service once he had been posted away from Ronald's squadron in the weeks after his crash at Shoreham.

There had been an extended period as an instructor on combat tactics where he strove to impart his experience to the novice pilots, a brief period "flying" a desk, before returning to active flying in the autumn of 1944 just after the failure to make the breakthrough at Arnhem. Like Ronald he had spent the late winter and early spring of '45 flying close support missions for the advancing 8th Army, but an ironic twist of fate had grounded him in the dying days of the war – someone had carelessly left an inspection cover off a drainage channel and he had fallen into the hole, in the night-time blackout that still prevailed on their captured Luftwaffe airfield. He broke his leg. At the time he did not know whether to be angry or glad, but the accident had guaranteed that he survived the war. His first posting on returning to active duty had been to Berlin, where he had bumped into Hutch.

Although he was offered a short service commission, after his tour of duty ended in Berlin, he elected to leave the RAF in 1949, not wishing to take the conversion course to jet fighters. He had felt that he had done his fair share of service to king and country, so with the Berlin Airlift in full swing and trouble in Korea looming he thought it was time to get out. He joined his father's animal feeds business which was just getting back on its feet in the post war recovery.

Keith had been entirely happy in many ways. He had married Mary in 1955 and although fatherhood had come to him later than average, three children had been born. The twin boys had gone on to success in the London Stock Exchange and his daughter, to his delight, had come into the business with him, ultimately taking over as chair and chief executive upon his own retirement.

During his time with the company he had even managed to continue his love of flying. He bought a two seater Cessna light aircraft which he piloted from the airfield near the company's headquarters in Ipswich to meetings with customers all around the country.

As Keith chatted away, Ronald had to suppress a tinge of envy at Keith's evident and acknowledged good fortune. Keith said openly that he lived his life to the full, as an obligation to all those friends and comrades in arms who had not come through the war, or had survived, but been so damaged that they were never able to function fully. Nowadays it was called post-traumatic stress disorder. For Keith there had been a simpler view – there was only just so much killing and destruction that one person could take and he knew he had reached his limit.

With that thought, Ronald wondered if the fancy label answered much of what seemed to have affected him throughout his life, which was not helped, and probably made much worse by the tragic death of Libby. Perhaps if the baby had survived, things might have been different – a future to cherish, but that had been taken from him and his second wife had made it clear that children would form no part of their life together.

He supposed that, in the way he had "lived" during the war, with certainty and purpose, with fear and hope, hope for a better life, but since the death of Libby when hope ended, he had merely functioned. After the war he had taken the old fashioned way into accountancy – in-service training and night study – and made a reasonable success of it, rising to the position of senior partner of a medium-sized county practice by the time of his retirement.

He had been a magistrate for a while, joined the local Rotary club to serve his community, gaining a certain level of personal recognition and respect, but deep down he knew he was marking time.

After Libby's death he had, in his darkest moments seriously considered suicide, being unable to see any future without her, so great had been their love. Torrie had supported and counselled him, gradually driving away the darkness, helping him to see a future until sense had prevailed, because he had come to recognise, like Keith, that by a miracle he had been granted the life denied so many.

Upon reflection, as he lay back in the deck-lounger, feeling the growing strength of the mid-morning sun and only half listening to Keith's life story, he judged perhaps his own had not all been bad. He had done his best, led an honourable life and doted unreservedly on Torrie's children, seeing them as his proxy future.

Despite Torrie's gentle protests, he had been generous, very generous even, to his great nephews and nieces, stating that whatever he did not need, others should have and benefit. It would please him to see them enjoying his gift in whatever way they saw fit – he attached no strings and made similar arrangements through his will, after substantial bequests to a variety of the armed forces benevolent funds.

A blast from the ship's siren jolted him back to reality. He surfaced to find Keith sitting on the edge of his lounger, laughing. "Welcome back, you've been sound asleep for the past hour. I realised that I was talking to myself, but I hadn't got the heart to wake you. You were muttering to yourself, but no, you did not say anything to embarrass yourself."

"Thank God," breathed Ronald. "I have been told by Torrie that I am prone to talking in my sleep, shouting sometimes, which is probably why she puts me in the guestroom at the far end of her house. Doesn't want me frightening the grandkids."

"We are nearly there," said Keith indicating the low-lying Danish coastline and its sandy beaches just off the port bow of the ferry. They could feel the boat beginning to make its turn to starboard around the island of Fano, with its large wind farm. The island acted as a breakwater to shelter Denmark's main port on its west coast from the worst of any North Sea storms.

Within minutes the harbour came into sight with its distinctive crenulated watchtower as the ship's tannoy instructed the passengers to return to their vehicles. The butterflies returned to Ronald's stomach, but this time there was no doubt as to their cause.

Collecting their cases from the cabin, they descended to the car deck where they waited with growing impatience for the docking process to be completed. To the accompanying cacophony of metal grinding against timber, shouted commands over the loudspeakers, the trucks and lorries around them rumbled into life, belching diesel fumes into the cavernous expanse of the car deck.

Keith started the Jaguar, ensuring the air intake was firmly shut, as a crack of light appeared at the top of the bow door. With a final resounding thud, the ramp fell to the quayside, flooding the car deck with weak sunlight.

CHAPTER 21

"Time to go," said Keith as he eased the Jaguar forward in response to a deck marshal's instruction. Ronald's stomach tightened as the Jag passed slowly over the ramp and bumped gently down onto Danish soil. Ronald took a very deep breath and tried to stay calm.

Large signs reminded them to drive on the right as they cleared customs formalities and headed out of the port facility, crossing the adjacent railway tracks, while Ronald collected his bearings. Working from the internet printout, he advised Keith to turn right onto Route 24 south-eastwards in the direction of the cathedral town of Ribe.

"We know that there are any number of possible locations because Hutch deliberately left out part of the map reference, so we'll start as agreed by going down to the south."

Once they cleared the suburbs, Keith drove sedately out into the open, flat Danish countryside on roads, pleasantly free of traffic, and onward through isolated villages each with its white painted church. South of Ribe with its magnificent cathedral clearly visible from the by-pass, Keith commented, "Must have been quite a landmark for our bomber boys on a moonlit night." Ronald grunted as he drifted back in time. Cathedrals had always been highly visible marker points: Lincoln, Grantham, St Paul's, Rouen, Hamburg, Cologne, the list was endless and it just depended on your point of view – nearly there or nearly home. Nearly home: the Brighton Pavilion had been his cathedral.

Returning his concentration to the present with a shake of his head, Ronald advised a right turn heading southeast on a minor road until Ronald asked him to drive a couple of miles further and then to park. Five minutes later they were stopped at a small crossroads, parking across the entrance to what appeared to be a gravelled field track which stretched away, straight as an arrow into the distance. Keith switched off the engine and they sat for a moment listening to the ticking of the cooling metal as they gathered their thoughts.

Climbing out of the car they surveyed their surroundings. Long fields, some ploughed, some still in crop stretched away in all directions, separated by rows of stunted fir trees acting as a windbreak against the prevailing westerly winds. From where they stood there was not a building in sight, the only form of construction being an isolated wind turbine more than sixty metres high, the three-bladed propeller turning slowly in the steady breeze, mocking their endeavour.

Keith blew out his cheeks. "There's nowhere here to hide a toy plane let alone a full sized fighter. We are never going to find it," he groaned.

"Have faith. Faint heart never won fair maid," quoted Ronald. "We never thought it would be easy. We learnt search and rescue all those years ago, so we'll put it into practice now. The map reference is suspect anyway and could cover a square ten kilometres on a side, a hundred square kilometres, so Ill set up a grid centred starting from here, heading generally northwest, then we can try to drive it before night falls. It will be tough, but with the country being so flat we should be able to see far enough to cover the area in three or four sweeps. We can, we hope, disregard the villages and concentrate on the countryside and as remote a location as possible, with enough space to land and take off. Easy peasy as they say," he concluded with a wry laugh.

"Aye, aye Skipper," replied Keith with mock servility.

Spreading the map on the long bonnet of the Jaguar, Ronald quickly sketched a search grid in pencil, and then traced the most efficient search pattern with a pink highlighter pen, avoiding the few small villages wherever possible.

To assist their search, Ronald had brought a powerful pair of binoculars, but three hours later, having completed the search grid, they had failed to identify a single site that they felt they could classify as a "probable" and no more than two "possibles". However both of these had severe drawbacks because both had natural features clearly of great antiquity which would have made landing and taking off very difficult for a fighter the size of a Tempest.

Dispirited and tired at the end of a long day, they agreed to suspend operations and to seek a kro for the night and to revisit the "possibles" the next day. Checking his list from the internet, Ronald pointed to an entry for a pub they had passed at the north end of the search grid, so Keith turned the car round and headed off at speed toward their hotel for the night.

A quarter of an hour later, they found the small hotel without difficulty. Keith had tried to memorise some simple Danish phrases, but they soon established with the proprietor that her English was far better than their Danish and there was some amusement at her attempts to correct his pronunciation.

Their room was simply furnished in the Scandinavian style, comfortable, spotlessly clean and extremely quiet. Showered and refreshed, they went through to dinner. They seemed to be the only guests staying that night.

They found the bar and Keith started on the local draft beer declaring he needed to wash the dust from his throat. Ronald hoped that they were not in for a repeat of the previous evening, but Keith announced that his thirst was quenched after a couple of glasses while Ronald contented himself with a glass of white wine – Keith helped him finish the bottle over dinner. Ronald would have preferred a good red wine, but found that as his age advanced, the reds gave him palpitations, which, alone at night, he found unpleasant and worrying. Dinner on the ferry was a lapse he did not intend to repeat. So, reluctantly, he followed his doctor's advice and tried to stick to the whites. Keith said that he was not fussed either way, so long as someone else was paying.

Over dinner, Ronald found Keith's company and conversation amiable and began to regret his lifetime refusal to have any contact with anyone from his old squadrons. In fact as the evening progressed he found he was able, almost for the first time, to recall some wartime actions and events without the feeling that his innards were about to burst into flame.

Once coffee had been served, Ronald extracted from his travel folder the original copy of the code and placed it on the table between them and contemplated it thoughtfully for several seconds, until he said to Keith, "You know, I think I've changed my mind. I really don't think we saw anything today that was even remotely possible as a landing ground."

Keith nodded slowly in agreement as Ronald continued, "So if you're game I think we should head north first thing tomorrow and west, more toward the coast, and try to follow the bearing as close as we can."

"Well, what do you reckon?" Keith asked, the next morning, after they had completed a half hour drive north and west toward the coast. He had a hopeful note in his voice.

"I think this could be it," Ronald replied. "It's old, certainly old enough from the looks of it, and it's big enough. You would surely get two fighters inside with a bit of room to spare. It's isolated, much more so than anything we have seen today and far bigger than anything we looked at yesterday and, on top of that, it has access to a proper landing strip."

"There's no obvious sign of much change to the field and surely any changes after the war would have made it smaller than we are seeing now, but even so, it would have been touch and go getting a Tempest off," said Ronald, more to himself, but Keith grunted his agreement.

"A Spit would have been OK, but another couple of tons..." Keith did not finish his comment as he fell to seeing in his mind's eye a Tempest at full throttle, bouncing across the rough grass, desperate to become airborne.

Ronald followed his thoughts as he peered at the far end of the field. He pointed through his side window.

"I don't suppose that barn, the one just the far side of the perimeter fence, would have been there in the '40s. That would have helped with the take-off a bit. Anyway, if there's nothing here, then it's all academic, but if there is, then it proves Hutch was one hell of a pilot."

Turning back, Ronald said, "Come on, let's go and take a look."

The old weather-beaten hangar stood like a wooden monolith three hundred yards away, its dilapidated timbers and panelling showing signs of long neglect, twisted or warped from the extremes of Danish weather so close to the west coast.

On the other side of the airfield, and slightly to their left, a cluster of buildings including a modern metal-clad hangar showed that times had moved on. There was a small compact control tower with green tinted windows, topped by an orange windsock, almost horizontal in the stiff westerly breeze. The small radar scanner was stationary. Half a dozen light aircraft, mostly two-seaters were ranged in front of the tower, tethered head to wind. The presence of just a couple of cars and one light van seemed to indicate that this airfield was now dedicated only to weekend leisure flying. For the moment, the aerodrome appeared to be deserted, which served their purpose. Nevertheless, the grass airstrip was neatly cut, but this only heightened the feeling of decay that pervaded the old wooden hangar.

Further to their right, on the far side of the hangar, perhaps a third of a mile distant, they could see, viewed through Ronald's binoculars, the long thatched roof of an old farmhouse. To its rear, a number of outbuildings, some wooden, some finished in corrugated iron sheeting, appeared all to be in urgent need of refurbishment.

The field between the farmhouse and the hangar was, by contrast, clearly in current use, half ploughed with the remainder still bearing the stubble of the year's harvest. A flock of gulls, like scattered hailstones, searched for morsels in the newly ploughed almost black, sandy soil.

It was Keith who pointed out that, apart from the massive front doors, the hangar itself appeared to be wholly sited in the farmer's field and they could see clearly where the plough had been worked around the far end.

"Do you think that could mean that the hangar belongs to the farm?" queried Keith, as he tried to stretch his legs into the Jaguar's foot well.

"There's only one way to find out," Ronald replied, opening his door and steadying it as the wind tried to wrench it from his grasp, "and even if it does, I'm not going over there and knocking on their front door to find out."

"Come on, let's go and have a look," and so saying, he levered himself out of the car, leaning against the open door while he found his balance.

"Next time, will you please park nose to wind," he said with a chuckle as he buttoned up his new overcoat, bought specially for the trip, and pulled his herringbone tweed cap tight down over his windblown hair.

"This is when I am reminded of my age. Bloody legs just won't work like they used to – get so stiff these days." He rubbed furiously at his thighs to get them moving.

Joining him at the boot of the car, Keith unlocked it and waited while Ronald ferreted inside his travel bag to bring out the smooth aluminium plate and the smaller zippered black case.

"Ready?"

"Ready, Skipper," Keith replied.

"Wish you would stop that stuff. We left all that behind long ago," Ronald retorted, a little sharply.

Keith was unabashed. "But it's all back, here, with us now. I can feel it round us. Bit creepy really," and he shuddered, pretending he was shivering from the chill in the air.

"Don't be so bloody daft," said Ronald, contrite. "It's just you, me and, and…" but then his voice trailed off. "Oh, sod it. You've got me going now, you old bugger," punching Keith lightly on the shoulder. "Bring your tools and we'll see how far we can get before someone tries to arrest us."

With that, Ronald set off across the short springy turf, leaving Keith trailing behind and struggling to carry tyre levers and trenching tool as well as the metal detector, which he still insisted in bringing along.

It only took a couple of minutes to cross the short distance to the front doors of the hangar, where they hung on their rusted overhead tracks, groaning and grinding slightly as they flexed in the face of the strong breeze.

There were no telltale signs that the doors had been recently opened; spiders' webs stitched across the joining faces of the two doors, but by contrast the heavy padlock was rust-free and looked well oiled.

Although there was a narrow gap between the doors, Ronald could see nothing inside, not even when he pressed his eye tight to the slit. The skylights, set high on the curve of the roof, seemed to be too dirty or abraded by years of windblown sand to admit anything but a faint glimmer of light to the interior.

At the side of the building, just beyond the end of the framework for the door-tracks, they found a gap in the hedgerow. They slipped through to stand on the scrubby margin of the field and picked their way along it, moving with some difficulty, as brambles and dwarfed thorn clutched at their clothing, until they reached the side wall of the hangar.

From there they made better progress, skirting round the decaying tubular skeleton of what had once been a light aircraft half buried in a tangle of grasses.

"Not quite what we are looking for," commented Keith under his breath. Ronald gazed at it with passing curiosity. Somehow the shape seemed vaguely familiar.

Then, to their surprise they came across a door let neatly, almost as though secretly, into the wall, so fine was the fit of the door in its frame.

"We'll come back to this in a moment. It looks like our only hope of getting in. There's no way we can get through that padlock on the front," said Ronald as Keith ran his fingers lightly over the door's surface, seeking a crack or fissure that might give him some leverage.

"In the meantime, I want to check out an idea I've been toying with, a way in which they might have hidden the 109. If the figures stack up, I'll explain. So for now, will you take this aluminium plate down to the far end, at the back of the hangar and hold it vertical so that I can see when I get to the front? And, when I give you a shout, try to hold it very, very still. I'll try to get a reading from this."

Holding out the black case which he had brought from the car for Keith to see, Ronald unzipped it and took out a yellow rectangular laser operated tape-measure, switched it on and aimed against the side of the building to check that it was functioning correctly. Satisfied that it was, he motioned to Keith to set off, and then turned and made his way back to the front of the hangar.

His progress, as he neared the doors' framework, was hindered by an increasing amount of rubbish in what he thought had been a dump for all unwanted items from the hangar or the farm; strips of corroded aluminium, rusted paint cans, coils of old electrical wiring and, further on, an old workbench largely eaten away by woodworm.

In the final yards, he found it increasingly difficult to find a safe foothold, so he supported himself against the wooden wall of the hangar, until he reached the front doors' frame. He was puffing heavily from the exertion, his heart pounding in his chest.

Doubting that this was the most sensible decision of his lifetime, he turned and, taking a moment to catch his breath, with a shout of "Ready" he carefully aimed the laser in Keith's direction, sighting with trembling hands to obtain a return from the metal plate.

At the far end he could see Keith hunched over the plate hoping to catch a glimpse of the telltale ruby spot of the laser, intoning at regular intervals, "No, nothing yet." The reading on the measure's screen remained resolutely and frustratingly blank. Gradually it dawned on him that to hit the eight inch plate with the laser at forty yards or more was like trying to hit a FW190 from half a mile, so small was the target.

As he cursed himself for a fool because he had not brought a larger reflector, he decided to abandon the precision approach and opted to try getting a reading from the sidewall of the hangar nearby, which was successful initially, but no sooner than he had turned the beam away, working down the side, the reading went blank once more.

With a growing feeling of desperation, he then tried waggling the laser in Keith's general direction in the hope of getting a response until, to his great relief, a reading appeared fleetingly in the display window. Steadying his hand, he heard a triumphant shout from Keith and at last the reading settled to 40.2 metres. "Got it!" he shouted. "Thank God for that!" floated back on the breeze.

"Meet me at that door," Ronald shouted back as he began once again to thread his way gingerly through the tangled undergrowth, looking carefully ahead to avoid any hidden snags or anything that might trap his ankle. Then, as he cleared a space for his foot, a small rectangle of black and silver coloured metal, buried deep in the undergrowth, caught his eye.

Teasing it out from its resting place where it had obviously lain undisturbed for many years, his heart began to beat a little faster as he started to decipher the letters and symbols engraved on to the silver areas of the plate.

By now, he could see that Keith was already waiting for him back at the door, so he tucked the identification plate into his overcoat pocket and hurried forward. "Sorry about that," as he reached Keith. "Stupid of me to think that such a small reflector would be big enough, but I wasn't too sure I could get a return off your body."

"That's OK. I wasn't sure whether it was you, or me that was the more shaky. Did my best to keep really still in this breeze. Anyway, what was the reading?" Keith enquired.

"40.2 metres."

"Ah-ha," said Keith, with a pleased grin on his face. "I wasn't so far off. I paced it out at forty-five yards." Ronald gave him a withering look in response. "But it's not so much the outside that matters, it's the inside, so let's try and get the door open."

"By the way," said Ronald, "talking of small metal plates, what do you think of this?" He fished in his coat pocket and handed the little plate to Keith who inspected it closely, turning it round and round in his hands.

"Well," he said slowly, "it's obviously an identification plate; look at the hole in each corner where it would have been riveted, made of aluminium or some such," but before he could continue, Ronald interrupted. "Look at the top line. Doesn't it say BAYERISCHE. Look closely for me. My eyes are just not good enough."

Keith scrutinised the plate once again, holding it as close to his eyes as his focus would allow, twisting it one way and then the other to catch the light, before replying lightly, "Well, if you were hoping it would say FLUGZEUGWERKE, then I'm sorry to have to disappoint you. It's MOTORWERKE, probably off an old BMW motorbike. Pity."

Then, seeing Ronald's face fall, he added, "It would have been nice to get confirmation the easy way, but it's what's inside, assuming it's there, that matters. Anyway, I doubt they would have been so careless as to leave a shred of evidence lying around, to be found like that."

"No I guess not," said Ronald grudgingly, unwilling to admit defeat, "but a clue, a hint, just to tell us we were on the right track, would not go amiss. But as you rightly say, we need to be inside, so let's have a crack at that door."

CHAPTER 22

Without an external handle to guide them, it was not immediately obvious on which side the door was hinged, or even whether it opened inwards or outwards.

"It's a right-handed world," said Keith, after a moment's thought, "so let's work on the assumption that it's hinged on the left side."

Ronald gave a tentative push on the right side about three-quarters of the way up. Nothing seemed to move, then Keith edged Ronald to one side and put his shoulder to the door and gave it a firm shove, but still nothing. Using Ronald for support, Keith tried a kick with the sole of his foot, but only succeeded in jarring his leg.

"Oh, hell, nothing ventured, nothing gained," joked Keith. "I might as well be wearing a stripy top, an eye mask and a bag marked SWAG," conjuring up a comic book image of a burglar, as he reached into his waxed windcheater and pulled out the pair of tyre levers.

"Now let's try and get it to open outwards." Keith inserted the tip of one of the levers into the right-hand door jamb and began to waggle it from side to side with his weight behind it, until he had wedged more than a quarter of an inch of the lever into the seam, widening it just a fraction. As Keith pushed more firmly, it seemed to Ronald that the door might have moved another millimetre or two.

"I think we might be getting somewhere," Keith growled through gritted teeth, but with a note of excitement growing in his voice, "so while I hold this one in place, you put the other lever in a bit lower and put some pressure on it. Then I'll try and work mine in more. If we do it together, in sequence, then we should get the damn thing open – or get ourselves arrested in the trying."

Little by little, working together, Keith's lever bit deeper and deeper into the wood, forcing the timber outwards, creaking in protest, until without warning, the door popped open, almost throwing them off balance as it swung wide.

"We've bloody done it," exclaimed Keith, punching the air, before looking furtively around in case they might have been observed, but the field was empty and there was no sign of any traffic moving on the road.

Taking a very deep breath, Ronald, followed closely by Keith, stepped cautiously into the gloom of the hangar, standing for a moment on the bare earth floor as his eyes grew accustomed to the darkness. The odour of dampness, the smell of oil, the faint scent of aeroplane dope reached his nostrils, triggering memories of his own childhood.

In the dim light filtering down from the clouded skylights, they could see that the whole of the far side of the hangar was taken up with the trappings of a once-active workshop; a workbench, rusting tools hanging untouched perhaps for decades on their wall-racks and, standing to one side, the twin cylinders of an oxy-acetylene welding kit, still upright on their trolley. A pair of darkened welding goggles, suspended on perished elastic, dangled from the pressure valve.

Over to their left, toward the front doors, they were surprised to see in the darkness the faint outline of a small biplane. Removing a flashlight from his coat, Ronald trained its beam to reveal that it was an old De Havilland Tiger Moth, once silver in colour, but now dripping in dust and cobwebs.

Clearly it had not moved for years for its tyres were flat and its fabric covering was shredded, hanging down in sheets to expose the inner structure.

"My God, it's like a time-warp in here," said Ronald. "I did my first solo in one of these. This is a bit of a sad old girl, definitely in need of a large dose of TLC. I shall never forget that moment when I lifted off the runway for the first time on my own. I thought I owned the skies."

"Me too," echoed Keith. "At least until it came to putting her back down, then I went a complete blank. Could not seem to remember a thing the instructor had taught me and the nearer I got to the field the worse it got. The whole of my approach was wrong; too high, too fast and nearly too bloody late, but then some instinct for self-preservation took over and I thumped it onto the deck so hard I thought the undercarriage was bound to break, but at least it stayed down."

"When I taxied in, I was rehearsing how to tell my parents that I had been scrubbed from flying, but the instructor, can't even remember his name now, was quite relaxed about it. I think he was just relieved the Moth was still in one piece, but not half as relieved as I was – although I tried not to show it."

Ronald laughed at the memory. "My solo was not too bad, better than yours, I think, but you should have been there to see my first landing in a Tempest. I never knew a plane could hit the ground so hard. It was more like an accident that didn't happen, than a landing. I was still shaking from the impact when I got back to dispersal. The fitter even congratulated me, quite genuinely, without a trace of sarcasm. There had been a couple of write-offs that day, so mine was an improvement. God bless Hawker's for building something that even I couldn't wreck."

"I'll drink to that – if you'll give me the chance," said Keith with a slow wink. "Shall we have a closer look at the Moth?"

Approaching the plane with some care, Ronald, out of idle curiosity, lifted a section of the torn fabric covering which was hanging down from the mid-section of the fuselage and almost tenderly lifted it back into place saying, "It would take more than my model aeroplane skills and a pot of glue to fix this," when Keith suddenly exploded, "Jesus, Ronno! Look! Look! You wanted a hint and you've got a bloody signpost. Get your torch on it, man!" as he shook Ronald firmly by the hand, pumping it up and down in his excitement.

There, faintly, but perfectly stencilled on the silvered canvas, was a large, red number eight.

"Oh, Jesus, Ronno!" he repeated excitedly to himself. "It's here! It's bloody well here. I know it is. I can feel it."

Even in the dim light, Ronald's breath caught in his throat as he began to trace the outline of the number while he passed the torch to Keith who switched it on at once to illuminate the side of the plane.

"My God, it's incredible. After all these years Hutch gives us proof positive and, look here." Ronald was pointing at the rectangle that formed lower half of the eight "That shadow, although it's so faded where most of the paint has flaked away, I think that once, there was a black chess knight. Wolfgang and Svenn together in the skies once again."

Ronald fell silent for long moments until Keith could stand it no longer and turned the torch onto Ronald's face to find tears rolling slowly down his cheeks.

"Don't you go getting all maudlin and sentimental on me, Skipper. We do still have a job to finish."

"Yes, you're right, I'm sorry. Just at that moment, your ghosts got to me and I felt them here, all around me. I felt such a rush through my body, sixty years of memories in a split second that, seriously, I wondered if I was dead. I could clearly see Hutch standing next to you, but it was the picture from The Times so it's just my imagination running on overdrive.

"Come on," Ronald continued, "it's time to crack this nut, before I lose the plot completely."

"Good man," replied Keith. "We've come so far and I get the feeling that there might be a bit more to discover yet. Like, why here, and not somewhere else. Why not Sweden? Loads of German aircraft made it there to be interned, and, as the crow flies it's probably nearer, straight across the Baltic with far less risk of being shot down. Just as you tried to stop them at Grossenbrode''.

"True. I guess I never looked at it in that way. I have become so enmeshed in following the clues left by Hutch that I never gave a thought to why they came here. If they had gone to Sweden, they really would not have needed Hutch and it should have been safer for Svenn in particular. Wolfgang could have faced nothing worse than being extradited back to his home country. Even though his home was in Berlin, surely no-one would have forced him to go back behind the Russian Iron Curtain. But then, of course they did not have the benefit of knowing how things were going to turn out after the war ended. Back to the burrow, I guess." Keith nodded slowly in agreement. "What was it they used to say? East, West, Home is best."

With Keith's question remaining largely unanswered, Ronald turned and walked round the tattered wing of the Moth, wiping his eyes as he went, and took the laser measure from his pocket. Keith joined him at one of the front doors as Ronald placed the measure against the inner face and switched on.

Instantly the screen lit up with a reading from the far end. "Thirty-seven point eight metres," Keith read out aloud from the glowing display.

"Look, there is a difference, two point four metres or just about seven and a half feet, maybe a little more," as he did a bit of quick mental arithmetic. "Enough room to hide a Messerschmitt? Surely not, unless you chopped it up into little pieces," he said with a tone of voice which made it clear that he only half believed it.

"The damp in this place is beginning to get to me, my feet are freezing, and I don't need any more problems with my circulation, so let's take a look and see what we can find, before whoever owns this mausoleum realises the door is open and they have got visitors."

Keith fidgeted uneasily, stamping his feet on the damp, oil-soaked earth. "I hope you did not mean that literally. I hope we are not going to find bodies. A graveyard for an aeroplane maybe, but bodies – I bloody hope not. But we should get on. It's time."

Putting his arm around Ronald's shoulder, Keith steered Ronald back down the length of the hangar, round the decaying Tiger Moth and back towards the pool of light that was flooding through the open side door, bringing with it just the slightest feeling of warmth, as the skies began to clear.

For a moment, Keith paused and turned to look back at the Moth with a puzzled expression and then his face broke into a broad grin and he burst out laughing. "How could we have missed it?"

"Missed what?"

"Missed the meaning of that bit of the last line in the puzzle we couldn't figure out. The bit that said DH82. It's so obvious – once you know the answer!"

Ronald blinked. "OK. Enlighten me, if you must."

Keith laughed, this time at Ronald's discomfort, relishing the moment to exact a small revenge for when Ronald had been the one to see the SWEN clue.

"The Tiger Moth: it was DeHavilland's Type 82 – DH82, see! Hutch must have been here. He was telling us what to look for and here it is. The final bit of the puzzle solved, done and dusted." He made a mock bow in the Moth's direction.

Ronald rolled his eyes. "Very droll. Dusted is something of an understatement!" Then he pointed Keith back to the job in hand.

Now that their eyes were more accustomed to the fragile light they were able to inspect the end wall of the hangar. At first sight there was nothing to arouse suspicion. It would have taken a practised eye to detect that the construction was not contemporary with the original construction of the hangar, as it reached seamlessly from floor to roof. The coating of accumulated spider's web with its burden of dust and desiccated insects helped to disguise the builders' mistakes; panels split and nails not fully driven home in their haste, but hammered over and flattened into the woodwork.

Looking for some sort of tool that could help them probe the cavity, Ronald wandered over to the workbench and started sorting through some of the dirt-laden materials lying on the top.

After a moment he said, more to himself than to Keith, "Ah, I think this will do nicely," and then over his shoulder to Keith who was trying without any success to wedge one of his tyre levers into a crack in the panelling, "Hang on a second. Before we start pulling things to bits and finding we are still in the wrong place, I want to try to probe the cavity." In his hands he held a rusty section of reinforcing bar about six feet long and half an inch in diameter.

"I have seen a few knots in the old wood and I want to try and knock one out and push this through. There might be a brick skin behind."

Keith gave him a sceptical look with a raised eye brow for emphasis. "You go ahead, but don't forget it was still wartime and I can't think they had time to start house-building."

By this time, Ronald was bending down, peering at a knot in the timber cladding some three feet above the floor and about a quarter of the way in from the outer wall. Holding the rod in his hands as though it were as snooker cue, he gave the knot a tentative knock with the tip and then, because it refused to budge, a much sharper blow. This produced a satisfying crack as the old, dried circle of branch wood surrendered under the onslaught and disappeared from sight into the blackness beyond.

Sliding the tip of the rod into the aperture, Ronald began to push it slowly through. It met with no resistance, even when he had inserted it to its hilt.

Ronald groaned with annoyance, swore softly under his breath, withdrew the probe, and shuffled sideways until he located another knot near the centre line of the wall and a foot or so higher up. A moment later, the knot surrendered its place, with little resistance, to the point of the rod. Again he pushed the rod slowly into the hole, but, this time, with less than twelve inches inserted, the rod came to a stop with a muted, metallic clonk.

"Yes, yes, yes!" Ronald repeated quietly, as he tapped the hidden object, time and time again, as though the resulting sounds were music to his soul. His heart began to beat faster with the excitement that was building inside him. "The picture at the museum could be right!"

Passing the rod to Keith, he said, "Here. You try. Go a bit higher." He pointed to a knot further to the left.

Keith attacked the wall with less finesse and, in a second, the knot was out and the rod sliding through the aperture, penetrating deeper into the cavity until, with almost half of the rod inside, it came to a halt with a similar, but more muffled clang. "There's something further back," whispered Keith, "and if I push down on this end I can feel that the tip is moving up across something which is curving away slightly. Part of the fuselage, do you think?"

Ronald nodded his agreement. Then they set about finding more points where they could push the probe through so that, after ten minutes, Ronald called a halt. In his mind, he had built a dot-to-dot outline of what was hidden behind the wall.

"Back there," pointing through the wall, after they had measured between some scratch marks they had made in the dirt on the floor, "we have something that is at least twenty-five feet long and, as best we can tell. not more than six to eight feet high, certainly higher to the right than the left, apart from that one sounding a little higher up, on the extreme left."

"Right now, we could walk away and with a bit of luck no-one would know we had been here, if we made a bit of an effort to cover our tracks. So now, it's decision time. As Michael Miles would have said: 'Take the money, or open the box'?"

"It's been years since I heard that old catchphrase from the TV," said Keith laughing. "Open the box," he shouted, mimicking the television studio audience of the long gone days of the 1960s. "Open the bloody box! We've come too far to walk away now, and besides, there's no money, unless it's German gold of course." He was so amused with his own joke that he fell into a fit of coughing that left him breathless.

"Go find something that we can use to rip these planks off and take a look-see," he wheezed. "But before you do, just humour me and roll that dice."

Doing as he was bid, Ronald delved into his jacket pocket, brought out the little yellow die and let it tumble on to the top of an old forty-five gallon oil drum, where it bounced once, spun on a corner and chattered to rest – six.

"What else could it be!" said Keith with a smile that said they were nearing the end of their quest.

Searching across the workbench, Ronald eventually came up with a lump hammer, short and heavy, as well as a builder's bolster and, with a look of triumph in his eye, he also produced a robust crowbar with a curved hook at one end for greater leverage.

"Let me make a start," Keith begged. He had already taken off his jacket and rolled up his sleeves. Before Ronald had chance to reply or protest, Keith had relieved him of the hammer and bolster, inserted the blade of the bolster into a hairline crack between two panels and struck it a mighty blow with the hammer, which he had been hefting in his right hand.

The sound of his blow, like the crack of doom, startled both of them as the whole of the wooden wall seemed to reverberate under the impact. Dust and dirt showered down from the roof.

"Christ!" exclaimed Ronald. "That's enough to waken the dead. Can't you do it a bit more quietly?"

"Open the box, you said, so that's exactly what I am going to do and no more pussy-footing around," Keith replied, through clenched teeth, as he struck the bolster again and again. Ronald winced at the row, certain that they must be discovered. He stepped quickly to the doorway and was relieved when he found no-one in sight, no sirens wailing in the distance. In fact, the scene was as peaceful and serene as ever. The cloud cover was lifting and held the prospect of a better end to the day. He swept the horizon once more. A split-second glint of light, from the direction of the old farmhouse, caught his eye, but then it was gone.

"All quiet, Skipper?" Keith enquired with a hopeful look on his face. Ronald nodded. "Think so."

"Right then, Red Two attacking now!" Keith intoned in the jargon of sixty years before.

Ronald took a sharp breath as Keith raised his striking arm. How long ago had he been Red Two, following Hutch, Red One, Baltic Leader, into oblivion, into the living hell that had been Grossenbrode? Now they were just inches from finding the answer and Hutch had passed the mantle of Red One to him. Then the moment for self-doubt was gone as he watched Keith, almost as though in slow-motion, driving the head of the lump hammer against the shaft of the bolster with all his strength.

Seconds later, hammering furiously, no longer caring how much noise he made, Keith had the bolster driven fully into the joint and he began to beat the bolster over to the side, gradually raising the end of the panel proud of the surface until there was a slight gap, just enough to allow him to insert the tip of the curved end of the crowbar. He tapped it firmly into place to give it good purchase.

"Right, let's go for it. Give me a hand here," and together they gripped the free end of the crowbar, pulling on it with all their weight. Gradually, the panel began to lift free with the accompanying screech of rusty nails, parting company with their timber bed where they had remained undisturbed for more than half a century.

Moving the crowbar round, they pushed and pulled once more until, with a final squeal of protest, the panel dropped to the ground at their feet, dragging forth another cloud of dust and dirt which enveloped them from head to foot.

Peering into the hole, it seemed the aperture was unnaturally dark so Keith pushed his hand through and gave a sharp, incredulous exclamation of surprise. "There's something like a curtain hanging here! Maybe some sort of blackout curtain. Perhaps they wanted a second line of defence in case someone took a peek. I think we'll leave it be for now and finish getting the wall down."

For another half hour they worked on, panel by panel, until they had removed a section almost twenty feet across and six or seven feet high at the centre, when they decided they could physically do no more. Like a magician's trick, the curtain continued to obscure what lay beyond.

Keith was perspiring profusely, mopping his brow with an increasingly grubby handkerchief, while, in calling the halt, Ronald readily admitted that for half the time his help had been more by way of moral support, than any strength of arm. In his own words, he said he was completely buggered.

"Let's have a breather," gasped Keith as he dragged over two small oil drums to act as a pair of makeshift seats, attempting, but largely failing, to wipe them clean with a scrap of rag. "You appreciate we don't have anywhere booked to stay tonight," as he surveyed his filthy hands and dust-stained clothes.

Then he looked at Ronald and burst out laughing. "You look as though you have just come up from a shift at the coal face in your Sunday best."

From his backpack, Keith produced a large bottle of mineral water which they consumed slowly, sitting in silence, side-by-side in the strong sunlight, which was flooding through the open door as the sun sank through a now largely cloudless sky toward the western horizon. Both of them were deep in thought, each beset with a myriad of memories and a plethora of possibilities. Keith spat a mouthful of dirt onto the floor.

"Hutch must have loved those guys, to have gone through all this," said Ronald, breaking the silence, which had been almost total apart from the sighing of the wind. Even the gulls in the field had ceased their chatter.

Faintly, in the distance they could hear a tractor working in a field, but they seemed to be in an oasis of tranquillity. None of their activities had, so far, attracted any attention and Ronald prayed inwardly that it would remain that way. Keith poured a few drops onto his handkerchief in a vain attempt to clean some of the grime from his face. They shared the last of the water.

"Time?" Keith asked wearily.

"Time." Ronald nodded, as he stood, rubbing the small of his back to ease some of the discomfort that was seeping through his body.

Taking a firm grip on folds of the curtain, Keith pulled down with all his strength until, from above, out of sight, there came the sound of tearing cloth.

A second later the complete curtain collapsed about Keith as he dragged it back with him into the hangar, swirling it to one side with a flourish, like a matador teasing a charging bull. A veil of dust drifted down, fogging their view of what lay beyond: a tantalising glimpse, a ghost becoming flesh.

Together, they stood speechless for a few moments while the air cleared as they stared into the void, now brightly illuminated by a shaft of golden light lancing through the open door from the setting sun. The profile of a World War II fighter was unmistakable and, like the legendary Holy Grail, it drew them closer. Words choked in Ronald's throat.

"Oh, bloody hell," breathed Keith. "It's a K, their last version," as he surveyed the aircraft in front of them. "Look at the green and white 'Defence of the Reich' band near the tail. It must have been almost brand new."

"Look at the Red Eight," whispered Ronald as he pointed at the large number eight painted almost the depth of the fuselage just behind the cockpit. "Look at the red eight!" he repeated, as though he could not quite believe his eyes. "Bloody hell is right; we've found it!"

In front of them, still partially obscured by the wood-work, standing on its own undercarriage, was, in almost pristine condition despite the coating of dust, a Messerschmitt 109 K, the last of a design dating back to 1934. The wings had been severed from the fuselage, crudely but effectively, by what appeared to be the work of an oxy-acetylene gas torch, then folded back against the fuselage, like the wings of a bird at rest. The white-bordered black cross of the Luftwaffe looked freshly painted. It sent a shiver down Ronald's back to see the hooked swastika on the tail plane.

The cockpit canopy was closed.

"Sat in one of these in '36. Never thought I would be this close again. That thirty millimetre firing through the propeller was the scariest thing I ever saw – such a slow rate of fire, *boomp, boomp, boomp*," said Ronald as he banged on the side of the oil drum to simulate the firing rhythm. "But if just one of those got you, it was curtains. I remember when…" but he did not finish.

"You may have sat in one," answered Keith, "but the nearest I got was when I nearly collided with one over France a bit before D-Day. We went head to head and we were both firing when I closed my eyes. The last thing I saw was that ruddy cannon blinking in the middle of the yellow spinner with the two machine guns, on top of the engine, chattering like bonfire sparklers. When I opened my eyes, he was going down with smoke coming from the engine so I claimed a probable and said a big 'thank you' to Him up there." He pointed skywards.

"We all prayed pretty hard in those days," agreed Ronald, "even though I was not particularly religious, more superstitious than anything. Like my dice – they gained a significance completely out of proportion, but they worked to give comfort to some of us."

"And they were loaded and you knew it," retorted Keith. "Good job you didn't use them for gambling. The lads would have lynched you if they had found out," he continued, in the good-natured banter that was growing between them.

"Right, I want a closer look and I think I saw a ladder somewhere back there."

Ronald stayed resting on the oil drum, as he continued to admire the mottled paintwork, thinking that perhaps the camouflage shades of grey streaked across the fuselage were a comment, a reflection of the state of Germany in 1945 – a grey country, pulverised and wasted with a grey, uncertain future.

He remembered how glad he was to have got back to the greenery of a late English spring, back to the girl he loved, a future full of promise and colour, until. Until…

"Give me a hand, will you?" Keith broke into his thoughts and he turned to see Keith struggling to carry a stout, heavy wooden ladder.

"Help me lift this over and push it up just behind the cockpit. I want to have a good decko."

After ensuring that the ladder was lodged securely in place, Keith took Ronald's flashlight and with stiff legs, climbed over a low-point in the wooden wall and started up the ladder, just a rung or two, before he paused, then came back down, looking at Ronald with a puzzled expression. "Before I start poking around, tell me how you knew, that the plane was in there." He waved the torch in the direction of the void. "Lucky guess, or what?"

"Well, it was a bit more than that, although we did get lucky that my idea came up trumps, but it all came from a picture I saw that first time at the air museum. Only caught a fleeting glance that time, and really I forgot about it, so I went back to the museum a few days ago."

"And, it showed...?" Keith interrupted impatiently.

"It showed a 109, minus its wings, being towed backwards by its tail wheel."

"Well, I'll be damned," said Keith quietly, while he re-ascended the ladder, giving a running commentary as the shaft of torchlight swept from side to side, illuminating the unseen parts of the plane.

As his head disappeared from sight, the beam of the torch shone downwards and Keith said, "I can see that the ammo covers on the top of the wings are off so they must have got rid of the shells somehow. They cut off the left tail-plane, so that they could stay within the width of the undercarriage. Incredible."

Then, as the beam swung to the right, he added, "Two of the blades of the prop are wedged against the outer wall so they only had to chop about a foot off the third. Not in a thousand years would I have believed that you could get a plane into such a small space and do so little damage!"

"That's what they were relying on," Ronald agreed with a hint of admiration in his voice, "and it worked for almost sixty years. Incredible, as you say."

Keith's body disappeared a little further out of sight as Ronald heard him say, "I'm going to have a look in the cockpit." and from his seated position he could see Keith's arm reaching down on the far side of the canopy. He could hear Keith grunting at the effort of lifting the canopy followed by a sigh of satisfaction as slowly, on creaking hinges, unused for more than a half century, the canopy began to move.

"Got it," exclaimed Keith, as the canopy fell outward and locked into place on the right side of the fuselage.

At that moment, another voice broke into Ronald's awareness, accented, but somehow so familiar that it froze him to the spot.

"Oh, Ronnie! Dear Ronnie, you came. Just as he promised you would!"

Ronald whirled round, shielding his eyes against the blinding sunlight, seeing only the outline of a slight figure silhouetted in the doorway, leaning lightly on an silver-topped walking stick.

"Do please be careful!" the voice implored, taking his mind back seventy years to the memory of a pretty, dark-haired young girl stepping out of a red and cream Mercedes at the foot of the steps in front of an art deco house, long ago destroyed in the suburbs of Berlin.

"Karin?" he said, when he finally found his voice, hardly daring to believe. "Is that really you? I thought you were dead," and then realising how ridiculous that must have sounded, he added hastily to cover his embarrassment, "I'm so sorry. It's a bit of a shock after all these years."

As he spoke, the elderly woman walked slowly into the hangar to stand in front of him, white-haired, a touch of powder to her face, rouge to her lips, but unmistakably Karin. Reaching up, she put a soft hand against his cheek, brushing away a little of the dirt that coated him, then touching so gently the barely visible scar that still creased his forehead, tutting softly. So like Libby that first day. His heart lurched.

In an old-world gesture that came from deep within him, he took her hand and pressed it gently, tenderly to his lips, caressing her skin with a fleeting kiss.

Before they could say anything more, Keith's voice floated down. "Is there someone there? I thought I heard voices. The pilot's seat is missing, but otherwise it's in factory condition. Unbelievable," he continued as though not expecting an answer to his question.

"Keith," Ronald called, "I think you had better come down. There's someone here I would like you to meet. A very dear friend."

"Right – ho, Skipper," came the cheery reply and Keith began to descend the ladder. When he reached the bottom he turned, saw Karin for the first time and said, "Good Lord!" before collecting himself and offering his hand, having first endeavoured to wipe it clean of its coating of dirt and dust on the seat of his trousers.

"So, this is Keith, who Hutch was so certain that he would come and help Ronnie find us," said Karin, taking Keith's offered hand, and which it seemed to Ronald, Keith took just a moment longer than necessary to release.

"It is a pleasure and an honour to meet you, Karin. Ronald has told me a great deal about your meeting in Berlin, but his description of you did not do you justice."

Karin smiled and gave a little laugh at the compliment, but as they continued to exchange pleasantries, Ronald was looking back at the opening in the wall, and the aeroplane secreted within its cavity, as he began to appreciate the enormity of what they had uncovered.

For an instant, he felt a hot surge of anger toward his old comrade in arms for involving him in his intrigue, for dragging him out of his comfort zone of old age, but as quickly as it arose, the anger subsided.

Hutch had kept a trust for so many years and, in a flash of profound understanding, he saw that now it was his turn, in a different world, one that had put fascism to its proper place in history, to put Karin's mind to rest and release her from her burden.

He wondered how, day by day, she had managed to live with any peace of mind, knowing that the secret, which was holding her brother and cousin in safety, could be exposed at any moment, not to mention the risk to which she and her parents had put themselves. Being found to be harbouring an enemy alien was a "go straight to jail card" and God knows what would have happened if the truth about Svenn had ever come out in his lifetime.

In thinking about Karin's brother, he realised he had assumed Svenn was no longer alive, but what if he were? What then, if the story came out as he believed Hutch intended? A war crimes tribunal, and what of Wolfgang?

With all of these thoughts swirling round in his head, making him slightly giddy with their implications, he must have spoken Svenn's name out loud because Karin turned toward him, shaking her head slightly and said, "It's a long story and I'll tell you it all later. I also have something for you to read, but for now we should go to the farmhouse so that you can clean up a little; well, actually rather a lot!"

Looking at Keith, Ronald burst out laughing as some of the tension he felt started to drain away. "If I looked as though I had done a shift down the pit, then you look as though you have been down there a week. You should see yourself in a mirror. You are absolutely filthy and covered in cobwebs," he joked. "And anyway the light is starting to fade, so it's time we packed up for the day. We still have another day and a half, till the ferry leaves on Thursday."

Quickly Keith responded, "I've been thinking about that and I think we might need a couple more days to sort all this out. So, if you have no objections, we'll ask Karin to speak to the ferry company to see if we can defer our return a couple of days, maybe to the weekend. I've nothing booked till the middle of next week."

Ronald did not demur, for in truth he did not have anything booked – ever – apart from dental and doctor's appointments these days which seemed to be the highlight of his social life. Although he visited his Rotary club from time to time, mostly when he needed an excuse not to cook a meal for himself, he had no special friends and Torrie was too far away to visit on anything but an occasional basis.

Much as he had grumbled about it, this, his eighty- fourth year, thanks to Hutch, had been the most interesting, most challenging year in a very long time and it had helped him shake off the nagging suspicion that, of recent time, all he had been doing was waiting for the inevitable.

Keith's suggestion that they stay a few more days had aroused in him the realisation, that, in fact, he did not want to leave Denmark until he had tied up all the loose ends; but whether this was for Hutch, for Karin or for himself he was not entirely sure. Probably a mixture of all three, but with hardly a second glance at the 109, which was beginning to merge back into the shadows as the sun sank below the western horizon, he took Karin gently by the arm and together they stepped out of the hangar into the fresh autumnal air. The sharp breeze of the afternoon had dropped to a whisper, easing the chill in the air.

Glancing back, he saw Keith with his mobile phone held at arm's length, then the stuttering light of its inbuilt flash as he took a series of photographs before he too left the hangar, carrying his metal detector. "Didn't need this after all," he said, with a touch of regret in his voice, as he wedged the door firmly shut.

Across the field, they could see Karin's small blue Volvo parked next to Keith's Jaguar. There, she waited patiently until Keith had made some makeshift covers to protect his beloved cream leather seats from their grimy clothing. "Don't touch a thing; try not to sit down," was his warning to Ronald as he slid gingerly onto the old picnic rug that Keith had carefully laid into place. Ronald responded with a weary, tolerant smile and a very Anglo-Saxon gesture.

It took only a minute to follow Karin's car along the minor road around the farmer's field, until she turned onto a short length of track which led into a cobbled courtyard at the back of the single storey farmhouse, with its long, moss-laden, thatched roof.

She welcomed them into the low ceilinged vestibule and then directed Keith to a shower room at the end of the hall and took Ronald to a guest room where there was an en-suite bathroom.

A large fluffy bath towel was already laid out with a selection of toiletries, which caused Ronald to wonder just how long they had been under observation. He showered at length, watching the grime of the day swirling round his feet and then, feeling refreshed, he dressed slowly in clean clothes, reflecting on the rapidly moving events and how they might be resolved.

He did not trouble to shave, but instead took a little of the offered aftershave, a popular English brand that reminded him of his cigarette lighter, combed the remains of his thinning locks, straightened his shoulders and headed off in the direction of the voices he could hear coming from the kitchen, which he had noted as they first entered the house.

When he entered the brightly lit, modern kitchen with its lime washed cupboards, black granite worktops and a freestanding cooker with an overhead extractor hood, Keith was already in animated conversation with Karin, who seemed to be apologising for her faulty command of English. On the windowsill immediately in front of the sink, facing the hangar lay a small pair of binoculars. To one side, a percolator was filling the house with the tantalising aroma of freshly brewed coffee, and Karin was in process of placing a few small cookies on a blue and white patterned plate.

"These will keep you going until I can prepare some dinner and I will make up beds for you as it is already too late to be looking for accommodation at this time of day," she said, waving away their protests and beckoning them to go with her through to the lounge area.

Ronald followed her lead and Keith brought up the rear carrying the tray of coffee and biscuits, which he placed at one end of a low, granite-topped coffee table, next to a large white envelope.

A shaded lamp, hung low over the table, cast a circle of light onto its surface, in the centre of which the envelope lay, like an actor in the spotlight, waiting to play its part. As he eased himself into the comfortable leather armchair, with Keith opposite, Ronald could see, to his surprise that the envelope bore his name, with title and decorations, written neatly in green ink in Hutch's backward sloping hand. 'Sq Ldr R.O. Wallace DSO, DFC'.

While Karin poured coffee, motioning for them to take cream and biscuits as they pleased, she said, with great, aching sadness in her voice, "Hutch brought this for you a few weeks before he passed away. He knew he was dying and asked that I keep it safe until you arrived. He was so certain you would come that I never asked what I should do with it, should you not. But I am so relieved that his faith has been rewarded. Please read it while I prepare the dinner." The words drifted over her shoulder as she left the room.

Ronald looked across at Keith, whose face was only half lit, to find an encouraging smile. "Go for it, Skipper," he said, "before Hutch gets cross with us." He waved his hands in an open gesture to indicate the ether about them.

Grunting with mild irritation at Keith's slightly tongue-in-cheek approach, Ronald gave him a withering look, but leaned forward, his hand trembling a little, hovering over the envelope, as he reflected that this was the second letter in a year from Hutch. Then, accepting the inevitable, he lifted the envelope from the table and began to open it, slitting the flap carefully with a small penknife which he had taken from the pocket of his waistcoat.

With something akin to the reverence due to a great work of art, he slid a manuscript of more than a dozen sheets into his lap, put on his spectacles and started to read, his lips moving slightly as his finger moved across the page.

"It's from Hutch," he said, unnecessarily.

CHAPTER 23

14th July 2002

Dear Ronald,

Old friend, and I still think of you as such, even though we have not met for so very many years, I owe you an apology, probably many apologies and also an explanation for everything I have put you through. I should start with an apology for not having had the guts to face you, but I just was not that brave. I hope you can understand. Of course, if you are reading this it does mean that I am dead, which does also mean, thank God, you cannot question me on my motives for what happened so long ago.

By now, you will have worked out much of what happened after the raid on Grossenbrode when I disappeared for those three days, but I will take a few moments to fill in, where there may still be gaps in your knowledge.

I guess I owe an apology to Keith for dragging him into this as well. He never knew how close he came to uncovering the truth. When I met him in Berlin he caught me completely unawares. I had absolutely no confidence that I had managed to put him off the scent. They say that the truth can be stranger than fiction, and perhaps that's what saved me.

To have had our secret uncovered at any time would have condemned three people to be exposed as the world saw fit, victor or vanquished, as traitors, possibly even war criminals in the early days. Certainly I would have been court-martialled, and to a degree I would have accepted that if I could have been sure that the other two would not have been cast into the public spotlight. No, it was better for them that it worked out this way.

I want you to know that to this day I have carried a burden of guilt, not for what I did, but for what I did not do – which was to do my duty.

As I led the attack that day, I knew that, despite my instruction that no one should make more than one pass over the sea plane base, I knew that, in the absence of the Mustangs getting in to help, I as leader could and should have gone round again to draw the fire of the gunners. That might have divided their fire and given some protection to the incoming waves. I did not then do my duty, and you Ronno, thank God, you disobeyed orders and you did my job for me.

As I turned away, to the south not the north as I had ordered I was almost physically sick as I looked across at the anti-aircraft fire coming up at the second and third waves. I could not believe that the Germans would put up such a defence at that time of the war; the flak was incredible, just about the worst I had ever seen and I assumed that the intelligence reports about the Germans' escape plans were right.

When eventually I returned to our airfield, the war was to all intents over. Monty was at Luneburg and negotiations for the surrender were in full swing. I was stunned by the news that the third wave in the attack had been wiped out to a man, and I think something in me died that day. Perhaps that's why I went abroad for so long. I could not face the prospect of meeting up with old comrades who might start asking awkward questions.

I owe you a debt of gratitude for writing those letters to the families before I got back. It crossed my mind that you might have written one for me. Did you? You can tell me when we next meet!

Maybe you noticed that I ignored my own order to jettison the drop tanks. Now you know why. I thought I was going to have to fuel two planes through to Denmark.

Once I was sufficiently far away from Grossenbrode, I set course for the airfield which the Germans had built adjacent the A5 Autobahn. I had the co-ordinates and I set a compass bearing and went low and fast, so low that I went under power lines and through tree tops. At first, I had my heart in my mouth that the Germans would put up fighters to protect Grossenbrode, but there were none. As we know now the break-out was just a rumour and they hardly had a plane left anyway.

In fact, the danger was not so much from the Germans but from the Russians once I crossed the Elbe. At the speed I was travelling they were getting very little warning of my approach. The silhouette of the Tempest was not much like any German plane – a 190 possibly- and thankfully any flak was well behind me. Occasionally I got a wave and I rocked the wings in reply to keep them happy. I knew I would be on a reciprocal course on the way back so thought a bit of goodwill would do no harm.

When I arrived over the A5 I was completely stumped. I could not see any trace of the airfield. The camouflage netting in the tree tops was so good.

I flew up and down what I thought was the correct section of the motorway, twice maybe three times, getting increasingly desperate, but at last I saw a green very light go up almost at the far end of the main straight, which was about 5 miles long. This was used as the runway. Their jet fighters needed much more concrete to get airborne.

Luckily I made a good, if bumpy, landing and turned off at an access point where I could see someone waving to me. It was Wolfgang in his flight suit and he directed me straight into the trees.

Once inside, I was staggered by what I found waiting for me. The gates to what was, in effect, a giant hangar carved out of the forest, were made as trolleys on wheels, planted with mature trees and shrubs so that when they were closed, they were designed to look like a continuous piece of the forest edge. We did not bother closing the gates. We had to take the chance that no one would find us, either the Germans or the Russians. I dared not switch the Tempest's engines off and the Prussian Queen (I knew you would spot that sooner or later in the code) did me proud, although she was bloody hot by the time we left, standing all that time on tick-over.

I had a few moments to look around whilst we got ready. There were planes everywhere – all jets, dozens of them. Komets, the crazy little rocket fighter, and ME 262's – they were beautiful. Arados, a larger twin engined bomber, even some Volksjager – the ones with the jet engine mounted on the back, still in their packing cases. There was loads of ammo, rockets and all sorts of weird stuff I had no time to look at. Just one problem; not a drop of fuel, not for the jets anyway although ironically there was loads of juice for our sort.

Wolfgang had already refuelled his – a brand new Me109, the latest K series. It was a real beauty, special mottled grey paintwork and that red 8. I had a devil of a job working out the code so that only you and Keith should recognise the two most important clues.

There was absolutely no one about. The Luftwaffe had abandoned the airfield and the Danish Regiment of the SS had set off "en masse" westwards to try and break through to the Elbe, in the hope of surrendering to the Allies. It goes almost without saying that, to a man, they did not make it.

The Russians had encircled Berlin with two rings of steel, one from the north and one, further out from the south which eventually stopped at the Elbe. Somehow we were in a quiet spot between the two.

Actually I don't think they really knew anything much about this airfield. I learnt later that their use of photo reconnaissance was very limited. They only had one weapon in their armoury – people. They sorted out each obstacle as they came to it, no matter what the cost in personnel. There were plenty of fresh supplies waiting in the East. God knows what Hitler thought, when he decided to take that lot on.

I digress. Please forgive me for being so long winded. It may not be my last will, but it is my last testament. If you are not reading this, then it is gone forever.

I was on the ground for only 20 minutes or so. Once we knew Wolfgang needed no fuel from me, I pumped the remaining contents into the wings from the drop tanks, refilled one and then we dumped the other.

Once we were ready, Wolfgang took me over to Svenn who was lying on a stretcher. He had been quite badly shot up in a skirmish with a Russian forward patrol, before the Regiment left. Although he had been patched up by a field surgeon, who had removed a bullet and some shrapnel, he had lost a lot of blood and was pretty weak. He had been lying there for a day or more with only a bottle of water and a Schmeisser machine gun for company. He had persuaded his commander that he was not able to travel and would take his chances, rather than slow them down.

The only way to get the two of them into the Messerschmitt was to take the seat out, and then fly with Wolfgang using Svenn as his cushion. It was a hell of a job getting him up onto the wing because he was pretty much a dead weight and in the end we had to haul him up with a piece of rope round his chest. We padded him up as best we could, then Wolfgang climbed in and sat on his lap.

Svenn gave us directions to our destination.

There was so much room under the tree canopy that I was able to spin the Tempest round on her brakes and then I followed Wolfgang out onto the Autobahn. All the while we were there, you could hear and feel those big Russian guns firing into Berlin, but outside, all was quiet.

We had to go north to take off, so with the bit of a tailwind blowing it took us quite a lot of road to get into the air, but with five miles straight and level it was not a problem. Both our aircraft were armed "just in case" and then we were away, side by side, as low as *we dared, as fast as we dared. At ground level, the Messerschmitt and the Tempest were pretty much a match for speed.*

We had agreed that, over the Russian lines I would go in front, in the hope that they would recognise the Tempest and be confused by the second aircraft for just long enough, to give us a fighting chance of getting away. And so it proved. We were fired on several times and although the Messerschmitt was hit in a couple places, there was no serious damage.

Once we crossed over what we thought was the Russian front line, Wolfgang led, assuming that, as we went further north, we would fly back into territory that was still German held. As you know now, a lone Mustang started sniffing around, obviously confused by the pairing of an English plane and a German one.

After perhaps half a minute flying parallel to us, he turned in and, rather than give him any choice at all, I signalled Wolfgang to continue; then I turned on the Mustang and gave him a quick squirt, to see if it would put him off. Fortunately it did the trick and he backed off. I wonder what he put in his flight log!

I can hear you asking what would I have done if he had closed properly and fired. I think you know the answer to that. I was already in too deep to fail.

I caught Wolfgang up just before we got to Grossenbrode. I gambled they would have too much on their plates to bother with us, but it was with a heavy heart that I saw the remains of at least four Tempests on the ground. We went slap over the top of the base at zero feet. Some of the survivors even shook their fists at Wolfgang, thinking he was too late. It was, after all, only a couple of hours since we had first arrived and attacked.

On we went, skirting round Kiel and then Flensburg, well out over the sea to avoid their formidable anti-aircraft defences.

Then, when I judged it right (it was a bit hit and miss) we turned north-west and headed inland into Denmark which at the time, was still under German occupation. In fact their military airfields were heaving with aircraft, following their decision to pull out of Norway.

We were probably at the greatest risk during this time, but we ploughed on, flat out, so it took us only a few minutes to reach the centre of Jutland. Then I put Wolfgang into a holding pattern whilst I gained height. You know how flat the country is so I must have stuck out like a sore thumb. After about 10 minutes (how very long that seemed), I spotted Strauning. Wolfgang indicated he was getting pretty low on fuel and signalled that he should lead me in. It was a desperate gamble that the Germans had not used the field, but as we came in over the hangar, I could see it was deserted.

Turning over the end of the field, I realised there was no chance of a dummy run. The Messerschmitt was on a one way ticket. Whether I could get down and back out, would be another matter altogether. Wolfgang went in first and made a classic 3 point landing, taxied up to the front of the hangar and then climbed out leaving the engine running. I followed him in as low and slow as I could manage, dropped the Prussian Queen onto the strip just inside the perimeter fence and nearly stood her on her nose trying to stop before I hit the tail of Wolfgang's plane.

Ronald paused in his reading as the images conjured up from the page were given flesh by the day's discoveries. He could see Hutch, an old man now, knowing his end was near, hunched over a desk, pen in hand, fighting the spasms of pain as he made his confession. A pronounced shakiness in the handwriting, here and there, evidenced his agony and then the confidence returned, perhaps supported by an intake of strong painkillers, racing against time to complete his endeavour, clearing his desk and his conscience before the final judgment. A polite cough from the far side of the coffee table, Keith expressing his impatience, returned his thoughts to the letter. Ronald offered an apology with a lift of his shoulders.

Karin had already spotted us and together we pulled the sliding doors open. Wolfgang taxied inside. I swung the Queen round so that she was facing back down the field, and switched off with a very long prayer that she would restart. With a bit of a struggle we pushed her backwards inside. The two planes fitted, tail to tail, with room to spare.

Frankly, having got that far we were totally exhausted and not quite sure what to do when, as though out of nowhere, Karin's parents appeared and then we were all in a huddle together, celebrating the reunion, until a shout from above reminded us that Svenn was still in the cockpit. Getting him down was somewhat easier. The field surgeon had done a good job; the wounds were weeping, but with her training as a nurse, Karin was able to manage his injuries and change his dressings in the weeks that lay ahead.

Karin had grown into a fine looking woman, with lovely dark hair, although she was very thin as a result of food shortages during the war. The Germans left them with enough food, just enough on the farm and commandeered the rest.

There was almost a moment of tension when Karin suddenly realised that she was hugging the enemy. She had not seen Wolfgang since a family visit just before the outbreak of war. I watched her step back with a frown clouding her face, but then she threw herself at Wolfgang squeezing him even harder and saying thank you, over and over again.

Karin said that the behaviour of the German troops had become quite unpredictable, since news of Hitler's death had filtered through. She had been listening to German broadcasts on the radio they had hidden in the roof of the farm house and had heard the rallying calls, urging the German troops to greater efforts in the defence of the Reich. From the English broadcasts, they knew that the Russians were in Berlin and the British were in northwest Germany with the Americans, but with all the German troops coming down from Norway, no-one could predict what might happen. All sorts of rumours were flying around. The Germans might make a last stand in Denmark or they might even try to do a deal with the Allies, to give them a notional German state in Denmark.

Afraid we might be discovered at any moment, we hurriedly closed the doors and then we carried Svenn across the fields to the farmhouse. They put up a bed under the eaves where Svenn would have to stay until he was fully recovered.

In all honesty, we were really stumped for what to do next. So far everything had gone to plan, but what next? Somehow, at least for the time being, all the evidence had to disappear. The people side of it was not a problem, well not too much. Wolfgang was all for giving himself up to the Allies when it was all over, but Karin would not hear of it. Svenn, she thought could explain his return as having escaped from a labour camp. They were fairly sure that no-one actually knew he had volunteered to fight for the Germans, but what about the Messerschmitt?

We held a council of war that night which went on into the small hours. We talked about burning the Messerschmitt or cutting it up and burying it outside in the field or even under the floor of the hangar itself. We all slept badly, fearing the worst, but the next morning the German activity was no greater and there was no sign of anyone sniffing round the hangar.

It was a beautiful spring day, the larks were singing and I can recall commenting that this was the first day I could remember in years when there were no sounds of war; no rumble of tanks, no thunder of guns, no murmur of distant aero engines. Little did we know that the surrender was less than seventy-two hours away.

Once we were back in the hangar, we stood looking at the two planes. Wolfgang said how much smaller and lighter the 109 was in comparison to the Tempest, but as we walked round and round, almost literally in circles, I found myself standing in front of the 109, staring up at its fuselage and down at its undercarriage, when a thought struck me.

It occurred to me that, unlike the Tempest, the undercarriage was mounted as part of the fuselage at the wing root, which meant that the wings played no part in supporting the plane on the ground. One of the problems we had discussed the night before was how physically, if we cut the plane up, we could move things, like an engine block, without heavy lifting equipment. As I pondered this problem, I realised that, without the wings, the airframe was no more than 48 inches wide and would be standing on its own slightly wider undercarriage. That way we should be able to push it around without the need for any sort of lifting equipment.

I remember gathering everyone at the front of the 109 and starting to explain what I was thinking. While we were talking and planning, I realised that Svenn's father, Peder, had disappeared, but he was back shortly, dragging along an oxy-acetylene kit from the farm. The gauge indicated the tanks were nearly full, and although the hoses looked a bit ropey, we would have to hope for the best.

Before he could start cutting, we had to climb up on the wings, unscrew the covers and remove from the feeds as much of the 20 mm ammunition as we could reach. The 30 mm, we could not get at and it's still there to this day, so be careful!

Then it was up to Peder. He cut along underneath the wing just outside the undercarriage leg, then across the top of the wing as far as he could, from the front and then the back. We had a bit of a problem with hydraulic fluid bursting into flames, but we managed to beat the fire out OK – a bit scary at the time. Finally we got him up into the cockpit and he made the last cut along the centre section of the wing. As it started to bend under its own weight, we pulled on the tip until it came crashing down with a terrible groan of rending metal. You could almost see a lump in Wolfgang's throat, as his Red 8 was butchered.

After we got the other wing off we dragged them both clear. The prop had to come off, well just the tip of one blade, but amazingly it was only made of wood; wartime shortages I suppose. We were going to leave the tail plane untouched, but this left it sticking out too far, and so the left elevator was taken off with the torch and we were back to being within our target.

It took us quite a while to prop one of the wings up against the back wall of the hangar, to push and pull and shove the remains of the fuselage tight up against it, and then to stack the other wing up against the outer side. It looked like a great, damaged dragonfly by the time we had finished. I watched Wolfgang standing by the plane, his hand on the body, almost caressing the red 8. I knew how he was feeling. The bond between pilot and plane can be special and this one had saved his life. He would never see it again if all went well.

All of this had taken the best part of the day. It shook me to know that little over 36 hours had elapsed since the attack, and I did not know whether you were dead or alive. For the rest of the day we started to build the framework for the panelling that was going to hide the 109.

That night, we decided that I would have to leave the next day and I chose to go just before sunset, so that I was flying out of the sun. I would have to take the shortest route. We ate our dinner in sombre mood, but a glass or two of Schnapps helped to lift our spirits. I guess it was more than a glass or two because I woke the next morning with a real headache.

Working like furies, we had the framework finished by mid-morning and by mid-afternoon the panelling was up far enough, so that only the tip of the tail-plane and the top of the cockpit canopy were still visible. Then it was time for me to go.

When we had finished our farewells – how I hugged Karin to me – we pushed the Prussian Queen out into the late afternoon sunshine. Then, up I went into the cockpit and Wolfgang helped to strap me in. We said not a word – I don't think we could. Like his father, he had once said to me "Befehl ist Befehl" and I know that if ever our paths had crossed in the air we would each have done our duty, but that was all over now. With a nod and the faintest of smiles, he patted me on the top of my flying helmet and slipped down off the wing.

I selected a fresh cartridge for the Kaufman starter, went through the usual pre-flight checks hurriedly, and pressed the starter button. The cartridge fired, the propeller turned briefly, but the engine did not start. Second cartridge, same result. Frantically checking round the cockpit, and with worried faces gazing up at me outside, I tried to calm myself and went through the checks again. It filled me with embarrassment when I realised I had not switched on the magnetos – no spark at the plugs – a stupid, basic pupil error. Perhaps it was understandable in the circumstances, but it could have proved fatal.

With a noticeable tremor in my hand, I selected the third, and my last starter cartridge, switched on the magnetos, literally closed my eyes and pressed the button. The propeller began to turn, to my indescribable relief, faster and faster until all the cylinders caught. I felt so exposed at that moment and, if a German patrol had been passing, I knew I was dead meat.

With the prop-wash lashing back against the hangar doors, Wolfgang and Peder held onto the wingtips while I ran the engine up to full power. I wasn't sure if the brakes would stand up to this treatment, so Peder had split a small log in half to act as chocks for the wheels. The Queen tried to slide forward as I had anticipated, but the chocks held. I pushed the throttle to the wall and jerked my thumb upwards. On my signal, Wolfgang and Peter pushed up on the wingtips as hard as they could, I released the brakes and we popped over the chocks and sped away across the field.

With the perimeter fence approaching far too quickly for my liking, I began to fear the worst, but at the last possible second I felt the controls bite on the air and I physically lifted the Queen off the ground. I sensed that the wheels had touched the top of the fence – in fact I flattened it.

Then I was up, turning to the west, then round once more, no more than fifty feet up and straight back over the airfield, over my friends who were waving madly, rocking the wings in reply, over the hangar, a turn slightly to starboard, then I headed due south. If I made it back, I knew I would have an awful lot of explaining, or lying, to you and the others. I had succeeded in what I had set out to do, possibly at the cost of the lives of good comrades, and I knew the time had come when I would find out whether I had to pay the price.

On I ploughed, at rooftop height, over the once great cities of Hamburg and Bremen, now burnt out shells looking more like ruined battlements than the homes, shops and offices they once were. Even the great flak zones, that we had avoided for so long, had fallen silent.

Just once, north of Bremen a single gunner fired on me; one 88 mm shell bursting closer to my port wing than I liked. It was as though he was saying "Well, that's it lads, the show's over and you can all go home."

Closer to our base, I flew over Luneburg Heath. A squadron of American P38 Lightnings were flying patrol over what was going to be the surrender site. Two of them flew up, one on either side, looking me over, but then with a salute, they peeled away and rejoined their patrol, knowing I was one of the good guys. If only they had known the truth!

By now it was getting dusk, but ahead I could see the flight path lights. That's how confident we had become and so I took the Prussian Queen up one last time, up into the waning sunlight where we looped and rolled, dived and climbed and then I cried in the cockpit, wept as I had not done since I was a child. Guilt, shame, relief, anger, all muddled up in a man just turned 26 and who had been at war for more than five years. Too much.

I brought the Queen down, kissed her onto the deck, taxied over to the dispersal bay, switched off for the last time and walked into the mess, where you just looked at me, like I was the proverbial bad penny – always turning up. Not a "where the hell have you been" or "Christ, I thought you were dead" just a wave of the hand. You did probe me a bit later and I fobbed you off without much of a protest.

So there it is, old friend. I can imagine you sitting at Karin's dining table reading this. Now you know the how, but you must be asking yourself why.

I know I have only a brief time left to me so I can acknowledge the why for what it was. It was love – the love of a man for another, in brotherhood, in friendship, the way one human could give everything for another. I had formed a tremendous bond with Wolfgang in the short time I had known him.

We continued to correspond right up to the war, as you did with Karin. She loved her brother, Svenn, more than life itself and so the two seemed to come together quite naturally. At least that is how I saw it – saving just one person from the awful chaos created by Hitler and his Nazis brought some form of redemption. Svenn fought out of conviction, so to save him with Wolfgang had about it a neatness, a perfection to it, no matter how misguided you might think it now.

How did we set it all up? Well, that's going to have to remain my secret. Suffice it to say, that there was a lot more communication going on throughout the war than most people realise and few will admit even today, and, as the war's end was nearing, even directly between the combatants. We made use of that, but there are still people alive who were involved and I have no wish to expose them –

they are still entitled to their anonymity; client confidentiality as Colin Farrell once put it to me.

Was it worth it –oh yes, on balance. Two good people were saved and some happiness planted for the future. Although I went back to Strauning from time to time, (largely in the hope that I could reassure Karin), Svenn recovered and lived the life that he would surely have lost, trying to fight his way to the Allies, or in some godforsaken Russian labour camp working to repay his share of "reparations". It is my atonement for what I did not do.

I started with an apology to Keith for involving him in all of this, and I finish with my thanks to him. I never doubted that you would solve the puzzle given enough time, but sadly that is something we have so little of left to any of us. I knew Keith could help shorten the timetable, once he got to thinking about what happened in Berlin.

There is so much more that Karin will be able to tell you. I simply do not have energy left in me to write any more. Give her my love.

Do I have any regrets? Yes – three

Firstly, I wish I could have seen the look on the faces of those Russians when they got into that airfield and found an English drop tank.

Secondly – that all of this had to remain a secret and that Karin, and her family had to live a lie for so long.

Thirdly – well I think you know what that one is, and, although I am about to discover the mystery of eternity, it does not, sadly, include being able to turn back time. I am sure she will be waiting for you.

See you in the Sky Lounge.
Your old pal,
Hutch

Putting the letter on the table, Ronald passed it over to Keith to read. It appeared that, in his closing remark Hutch, despite the advanced state of his cancer, had not lost his sense of humour, but he could see that, from time to time, the handwriting was reduced almost to a scrawl as his illness took its toll on his body. Keith read for nearly three quarters of an hour, re-reading some passages, in a silence that was almost complete, but punctuated by an occasional expletive.

All the while, Ronald stared through the small low windows, so typical of Danish architecture, at the serene landscape, both seeing his life in snatches of fast forward as well as wondering what life must have been like when it was subjected to almost six years of German occupation.

As the shadows lengthened, Keith finished reading and pushed the letter back to Ronald. All he said was, "Well, would you believe it. Must have cost him dear to put all that to paper," before rising from his chair and walking out of the room, towards the cobbled courtyard.

Moments later, they heard the Jaguar crunching down the drive, but within half an hour he was back, brushing cobwebs from his coat, metal detector in hand and a rather smug look on his face as he brandished the detector saying,

"I told you this would come in handy. I've been back to the hangar. I climbed in behind the panelling. There is a very strong return in the corner, just as Hutch suggested, so I think all the ammo must be buried there. That's got to be sorted out somehow."

And that, thought Ronald, as the full implication of what they had done hit him, is probably the least of our worries.

CHAPTER 24

The next morning, Ronald woke early, his mind confused, feeling that he was in a strange bed in a strange land, but a land in which he felt entirely at ease. The local landscape reminded him so much of the flat open spaces of his home county, between the Wolds and the sea. He loved the big sky.

Finding himself the first to rise, he set about percolating some coffee, no chance of tea, and then, after exploring the cupboards and drawers in the low-ceilinged kitchen, he laid a breakfast table for three, wishing he had his Times to comfort him. There were still unanswered questions.

Faint noises from the far end of the house indicated someone was on the move, so he perched uneasily on the edge of one of the chairs in the living-room until, five minutes or so later, he heard light footsteps coming slowly along the corridor, which ran the length of the building.

When Karin entered the room, her face fleetingly wore a puzzled frown, but then it lit with a bright smile as she walked over to him, cupped his face in her hands and kissed him lightly on the forehead.

"Hutch used to sit just like that, when he visited, and just for a second I thought..."

"Did he visit often?" Ronald asked as Karin's voice trailed off.

"No, not really, perhaps once every four or five years after he moved to Hong Kong and the last time was when he brought the letter. He was very sick, he looked terrible, but it mattered so much to him that he make the effort to come over here. He wanted to make absolutely certain, once and for all, that I was happy he put you on the trail."

"Were you, really?"

"Oh, yes. Of course. To share this burden which I have borne for so long, and, of course, to be given the chance to see you just once more. You know I was very fond of..." but she did not get to finish her sentence.

"And here we all are," boomed the voice of Keith, startling them both as he came unnoticed into the room. Karin turned, greeted Keith with equal warmth and then disappeared into the kitchen.

Over breakfast, Karin announced that she had an appointment at the city hospital fifty miles down the coast which would take her away for most the day and so, mid-morning found them in the Jaguar purring northward on silky-smooth roads through the pretty town of Ringkobing with its white-painted houses and their red tiled roofs. Then they headed due west, towards the coast.

Turning once again north, they followed Karin's directions until they reached the remains of the coastal fortifications which had formed the northern end of Germany's Atlantic Wall. Karin had made them a flask of coffee and they spent the rest of the morning investigating the bunkers, strong-points, and the massive gun emplacements, now staring vacantly out to sea, all half-buried in the advancing sand dunes.

Bracing himself against the west wind, which was steadily rising, and shouting to overcome the roar of the sea, Keith commented, "What a bloody waste of time! Don't think these would really have stopped anything. Flat as a pancake." Ronald nodded his agreement, imagining a succession of German soldiers thankful to sit out their war, but always steeling themselves anxiously for the attack that would never come.

Just for a moment, he tried to put himself in the shoes of a foot soldier at the southern end of the Wall in Normandy, Allied or German, at the start of D-Day. He wondered if there was such a thing as a scale of fear. Did what he felt at Grossenbrode get anywhere near what they must have felt? Somehow he doubted it. How could anything match that slow, relentless, unavoidable, inescapable tidal wave of history, driving a man forward, where caprice, fate or whatever you called it, decided whether he lived or died.

"I'm freezing," shouted Keith, breaking into his thoughts. "Time to find a pub." Ronald nodded as they started their descent, along the well-trodden paths through the dunes, to the car park where they shared the coffee while the Jaguar's powerful heater gradually warmed them through. Keith remembered that he had seen a restaurant in the coastal resort where they had turned north, so he headed back.

The restaurant was busy with tourists, mostly from Germany, but they managed to find a table near the window, ready laid with sparkling cutlery and glassware set on a damask tablecloth. Style was everything. Knowing Karin would not be home until late, they had a leisurely meal while discussing the knotty problem of what to do about the Messerschmitt.

Keith argued forcibly, for Karin's sake if no other, that the only proper, sensible solution was to inform the authorities – Danish police, or their Air Force or Bomb Disposal. Keith declared that he was not inclined to go digging to prove whether the response on the metal detector was scrap metal or the ammunition. "If there's tracer down there, then it might self combust, when it gets exposed to the air. Not as quick over a hundred yards as I used to be," was his final comment.

Initially, Ronald had argued that it was best to let sleeping dogs lie, even suggesting, half-heartedly, that they go as far as re-fixing the boarding, but gradually he came round to Keith's way of thinking. It was, of course, far too late to try to put the genie back in the bottle, and the whole purpose of their quest was to release Karin from her burden. To do otherwise, he accepted, would be unthinkable.

They agreed they would discuss it with Karin at an opportune moment, but in the meantime Keith offered to ring a couple of his contacts in the RAF to see if they could offer any help.

On the way back to the farmhouse, by a different route with Ronald navigating, and travelling at the regulation fifty miles per hour they rounded a corner to find the road, deserted of traffic, stretching out before them into the distance. Without a second's hesitation, Keith floored the throttle, the automatic gearbox kicked down and the supercharged four litres of Jaguar's precision engineering snarled its response, hurling the car down the straight.

Ronald sat back, pulling the seatbelt just a little tighter as he watched the speedometer needle out of the corner of his eye, climb through one hundred and ten miles per hour, then one twenty, then one thirty with no sign of Keith easing off the throttle. Turning in his seat, he looked at Keith with a raised eyebrow. Keith was grinning broadly.

"One forty-five," he shouted over the rising wind-noise and pointed to the speedometer. "I knew she could do it!" and he roared with laughter as the needle held steady and the tarmac disappeared under the bonnet at an astonishing rate.

"For God's sake!" Ronald shouted back. "Either get the wheels up or cut the throttle. We need one or the other to get us round that bend!" pointing through the windscreen at the onrushing corner.

"Right ho, Skipper," came the calm reply, as Keith took his foot off the accelerator and began to apply the brakes with some force. The Jaguar rocketed into the bend and Ronald began to steel himself as the tyres started to squeal in protest, but then under Keith's skilful handling they were through, and on to the next straight.

As he began to unwind the knot in his stomach, Keith punched him lightly on the shoulder.

"God, I needed that. Wonderful. That was one of my 'ten things to do before you die' – getting the old girl flat out just once. I'm not ready for my box yet!"

Then he continued, "I know it's usually fifty, but I've had to compromise. I'm doing the world cruise next year and I've done meeting the Queen so that leaves six, well maybe five, if coming to Denmark counts as doing something utterly daft."

After he had done the maths, Ronald asked, intrigued, "There's one in there you have not told me about. Care to explain?"

Keith laughed. "Well it's not about getting laid, if that's what you are thinking. That's number eleven, reserved for the cruise. Got to have something to look forward to," he said with a mischievous smile.

"Actually, it was to get rip-roaring drunk in the company of a friend who would put me to bed and not be critical or judgmental. You did that very nicely for me on the way over, thank you."

Ronald decided not to elaborate on his top ten, realising that he really did not have one. Ambition seemed to have withered a long time ago. Perhaps, he thought, he should have a top five at least, but nothing came readily to mind, so he changed the subject, saying, "When you came on to that straight and opened the throttle, I was back with Hutch on that autobahn. I'd been trimming her up and pulling on the stick long before you got to the one thirty."

"We miss it and we miss him, don't we?" Keith replied with a sigh, as he switched on the cruise control and let the Jaguar take them home. Ronald found he could not agree more.

CHAPTER 25

Back at the farmhouse, Karin was already home and, as the shadows lengthened, they sat chatting quietly as though, at least for the time being, they were unwilling to return to their examination of what had occurred in those last days of the war, and in the aftermath of the German surrender.

Perhaps they all knew that this was to be a tale of dark days and dangerous times and that it was not a tale to be told comfortably by the harsh light of day. They still needed the shadows to hide in, to soften the reality.

Finally, as dusk began to creep stealthily over the farmhouse, to cocoon it from the present, it was Keith who could no longer restrain himself and returned their thoughts the past, to Hutch's letter, which had raised as many questions as it had answered.

"Before I explain anything else, I think you should try to understand what it was like to live here in Denmark throughout the war years." Karin paused, as though marshalling her thoughts, before continuing. "Never having been invaded, it's hard for you to imagine such a thing – being occupied by an enemy, that is."

"For a moment a little history. No, not too much, I promise," noticing Keith's alarmed expression, "but you may not know that the part of Denmark where my family lived, and where I grew up until I was a teenager, had not always been Danish. In fact, that area in the south was under German control for more than half a century, captured from Denmark at the end of what we called the Three Years War in 1860. It was only returned to Danish ownership after the Treaty signed at Versailles in 1919.

"Thus for some people, there were mixed emotions and loyalties when the intentions of the Germans became clearer after they invaded Poland. Across Europe, as you will remember, the fascist parties had been on the march, even in England where you had Sir Oswald Moseley and his Blackshirts. We too had a fascist party and the Germans knew that any move against Denmark stood a good chance a sympathetic reception in the south. Three generations had lived and died "German" in those parts.

"When the invasion came on 9th April 1940, a full month before France, it was a walkover. Virtually no resistance was offered. In fact the Germans proclaimed it to be a protective occupation; to protect us, as they said, from the expansionist plans of France and England. What a joke that was, but faced with such overwhelming forces, the tiny Danish army mostly stayed in its barracks as the Government capitulated. The King stayed to support his people and so it remained until 1943, while our country melted into a fog of obscurity, living an uneasy co-existence with the occupying German forces.

"For our family, that inner conflict was terrible. My parents had been born German, but I had grown up Danish, Svenn too. My aunt, who I adored, was married to a senior member of the German Nazi party, as I wrote to you many times," she added, looking directly at Ronald in a way which almost seemed to accuse him, personally, of failing to prevent the unfolding tragedy.

"Svenn, however, had grown up strongly attracted to all things German and became increasingly immersed in the fascist ideals. I begged him to give it up, but he would not listen to me and our arguments became more and more heated, which often left me in tears. He once accused me of being a traitor to our heritage. Much as I loved him, I slapped his face and we hardly spoke for days.

"After the outbreak of the civil war in Spain, Svenn wanted to go and fight for the nationalists, but my father would not hear of it. After all, Svenn was only sixteen at the time! The trip to Berlin that year really only made things worse, but for a while, Father held sway with the argument that we could not manage without him on the farm.

"Svenn continued to argue that fascism was the only true defence of the cultured world against the dark clouds of bolshevism. That was one of his favourite phrases, especially when he was trying to justify his position. For a while, he was confused by the non-aggression pact Germany made with Russia, but I am certain he was in touch with Uncle Otto, because he soon started saying that the pact was all part of a bigger plan. Events proved him right.

"Then in early 1939, fearing that there would be a war in Europe, once he had seen the German takeover in Austria the year before, my father became convinced that Germany intended to retake that which had been theirs for almost sixty years. He regarded himself as Danish and although he loved his sister-in-law, Elise, dearly, he decided to sell up and within weeks had moved all of us here to this farm, over my mother's protests. He completely ignored my complaints that I would be losing contact with all my school friends. He said he would not rest until we were on what he called 'proper' Danish soil. Much good did it do us," Karin added, with sadness tingeing her voice.

"Anyway," she continued, as Ronald and Keith sat listening intently, "within weeks Germany attacked Poland, you declared war on Germany, my father insisted he had been right all along, and what happened? Nothing, for months! The Sitzkrieg, or the Phoney War as you called it.

"Christmas 1939 came and went and still nothing happened, except there was a growing, dreadful sense of foreboding. On the farm, life continued as before and I continued to go to school, dreaming of becoming a nurse, of going to college in Copenhagen, and, by this time, of getting away from it all, to lead my own life.

"Father talked about emigrating, but of course, by then, no one would buy the farm, so we continued like a ship in the olden days, sailing, unstoppable, towards the edge of the world. As winter receded, father began to prepare his fields for the spring crops, just as though nothing was going to change, but then we woke up one morning to find the Germans in our village and our little ship had sailed off the edge.

"So began five years of occupation. Father continued farming, Mother continued to be his wife. Little changed and yet, everything changed. You might be surprised to know, Ronnie, that I received your letters written in March of 1940, forwarded from the old address, although they had been opened by the German censors. Because you had written in terms which were, shall we say fearful, the Germans crossed nothing out, as though to express their power. I was miserable because I could not reply to you."

Karin looked into Ronald's face with tears welling up in her eyes, as the pain of sixty years could not be easily washed away. Ronald made to get up, to comfort her, but she waved him back.

"No, Ronnie, it's alright, really, but I have to do this. It's what Hutch wanted, so just let me continue." Ronald sank back into his chair, wishing for a moment that he had turned back that day on his way to the air museum, but now it was far too late for second thoughts.

"Anyway," Karin continued, forcing herself to pick up the thread of her saga, "at home the atmosphere got steadily worse. Svenn secretly welcomed the German invasion. He saw it as a protection against communism and said it was good that we would have the strength of Germany to be around us. He had frequent, heated rows with my parents.

"Then in the spring of 1941, Otto and Elise turned up at our farmhouse, unannounced and in complete secrecy. They swore us to silence, but they did not need to. We had been careful not to tell our neighbours of our German connections. I am sure you can imagine what might have happened if it had got out."

Keith nodded his understanding. "Saw what happened in France after the liberation," he grunted cryptically.

"Despite everything, we had such a happy time. Otto's car was laden with provisions, which we eked out over the following months. Why did they come? Guilty conscience perhaps, or a last chance to say farewell. I am certain that Otto told my father of Hitler's intention to attack Russia, to warn him that, when it happened, things would never be the same again.

"They stayed two, perhaps three days and then they were gone. Mother cried her eyes out and Svenn begged to go with them so that he could enlist in the German army, but Otto refused to take him saying that he was still too young and that he was needed at home. It did not convince Svenn, especially when he learnt that Dieter was already in training with the Luftwaffe. He went around under a cloud of anger and depression in the following days, making life ever more miserable for us.

"To make matters worse between Svenn and myself, I discovered after they had gone back to Berlin, that Otto had given Svenn a letter, a sort of safe conduct pass that he could use if or when he decided to join the German armed forces. I did not dare tell my parents about it.

"The parting was terrible. I heard Uncle Otto asking my parents to move all of us to live with him, at least temporarily, in Berlin, but he knew it was a forlorn request. My mother and aunt clung to each other as though they would never see each other again. They were right.

"After that, the Germans left us largely in peace. Father told me later that Uncle Otto had left word, he apparently had that power, that we were to be treated with a light hand. Later in the war it served me well. Otto had also ordered that the old hangar at the corner of our land should not be requisitioned. We were instructed to store our farm implements there. Perhaps uncle Otto hoped we might have a better life that way, but at the end it was to no avail and the equipment was taken for the 'benefit' of the German war effort.

"By that time, of course, Svenn was long gone. When Germany invaded Russia, propaganda posters began to appear, urging Danish young men to join the fight against Bolshevism. Svenn needed no second urging. Within days we found a letter on the kitchen table telling us that he had gone to follow his conscience."

Karin wiped her eyes with the delicate embroidered handkerchief that she had been holding and twisting between her hands all the while she spoke.

"Somehow we had to explain his disappearance so we pretended he had been taken into one of the work battalions that had been formed to build the coastal defences you went to see today. Many of our young, and not so young men were, shall we say, obliged to work there. Alternative forms of employment were available." Karin left the comment hanging in the air.

"Svenn was gone for months before I heard anything from him again."

Then, realising the room was almost complete darkness, Karin apologised and switched on the lamp which hung low over the coffee table around which they were sitting, to leave their faces in deep shadow. Making her excuses, they heard her go through to the kitchen, the rattle of cutlery and crockery and, with the puttering of a percolator, the aroma of strong black coffee drifted through to the lounge.

This reminded them that they had not eaten for hours and it was a welcome relief when Karin returned with a tray of open Danish sandwiches, a large flask of piping hot coffee and a small bottle of almost frozen schnapps, which was rapidly frosting over after its removal from the freezer.

Setting the meal out on the coffee table, Karin indicated they should help themselves, poured each of them a coffee and decanted a measure of schnapps into three tiny glasses. As they began to eat, Karin raised her glass holding it close to her lips inviting them to join her in a traditional Danish toast. Downing it in one gulp, she sat back, escaping from the circle of light which plunged her face into deep shadow. After a moment, she cleared her throat and continued in a stronger voice, as though the ice-cold alcohol had lifted years from her shoulders.

"Ah, Svenn. What a wonderful brother he was; handsome, loyal and brave, headstrong and reckless. My Black Knight. I don't think he really thought through what he was doing, but he had a passion, a belief and I loved him for it. We were so close," she said with a catch in her voice. "When we next heard from him he was in Poland, training with the Nordland Division of the Waffen S.S.

"Despite the war, the German forces postal service was remarkably efficient and we received a letter from him every couple of months. Always the same thing: bland, reassuring comments so as not to worry the family at home.

"Perhaps, because they were written in Danish, the censor missed the fact that there was a code hidden in the text. It was childishly simple. All I had to do was count the first, second and third letters up to ten then back to one, then back up and down until the text was finished. Afterwards I wrote the sequence down backwards to get the meaning.

"What it told me was very different. I followed him from Poland to Latvia as Germany's situation began to deteriorate after Stalingrad. He wrote of desperate fighting and much killing in early 1945 in a failing rearguard action. The German High Command was so impressed with their regiment's unswerving dedication, their almost suicidal devotion to duty, that they were evacuated by ship – the last ones out as the defences collapsed. It was a miracle that they were not sunk by a Russian submarine in the eastern Baltic. Many such ships, even refugee ships were attacked, with incredible numbers of fatalities, right up to the end of the war. The Russians were not in a mood to show much mercy.

"The letters, more brief now, continued to arrive and I learnt that he was in Berlin as part of the final defence. It was the beginning of March '45 and that was the last letter I had from him, but not the last communication. In all that devastation, his regiment was ordered to the west of Berlin, into Charlottenburg of all places. I always wondered if Uncle Otto had something to do with that."

Karin paused, eyes closed, as she struggled to complete her story. The silence extended. She drew in a deep breath, but her eyes remained closed, although her lips moved as though she were in conversation, in a debate with herself.

Keith leaned forward to see if she had fallen asleep, but Karin suddenly opened her eyes, smiled sweetly at him and continued as if there had not been a second's interruption.

"Towards the end of the second week in April the telephone rang." She nodded in the general direction of the hallway. "We all jumped out of our skins. We were forbidden to use the phone because we knew it was monitored all the time by the German security."

"After the uprising in 1943, when the Germans dismissed the Government, active resistance began to take shape, although it was never on the scale of the Marquis in France. Denmark, you know, is a small, flat country with none of the hills and mountains which were available to the French resistance as hiding places. I became a resistance worker in the summer of 1944, after D-Day, carrying messages between members of the resistance, messages which I had to memorise. We never, ever wrote anything down or used the phone.

"Resistance was limited mostly to blowing up a few trains and the very occasional attack on a truck, but the resistance leaders issued specific instructions that, even when substantial amounts of small arms, ammunition and explosives were being parachuted in at the beginning of 1945, the armed resistance groups, which were never more than ten strong, should not enter into direct combat with German units. Hit and run was our watch-word.

"Regularly, I carried pistols and ammunition in a false bottom to the basket on the front of my cycle. The Germans never suspected someone who looked like a schoolgirl, could be helping to arm the resistance. I became really good at pretending to be a lot younger than I really was, and I had a set of false identity papers to match.

"From the beginning of 1945 we knew the end was coming, but the when and the how were the big questions. Refugees from all over northern and eastern Germany were pouring into Denmark; civilians, wounded soldiers, more than a quarter of a million by the war's end. The civilians were forcibly billeted with Danish families which produced terrible tensions, but we were somehow overlooked.

"Rumours were rife that the Germans would make a final stand in Denmark and towards the end of March, as the resistance attacks increased, the attitude of the Germans became very aggressive. My father forbade me to go out and for once I obeyed, so it meant that I was at home when the phone rang.

"I remember my hand trembled as I lifted the receiver. Before I could say anything, there was Svenn's voice and I know I screamed. He was in Otto's house, or what was left of it, and found the phone was still working. We spoke only for a couple of minutes, at the most. Even over the phone I could distinctly hear the rumble of gunfire. Svenn told me they had been given permission, as a regiment, to fight their way out and try to get across to the River Elbe, where the Americans had come to a halt. The Russians had mostly encircled Berlin, but he said there were corridors where there was still just a slim chance of escape.

"Then he said, surprising me completely, he had met Wolfgang and *we*, that was his word, not I, would be home soon, but before I could ask him anything he just said, "Love to you all, especially you little sister. I'm sorry that..." but he never finished the sentence because the line went dead."

"We knew Uncle Otto's number and tried phoning back, but could not get through. Having believed Svenn was already dead, we were given hope, only to have it snatched away. Mother cried for the rest of the day and Father asked me, time and again, to repeat what had been said in the phone call. Each time, we came back to what Svenn had meant by 'we'."

"We heard no more until a week later. I was outside in the yard when a Messerschmitt 109 flew over. I recognised it at once because I had seen so many during the occupation. It was escorted by a British fighter of a type which I had never seen before. At that moment, I hoped our prayers had been answered. With no thought of how the future might unfold, I ran like the wind, to begin opening the doors of the hangar.

"How I managed to get those heavy wooden doors, even partly open, by myself I will never really know. I think hope and fear in equal measure gave me strength and I stood open-mouthed watching the Messerschmitt taxiing in, piloted by Wolfgang with Svenn behind him, his head lolling to one side. For a moment, I feared my brother was dead, but then he moved his head weakly and I knew our prayers had been answered.

"Then I saw the pilot of the second plane was Hutch and I believed a miracle had been granted to our family. Our joy knew no bounds. You have both read Hutch's letter and seen how we managed to hide Wolfgang's plane."

Neither Ronald nor Keith had stirred for so long, listening to Karin's description of another world in another time, that Ronald wondered if Keith had fallen asleep, but then Keith shifted in his chair and posed the question that had been running through Ronald's mind as well.

"OK, so you had got your brother and your cousin back, almost from the dead. On the one hand, you would want to celebrate, but on the other, hadn't you just given yourselves two enormous headaches, which could have landed your family in serious hot water?"

Karin took a moment before replying, "Yes it's true. Only when Hutch was preparing to leave, did we really begin to think about what we were doing. Under our roof we had a German Luftwaffe pilot, who would certainly be treated as a prisoner of war. But as the son of a high ranking SS Officer, one of the early members of the Nazi party, he might have been sentenced to a lengthy period of imprisonment, or, possibly, he could have been shot. We just did not know. We also had a former member of the Danish Regiment which, assuming the Allies won the war, was going to place Svenn in a very difficult position if he were ever discovered."

"Perhaps you won't know," she continued, "that more than five thousand Danes volunteered to fight for the Germans. In fact the Germans were able to recruit regiments in almost all the countries they occupied. Anyway, almost half the Danes who volunteered were killed in battle during the closing months of the war and, later, many were sentenced to death and executed by our own country for what was seen as their treachery. We did not know this at the time, but we were sure Svenn was in very great danger.

"In the last week of April, the Resistance Council of Denmark published regulations for the conduct on the war against the Germans if there were open hostilities, even though everyone was praying that they would surrender without firing a shot.

"Thankfully the Germans stayed in their barracks but another set of regulations were published at the beginning of May, this time on behalf of the Allies, dealing with the treatment of refugees, deserters, and the thousands of German soldiers, some of whom were already marching, in columns, back toward Germany.

"By now a new fear had arisen, which was that the Russians might invade Denmark even before the end of the war. As your Mr. Churchill recognised, one time allies were really allies no longer.

"The fear of Russia was very real. There is an island in the Baltic, halfway between Denmark and the eastern Baltic countries such as Estonia and Latvia, which is Danish. It's called Bornholm. The Germans occupied the island in 1940 and used it as a radio listening post and weather station, but in May 1945, when the German commander insisted that he wanted to surrender only to the Americans, the Russians bombed the island even though the formal surrender of all German forces had already been signed. Many died. What the Russians might have done to Svenn did not bear thinking about, especially when you know that Russia did not give Bornholm back to Denmark until 1946.

"Anyway a few days later, just after Hutch had gone, the British tanks arrived in our part of Denmark and we knew then that our war was finally over.

"We held a family meeting. We decided that we would hide both Svenn and Wolfgang in the attic of our farmhouse for as long as it took to work out how to 'produce' them. They both agreed, and only came out at night for exercise and fresh air. This went on for months.

"In Svenn's case, we decided that as a cover story we would say that he had been taken, as part of the forced labour, to work in a German factory just north of Berlin. He would say that when the Russians over-ran the area and started to ransack the factory, he managed to escape to join the hundreds and thousands of refugees streaming westwards across northern Germany."

'*The dirty, the dispirited, the desperate, the ants*', thought Ronald as he remembered his wartime patrols in those early months of 1945. Suddenly, without warning, in a flash as though the entire room was flooded with daylight, he was back in the cockpit of Miss Faithful, flying down, once again, his own road to damnation.

Ahead, two long, ragged columns of people, separated by no more than fifty yards, are trudging slowly across a barren, snow-covered, almost featureless, landscape toward a small village a mile or so distant. To left and right, the burnt-out remains of trucks and tanks scar the pristine snow, evidence of an earlier engagement.

Flak begins to weave toward him from the far edges of the village, threatening to engulf him in their crossfire and giving covering fire for the advancing columns.

Wehrmacht soldiers or refugees? Soldiers escorting PoWs? Decide. The flak whips past his wingtip. Decide NOW! Left or right, or not at all. Do your duty. Touch of right rudder for the right-hand column. People starting to turn and stare in fear. No time to take a second look. God forgive me, if I am wrong!

Cannon and machine guns shake Miss Faithful to the core, as both columns try to dive for cover, too late. The ground is hard and white, like a bleached billiard table being seeded with red. Fate will decide whether they live or die. Out of the corner of his eye, on the flank of the column as it dissolves under his guns, he sees... but then the picture freezes and the darkness swallows him.

"Skipper, are you OK?" The words come to him from a great distance. "Skipper!" more insistently, dragging him back

A soft hand touches his forehead. "Ronnie, dear, did you faint?" He shook his head to clear the fog. He opened his eyes and, as the room came back into focus, he found Keith staring at him anxiously while Karin was kneeling at the side of his chair with a moist cloth in her hand. He could feel its soothing effect on his brow.

"Christ, Ronno! For a moment, I thought you were done for. Scared the hell out of me!"

"No, I'm OK. Think I must have nodded off for a second or two."

Keith gave him a sceptical look. Then, with a sense of wonderment, Ronald added, without explanation, "I saw him!"

In that moment, before the picture froze, he had seen a soldier, heavy machine gun cradled in his arms, staggering under the recoil while the ammunition belt wriggled like a live snake, as it fed through the breach. A gesture of defiance dribbling from a defeated army. At last, after sixty years, he knew that he had not made the wrong decision. He saw also that he could be forgiven.

"No, really, I'm fine," he responded, with a certainty. "Let's continue."

Karin looked at Keith, who gave her an encouraging smile. "If the Skipper says he's OK, then who are we to argue?"

Karin gave a little laugh of relief, but only continued after she had received a reassuring look from Ronald.

"If you are sure?"

Ronald nodded, more certain than he had been in many years.

Karin continued, "We worked out a date when he 'escaped' and then, allowing him progress west at the rate of ten kilometres a day, we got him to 'arrive' home in the third week of August 1945. By that time Denmark was bursting at the seams with refugees. Your troops were building special camps for them, so that one refugee, more or less, made no difference.

"We kept the secret for the next fifty years until his death in 1996. Unlike you, Ronald, he never married, but like you he never had any children, even though for quite a time he lived with a woman from the next village, but eventually they drifted apart. He did however love my two girls. I had married a teacher in 1952 and my daughters were born in '55 and '57. My husband Jacob died of cancer when the girls were well into their thirties, and by then, my parents were both very old and in need of care, so I sold up and moved back here to look after them, as well as Svenn, until the end.

"All of the farm's land is rented out now and as you will see I have converted some of the outbuildings for holiday lettings so that I still have an income. Sadly there is no one to take over from me, and when I am gone it will all be sold."

As she paused, Ronald said, "Oh Karin, if only I had known," but she cut him off, saying fiercely, "No, Ronnie, you could not have known, no-one could. Even for all of our friendship before the war, I could not risk telling you. I knew that I would hurt you, but there was so much more at stake."

"But why tell now?" interjected Keith. "Why not leave it all a secret to be discovered after your death?"

"Well," replied Karin, "it was not just about me, or Svenn or Wolfgang, it was about Hutch as well. I believe he needed forgiveness, and this was his way of having one of the most important people in his life understand what had happened."

"Me?" said Ronald in a baffled tone.

"Yes, you. He loved you like a brother, even though you could not have realised it. He so wanted you to know what had happened on that last raid. He carried a crushing burden of guilt for those who died, and he wanted some understanding, if not forgiveness from you even if it had to wait until after he died."

For once, Ronald was lost for words and it took Keith to bring the conversation back to the reason for their visit.

"But what about Wolfgang? He was listed as 'missing believed killed' by the Germans at the end of the war. How did you bring him back?"

Karin closed her eyes and brought back more memories of so long ago as Ronald said gently, "I know how hard this must be. It took me weeks to decide to come here and then I only managed with Keith's support, so I do understand. Please, take your time."

Karin remained motionless breathing deeply then with a sigh that seemed to express years of loss and disappointment she went on:

"Poor Wolfgang." She sighed again, but then continued, her eyes still closed as though to distance herself from the final chapter in her story.

"You know, at first there was the euphoria, the excitement of his survival and escape, but this was soon tainted by the realisation that at only twenty-five years of age he believed his whole family had almost certainly been wiped out. There had been no time for him to grieve, even for Dieter who had been killed the year before. What must have happened to his mother and father had been so quick that he had not had time to take it in. At least for Dieter, they had managed a funeral of sorts."

She paused again, clearly feeling Wolfgang's pain before continuing in a whisper, "They were my family too, remember. Once the Wall came down in the early nineties I always intended to go back, to see if I could find out anything about my uncle and aunt, but

I could not bring myself to do it, and now it's too late." A sob escaped her lips and she dabbed at her eyes.

"Anyway, as the weeks passed, his mood deepened and he found the enforced isolation tiresome and depressing, especially after Svenn, as Wolfgang saw it, was given his freedom.

"As the summer turned to autumn, and the nights became longer, not even the extra time he could spend outside seemed to help. He joked, darkly that the German eagle had become a German owl, with its wings clipped. And so his moods deepened steadily until we thought he was on the edge of a sort of madness.

"He wanted to leave, to take his chance. He said he might as well swap one form of prison for another, where there would be at least some hope of parole. In fairness, we still had not come up with a way of getting him "out" so the farm really was his prison. He even talked about joining Dieter, of ending it all, so that his record would say that he died with honour, but Svenn talked to him for hours and he seemed to calm a little."

Karin opened her eyes, her face brightened and with a faint smile on her lips she continued, "Then the most extraordinary thing happened! One night, just before Christmas 1945, in the early hours, our dogs went crazy. I heard my father shout at them to be quiet, but they would not settle and kept on barking and clawing at the kitchen door to get out in to the yard. Normally, they never bothered with the wild animals roaming round the farm, so we guessed it must be something different.

"Eventually we were all out of bed and dressed warmly. It was a bitter cold night with a heavy frost and light snow. Father armed himself with the little rifle he used for shooting rats. He had managed to keep it hidden right through the war. Svenn found a big, heavy spanner. We lit our kerosene lamps and then we let the dogs out."

She paused again, as they followed her mind's eye to the back door of the house, not twenty feet from where they were sitting.

"Without a second's hesitation, the dogs went straight across the yard and we followed them, our feet crunching the frost, into the barn as the lamps cast flickering shadows on the walls. It was still such a novelty to be outside, at night, with an unguarded light after four winters of darkness.

"The barn was where we stored what was left of the hay and fodder for the two or three cows that my father had managed to buy since the war ended. All the hay was piled up in the back corner and the dogs were already there, at the foot of it, barking furiously. Try as we might, we could not get the dogs to calm down.

"My father was afraid that there might be a German deserter hiding somewhere in the pile of hay, so he and Svenn shouted in Danish that they had a gun and that whoever was there should come out. There was no reaction. By this time, Wolfgang had also come out to the barn and then he shouted in German for them to come out with their hands up.

"Almost immediately, as his words rang out, there was movement under the surface and next, a pair of hands appeared, and there was a muffled reply. I watched as a figure, a dirty dishevelled tramp rose to his feet, hands held high and begin to shout in German, 'Don't shoot, I'm...' but before he could say another word, Wolfgang charged into the hay, shouting, 'It's Werner'!"

Ronald sat bolt upright, incredulous. "Werner, are you serious? In God's name how?"

Karin held up her hand to quieten him. "All in good time. I will explain."

"Wolfgang scrambled to the top of the stack, threw his arms round Werner and they both tumbled, locked together, down to our feet. Only when he was close by could I recognise him. He was so thin, filthy and, as it turned out, infested with lice, but Wolfgang was so happy, ecstatic that he had a small part of his family back.

"We tidied him up as best we could, we burnt his clothes and," Karin smiled at the memory, "we bathed him in an insecticide for the cows to get rid of the lice. Mother would not have him in the house until he was clean.

"Little by little, over the coming days, he told us his story. In August 1944, shortly after the failed plot to kill Hitler, Otto's protection finally ran out. He was arrested by the Gestapo and taken to a concentration camp north of Berlin, Oranienburg I think it was called, which was for political prisoners. It was not an extermination camp as such, so he survived for almost nine months, slowly starving, until the Russians overran the camp in March 1945.

"The last thing Uncle Otto did before the Gestapo came for Werner, was to tell him to make his way here, to our farm, if he was lucky enough to survive and was not taken to the east by the Russians. I also think in some strange way Otto repaid the debt to Werner from the time he looked after Auntie Elise before Otto was repatriated in 1919, by arranging for him, despite his Jewish origins, not to go straight to one of the death camps."

"Was that possible?" asked Keith, hardly able to take in the events of sixty years ago. "Do you really think he had that power, that authority?"

"I really don't know, but there Werner was, when he should have been dead. He told us that when the Russians opened the camp, he managed to persuade his liberators that he was sympathetic to their political outlook. It wasn't very difficult for him. Some of the advance troops were not very bright. He had learnt enough of the jargon from when he lived on the streets in the twenties to keep the Political Commissars happy once they arrived to take over the running of the camp from the Russian army at the end of April.

"The Russians did bring food, of a sort, so for that month Werner regained some of his strength and hoarded what he could. He stole a civilian set of clothes and took his chance to slip away from the camp while the guards celebrated the capture of Berlin. They were all, he said, very, very drunk, firing their machine guns into the air and, once it all started to get out of control, he made his getaway with what food he could carry. Then he went to ground for a couple of days, living rough. But he was used to looking after himself; he learnt that the hard way during the Great War and afterwards.

"Then he went westwards as fast as he could, by day or by night towards the Elbe. One or two crossings were still open, but not for long. The Americans were on the west bank facing the Russians on the east, but the stream of refugees was so great and the Russians were stretched too thinly on the ground to check everyone so he kept going. Sometimes he pretended to be a father to a family, once he dressed in a woman's cloak – anything to blend in, to avoid being noticed, because he had no papers.

"There was a terrible risk that he would be caught and arrested as a deserter. There were German units surrounded in pockets, and soldiers were trying to get to the Allied side, knowing what their fate would be if the Russians took them to their labour camps

"After a couple more days he reached the Elbe, and found a railway bridge. It was still standing, despite being bombed, but it was just usable as a footbridge, although the track was twisted and tipped over at a crazy angle. He went across as part of a family, helping them carry some of their belongings. So many refugees were crossing, that the Americans could not possibly check every one. They were just looking for "war criminals". The Russians blew the bridge up shortly afterwards to close that escape route.

"So he got through the American's front line and went to ground again, to rest and rebuild his strength. He was really very weak after his time in the camp. It took him the next seven months to work his way through northern Germany. He managed to cross the border into Denmark, he would not say how, and arrived with us just in time for Christmas."

"Bloody hell!" said Keith, "Unbelievable – some Christmas present!"

Karin laughed out loud. "Yes, you could put it that way. Certainly it was by far the best present for Wolfgang. Werner's arrival cheered him enormously and we did manage to have something of a family Christmas.

"The following months saw Werner and Wolfgang growing ever closer, not just good friends, but more like father and son. Wolfgang needed a father figure and Werner had been close enough over the years to provide that. But we had still not worked out how to bring Wolfgang back.

"I think that's why my father bought the aeroplane. Wolfgang was getting restless again, so my father thought if he had a plane, it might give him the freedom in the air which he could not get on the ground. It worked for a while. Wolfgang was happy once flying restrictions had been lifted by the government. Then, one day, in the spring of 1949, he was gone for a long time and we thought he had flown away, but he came back. I think somehow he was preparing to say goodbye.

"We parked the Moth in the hangar exactly where you found it yesterday. He never flew it again.

"Perhaps he had done a reconnaissance, because, about a week later, we found that he and Werner were gone. They left us no note or explanation, just this." Karin reached in to the pocket of her cardigan, taking out a small slip of paper, spotted with age, unfolded it, and placed it on the coffee table between them. It bore only one word 'DANKE' and beneath, the signatures of Wolfgang and Werner.

"We never heard from either of them again. Our government was in the process of sending all the refugees, all the displaced persons, back to their own countries and I think they took the opportunity to melt into the crowd. For years afterwards I looked in the papers for any signs that they were still alive, but of course there was nothing. Eventually I gave up looking. I had my own life to live."

For a moment, Karin slumped back into her chair as though exhausted by the process of recalling such painful, stressful memories.

"How did the family react?" Keith asked.

"I think we were relieved, saddened, but relieved that it was all over. I suppose we were a little selfish in being glad that we had Svenn back and that we no longer had the problem of Wolfgang."

Karin's hand flew to her mouth, "Oh, I did not mean to put it like that! It's just…" but before she could say another word, Keith leaned forward and placed his hand gently on the back of hers, stroking it lightly.

"It's all right, we understand, we really do. Everyone meant for the best and I guess the best came out of it. Wolfgang was out of his prison, with a friend he trusted, and so he took his chance. The odds were a damn sight better than they were in'45. You could say he had a second chance."

"Would have been nice, though, to know what happened to him, to tie up that loose end." His voice ended in a whisper.

Ronald tried to picture Wolfgang and Werner adrift somewhere in northern Europe and wondered how they could have survived, aliens in their own country. The thought that they would almost certainly have turned to petty crime was irresistible. Werner would have known how.

"Well, I'm off to bed," said Ronald, to break his train of thought. "I'm whacked, very tired," he added, seeing Karin's puzzled look as she struggled with the translation. "But before we call it a day," he refilled the tiny schnapps glasses, "I want to offer a toast. I remember it from my last night in Berlin in 1936. It was right then and I believe it to be right today." Karin nodded, remembering the occasion.

They raised their glasses as Ronald proposed, the scene as fresh in his mind as though it were yesterday, "Family and friends."

"I'll drink to that!" replied Keith, as he replaced his now empty glass on the table. "Family and friends. God bless 'em all"

Karin rose slowly from her chair, assisted by Keith, and walked slowly from the room, leaning a little on his arm. "Night, night, Skipper," came Keith's cheery parting words, adding in a light-hearted way. "Don't be too late and don't forget to put the lights out."

"Yes, mother," Ronald responded with a chuckle, but quite how long he sat there, an hour or two, perhaps three, surrounded, suffused, enveloped by seventy years of memories and emotions, he was not certain.

In the early hours he rose, stiff limbed, staring around the room, in which so much of the drama had unfolded, as though to discern the ghosts of his past. Then, killing the lights in the room and the corridor as he went, he slipped wearily into bed, cocooned by the duvet, reliving the moment when the dogs barked in the middle of the night.

CHAPTER 26

Mentally and physically exhausted from the exertions of the day, one which he found had been the more demanding than perhaps any since the war, certainly any since the day of Libby's funeral, it occurred to him that he might just possibly be sleeping in the room that had once been Svenn's.

Whether or not he was right was of no matter, but the thought comforted him, bringing to him a sense of family that had in part been absent, missing from his life for so long. Again, it brought back memories of those days in Berlin, now more than sixty-five years previously, when they were all young, strong and beautiful – he hesitated to use such a word about himself – with their whole lives to look forward to.

The vivacious Karin, to whom he had taken such a shine, and who knew what might have come to be, but for the war. But then there would have been no Libby, and he sighed deeply as he put out the bedside light and began to drift off to sleep.

The glamorous Elise; well, as a fifteen-year-old largely ignorant of the ways of the world, he had found her to be like something out of a Hollywood movie with her couturier wardrobe, her skilful use of cosmetics, her ability to be the perfect hostess for a society dinner – such a contrast to his own mother who, bless her, was homely, a true home-maker and completely content with her role in life.

Max, the handsome test pilot, who was always courteous, always considerate to the young Ronald and whose love of flying had so inspired him.

Wolfgang and Dieter, growing up in the belief that they were going to play their part in creating a new Germany, the receptive vessels, like much of the German youth of the day, of ideas and concepts, some of which were honourable and decent on the outside, like a shiny apple, but which contained the seeds of its own corruption and the maggots of its own destruction.

Not for the first time in his life, Ronald pondered the mystery of why he was he, and not one of them; and, had he been, what different choices, what different dilemmas might have been forced on him.

Other faces: Werner, the loyal part Jew, and Otto, who tried to protect him from a system that would ultimately destroy everything.

Otto, the master of deception in so many ways; genial, humorous, too worldly-wise by far, but a patriot who seemed to ride the darker side of the Nazi dream less easily than some.

Then, Regina, the beautiful Regina; there was no other appropriate word to describe her and for whom Hutch had fallen so completely; what of her, he wondered. What had been her fate in the months after the Russians took control of so much of the former German Reich that was to last a thousand years?

As sleep began to take him, another tiny bell began to ring at the back of his mind, something that he might have seen or read since this whole business with Hutch began, but whatever it was, it eluded him and he fell asleep, hearing once again those gentle tones of the dance music he had played in the minutes before he had proposed to Libby. Until.

Yet again, he dreamed the dream. Yet again, he was in the cockpit of Miss Faithful, hurtling earthwards, the prized Messerschmitt jet fighter in his sights. Yet again, the speed was building beyond his control, but then as his thumb moved to the firing button, as it always had done, he found instead that, this time, he still had control, and the joystick came back into his lap. He flared Miss Faithful out, the engine no longer racing, to fly alongside the German aircraft and as he looked over he saw that the pilot was Wolfgang, smiling and waving; but before he could respond, a third aircraft joined them to fly in perfect formation and he realised to his amazement that it was the Prussian Queen with Hutch, young and vigorous, at the controls, laughing and holding a little brass bell which he was shaking: ting-a-ling-ling, ting-a-ling. With a final wave, so reminiscent of that moment before Grossenbrode, Hutch gave a shrug of the shoulders – on with the show – and turned The Prussian Queen with the German fighter, away to starboard, and they began to slide from sight into the swirling haze, the sound of the bell continuing to ring faintly.

For a while, Ronald followed them with his gaze until they had completely faded from view, feeling somehow released, his hands resting, relaxed, on the control column, then he looked forwards into the blinding light of the setting sun.

He woke with a start, momentarily disorientated in time and space, dazzled by the early morning sunlight which had turned the pale yellow blind at his window into a golden furnace. He lay for a few minutes gathering his thoughts and then, as he once again smelled the aroma of freshly percolated coffee, he raised himself slowly out of bed, quietly bemoaning his ageing limbs and walked slowly through to the bathroom to shave and freshen himself in the shower.

Quite how long he stood under the curtain of water, he did not know, but as he dried himself and dressed, he felt in some way that another of his demons might, at last, have been banished, even though the little bell continued to tinkle in a corner of his mind.

As he walked through to the kitchen in pursuit of the coffee's aroma, he found Keith, once again, deep in animated conversation with Karin. For a moment he felt a fleeting pang of jealousy, but then it was gone, as Karin kissed him lightly on the cheek in greeting.

"Har du sovet godt?" she enquired, then apologising with a laugh, she translated, "Did you sleep well?"

"Yes, fine," he replied, then added. "No, actually it was better than fine; I slept better than I have done for years. Just out of interest, you didn't hear me shouting did you? I know I do sometimes. Doesn't matter when I'm on my own, but a bit of a bother when I'm in company."

Both Karin and Keith shook their heads, to his relief, and then Karin added, smiling, "Even if you had, I don't think Wolfgang would have minded. It was his room I put you in."

A shiver ran down Ronald's spine, as Karin invited them to the dining table where she had already laid a light breakfast of fresh rolls and a selection of cheeses and meats. While she poured them each a cup of strong black coffee, she asked, "If you feel up to it, Ronnie, there's something I would like to show you. I think you might like to see it too, Keith. You will need your overcoats, but it's only a little walk." She did not elaborate further.

Ronald ate his breakfast largely in silence as he listened to the continuing discussion between Karin and Keith about their family histories. He thought to himself, looking at their obvious rapport, "Well, why not?" and he regretted his earlier moment of jealousy, and joined their exchanges with stories of his own nephews and nieces.

When he told Karin about Libby, her eyes filled with tears. "Poor Ronnie," she said sympathetically, laying a hand on his arm, but he took her hand in his, saying she should not concern herself as it was all a very long time ago. Keith saw from the expression on Ronald's face that it was, in fact, anything but.

Breakfast over, Karin sent them to fetch warm clothes and, suitably dressed against the cold autumn morning, she ushered them out of the house and down the stoned track to the road. There she said, "Walk with me," as she linked arms, with Keith on her left and Ronald on her right, steering them down the quiet village street, past neat bungalows with well tended frontages, mostly of dwarf conifers set in gravel beds. She gave a running commentary on who lived in each house, and who was related to whom, heightening the sense of community and peace that Ronald had felt since he arrived.

They walked on, still arm in arm, undisturbed by any traffic, past the village hall, the village school, a neighbour's farm with its modern barns and equipment and then still onwards, until Ronald began to understand that Karin was leading them to the church at the edge of the village. Like most Danish churches they had seen so far on their travels, this one was of the familiar style, small, white painted with a grey-leaded roof to its short tower, which was topped with a simple weather vane.

This village church was set on a slight rise and circled by a ring of plane trees, now losing their leaves in the advance of winter, to expose their branches, bent and twisted by the violent winter storms which raged inland from the North Sea only a few miles away. In cast-iron numbers fixed, black on white, below the clock on the side of the tower facing them was the date, 1886.

"All my family are here," said Karin, as she conducted them through the wrought-iron lych-gate, set in the dry stone wall that surrounded the church and its graveyard. The church grounds were a revelation to both Keith and Ronald, quite unlike anything they had experienced back home. The whole of the graveyard was perfectly manicured; narrow paths of fine grit were bordered by strips of carefully mown turf which fronted the burial plots, separated individually either by low, square-cut box shrubs or by taller screens of well tended copper beech, now turning to their autumn colours.

Quietly, Karin led them past rows of gravestones, mostly of black or pink marble, each chiselled with a star to signify the birthdate and a cross infilled with gold to signify the death. They moved on unhurried until, in a corner under the west wall where there was some shelter from the wind, Karin stopped in front of an extended plot, encompassed by a beech hedge.

"Here we are," she said. "My mormor, my mother's mother," indicating the headstone on the extreme left, then as she moved slowly to the right. "Farmor, my father's mother, then farfar and finally morfar," without feeling she needed to translate further. Then she pointed out the graves of her own mother and father, Anna and Peder.

Next lay the grave of Svenn, marked 1919 – 1996, and Karin bent down to place a single red rose at the base of the stone. Ronald stood for a moment head bowed, remembering. Recalling so much, in a kaleidoscope of memories.

Then, looking at the empty space beyond, Karin said a simple, matter-of –fact way, "That one's mine – my husband is in his village."

As the sense of family once again folded about Ronald, he vaguely noticed out of the corner of his eye, that there was one more headstone at the far end of the plot, in front of which Keith was now standing. He thought, but was not sure, he heard Keith say under his breath, "Oh, hell's bells!"

Next, Karin was at his side. Standing silently, she seemed to push him gently toward the last stone. Keith had turned away and was blowing his nose loudly as Ronald began to read the inscription. For a few moments his mind was unable to take in what he read. He felt Karin's hand, gentle and comforting, at his elbow.

With the same Danish symbols of a star and a cross, he read:

Richard "Hutch" Hutchinson 1919 – 2002.

Below, there were engraved some other words, in Danish, that he could not understand.

Choked with emotion, he turned to Karin who was smiling tenderly. She took a handkerchief from her handbag and wiped the tears that were trickling down his cheeks.

"His body was flown over just after Christmas to be with, as he put it, *his* family. I had already agreed that he could share our plot. After all, he gave me back my family, so how could I refuse."

"No, indeed," was all that Ronald could think of saying, as he began to feel slightly faint, battered by the emotions swirling through him.

As he struggled to regain a degree of composure, he pointed at the other words on the stone and asked, with a strong feeling that they must be significant, "Please translate that line for me."

Keith came back to them, still wiping at his eyes. "Bloody cold wind," he muttered.

Karin took a deep breath and read them aloud:

Hvil i fred med din Dronning.

Next she said, "That last word *Dronning* means Queen." And, seeing that there was no reaction from Ronald, she added, "The complete line means '*Rest in peace with your Queen*'." Still there was no reaction, no inkling of what the stone was telling him.

"Think, Ronnie, who was his Queen?"

Not understanding, Ronald replied, "Queen Elizabeth nowadays, or Queen Mary during the war. I don't see how the two are connected."

"No, Ronnie," Karin said gently, as she continued to dab the handkerchief to his cheek, reaching up with a gloved hand to tenderly stroke a stray lock of his hair back into place. "Not that sort of Queen; another sort, more personal. Think about it."

At his side, Keith suddenly exploded, "Oh! Jesus Christ!" and then, acknowledging their surroundings, he began to apologise to Karin who stopped him, saying, "Just let him think for a moment, shall we? You have worked it out, haven't you?" as she slipped her arm through Keith's and took him a little to one side.

"Yes, I believe I have, as incredible as it all seems."

From a few paces distance, they stood quietly and observed Ronald wrestling with the puzzle, watching him as he talked to himself, repeating the word "Queen" over and over again. Then in the middle of his ramblings, they heard him say just once "Queen, Queenie", but then he was off again muttering and gesturing, until suddenly he stood bolt upright and exclaimed, "Surely that's not possible!"

Then he turned his eyes up to the skies and Keith shouted, "Oh Lord, I think he's going to faint again," as he rushed to Ronald's side to catch him in case he fell. He found Ronald mumbling, "Regina, I can't believe it. He found Regina. I think I need to sit down for a moment." Keith helped Ronald over to a stone bench nearby where he settled him to recover his composure.

Ronald's mind was in chaos, the little bell ringing ting-a-ling, as he tried to put some order into the thoughts that were threatening to overwhelm him. As he grew calmer, he looked up to Karin for an explanation, a bewildered expression clouding his face.

Karin came to sit beside him, and, taking his hands in hers, squeezing them tightly, she said, "It was not just Svenn and Wolfgang that he rescued; he also rescued cousin Regina with whom he had been so deeply in love, since that first time they met in Berlin. That's why Keith saw him in Berlin in 1945. He was trying to discover if she was still alive. It took him months to find her, and then another couple of years to smuggle her out of what had become

327

the Russian Zone, which later became East Germany, but before they got round to putting up the Wall.

After that, he took her out to the Far East, to Malaya, where not too many questions would be asked while she recovered from her," she hesitated as she tried to find a suitable word, "her *treatment* at the hands of the Russian soldiers. He told me that she was very damaged and had to spend time in a private hospital where she had some surgery, but she was never able to have children.

"They were so in love. They had a happy life together in Hong Kong and then when she died shortly after they returned to England, Hutch told me he wanted her ashes to be buried with him here."

Turning toward the grave, Karin added, "She is there now and they are together for all time." Karin sighed in a contented way.

After a moment she laughed. "You never saw the clue, did you?"

"What clue?" Ronald asked in amazement.

"Hutch thought, hoped, you might spot it in The Times. He told me it cost him a slap-up dinner and a case of champagne to encourage, yes that was his word, to encourage the writer to include her pet name in the obituary. Wives normally get a full mention by name, so Hutch told me." *Ting-a-ling.*

As she finished speaking, Ronald ripped open his overcoat and plunged his hand into the inside pocket of his jacket, drawing out his leather wallet. Riffling through some papers, he pulled out the old cutting from The Times. Opening it with trembling hands on his lap for Keith to read, they found at the very end, the note, unread in almost a year, which recorded that Hutch had been predeceased by his wife Queenie.

"Oh God," said Keith. "Queenie, Regina; PQ – the Prussian Queen. It's been there all the time."

"Bluff and double bluff," said Ronald as he stood up from the bench and walked unsteadily back to the gravestone, wishing for once that he had his walking stick for support.

Placing his hands on the cold stone, to steady himself, Ronald said quietly, "Rest in peace, my old friend, with your lovely queen. I'm sorry I was such a dunce from time to time. No more surprises I hope." Then he leaned forward and placed a kiss on the top of the stone.

As he straightened up, Karin delved into her handbag and brought out a small candle in a white protective case with its own inbuilt windshield. "I thought you might like to light one of these –

it's the Danish way," she said as she handed him the candle and a box of matches.

Taking them from her with a look of gratitude for her thoughtfulness, he knelt down with some difficulty and placed the candle at the foot of the stone, striking several matches before the candle was lit and burning brightly in the swirling breeze. For a moment or two he gazed at the flickering flame, reliving the time when a young girl tied a red white and blue scarf around the neck of his friend, binding them together in love. Then Keith helped him to his feet.

Rubbing his back to ease the stiffness, Ronald turned to Keith and seeing the tears in his eyes, mirroring his own, he said simply, "I think so, don't you."

Keith instinctively understood what was meant and then, as one, the two old soldiers turned smartly to face the grave, straightened their shoulders and saluted, hands held to forehead for a full, silent minute.

"Goodbye, old friend, God bless," said Keith as he turned and walked with Ronald and Karin, once again arm-in-arm, without a backward glance, out of the graveyard as Karin said, "I will look after them for as long as I can."

Once they were back at the farmhouse, Ronald felt empty, drained and overwhelmed at one and the same time. It was done. All the pieces of the puzzle had been found and put in their proper place – but at what cost?

Suddenly, he was seized by the need to walk, anywhere, alone and so, making his excuses, he left and walked out of the village, into the flat open countryside, away from the church, away from Hutch and his surprises. As he battled against the stiff headwind, he prayed there would be no more, that the episode should be closed as quickly as possible. He realised that he was beginning to think of home and that he was regretting the decision to delay the return ferry.

He walked on in a great circle which unavoidably brought him back past the church. Like the centre of a whirlpool, it drew him toward its heart and as he sat once again on the stone seat, the peace of his surroundings enfolded him. Briefly, he wished he had the soothing effect of a cigarette, but that was all done with long ago – when the killing ended.

At length, having stared unseeing at Hutch's burial plot, muttering to himself from time to time, he felt the cold seeping into his bones, but he had reached a decision which sat comfortably on him, so he rose, standing for just a moment more in front of Hutch's stone, bareheaded.

He whispered a final farewell and, glancing back only when the curve of the path began to cut off his view, he walked purposefully back towards the farmhouse. His mind was clear and untroubled. He had forgiven and been forgiven in return.

Pleasantly tired, and slightly mud-bespattered, he entered the farmhouse to find Keith and Karin waiting anxiously for him in the lounge.

"Oh, Ronnie I was beginning to get a bit worried, going off like that, but Keith was sure you would be alright."

"I'm sorry," said Ronald. "I should have explained, but I just needed to be on my own, to take it all in. It's been so much, in such a short space of time. Then that business with Regina; what they both must have been through. It really shook me."

"You know, when all this started I cursed Hutch for dragging me into his schemes, but at the church I felt so guilty, to have doubted him for a moment."

As he spoke he noticed two fat envelopes of the same type as had contained Hutch's letter, lying on the coffee table, one addressed in Hutch's handwriting to himself and the other addressed to Keith. He looked at Keith who answered his enquiring face with a shrug of his shoulders and the slightest shake of his head.

"Do you know what these are?" he asked Karin.

"Yes, I do. It's Hutch's thank you to both of you for having faith. Open them."

"Here we go again," Keith spluttered, as he reached forward, grasped his envelope, slipping his finger under the flap to rip it open.

"Oh, bloody hell!" was all he could say, as a bundle of dollar bills fell out onto the table. He stared at them open mouthed.

"There are ten thousand dollars for each of you," said Karin softly, "to do with as you please; to repay some of your expenses in coming here, to give to charity, to give to your family, whatever you like. He insisted on doing the same for me. I am giving mine to our church, so that the family graves, including his, will be cared for long after I have gone."

Ronald, who had remained silent, placed his index finger on his unopened envelope and pushed it across the table toward Karin and said, his voice cracking with emotion, "I think I would like to do the same, but on one small condition. Could you arrange for his stone to have some words added?"

"Such as?" enquired Keith. "What...?"

Ronald held up his hand to silence Keith, before he continued, "I would like to suggest, with your agreement, Keith, these words: *'Remembered with honour by his friends Ronald Wallace and Keith Watson'.*"

"Bloody good idea," said Keith. "Might even have something like that on my own." As he coughed loudly to cover his feelings, shuffled the bills together and placed them neatly with Ronald's envelope. "Job done."

And indeed it was.

CHAPTER 27

Late one afternoon just before the New Year, Ronald took out, for the last time, his wartime suitcase. From it he extracted the small yellow die, and rolled it – it came up three. He rolled again – five, then a two. Intrigued, he rolled again and again until, at last, there was a six. He grunted with amused satisfaction. The power of the dice over his life was gone, their role at an end. He was tempted to throw the die into the waste bin, to be rid of it once and for all, but the talisman was too strong and so he tossed it back into the case. He did not look to see how it landed.

Next he took out the silver Dunhill lighter, turning it in his hand, noting the scratches and dents of a war's service; then he filled it with fluid and lit a cigarette, his first for more than fifty years. He sat for a moment, reflecting, watching the smoke curling upward into the shadows.

Then he took out the small, engine-turned, silver photo frame, the silver tarnished with age almost to black and set it where he could see it on top of his bureau. The newly-wed couple stared out at him, smiling, arms around each other, full of hope for the future.

Lastly, he removed the cellophane wrapper from a compact disc which he had just purchased over the internet. It had taken days of patient research to hunt down the particular piece of music he needed to hear one more time. With exaggerated care, he loaded it into the player.

Selecting pen and paper, he started to write the letter he had promised himself he would send to his little sister – for he always regarded her so, even though they were now both well into their eighties.

28th December 2003

Dearest Torrie,

All that follows, which you will read with the long letter from Wing Commander Hutchinson, Hutch, will tell you everything about my wartime service. I have never been able to talk to you about it, unlike you who could not wait to tell me about your time on the south coast guns. It is all so very long ago, but I want your kids and especially the grandchildren to understand what we did and, as a result of my recent trip to Denmark, a big gap in that history has been filled. I have now come to terms with everything, well, almost everything.

Keith Watson stayed on for a few more days to help Karin with telling the Danish Authorities about Wolfgang's plane. What a kerfuffle there was and I was glad to be out of it. As you may have seen in the press, Germany and Denmark are now arguing who should have it. Flying home was infinitely preferable to another ferry crossing. I think I have been through every emotion possible, but in the end I am proud of what we did. If it was Hutch's intention to release us, especially Karin, but perhaps me also from the prison he and the War had created, then he certainly succeeded, thank goodness.

He continued to write for an hour or more, then he rested, his hand poised over the paper, as the track on the CD he wanted now to hear so much filled the room.

Until there are no stars to shine,
There's no such thing as time,
I'll love but you.

Looking up at the picture he ran his fingers across the glass, lingering on her face and wondered how long it would be until...

Until.

The appropriate arrangements have been made. He is ready.

CHAPTER 28

The following spring, on a bright clear morning when he sat, as usual, at the dining table reading The Times, Ronald heard the sound of footsteps on his drive – the postman he assumed – but then was surprised to hear the doorbell chime.

Releasing the security chain and opening the door, he found his regular postman offering him a letter by registered post. He signed for it with some reluctance. It had been his lifelong experience that such communications rarely brought him any great reward or pleasure.

The brown manila envelope seemed to be stiffened with card and was addressed to him with full military decorations. For a moment he wondered if it was another communication from Hutch. Perhaps he feared it might be.

With his reading glasses perched on the end of his nose, he carefully slit open the envelope and removed what appeared to be a newspaper cutting and a further sealed envelope, which he put to one side. Unfolding the cutting, he scanned it slowly, until, chuckling helplessly he said, "Keith, you sly old fox."

Then, still chuckling to himself he opened the sealed envelope and drew from it a single sheet of white card, silver embossed. The card requested the pleasure of his company at the wedding of Mr. Keith Watson to Ms Karin Marssen.

CHAPTER 29

The Times Register; Tuesday October 14 2008

Squadron Leader Ronald Orville "Ronno" Wallace

British ace who fought the flying bombs and into Northern Germany.

Joining the Royal Air Force in 1941, Ronald Wallace was one of the last of the home-grown fighter pilots who served throughout the remainder of the war until the cessation of hostilities in May 1945. Classified as an ace for five combat victories flying Spitfires during sweeps over France in 1943, he was hospitalised for an extended period following a crash landing in the summer of that year.

Returning to combat duty in the spring of 1944, his squadron converted to the Hawker Tempest fighter in readiness for the D-Day landings, but he was diverted to counter the growing menace of the German V1 flying bombs. He was awarded a Bar to his DFC for shooting down eight flying bombs in July 1944, the last of which nearly cost him his life when it exploded in front of his Tempest. He survived the destruction of his aircraft, but was hospitalised again, not returning to active duty until early 1945.

His squadron was then continuously engaged until VE Day, in support of the advancing ground troops and he was awarded the DSO for his part in the raid on the Grossenbrode seaplane base on the Baltic coast which was carried out after faulty intelligence indicated that the German High Command had broken out of Berlin and were attempting to escape to Sweden. The raid suffered 50% casualties and was, on May 1st 1945, the last organised combat sortie by the RAF.

Educated in London, he visited Germany in 1936, meeting Adolf Hitler briefly, during a holiday with his father Alfred Wallace whose role then, and during the war remains covered by the 100 year rule of the Official Secrets Act.

After the war, Ronald Wallace left the RAF, qualified as an accountant and practiced in Lincolnshire until he retired as senior partner.

In 2003 he received a communication from the late Wing Commander Richard (Hutch) Hutchinson – (Times obituary: October 19 2002) which ultimately led to the discovery, with Flight Lieutenant Keith Watson DFC of a largely intact World War II

Luftwaffe Messerschmitt 109 fighter, hidden for almost sixty years in a barn in Denmark. He recorded the part he played in these events in his autobiography *The Last Role of the Dice* (published 2005) in collaboration with Keith Watson.

His first wife, Elisabeth, predeceased him in 1947 and his second marriage ended in divorce. There were no children.

Ronald Wallace DSO DFC and Bar, accountant, was born on September 23 1920. He died on October 11, 2008, aged 88

EPILOGUE

The gravestone, of polished black marble, gold lettered, is set in the tiny churchyard, next to one hewn from a block of grey slate, now leaning slightly, and inscribed:

'Elisabeth Wallace 1923-1948. At peace with her child in the hands of God'.

Rosettes of yellow and green lichen are beginning to stain the surface. A single, fresh, red rose lies at its base.

An elderly couple stand in front of the new stone. She, silver haired, is helping the man rise from the spot where he was kneeling and has just lit a white candle, the flame burning straight and clear under its protective cap in the cold, still, damp autumn air. Together they read the words on the stone:

Ronald Orville Wallace 1920-2008
Rest in peace with your beloved Libby
Remembered with honour by his friends

The man straightens his back, removes his hat, salutes in silence and then, supported by his wife, he bends forward to place two small, yellow cubes on the top of the stone. His fingers linger for a moment longer on the cold, polished surface.

The two dice shine like a tiny beacon as the couple turn and walk away, arm in arm, into the gathering mist.